Betsy

Praise for *Mason's Retreat*,
a *New York Times* Notable Book of the Year,
and a *Publishers Weekly* Best Book of the Year

"Tilghman gives us richly drawn characters, shimmering detail, and an irresistibly moving theme. . . . [This novel] comes close to pure, exhilarating perfection."
—David Wiegand, *San Francisco Chronicle*

"A superb first novel from Tilghman that portrays with tenacious intelligence and wrenching intensity the nuances of family unhappiness and conflict. . . . Echoes of *The Great Gatsby,* William Styron's *Lie Down in Darkness,* O'Neill, and Faulkner add further resonance to a novel that stands . . . as a stunning, individual achievement."
—*Kirkus Reviews*

"A magnificent meditation on the dynamics of family relations and the consequences of selfishness . . . Tilghman's first novel places him securely in the ranks of our most accomplished writers."
—*Publishers Weekly*

"Tilghman keeps the reader spellbound as his novel gathers momentum, spinning out a tale of the entwined power of history and fate. . . . His insights . . . are astute and heartbreaking."
—Colleen Kelly Warren, *St. Louis Post-Dispatch*

"*Mason's Retreat* is a brilliant book—full of wisdom and insight into the workings of the soul. The language is perfect. Every paragraph holds a treasure. This is one of the most thoroughly satisfying novels you will ever read."
—Kaye Gibbons

"*Mason's Retreat* is extraordinary—a brilliant novel with a flawlessly elegant style and great compassion. Tilghman successfully transports the reader to another time and holds him there transfixed."
—Jill McCorkle

"Christopher Tilghman has now taken his place in a line of classic American writers—among them, John Cheever, William Maxwell, and Wright Morris—who have written about the American situation with a clear-eyed moral authority and a capacious human sympathy."

—Edward Hirsch

"Impressive . . . strong and skillful . . . Tilghman is true to the moral tone of the time about which he writes."

—Maya Muir, *The Sunday Oregonian*

"Mr. Tilghman masterfully presents his own version of two abiding literary themes: waning wealth in which the humble prevail and the high-placed simply wither away, ruined by their own misdeeds, and the enduring land, which gives up none of its secrets, but rewards those who refuse to take it lightly. In every way, *Mason's Retreat* is a fine read, solidly crafted and a credit to Mr. Tilghman's growing reputation as a writer of merit."

—R. C. Scott, *Washington Sunday Times*

"Tilghman's thoughtful pacing and talent for setting the scene reward the reader with a satisfying and memorable understanding of a complex family."

—*Booklist*

"One of the most poignant, evocative, beautifully written novels this reader has come across in years."

—Susan Miron, *Miami Herald*

"Extraordinary . . . a revealing series of events that weave together such universal themes as history's effect on individual lives, the complexities of family bonds and tensions between the races. . . . Beautifully crafted drama."

—Peter Khoury, *Greensboro News & Record*

"Tilghman writes beautifully, with an eye for the subtle emotions that animate relationships among family members."

—Linda Falkenstein, *Isthmus*

"A richly satisfying story . . . His narrative, elegant, wise, and poetic, gets to the heart of each character."

—David Simpson, *The Virginian-Pilot*

MASON'S RETREAT

MASON'S RETREAT

CHRISTOPHER TILGHMAN

Picador USA
New York

Picador® is a U.S. registered trademark and is used by
St. Martin's Press under license from Pan Books Limited.

ISBN 0-312-15586-7

First published in the United States of America by Random House

First Picador USA Edition: May 1997

10   9   8   7   6   5   4   3   2   1

TO MY SONS

Matthew, Luke, and William

ACKNOWLEDGMENTS

I am very grateful to the Mrs. Giles Whiting Foundation, the John Simon Guggenheim Memorial Foundation, and the Ingram Merrill Foundation, for giving me time to work on this novel and on other works of fiction as yet unfinished.

Each time the French liner *Normandie* sails into my novel, it carries my debt to Frank O. Braynard and his *Picture History of the Normandie* (Dover Publications, Inc.).

Deep thanks to my editor, Kate Medina, and to my agent, Maxine Groffsky. No writer deserves the kind of support and guidance they give to me. And to Caroline, thank you, again and again.

MASON'S RETREAT

1

HARRY MASON CAN picture his grandfather, Edward, on the sundeck of the *Normandie*, early morning, August, a pebbly North Atlantic mist. He is wearing a suit made of yards of heathery Irish tweed, and the fronts of his double-breasted Burberry, flapping slightly, are big as sails. He has paused on the silvered teak decking for a second or two and is looking toward the horizon. His large palms have gripped the cold steel of the life rail, greasy with sea dew. The waves are silver-flecked, broad-troughed; the swell is deep enough to turn walking into a slight climb-and-run, and the stewards and deck crews go about their daybreak duties with counterbalancing shifts of their weight. Edward Mason judges it a mariner's sea, and it gives him strength to reflect on the timelessness of the scene. He had, until a moment earlier, been quite content and untroubled, but some passing breeze has reminded him of the uncertainties ahead, and now he must gather in his resources for a second or two. He assumes that those who see him in this nautical stance will not guess that he is performing damage control on his dreams. The man is good at this, especially when he has a lifeboat, in this case, the largest and finest liner in the world. Now isn't that a comforting thought? All around him the crew is at work. The smells of baked goods, of coffee and chocolate, blend with the sea mist into the narcotic essence of food. Edward Mason is one of those men who believe a fine appetite is something to give thanks for. He starts to feel a little better. He calms himself with the image of the outside *appartement de luxe* he has procured for himself, his wife, and two sons. He has made certain promises, mortgaged all to the French Line for this last extravagant passage, and, by God, except for a little too much vibration from the propeller shaft, the Frogs are delivering the goods.

When Harry Mason thinks about his grandfather and his life, it is often in the twin, blended image of the man and this ship as they sliced back and forth across the Atlantic for those few years before the war. He loved that ship, from its whaleback bow to the elegant stepping of its afterdecks; no drowning person ever clung to a shattered spar with more desperate strength than Harry Mason's grandfather gripped the *Normandie*. Every thwart and bulkhead adorned with gilt bas-reliefs, paintings by the latest rage, tile friezes, and carved sliding doors. The *Normandie*, the *Normandie*, huge but graceful, financial madness, the man's likeness, his brother doomed to die young.

Harry can hear his grandfather's voice, on this early morning in 1936, bellowing out of the fog. The crossing is in its second full day, and by now the entire ship's company—stewards, actors in the theater company, waiters—has experienced that voice; even Captain Thoreaux, standing stiffly on the wing of the bridge, has been distracted from his duties by a greeting projected from somewhere near the deck-tennis courts. The crew and passengers must be wondering whether there are two, or even several, of this large figure on board. Was he not taking a nightcap last night in the smoking room well after two, and is that not his voice out here somewhere in the deep mists of the promenade deck? Is that not he taking part in the regularly scheduled Sunrise Deck Walk, drawing close, suddenly a gray form above all the others, plunging forward like the clipped bow of this ship, rigid with turboelectric energy?

"A splendid morning," he is pronouncing. The ladies, one of whom is being pushed in a large wicker wheelchair, are delighted with his company. Two men amble meekly behind, just in front of three enormous Rottweilers followed by a pair of dark-skinned stewards with brass water cans and fireplace shovels. "I must say, Mrs. Francis"—Mason leans down to enunciate carefully to the woman in the wheelchair—"you were quite right to insist I come."

Mrs. Francis is an elderly American who makes transatlantic crossings frequently, always, it seems, just slightly out of phase with her husband, who has business dealings with the Germans. "Your wife and sons are still asleep?" she asks.

Mason reflects that Edith, his wife, is always up by now, by six, and usually earlier. This habit of hers had disappointed him when he discovered it on their honeymoon almost fifteen years ago. As for the boys, he has hardly seen them since they boarded. "My wife is enjoying the luxuries," he says.

"As well she should," says Mrs. Francis. Her speech is flat and coarse: her words are all business. Mason takes pleasure in language. It was this sort of embellishment, a depth and savor to daily things, that he and Edith had been seeking when they moved to England in 1922.

"No one gives wives of industry credit for the work we do," Mrs. Francis adds.

Her point is wide of the mark. Edith may deserve credit for things that she does, but not as a wife of industry: she has never set foot in the small machine tool company he owns in Manchester, and has certainly never come into contact with any of its employees or products. "Your husband is in the rubber industry?" he asks.

She waits for the purser, a smallish but intelligent-looking man, to tell Mason that Mr. Francis owns a large and important tire manufacturer in Akron. Mrs. Francis has taken the Trouville Suite and is regarded by the French Line as a catch.

"A fine company," Edward says, though he knows nothing about the tire business and the thought of Ohio, that blank American middle ground, fills him with horror. He grew up in Boston and Edith grew up on the North Shore of Chicago. "I must say—speaking as a rival—that American industry is a credit to us all."

"Then you've spent your whole career in Europe . . . ?" she says, inviting him to give a complete accounting of himself. She looks back at the other passengers, who have paused under the lee of the center stack, and then beckons to the steward pushing her chair to continue.

What can Mason say? He left the Sheffield School with his degree in engineering in 1916. He put in four years of apprenticeship in Boston, and then spent a year in England because his father believed the English to be the best engineers in the world, which, from his father, was praise that spoke not just of talent but of character. He came back to America to court and marry Edith, whom he had met when she was studying art in Paris the summer before, and then returned to England, having bought a company, Machine Tool, in Manchester, with his father's blessing and financial help. Should he tell this woman about those years, when he and Edith shone with youth, an effortless success on two continents, and when the works seemed to chug along with enough of Edward's attention for him to claim credit for its modest successes? Then the Depression had wiped him out. He was able to dance and parry for a number of years more, but now he had reached the end of the line. Not so uncommon a story, not an interesting one to this woman, Francis, who could only regard his failures as deserved. Mason decides to dodge. "Yes," he says. "Until recently my company has demanded close attention."

"Naturally."

"But I have never surrendered my American citizenship. Of course, my sons retain the right to choose at the appropriate time."

"Then you expect to remain in America?"

"For a year or two, certainly. I own an estate in Maryland. Badly managed in my absence, I'm afraid. It'll take some time to put it to rights." As usual, he has difficulty admitting that this, despite all he has tried to do in his adult life, this is where he is headed. For the benefit of his spirits, he adds that the estate has been in his family for almost three hundred years.

"It sounds pretty dull, but maybe your children will think it's fun."

They continue through the mists without talking for a few minutes, accompanied by a slight squeaking from the wheelchair each time one of the wheels makes a revolution. The junior purser flinches at the sound, as if he fears this most important passenger will have him thrown to the sharks. Mrs. Francis, Mason has observed previously in the dining room, is perfectly ambulatory.

Mrs. Francis shifts the conversation to matters that interest her more. "What do you think the English are up to?"

"In what respect?"

"With respect to the Continent, of course," she snaps at him. "You're enough of an American to keep your perspective, right?"

This is all becoming depressing. Mason regrets coming on the Sunrise Deck Walk, and he will not do so again, at least not with this woman as company. The politics of England, or of any country, for that matter, is not something he spends much time thinking about. His energies are consumed by his own negotiations and skirmishes. He wonders what to say, whether to try to bluff her, but suspects he will be immediately exposed. He decides to tell the truth, in some form. "My interests are cultural," he says.

She is irritated and gets to the point. "My husband is impressed with the new Germany. He believes"—she does not lower her voice in consideration of the purser—"the British are making a mistake throwing in with the French. When was the last time *they* won a war on their own?"

The woman's ominous suggestion that the British will pay for their mistake serves as sufficient warning to Mason that he'd better cut this one off. "I shouldn't think it would matter all that much."

She looks up at him, and her sneer makes him understand that he is an insignificant industrialist, a man of no vision. Fortunately, they have only a few more paces to go before they reach the railing. They are facing forward, looking down a ladder across the sweeping port wing of the bridge, its polished crew standing as rigid as spars. Mason stares out at the sea; standing here a moment or two will allow him to remove this woman from his mind and restore his interest in breakfast. Mrs. Francis clears her spotted throat loudly and directs the purser to push her back to her suite. She expects Edward to bid her good morning, and he knows he certainly should; more than anything else, his impeccable manners have been his salvation over the past few years, a priceless birthright from his father. But he cannot pull his gaze out of the funneled breeze over the bow; his face is forced into it like a compass needle as they head west toward the New World.

——

DURING THE TIME her husband has been strolling topside with Nazi sympathizers, Edith Mason has been sitting rather stiffly at a blondwood writing desk, writing a letter to her parents. The entire stateroom is blond—the paneling, the beds and dressing table— and while at first glance everything seems quite spacious, Edith has figured out that this illusion has been achieved by slightly reducing the dimensions of the furnishings; even the ashtrays and telephone are three-quarter size. Edith is not easily fooled, though she usually keeps the truth to herself. She would not remark on this miniaturization in her own behalf—she is only a little taller than the average woman and knows how to use her body, a slender woman whom men might describe, in more recent times, as athletic—but her husband has spent his life banging his head and stubbing his toe and bellowing about it, and she has come to notice any low door-frame and to cringe at any unexpected obstruction on the path ahead.

She is dressed in a frayed terry-cloth bathrobe, and her black hair, with its tightly marcelled waves, is lopsided because she sleeps on one side; one patch is squashed down to her gimlet eyes. People sometimes think she is Eurasian, but the truth is that her eyes and cheekbones and coloring may speak of a touch of Indian in her blood; her people were out in Illinois and Wisconsin quite early in the last century, not that there is much of the hunter-gatherer, the trapper, or the settler left in her family now.

She runs a hand back and forth over her exposed thigh; when she brings her mind back to her letter, she snaps the front of her robe shut and writes, "Dear M&D." Then she stops again. She would like simply to describe the voyage, tell them that Simon, at six, is still young enough to spend his days in the children's playroom, with its fabulous toys and Punch and Judy shows, and that Sebastien has spent his time prowling about, just as one would expect of a boy almost fourteen years old. But the fact is that her mother and father, home in Winnetka, Illinois, and her older and younger sisters are waiting for meatier stuff, explanations, apologies; they'll expect it all a few days from now in person when the family arrives for a visit. Edward will be summoned to her father's office to formulate a plan; she will spend hours and hours with her mother in her garden; the boys will be driven senseless with boredom. Edith loves her parents and forgives them their concern. She's fond of her sisters, too, even her older sister, Rosalie, who teased her as a child and has never liked Edward. But this visit—the first since the late twenties—is not one she's looking forward to.

When Edward announced, about six months ago, that he had decided to return to America to take over the family farm, she thought he was joking. They were living at the time in a huge borrowed flat that seemed abandoned, even with them in it. Anything would have been better than that, and it seemed to her that he was acknowledging this fact with a rather ironic, though bitter, twist. She laughed, as she had not done in quite a while; when things were good, much of what Edward said was funny. He was a man who sparkled when successful. Oh, she had said to herself, drying her eyes, we *do* still have our sense of humor. But one look back at Edward had told her the truth.

"You're not joking?"

"No. I'm not."

"That place of your Aunt Miss Mary, or whatever her name was? I thought you were going to sell it."

"Dear, I must make decisions about our family's circumstances the best way I can. This has been on my mind for a number of years now."

Edward did not claim to have ever been to the farm, a thousand-acre estate called—impossibly—the Retreat. He knew only that it had been in his family since his forebears escaped England during the Cromwellian revolution, and that it had been willed to him, as the family's oldest son, by a maiden great-aunt. She died a few years after Edward and Edith moved to England.

Yet, he said, as if acknowledging a truth he had previously resisted, the Retreat was one of the Chesapeake's great houses. Furthermore, she would be amazed at the ease and the amenity of plantation living, the abundant household help, a life that had not been possible in England for many decades. She would find in Baltimore, he told her, a center of American culture, and he expected that there would be many opportunities to attend functions and balls at the embassies in Washington. They would not be far from the city, he told her, perhaps three hours at most by car, probably less. "Even with the ferry ride," he added, having figured out that Cookestown, Maryland, was on the Eastern Shore of the state. Perhaps, he said, they would take a pied-à-terre in the capital. "It could be quite gay, I think."

"Oh, Edward," she said. "If you are truly determined to do this, all that matters is that the house is habitable."

Edith checks her watch: still before eight. There has been no thumping on the bulkhead from the boys' stateroom, which may indicate that they are still asleep, although Sebastien may well have slipped out hours ago. He is capable of moving silently; his father has punished him for eavesdropping, but it does not seem to make him change. From the time he could walk, Sebastien has prowled; when he is motionless, he lurks. As their dwellings became more and more modest over the past few years in England, he suffered cruelly from the lack of privacy; he has always needed more space than most children, and other children, especially, have a way of making him feel crowded. More than anything, she has taken hope from the thought that an estate in Maryland will give Sebastien air, sky, and land. For herself, she looks forward to light, to slanted rays of it, pools overflowing with it, a radiance of objects, sudden bursts and slow waves, the kind of light she remembers from her childhood on the Great Plains. Edith has spent the past few years starved of light in sunless flats and foggy streets. These are the simple visions that are sustaining her these days, sunlight in this mansion on the Chesapeake, or whatever it is, and room for Sebastien to run.

There is a tapping at the door; she recognizes it as the wake-up call of their steward. She goes to the louvered panel and thanks him. She bathes and dresses with some difficulty as the ship begins to roll a little. She does not know that this slight shift in the direction of the sea means that they will be facing some weather over the next day or so. She goes through the door to wake the boys. Everything is as she predicted: Simon is there, sleeping with his small lips slightly parted; his mouth is still a babyish bow-tie shape, and his eyes, restfully shut at this time, are big and kind. His head rolls a little with the sea; the vibration sets his red hair slightly afire. The bedclothes of Sebastien's empty bed are ragged, twisted and stressed down to the last fiber. She remarks, as always, the difference between her two sons and hopes that she does not love Simon more because—a coincidence in the name—he is so much simpler than Sebastien, in almost every way the dearer of the two.

She sits down to pat Simon awake. Simon loves stuffed animals, and there are several in the bed with him, including his beloved toad—his favorite, which is why his older brother calls him Toad. His body remarks on her presence and forms around her like plaster. "Simon," she says, shaking him at last. "Sweetie," she says.

He resists; this is one of the few moments of his day when he can be disagreeable.

"Time to get up."

"No," he answers finally. "My stomach aches."

Simon's excuse for everything is a stomachache. "You'll feel better after breakfast."

"No," he says again, pulling the pillow over his head.

She lets him pretend to fall back asleep. She looks around this stateroom: blond, blond. The French seem absolutely entranced with the blond look. She waits for him to make his move.

"Okay. Fine," snaps Simon. He flings back the covers and marches to the bathroom. Edward calls it the head. Last night at dinner he mentioned that perhaps they should buy a yacht, as soon as they were settled in Maryland and the farm income had reached a sufficient level. She did not argue with him about this—she knows Edward values his comforts too much to put up with cramped spaces—but the last thing in the world *she* wants to do is spend time on a boat. In the last six or seven years she has done all the floating with the tide, the traveling in the currents, she wishes to do. All she wants now is to be permanent for a while, anywhere. The Retreat could be a shack on the marsh, and if no one could come and kick them out, reclaim it because their daughter was moving back from the Continent—as Lord Belsen had done with their most recent flat—she'd be happy.

"Mother," Simon says when he returns, "I do not like Governess." He is referring to the woman—a Scandinavian—who administers the playroom.

Edith helps him into his shirt and shorts. In fact, she doesn't much like the woman either: when she first met Simon she squeezed him painfully on the shoulder and pronounced him too thin. "Too tin," she said, but clearly what she meant was that skinny red-haired English boys, sallow in complexion and shy in manner, effeminate little things, were not at all to her taste. "Oh, I think she's fine. It's just for a few days."

He sits to put on his shoes, and she joins him on the bed. "Will we have a new governess when we got to Maryland?" he asks.

Edith is not sure of the answer, but she suspects not. She does not want him to notice how unsure their future is, so she teases. "Yes. She is an Indian," she says.

The boy's eyes widen with pleasure; he can be fed all day on small jokes, rolling new bits around on his tongue like new tastes. This is where Simon is lovely. Unlike Sebastien, Simon can live in mirth.

"You are lying," he says. Lies are funny to people like Simon; lies are pictures: the woman in buckskins and feathers, with a papoose on her back, squatting not in a teepee but in the nursery in Cottingham. He laughs. Edith can see in his merry eyes the pictures as they unfold. When the Indian wants to wake the boys, she makes a war cry with her hand against her mouth; instead of sewing, she sits in the dayroom in the afternoons and chews on buffalo hides. He smiles again, but now he's ready to move on. "The Indians are all gone," he says.

"Of course they are," she answers. "I meant that she was a Negro." She's thinking of *Gone with the Wind*, which she has read, with mounting dismay and anxiety, as preparation for this move. When she was growing up, a colored woman named Florida had come in from Joliet two days a week to do laundry, and she had been a wonder of fashion and manner, by far the most stylish person who appeared in Edith's girlhood. If this book is any guide, there are no women like Florida in the South.

Simon's brow furrows; he knows that if they have a governess, she could be a colored person. Simon may never have seen a Negro— Edith has tried to recall when he might have, but she can't—and some of his friends in England, whose fathers fought the Zulus, have told him scary stories.

Edith reads all this and recognizes that she made a mistake. "I don't think we will have a governess," she says quickly. "You boys are too big, anyway."

All at once, as if they have crossed some sort of line on the sea (which they have—the quartermaster on the bridge has just watched the barometer lose an inch in the space of three or four miles), the ship begins to heave and roll vigorously. She can hear the whipping strands of wind, and reaches above Simon to close the porthole. The light is silver. "I think it will storm," she says.

"Fun."

She glances at her watch: a few minutes past nine. "We must go. Time for breakfast."

"May I have a sweet roll?" he asks.

She's thinking ahead now, to Edward at breakfast, to finding Sebastien; this private moment with Simon is done. She doesn't really hear him; she nods. "Where is Sebastien? Do you know?"

He shakes his head. Of course he doesn't know. Edith told Sebastien last night, very firmly, that he must not be late for breakfast, that he must be clean and properly dressed. None of these reminders were intended to give him permission to slip out early; she did not want his father to have reason to fault him.

Together, Edith and Simon back out of their stateroom and into the long passageway. It is now advisable for them to keep a hand on the rail as they head forward. Edith has hoped to see Sebastien skulking around at the end of this corridor, by the lifts. This weather has begun to make her nervous; she wonders what is really happening up on the decks. Wind, rain: is it slippery and windy up there?

She pushes the call button for the lift and as soon as the door opens she forces herself and Simon in. She thinks she should check the grand salon and the smoking room first; Sebastien likes those rooms, with all the mumbled conversations to overhear. When the door opens again, Edith moves down the staircases. She's good at spotting his sandy-brown head in crowds; she's had plenty of practice. She surveys the tables and chairs of the salon, but this room is so extravagantly designed and adorned that she can barely discern whether a single human is in there, much less her son. She grabs Simon's hand tighter and they walk briskly through. There are a few groups, but no Sebastien. She goes through the small doors into the smoking room; heads turn now: a woman and a boy. Edith is beginning to get very worried, and she has no use whatsoever for this roomful of men, with their florid faces and self-satisfied mouths.

She must be acting peculiar. Many people appear to have noticed her. Why shouldn't she be worried? What could have possessed her to give him the run of the ship, a boy who knows nothing of the water, a boy who can't even swim? He may be bobbing now in the froth of their path, waving for help. She pictures those paintings of Great Lakes shipwrecks that her father so loves—men with their heads slanted against the surface, cries for help in elongated o's, one arm raised to the lifeboat, already too full, as it recedes into the painting's back reaches.

"You're hurting my hand," says Simon.

"I'm sorry," she says, relaxing her grip somewhat. In answer, the ship shudders as it begins to plow through heavier swells. Edith notices that stewards and other members of the crew seem to have been called out to secure the ship's furnishings for rough weather, and she wonders what happens if someone falls overboard. Do they go back and look for him or just radio to other passing ships? She knows the French are wildly proud of the *Normandie*'s speed records, and she can only wonder what it would take to induce them to lose hours and hours in the middle of the Atlantic.

They get back into the lift, and the porter waits for her destination. She looks at her watch again: twenty past. She decides to go to the dining salon, make excuses to Edward, and then continue the search. Edward has never been willing to make accommodations for the children and pouts when they interfere with plans. Even when he was very young, Sebastien used to make himself late, or ask for something at an inconvenient moment, just for the sport of seeing everyone struggle.

Edith and Simon are led down the dining room and toward a grotesque statue of Peace. The French seem to love these oversized females and have put them at every promontory; this woman's huge breasts take Edith's appetite away. There, at the base of this landmark, are Edward and Sebastien. Edith drops her grip on Simon and stares at them. Simon rubs his hand. Edith is so busy feeling foolish and angry that she doesn't remind herself that the last place she expected to find Sebastien was breakfasting at his father's side.

Edward begins to rise, still holding on to this morning's edition of *Gangplank*, a full smile shining momentarily through the toast and jam. He's proud of himself; he thinks this is the sort of thing she wants him to do.

"As you can see, my dear, the boy and I have begun." He beckons toward Sebastien, who is nearly obscured by sweet rolls, jam pots, chops, kidneys, and eggs. Edith glares disapprovingly at this mound of food, which Edward notices. "The fatted calf," he says. He often peppers his speech with biblical references, some quite long and flawlessly recalled, but always as a joke and a revenge against his mother, who had drilled all these passages into his head in the first place. "The return of the prodigal."

She looks at him and realizes that he is mocking her, and she does not especially like it, still so fresh from terror. She glances quickly at Sebastien. "I was worried," she says.

Sebastien shrugs. "I'm sorry," he says, staring from his deep hazel eyes. She knows it is silly, a mother's superstition, the fruit of her darkest fears, but she has always felt she should not look too long into Sebastien's eyes, as if everything were written there. She loves him far too much to want to know his future.

"Don't shrug at me. I mean it."

"We've been having a splendid time," says Edward, interrupting, playing a very unfamiliar role: peacemaker, protector of children.

"You should have sent him back to get me," she says. Edward manufactures a contrite expression. She looks again at Sebastien, sitting behind his breakfast. He was a big child, a little fat around the middle and rounded in the chin; he's still big, but in the last year the loose flesh has melted and the fine bones of his face are coming through. He has dressed properly this morning, with a tie that is clean and unwrinkled. Perhaps she has overreacted. This *is* a rather unusual scene; she would love to have heard these two as they settled into the plan. Edward has given some signs that he will be an acceptable father when the time comes, but will Sebastien accept his father? He is old enough—and perceptive enough—to sense that there is something unjust about his parents' dominion over him; as a younger child he was stubborn, but now his resistance is becoming more active, part of a larger plan.

"I would like a sweet roll," says Simon. "I should like a chop like Sebastien's."

Edith quiets him, and is annoyed when Edward continues with his biblical reference.

" 'It is meet to make merry,' " he says to Simon, " 'for this thy brother was dead—' "

"Please, Edward," says Edith.

"A classical education . . ."

"I don't think making jokes about the Bible is education."

"I'm giving him culture, the greatest gift I have to bestow." He turns once again to Simon. "I will explain it to you. 'A certain man had two sons.' Absolutely fatal mistake, of course. No winning that game."

Simon is now hooked, and he reacts the way Edith expects: he giggles.

"It's not funny," she says to both of them.

The waiter is standing above them, and she orders a sweet roll and a chop for Simon, as if to buy him back from his father.

"The morning is quite beautiful," Edward says. "There is a strange, menacing color in the light. It's turning stormy, you know." He points to the water in his glass, the liquid surface holding level, rigid as a wafer, as the table tips. "We won't have any trouble, of course." He reaches for another piece of toast and takes a large, almost splintering bite. He has always chewed vigorously, crunching through foods like soup and pudding that don't seem to contain anything crisp or dense. His brow furrows somewhat. "That old hag Francis. Terrible." He finishes chewing and then wipes his chin; the huge napkin covers his face. "Has some damn deal with Germany on her mind."

"I don't think Americans will ever understand Europe," says Edith. "All they care about is Wallis Simpson."

"Oh," says Edward expansively, "we shall see. I suspect America has changed a great deal since we left."

Edith doesn't really care if America has changed. Edward left his America by design, fueled by disdain; if America is now a different place, that gives him license to return. Edith left her America rather carelessly, cast it off in an extravagant display of youth. She was only twenty, and moving to England seemed glamorous and fun; that was what Edward promised when he proposed. Her marriage and expatriation had shocked her friends and family in Winnetka, which added to her pleasure, but she had never intended to turn her back on them, or on America. In many ways, as the years passed, it had been her family and America that had turned their backs on her.

"Did you sleep well?" Edward asks, after a particularly long-hanging roll of the ship. A muffled chorus of groans goes up during this hang-time, capped by the clattering of a single silver plate cover.

"I have been having wild dreams. Don't ask me to describe them."

He reaches over and pats the back of her hand. "Of course you have. We are on quite an adventure."

Edith reflects that yes, this move is an adventure, at least, is a journey to a strange place, and yes, that would account for her dreams. She has spent months imagining a house in Maryland, helplessly attempting to fill in the blankness and uncertainty, and this has come out in dream as a visual cacophony. Yes, she thinks, Edward is right. She lets out a long, relaxing breath and is amazed by how much better she feels. As this great ship pitches and rolls through the glittering foam, she'd like to think they're going to a better life. As reward. For growing up. For being a good mother. For being, at base, loyal to her husband, as difficult as that has been; for trying to understand his pain over the past several years and for forgiving two dalliances—two that she knows of—with office girls, and the one affair that was really not forgivable, the one that in many ways had killed her joy, just the way the Depression had killed his. She knows she must start—must continue—to pretend that there is still hope in her, because maybe the real thing will follow. She makes herself smile, and though it is far from the truth, she adds, "Yes. A nice family adventure."

—

SEBASTIEN LOOKS UP from his plate in time to see her take his father's hand. There is no one on earth, nor will there ever be, whom Sebastien loves more than his mother, but he is not above finding fault in her. It makes him seethe to see her bright, hopeful smile, just as it makes him furious to see his little brother take humor from their father's blusters. Smiles and laughter are lies in the face of what he knows is the truth: that this "family adventure" is his father's final disaster. This place in America is simply the remains of the privilege. God knows what it is like. Each time they moved over the final few years in England the talk was the same, as if he couldn't see with his own eyes that they were on a downward spiral: if the new house was passable, the move was "a new start"; if the house was dreadful, it was "temporary." What, he wonders, does it mean when the move is an adventure?

Sebastien is a smart boy, despite an education thus far interrupted frequently by his father's latest theories or financial setbacks. He knows, for example, that if anyone at this table is playing the part of the prodigal son, it is his father. He doubts that anyone in Maryland will slaughter the fatted calf when they arrive. Sebastien knows far more about this family's finances than his mother does. He's seen and read the threatening letters; he's overheard the desperate transatlantic telephone calls to a bank in Boston; he knows the most explosive secret of all: that without his mother's knowledge, this last bit of luxury, the crossing on the *Normandie*, has been paid for by her parents.

He listens to them talk about the day. His father consults the *Gangplank* again, and notes that *Design for Living* is playing at the theater. There is a hat ball planned for the evening—how diverting! An illustrated lecture this morning on Diego Rivera and a talk on German rearmament. "That's one I'll avoid," his father says. "Mrs. Francis will be there, passing out armbands."

"Simon and I will go for a walk," says Edith. Simon is ecstatic that he will not be sent to the nursery and jumps up. She stands, and immediately two waiters come to help the family depart. One of them brings his father's coat, hat, and umbrella. The dining room is about half full; at the next table is a French family with a girl about Sebastien's age. She smiles at Sebastien, and he pretends not to notice.

By the time the family has wandered through the tables, and his father has stopped to greet an old man, who seemed heartily annoyed to have his breakfast interrupted, and they have proceeded up the grand bank of stairs and into the cloakroom, Sebastien has broken loose. He is suddenly so grateful to be free that a small, birdlike chirping escapes from his lips. He's moving rapidly down the main hall past the lifts, up the stairs opposite the entrance to the chapel, past the florist's and the gift shop. He has no plans other than to continue his searches through this ship: he does not know exactly what he is looking for—he never does—knows only that this ship has a heart somewhere, a place he can touch, an unseen X on the deck or a light shining from within a piece of steel. He has always needed to find this spot wherever he goes; he is haunted by it, especially because there always seems to be one, a place where everything makes sense for him, where there is rough balance. For a few years now he has wanted to explain this to his mother, but he is afraid. He knows it is odd—perhaps he is even mentally defective. He has already searched the boiler rooms, been caught by a stoker, and been brought roughly back to the passenger spaces and shoved into the gentler clutch of a tourist-class steward. He has spent an hour on the signal bridge, where the starched deckhands patted his head and indulged his presence until an officer came and sent him back down.

At various times he has come upon his father making his own sweeps, and once, as they were entering the tourist-class gymnasium from opposite directions, their eyes met. His father pretended to be lost and made a large show of asking for directions to the lifts. They did not speak to each other. He wants most to explore the stewards' quarters, the holds and storerooms. In the cutaway drawing of the ship, there is pictured an airplane stored in the garage on F Deck. It sits, darkened, still as a corpse. Sebastien wonders whether there really is an airplane on the ship, and whether it has a machine gun and can carry bombs. He wonders if there are German U-boats in the ocean. On the weather decks, he thinks he can hear the laughter of their crews coming up from the deep.

He's still standing outside the florist's, looking down the passageway toward the other shops. The shopkeepers are stowing their wares; deckhands are hurriedly setting up storm railings across the wider expanses of the ship's elegant spaces. As he moves forward, past the hairdresser's and the manicurist's, into the passageways of the *appartements de luxe*, he observes the stewards as they go door-to-door, preparing the passengers for a storm, lashing down steamer trunks, respectfully suggesting that picture frames, perfumes, and other personal items might be removed from tabletops. There is excitement in the air; everybody seems charged, as if this is the moment the ship will show its every quality. Sebastien knows he must find a place quickly where he can wait it out. The ship is pitching deeper into the troughs, and he knows now that he wants to be up where it is happening.

People have begun to take more notice of him, warning him back to the supposed security of his family's stateroom. He hates those looks, the same ones he used to get in London. The elevator operator eyes him warily, but takes him up. When Sebastien gets off the lift, now up in the ship's superstructure, he can hear the wind and the claps of waves on the steep sides of the ship. For a moment he hesitates, realizes that he is at the entrance to the winter garden, and decides to go in.

The door closes behind him with a hiss. The space is hushed by a deep blanket of fragrances: the light perfume of the blossoms over the sharper musk of soils, the slightly acrid burn of wet metal: cast-iron planters and lead-soldered watering cans. It seems stiller here, with the palms in their glassed-in planters waving only slightly, as if in a mild breeze. The light from outside is rose, as in the evening, and not a stark warning of trouble ahead.

He moves into the center of the room and is surprised to find that a single passenger, a young woman, has been watching him through the vegetation. She is pretty and she smiles at him. Her hair is brown and straight, and it ends in a slight wave on her collar, unlike the tightly marcelled coiffures of his mother and all the other women in the world. When she speaks to him, he can tell she is American. "It is rough out," she says, and then laughs at herself, because just then there is a huge handslap of water across the tall windows.

He smiles back; he has to remind himself to speak out loud. "My mother will be seasick. She . . ." he starts to say, but is stopped by the flash of an image: the ship sinking, a battered wreck, but this winter garden, with him and this woman safe inside, floating serenely away from the fray.

"She?" The woman has not let her face lose its bright, encouraging look, but Sebastien can feel the solitariness of this scene. This woman is alone in the winter garden because she needs to be.

"Oh. She was very nervous when we left. I don't think she trusts ships."

"And you?"

"I suppose we shall be fine. Don't you?"

"Of course we will."

"You . . . ?" Sebastien begins. He doesn't have anything to say, but he does not want to let her go. She is gathering up her coat and book.

"You're funny," says the woman. "You never finish your sentences."

"Oh," he says. He looks around this place, hushed like a churchyard; he can almost hear the drowsy gong of unhurried sheepbells. "You are American?" he asks finally.

"Yes."

"Do you know where Maryland is?"

Her expression takes on color now; she looks at him a little more closely. She tells Sebastien that she knows where Maryland is, and that a girlfriend of hers at Mount Holyoke—her college, she explains—lives in Baltimore, but she has never visited the city. She lives near Boston herself, in Massachusetts. "Do you know where Boston is?"

"Yes," he answers. "My father grew up there."

"But you're English?"

"I guess."

"Are you going to visit someone in Maryland? Are you on vacation?" she asks.

"No," he says. She looks at him quizzically, and he can well understand why, but before this moment, he's never said to anyone, much less to himself, that they were moving there to live. "My father owns a farm," he says finally.

"With horses? That will be fun."

"I suppose."

"You don't sound very happy about it."

He shrugs; he isn't sure he knows why she bothers to say this.

"Doesn't it matter?" she asks.

"If I'm happy about it?"

"Yes."

He shrugs again. His mother tells him not to make this coarse gesture, but often indifference takes over and he does it involuntarily.

The woman waits for him to respond further, and when he doesn't, she reaches for her tablet and pen. She gets up just as the ship plows deep, and for a moment she grabs the air, and then latches on to his arm. Her hand, where it brushes his wrist, is hot as a coin. She wedges her legs between the table and the chair. "Why don't you come back with me? We'll find your father."

"No," he says. "Thank you."

She gives him a wary look. "Can I trust you?" she asks.

"Yes. I shall be careful."

"Later on will you have tea with me?" she asks, and he nods, which satisfies her enough to leave him. He goes to the windows and looks out over the bow into the blackening sky. The changes are happening fast. He sees now that there is a deck area forward of the winter garden that ends with a high wavebreak to take care of weather coming over the bow. That is what is happening now— green seas breaking like thunder; when the ship rolls into the troughs, wave tops rise high above the smokestacks and spars. But this deck area, a broad expanse of silver planking, seems dry and secure. He forces open one of the doors and looks out over a hatch cover. The wind tears at his tie and his coattails, and the air is brittle, and dense with change; he is immediately soaked by a spray so fine and sharp that it doesn't even feel wet. He sees where the side-deck railing meets the brilliant white steel of the wavebreak, and he knows that it is right there, half in the wind and half out, that he wants to stand. There are lifelines strung on stanchions out to a door in the center of the break, and railings from there. He sets out into the wind and the whistle, leans hard, and keeps pushing forward until he hits the protection of the break, and suddenly he is becalmed, the plowing of this great ship into the storm is at balance in this sheltered spot. This is what he has been looking for. When there is a snap of wind that eddies around the deck, he hears the voices of the crewmembers who have been sent out to retrieve him. He looks back and above, at the bridge, and sees that officers are pointing and shouting at him. He doesn't care, he has made it now to his spot, and he's holding on to it, with a roaring ship behind him and an endless gray expanse ahead. He is finally at that place beyond human invention, and he is being lifted, by the huge waves and that tiny bow, by the muscular hands of the crewmen who are now trying to pry him away, by a momentary flight of his soul. Sebastien has never, ever, felt more free, and he knows that with a small wriggle of his arms he could escape the grasp of the cursing crewmen, alight the rail, and jump out over the water so far that only God could follow his flight.

And this is where Harry Mason pictures Sebastien, his uncle, as a young boy, in the grip of foreign-speaking strangers who are fighting their way back across the foredeck to the illusory security of the superstructure. This is what Harry imagines to be true. The rest he knows. How the *Normandie*, whose Blue Ribbon was then flying on the *Queen Mary* but was soon to be retaken, completes this crossing in yet another splendid display and deposits the family in the New World. In a few short years, those glorious salons and promenades, half submerged in the fecal muck of New York Harbor, will be cut off like gangrene, as if a thousand stewards had never served there, as if orchestras and theater companies had never performed there, as if no one had ever made love, or been denied love, in those beds now foul with harbor water. The seas will become what they have always been throughout history: a place for war, choppy with shattered debris, with weathered lifeboats carrying skeletons in the tradewinds. This war will save more than one failed career and rebuild, almost to earlier levels, thousands of family fortunes. This war, which nobody wants but everybody needs, is waiting ahead not like a storm or like a fire but like a promise. Harry knows what is to unfold in an old wreck of a house in Maryland, and knows that these events will haunt his father, Simon, for the rest of his life. Harry knows that this story, told to him over and over again for reasons that he can barely imagine, is now his to tell his own children, to be taken well or badly, to be believed wholly or in part, like a kiss.

2
_____

"WE'LL COME OVER tomorrow," Mason shouted into the phone. They were in a room in the Belvedere Hotel in Baltimore, and he was talking, at long last, with McCready, the farm manager at the Retreat. He had been trying to get him to a telephone for a week; he had understood that Miss Mary Mason, from whom he had inherited the place, had both a phone and electricity, and he was horrified to learn that the phone service had been allowed to lapse, as if vines had come into the house and strangled it silent. "What?" He cupped the receiver and said to Edith, "I can hardly understand a word this man says."

She tried to give him an encouraging smile. Simon was sitting on her lap, humming to himself, and Sebastien was staring out the window. The gaseous late-afternoon sun seemed to burn into the room, and the odors from the docks, from the workboats and streaked steamers, from the men and the horses, the cargoes and catches, were overpowering.

Mason listened for a moment more, his brow creased with confusion and dismay. He glanced down at the map spread on the bed in front of him. "The ferry lands at Love Point. On Kent Island. It must be at most ten miles from the Retreat."

"Edward. Don't yell at him."

"My dear, I will handle it." He had been saying this for days, as they cleared customs in New York and set out in two taxis to Grand Central Station—one just for the luggage—to catch the Twentieth Century Limited. This exhausting phase had not upset him. He'd enjoyed the Irish cabbie's hints about visiting America: Don't miss Grant's Tomb; carry your money in your shoes; avoid Jews and Italians. But once in Winnetka he all but had to sign an affidavit assuring Edith's father that in one year the bloody farm would be sprouting greenbacks. He had had to listen to lectures about bringing a business through hard times, when, really, it was nothing but astounding luck that Mr. Taylor owned a business that would flourish in the Depression: a bonded warehouse and moving concern.

"Tomorrow," Edward repeated for the last time. This conversation felt like speaking English to a Chinaman. Wasn't the request simple enough? Why had it taken such negotiation and explanation? Edward wanted to scream into the telephone, but simply signed off and threw his hands up into the air for the benefit of his family. He looked out at the faces, Edith's sharp eyes disapprovingly narrowed, Simon's innocent little smile, and Sebastien's blank, uncharitable mask. All their questions were upon him. Before he was married, Edward had not anticipated that a family would offer so many personalities to deal with; he'd thought mother and children would stand as one, their needs simple: lodging, sustenance.

"Well, then," said Edith. She dumped Simon out of her lap. "It's arranged."

"Yes," said Edward. "Yes." He raised his hands again, this time as if asking her not to shoot him.

"Perhaps we should eat. It would make us all feel better," said Edith.

Edward raised his left hand to his face, removed his glasses, and pinched the bridge of his nose so hard the pain spread through his sinuses and into his temples. Even food had lost its ability to cheer him. How was he going to pay for dinner, for this hotel room? He was down to the coins in his pocket. He had tipped lavishly on disembarking from the *Normandie*, but what was he to do? One's reputation on an ocean liner literally traveled round the world. Edward wanted to lie down and hold his breath until this all went away; he wanted complete stillness, the heartstop between clock ticks. This happened to him sometimes; sometimes this feeling had lasted for days, but he didn't have days now, not in this hotel room with his wife and sons and these masses of suitcases, pathetic storehouses of belongings, the only things salvaged from the defeat, a few good suits, his shaving kit. As his friend Lord Belsen had once said, a man is still a lord if he has his razor, but the remark wasn't amusing now—it probably wasn't then, though Edward didn't stop to recall the moment—it was a prophecy, an indictment. Oh, the waste and stain of it. He still had his hand on his nose, but he had relaxed his grip; his face now felt loose over the bones, as if he could rip it off, his last possession.

"Edward?"

She sounded like his mother. Perhaps she was his mother. He didn't really care anymore whether he gained her approval or not. Whose approval? Hers. Whose? This was getting confusing for him, and he was completely exhausted, much too tired to think, tired out. God! Tired, beat. "I'm very tired," he said, perhaps out loud. He would be fine if he could get some rest, and if he could stop smelling these damn cigars. He looked up, and it seemed to him that Sebastien was sitting at the window, smoking a huge, foul cigar, kissing a long noose of smoke straight at his neck. Put that out, Edward thought he might say. Somehow he had ended up lying full-out on the bed, his waistcoat still buttoned, lying like a drunk with his shoes on, unable to move. He struggled a bit. His father had died paralyzed and unable to say more than a word or two at a time, just his eyes moving, cancer having eaten his spine. Edward had come over from England for the event, and he sat through that mute week, wondering what one question he would ask his father if one could be answered. Nothing came to mind. His father died hearing everyone claiming to know his needs and wishes best: He likes the drapes drawn. No, he always loved the sun. The sun, the son—did he love the son? Do you love me? His father died being pummeled with questions: Are you comfortable? Do you need the bedpan? Can you hear me? Can you hear me? But no damn answers, not a single one. "I will give thee the treasures of darkness." Isaiah, Edward thought. A damn good line, but why did that pop into his head? Maybe he was dying. He struggled again, but his feet, damn it, his feet seemed tied.

"Edward," she said. "Stop squirming. Let me take your shoes off. You rest for a moment."

Rest for a moment. Yes. The very thing. Edith, yes, it was Edith. Quite right, as usual, she was. Damn fine girl. A little rest would help greatly. Maybe, after a nap, a little roll in the hay. And then a few details to attend to: number one, reconnoiter this miserable little ferry; number two, eat dinner; number three, talk to the hotel manager and explain that payment will be wired as soon as the family reaches the Retreat. Not, all things considered, a long list; he wouldn't even consider these items a challenge, were he at home in England. Yes, thank you, he thought, as a shoe traveled down the slippery length of his foot. It did feel much better to have those shoes off. Yes, that blanket was indeed a comfort. Just half an hour

would restore him. Remind me to tell you of Father's last words
to me. He ... He ...

—

EDITH LEFT THE ROOM, flicking off the light switch. She suspected that Edward would sleep through the night, and she hoped
he would; he deserved rest. She had watched him keep the visit
going in Winnetka, and it had touched her to see him make such
efforts, willing to ignore her father's snipes, trying to flatter her
mother about her terrible cooking. For enduring her brother-in-
law's advice on investments, Edward merited a Victoria Cross.

"Is Father ill?" asked Simon when they reached the elevators.
He was frightened by the American accents, by the noise on the
streets and the informal behavior of people passing by. The taxis
smelled odd to him, like boiled cabbage, and he hated the way a
boy had stared at him in the Pullman car. He wanted to pretend
that he was a prince, that his father was a lord, that his family was
on holiday and would quite soon be returning to their castle.

"He's tired," said Edith. "Men get tired," she added to her sons,
though she did not know exactly why, except that it seemed true
that men were allowed simply to get tired, and women were allowed
only to collapse.

Sebastien was at the far end of the hallway, looking out the
window, his fair hair backlit into a halo. Down below, he could
see the evening calm on the docks, fingers of traffic out into the
oily harbor, the slight bobbing of the schooners as a motor launch
passed by. She called to him, and when he had drawn up to her
side, he asked, "Is this what you pictured? Maryland?"

"Please, dear. No hard questions just now."

"But is it?"

She swatted him on the back of the hand. "I don't know what
I pictured," she said. "It seems fine."

It was early in the evening, but the hotel restaurant was quite full, mostly with couples. She'd forgotten this about America, that when people went out, it was almost always as man and woman, as a family, quite often, even with younger children. She liked being there with the boys, and she liked the interested looks they got: this lone woman and two sons.

"My stomach hurts. What is there to eat?" said Simon, putting down his menu. The items on this menu were strange, even for her—odd seafood and vegetables, crab dishes with obscure names. She ordered prime beef, which was one of the things of America that she especially missed during her years in England.

"When will we get to the Retreat?" asked Simon.

"Will you tell him to stop asking so many questions?" said Sebastien.

"Mother, Sebastien is being mean to me."

"Stop. Please," she said to them both. They were too many years apart to bicker directly, so when they quarreled—which didn't happen often—they did it like this, through her. She went back to Simon's question. "Tomorrow. We'll ride a ferryboat across the Bay. It will be fun."

"Will there be turkeys at the Retreat?"

She had told the boys about visiting her Aunt Emily's farm in Indiana as a child and being chased by the turkeys. Simon thought this sounded like lots of fun.

"I don't know. We'll have to see. Cows and sheep, certainly."

"And Negroes," added Sebastien.

"Slaves? Are they still?" Simon asked.

"Of course not," Edith snapped, but she could say no more about Negroes. She didn't know anything about Negroes—where they lived, whether they held jobs, whether they would be happy and simple or menacing and angry. She noticed a red-faced man at the next table, a man a little older than Edward, intently eavesdropping, and she moved in her chair to tip the balance of her face away from him.

"But there were," said Sebastien. "Father said there were slaves on the Retreat until Abraham Lincoln."

"Let's drop this," she said. When their dinner was done, she felt waterlogged with food. "Let's go see what Baltimore looks like."

They strolled down toward the harbor in the pale and mild warmth of the evening, along the wharves of Light Street with its row of steamship offices, most of them looking dilapidated, their entrances, once grand and welcoming, now boarded up, lesser doors cut into unpainted siding. "This is rather squalid," said Sebastien. They turned back into the city, toward a dome that appeared to be a large municipal building, City Hall perhaps. Friendly American faces invited them to enjoy the sights; there were monuments, parks, policemen at most corners. It became a fine walk, a restorative return to dry land, and Edith reentered the hotel feeling that in all its modesty, the City of Baltimore had done its best to welcome her.

As they entered the lobby, she was surprised to see Edward standing at the doorway to the dining room, deep in conversation with the man who had been intruding upon her during dinner. He was short and had a large nose; he was ugly, but in some way not unattractive, like an Australian. She looked for a way to sneak past them, but when she could not, she released the boys to their room.

"This is Mr. Hazelton," Edward announced with huge pleasure. "His mother was a Mason. He's boning me up on the family tree."

Mr. Hazelton bowed at her slightly. Edith found it a little difficult to believe this squat little man, with his studied European manner, was the product of a Maryland dynasty.

"A western shore Mason," Edward continued, as if he had grown up dividing his world between these two shores. "But they can trace their way back to the Retreat."

"My mother entertained Miss Mary often when she was here. Miss Mary's house was on Charles Street at Mount Vernon Place, as you know. We are just around the corner."

"Ah," said Edward. Edith did not think Edward knew of this place.

Hazelton picked up the slight hesitation. "She spent her winters here, of course."

"Naturally," said Edward, aiming a slight cough into his large palm, avoiding Edith's eyes.

Hazelton now turned to Edith. "I hope you didn't think I was being rude during dinner. I was enjoying your accent. We work hard to maintain standards, but it helps to hear the real thing."

Edith was not ready to accept this apology. All week, people had been mistaking her for English, which, oddly, irritated her, leaving her without a native land. "It isn't the real thing," she said tartly. "I was born and raised in Illinois."

Mr. Hazelton took a step back, as if physically pushed. "Yes," he said. "I see."

There was a pause, during which Edward glared at Edith. He turned back to Hazelton. "My man at the Retreat is positively unintelligible."

Hazelton's spirit returned. "Well, now, the Eastern Shore is at a further remove, isn't it?" he said, with a somewhat coarse laugh at the end.

"Still?" said Edward. Ah, he implied, the old Eastern Shore, never changes a whit.

"Oh, more than ever, now that the steamboats have stopped runs up the rivers. The ladies used to come over for the day. It's still very hard for me to imagine that this way of life is over."

Whatever this Hazelton was, he spoke with a yearning that Edith could understand, and she began to feel sorry for flattening him. "These changes are difficult," she said.

He acknowledged her sympathetic tone. "Oh, I guess they couldn't make it pay anymore." He waved in what Edith knew was the direction of the docks. "You can imagine the upkeep."

This was not a turn in the conversation that Edward had sought. He had awaked disoriented and flushed in his hotel room; he might well have sunk back into his humid despair had not his powerful hunger—he hadn't eaten all day—reminded him that life could always be made to improve by taking things one at a time. He had washed, dressed, and arranged a truce on the subject of money with the hotel management, and the evening began to appear potentially jolly, particularly after the chance meeting with a cousin, a man a good bit older than he but one Edward could call a peer. But this talk of the Eastern Shore was spoiling his appetite. "This Depression can't last forever," he said.

"Quite right," said Hazelton, though Edith could plainly see that the Depression was not what had saddened this rich man, that he had probably barely noticed it. "I was just saying to your husband that I would have been delighted to run you over in my boat tomorrow, except that she is in the yard for repairs. My son, Thomas, is always looking for an excuse to take her out."

"I gather the ferry is quite convenient," said Edward. "Just a block from here."

"Oh, yes. To Love Point. There used to be a fine hotel there, but I suspect it's gone now."

Edith considered this. "You make it sound as if the whole place has gone back to the savages."

"No, really. My friend Mencken forgets this, but some of our finest families are still there."

"Mencken?" she asked.

"Don't worry about him." Hazelton clearly assumed it was impossible not to know who he was. "His readers all know he writes for effect."

"Exactly," said Edward forcefully. "I agree." As usual, Edward did this beautifully, not really implying that he knew what or who Hazelton was talking about, but simply suggesting that on some deep level he had understood the point. Trust Edward Mason to keep up; no need to slow down a good conversation on his account. "Hazelton has invited me for a nightcap at his club," he said finally.

—

EDITH BID EDWARD and Hazelton good night, and turned thankfully to the elevators. The rooms were cooler now, brushed by a dry breeze. She went into the boys' room to say good night, but they were both asleep, drifting on a new continent. She looked down on those blameless heads on their American pillows; her love for them felt brittle, and the uncertainties she had subjected them to hurt like shards of glass. It had been time, past time, to give the boys a better life. Living in the wreckage of Edward's business, England itself falling further and further into disrepair—where could children find joy in that? And their parents' marriage, once so wonderfully impulsive and sweet—what could bitterness teach the boys? What kind of parent had either of them been these past few years?

She stood at the window. The twilight coming from behind the hotel was red, humming with red. The light cast a glow upon the stained white superstructures of the ferries and side-wheel steamboats, with their odd collection of names ornamented boldly under the arc of the paddle housings: *Potomac, Emma Giles, Dreamland*; in the twilight these derelict vessels could almost appear new. She looked down the long harbor, which the lobby captain had informed her was actually a river, the Patapsco. Out there, down the river, the light was skittish in the evening haze and she knew it was the Bay. She had already begun to feel this Bay around her; she could hear it in the people's voices and smell it in the air, the insistent stab of water right into their lives, the Bay's rivers reaching deep into the land to take whole towns into their clenched fists.

—

IT WAS FIVE o'clock in the afternoon of the next day before the family boarded the ferry. Edward had awaked late and had accepted an invitation to lunch from two of the men he met at the club. What a picture these clubmen painted of his new home! He heard about ignorant, toothless employees, lynch mobs, Negroes both murderous and unfairly accused. He heard about exhausted farms, failed canneries, fallen families, lines of the poor and indigent winding through baked, charmless communities that, almost as a special mockery to him, had stolen the names he cherished most: Salisbury, Cambridge, Oxford. He heard, finally, of Methodists and Quakers, and a temperance movement still so powerful that the Eastern Shore and the west were separated not merely by the Chesapeake Bay but by a schism between the wets—his people, after all—and the drys, and guess which side was which?

After supervising the hotel bellboys as they loaded the mass of luggage onto the deck, and letting them go without a tip, Edward settled Edith and the boys into a dark lounge. It smelled of coal and coffee, two smells Edward hated, but he was able to buy Edith a cup of tea and the boys some biscuits, and he took his leave to go forward into the fresh air. They were already in the middle of the harbor, moving heavily past a confused display of fishing boats, and schooners loaded with lumber high on the decks; a small runabout motored smartly past, carrying three men with briefcases.

The ferry rounded a buoy into the channel of the Patapsco and came to a course downriver. The river was lined with commerce, but ahead the banks were greener and lower, and out there the broad mouth of the river seemed to drink of the Bay like a whale. He heard the slosh of a slight chop, and then the ferry moved past the last of the points into a deeper, more powerful swell. The whole vista came into view, a seascape to the north and south, but to the east, a hazy and fragile promise of dry land, this Eastern Shore. Edward could appreciate this landscape, but who could really know whether he would survive it? He was lonely suddenly, and frightened, and he turned almost instinctively for Edith and discovered that, soundlessly, she had been there for some time. "There you are," he said.

"It's quite beautiful, really. Isn't it? It's like Holland."

"Oh. A little. Because the land is so low, do you mean?"

"Edward?"

"Yes, my dear."

"Perhaps things will work out."

This was the first time she had ever come close to saying this, through the trials of their past months, through evenings when they could hardly bear to look at each other.

"That's kind of you to say. I hope it can make up for some of what I have done. I certainly made a hash of things."

She put her arm around his waist. "None of it was your fault. None of the trouble with the works, I mean. You have done your best. We know that."

"We?"

"The boys and I. Even Daddy understands. The world doesn't condemn you."

He did not react to the mention of her father, though it helped a great deal to hear her say it. "I don't suppose I shall ever win much credit from Sebastien, but Simon seems to like me." He coughed into his hand; perhaps he was being a little too sentimental here, but the thought that Simon might care for him raised a scratch in his throat. He said, "I hope to win you back, Edith. You know I can do absolutely nothing without you. Through all my mistakes, I've always loved you."

Edward did not think that what she felt for him was love any-more—he'd given her too much cause for anger over the past few years; he'd let her see the pathetic side of his charm—but there was much of love in her manner, pieces of it: a tenderness at times. That was what he needed so badly, what he was asking for, those moments of refuge in the kindness of her heart.

She flicked a bird feather, a sea gull's, most likely, from his collar, and rested her hand there. "You don't have to win me back," she said.

That had to do for Edward, that kindly neutral, or neutrally unkind, statement, because the boys had come forward to stand with them, and the Eastern Shore was fast approaching. It was now the whole family, the Masons, lately of London, England, standing together, for better or worse, as features of the shoreline became distinct, a high stand of spindly pines, a water tower, houses here and there along the shore, and a small fishing village well to the south, offering a wharf that jutted hundreds of feet into the Bay.

"Look," Sebastien said. "That's got to be it. The red light."

Edward peered out; a ghostly form sprung up in front of him. It was time for him to lead again, to cast off his doubts, to be the first man to set foot on the new world. The whole pier was under a roof, and the dim lighting inside cast a shrouded glow on the water and made the structure appear to be hovering. There were several men standing in readiness, ferry workers, perhaps, and a few others leaning against freight and machinery.

The ferry nudged alongside the pier, and it seemed to take only a light tug on lines fore and aft to draw it in. The other passengers—the farmers, the politicians and county bureaucrats—had gone to their vehicles, and the smell of exhaust started to filter out through the seams in the ferry's bulkheads. The black passengers, who during the crossing had been full of chatter and cheer in the stern, were quiet now; as soon as their gangplank was across, the men and women moved off and fanned onto the macadam parking area, some cutting into tall marsh grasses and corn, some heading for a line of unlit cabins a few yards down the road, all of them into the night, the gloves of the women and the T-shirts of the men the last things visible.

The family stood on the pier as the ferry crew unloaded the bags. They made it clear that this was a kindness and not a service, but they did it cheerfully enough. The ferry departed. No one, among the last workers closing up, or the last passengers departing the landing, asked after their plans. Perhaps it would not have surprised anyone if these rich, foreign-looking people simply shouldered their luggage and melted into the cattails with the Negroes.

Edward walked down the pier and stared out onto the darkened lot. To one side there was a hotel establishment of some sort, probably what was left of the once-fashionable resort that Hazelton had mentioned. A breeze waved past, a rotten breeze from behind the crab shacks. Two of the black men had remained behind, waiting for a ride or lingering before returning home. Edward knew McCready was out there, in one of the three Fords in the lot. He could go hunting, but instead he stood rigid. He would outlast this man, he would bury him soon enough. He offered himself to be served; in England no one—a stranger, a bobby, a child—would pass by such a commanding figure without offering assistance. Here, perhaps not, but Edward would not give McCready the satisfaction of a single suggestion of doubt, no glancing at the watch, no double-checking the name of the ferry landing.

At last the headlights on one of the Fords lit up, and the car pulled around next to Edward. Edward stooped a little to talk through the window but continued to give the impression that he was standing unbowed. "Mr. McCready, I trust."

"Yes. That's me." He looked about fifty—though it turned out that he was much younger—with a wrinkled face, and black gaps between his teeth. His ears seemed enormous, and he grinned sleepily as he answered Edward, which made him seem simple-minded. "Dozed off there, I reckon."

"Thank you for coming," Edward said, his manners always larger than himself, but really he wanted to smack him, this miserable, foolish little man. Edward ignored the fact that he had not told McCready what ferry to meet, which meant he had probably been sitting there all day. "My family is waiting," he said. He put an accent on the word "family" that indicated he was talking not only about Edith and the boys but about all those Masons, living and dead, who had dominated cultural and political life on this wretched peninsula for the past three hundred years. "I do not know how you expect to carry us and all our luggage."

"Oh, right smart of room in a Ford. We can use the roof."

"For whom?"

McCready did not answer, but he headed down the pier to find the luggage.

He came back with a few smaller cases, and announced that they would leave the trunks and the rest of the luggage there tonight, and he and the hired boy would bring the truck back in the morning.

"Leave them here?" said Edward. He nodded toward the black men still loitering under the streetlight.

McCready seemed confused. "You wouldn't be thinking them boys there would touch those bags, would you?" The utter foolishness of the idea remained on his brow; he shook his head, as if now he'd heard everything—colored boys messing with a white man's things. "The onliest things you need worry about is keeping them away from buzzard droppings."

Edward didn't want to even speculate as to what this last comment meant, and Edith and the boys had come up behind, carrying a few more small items for the night. Her cheeks were darkened, her mouth drawn in with fatigue.

"My dear, get in and we will pack."

She thanked him, and after he and McCready put the things into a filthy and musty trunk, and after he closed Edith and the boys in the backseat, which smelled of sour milk and Bon Ami, he stood erect once more. He ran his eye across this now-familiar wasteland, the piers, the rotting hotel, the indolent night Negroes, the grasses, and out there, this tepid, brackish Bay. He was beside the water, and here, he thought, now, was the time to say what had long ago occurred to him as the appropriate words for this moment. He turned toward her, hands at his sides as if to accept a martyr's wounds, to permit the stones and arrows as they cut into his flesh. "This," he said, "this is our Babylon. But we shall prosper in spite of it."

"Oh, for goodness' sake, Edward. Just get in the car."

McCready drove them slowly over flat, dark land, through the sounds of peepers and bullfrogs, the alternating pungent odors of tidal flats and cow manure. In a few minutes they rose over a slight hump, and McCready remarked, "Them's the Narrows." None of the family had any idea what he said, all a single alien word, unintelligible to its roots. McCready offered nothing more during the cramped drive, which followed—though the family did not know this at the time—the slow arc of the Chester River from its broad mouth to its tightening channel. Soon they were rattling over bumpier roads, and then they stopped for McCready to open a gate. Once through, they were in the shelter of broad, high trees; the mossy air came to them, the dense stillness of a forest floor, a darkness for fireflies and red-eyed cats, the leaves above rattling like knives.

McCready came to a stop, yanked on the emergency brake, and said, "There it is, the Mansion House." He turned, as if to throw them all out of the car.

They looked, dumbly. Even Sebastien was taken aback by what

he saw through the car window. The house rose in front of them, with a long line of attached buildings to the left that ended with a small, freestanding backhouse. It was too dark to make out much detail, but it was clear that this was not the white-columned antebellum mansion Edward had described; this house was immense, but squat, ugly as a toad. Overgrown box bush, yews, and dogwoods reached above the first floor, and twisted shapes of ivy clawed up to the chimneys. Edith could smell the mildew from here. The shutters were closed, but at the peak of the center gable, one was hanging from a single hinge, and she had the clear feeling that she should not look too closely at that window, lest an eye suddenly appear in that empty socket.

There was a single yellow flame showing through the fanlight above the door. As they all stood in the spiky, wet grasses, the door opened—Simon gasped—and a woman in a dirty wool overcoat came to the top of the stairs.

"My wife," said McCready.

Edward had included, in his letters to McCready, the very reasonable request that the house be cleaned and put functionally to order before their arrival. He had expected the household to be a little creaky, like a man waking up from a long sleep. But he had envisioned, despite the modest tone of his letter, something almost joyful about the revival: a reawakening of custom and tradition, the full breeze of air coming into musty corners and closets, the sharp snap as the servants shook out the linens. He had fancied his arrival in a blaze of light from windows and a fanning-out of staff, and had wanted to arrive at night because the picture was so pretty in his mind.

He had known that everything would not quite equal these pleasant speculations—oh, Edward Mason had not learned nothing over the years. He was no stranger to accommodations that were in disrepair, and, by God, he had always tried to see the humor, or the charm, of the thing. He would do it again. But he would do more than that here: he had wagered all on this last chance, and he would give it his last breath. If this black hulk of a family ruin was what he had come to, so be it; he would accept its shelter. If running a dairy farm was what God had in mind for him, and if God would grant him just a crumb or two of success, and if Edith would stick with him, then he would do it gratefully, he would do it with thanksgiving.

He took Edith's arm and they walked up the steps. When they reached the top, Edward introduced himself, Edith, and the boys to Mrs. McCready.

She did not offer her name in response but did move aside to allow them into the house. She said, "The water ain't hook up. Dead rodents in the line, I expect."

"Lovely," said Sebastien.

They stepped onto the red tile of the foyer, under a hanging kerosene lantern; the chair, a Chippendale, in which Mrs. McCready had been sitting, lay in its weak pool of light. The ceiling was low in this small space, but through the etched glass of a partition the space opened into a cavern, a great hall and a curving staircase. Edith took a few steps into the house and was met by a wall of must and the distinct essence of wet fur. She gasped; her nose and lungs seemed suddenly packed with spores. She said, "Has it been cleaned?"

Mrs. McCready turned toward Edith, and it was clear that she was going to tell Edith that she herself was no cleaning lady. She was also about to list all her many responsibilities to her own family and to the farm. It was so clear to everyone that she was going to do this that she did not bother. "The colored wouldn't come unless the family was there."

"Why not?"

"Afraid of ghosts—"

"As are we all," interrupted Edward.

Mrs. McCready paused, but continued with determination. "They won't say it out loud. They just say, yes, they'll be there, and then they don't come." She shrugged: fact of life, fact of colored people. This was the point she wanted to make.

Edward moved on and stood in front of a brass switchplate with a dozen sets of buttons. He worked his way down the line, getting a hearty and reassuring report each time he punched, but there was no result.

"Ain't no electric in here," said Mrs. McCready after he finished.

Edward stood back, still eyeing the switches. "Then what, madam, are these?"

"Miss Mary had a Kohler, for when she was here. Used to be in the pump house."

"Used to be? Where is it now?"

"I can't correctly say for sure."

"I would like to know."

"You'll have to ask my husband," she said, and from the tone in her voice, it was plain to Edward that this generator was either chugging away, at this moment, in the McCreadys' basement or had long ago been sold to the earliest bidder.

"There's a mess of lanterns and candles on the hall table," she said, moving now to show the way.

Edward decided to drop the matter of the generator, for now, and followed the woman into the main hall. He could feel the rising of the ceiling. They walked across straw matting and gathered around a large table in the bend and rise of the staircase. Mrs. McCready lighted a few candles and lamps, and the hallway began to come into view. Beside them, reaching all the way to the second-story landing, was an iron parlor stove, isinglass still shimmering, as if it had been the one pulse of life in this deserted house for all those years.

"A fiery furnace," said Simon. He was delighted with his invention, so he repeated it. "The fiery furnace."

"We heard you," said Sebastien, but not with much sarcasm, because he, like his father and mother, was nearly stunned at what the slow gathering of illumination revealed. The place was huge, the rooms vast and square; it was Victorian, not Georgian. It seemed, more than anything, to have been inspired by the overgrown villas of the French Riviera, with a central hall providing a conduit for the breezes between the land and water sides, and French doors opening every room on two sides onto a broad, tile-floored porch. It was a house designed to catch the perfumes of the Mediterranean, or even of the Chesapeake, but a window had not been opened in years, and the air that night was the worst of it, thick with the odors of neglect: mold and moth, rot and rust. Long strips of Chinese wallpaper hung off the walls in spirals as if left over from a gay party. An animal—not a mouse or a rat, but something large, like a fox or a dog—had died long ago in the center of the hall, leaving only the black stain of its dried juices and a moldy skeleton. In the dining room, there was a table for twenty-four that was covered by a confused jumble of plaster and lath, rodent nests and locust cocoons, all of it given forth from a rotten, water-damaged ceiling. Edith wondered what kind of sound it had made, this crash, deep in some abandoned winter.

Whatever had happened to the first house, burned most likely, the contents had been saved or replaced. Through the decay, not to mention the dust and cobwebs, they could see that the place was crammed with things: furniture, pictures rising three-high on the walls, every horizontal surface awash in pieces of art, items of interest, objects of brass and stone, carved and built, made and found.

"Look at this," Simon hooted. He was holding up an Indian hatchet. He had walked back into the center of the hallway and was peering over a vast table, candlestick in one hand. "Aborigines."

"Indians," corrected Sebastien. But he came over with his lantern to see what else was in this grand stew of objects—an oval miniature portrait of a young man, a few Indian arrowheads, a brass model of a tractor, a lady's ivory-and-silk fan, a set of lacquered Chinese boxes, a book. Simon picked it up. *"Wild Animals I Have Known,"* he announced. He dropped it as they both moved on, entering what must have been a library, where they were confronted by the broad face and shiny black nose of a Jersey calf.

"Bloody hell!" yelled Sebastien. "It's stuffed."

Edward walked from room to room with a large green-shaded student lamp in hand. He held it up to the portraits, all these Masons peering arrogantly through the dull whitened sheen of their own private mildew. They didn't seem to mind their fate, but it was unimaginable to Edward that this place had been waiting for him all these years in such a state of suspended breath. Clearly, when Miss Mary died, no one had a clue as to what to do with the place. In England it would have been maintained as before, with little notice taken that one member of the household—the owner—was no longer there. In other, uncivilized, lands, the house would have been picked clean by distant relatives and villagers. In fact, his quick survey had revealed an array of objects that appeared quite salable; his English friends had been marketing such family heirlooms for years. But here they just closed the door, and would have kept it closed as the house settled slowly into its foundation, back to the earth. Edward supposed that what, in the end, surprised him was not the neglect of the house, but its lack of meaning, its absence of value for anyone but him, and, at that, it had taken over a decade of ownership before he set foot in the place.

—

EDITH MADE A quick tour through the bedrooms, which, unlike the first floor, with its Chippendales, had been furnished in High Victorian style: dense armoires and daybeds with carved dolphins for feet and bureaus with dragons' heads for drawer pulls. She opened windows each time she entered a room. Mud dauber nests lined the insides of the shutters, and she recoiled at first, but soon she didn't care what wildlife or organic matter she encountered, she just needed relief from this building's musty exhalations. She found blankets that were almost blue with camphor, but here at last was a smell that seemed clean to her, and she didn't mind laying them out on the beds. She looked for linens, but suspected that when she found them, she would find them all neatly folded, and rotted in piles, like leaves.

"Miss Edith?"

She had paused for a moment, bent over an old sleigh bed, wondering who might last have slept in it, and had not heard Mr. McCready coming up the stairs with their bags. She jumped.

"It's just me," he said. "Just me with the bags. Right sorry."

She shook her head to tell him not to be. This was her first good look at him, and through the special gloom of the house, she saw a friendly, almost clownish face. "Thank you," she said. "The boys would have brought those up."

"I expect you're all right tired, Miss Edith," he said.

Edith was making progress with the accent, and when he said "tarred," she knew what he meant. "We've come a long way." As she said it, her body slumped.

"You been through the rubs, but you'll settle out here. It will be real fine."

"You were kind to wait for us at the ferry. I'm sorry we were impolite."

"Oh," he said, dismissing her apology. "You're home now."

She looked at him and knew that he meant this, that she did not have to worry about being rude to him. He used the word "home"—which could mean so many things to Edith, so many bad things—as if she and her family were returning, and not arriving for the first time. As if she could expect forgiveness without asking for it. It was a generous thing for him to say, but he did not say it as if he were trying to be kind. She thanked him, but before he left, she had to ask him for a favor. "We haven't had supper. Could you . . . ?"

He had not expected this, and the solution was not easy for him. "Well," he said. "My wife . . ."

"Would she mind?"

He didn't answer.

"Would you like me to ask her myself?" She was speaking as if to a child about his mother.

"I expect that'd be best," he said. She went downstairs and found Simon, pockets full, waiting at the door. She put an arm around him and brought him along for protection as she asked Mrs. McCready if she had anything, anything left over, that they could have for dinner. The answer came back with the same sullenness, but there was no great explosion. If anything, Mrs. McCready seemed pleased that Edith had to ask.

Mr. McCready helped her set up a small table in the parlor, and when Mrs. McCready returned with some dry chicken, bread, beans, and applesauce, Edith set the meal out in the candlelight, with silver from the sideboard and bone china from a pantry. Mr. McCready was able at last to take his leave and to take his wife with him, and the family was left to itself, eating their first meal in this house.

The food was extraordinarily good; Edward even poured himself a glass of milk, surely the first time in thirty years. At the end, they all four got up in unison and headed upstairs. There was nothing Edith could do with the dishes, so she left them there, the forks still creamy with applesauce, the chicken bones still flecked with meat. It was a ghostly sight, she thought, as she blew out the candles. She had the sense that generations of Masons, the ones in the portraits, the ones who stayed on in the Retreat out of grief or returned in joy, she had the sense that these Masons were very much there and that they might settle down at this interrupted table and finish the meal. She would have liked to ask these ghosts to be gentle with her children and forgiving to her and Edward. She blew out the last candle and, in the darkness, wondered if it was really she passing through the room, or just a person standing in for a year or two, just long enough to get this part of eternity over with.

She lay down beside Edward under the rough wool of blankets. The sounds grew around her, the peepers and the clacking flutter of flying insects, the groans and creaks from the stairs and from the dark furniture: voices. The moon had come up, and because the light was soft, the truth of the house was bathed in mystery, as in a dream. She rolled over to shield herself from it, but with her back to the doorway, she felt exposed, as if a line of people were filing by, peering in like tourists. If Simon had one of his nightmares, she thought, she might begin screaming with him. The hours passed, and she dozed a little, but each time something woke her, it was as if she were being slapped, a jolt, the recognition of her fate.

3

FROM THE PROTECTION of a box bush overgrown with honeysuckle and poison ivy, he watched two black women arriving on foot. It was still misty; the sound of their steps over the oyster-shell lane were muffled by dew and by the slack air of sunrise. One of them, the older one, limped heavily, but her walk was strong and she was carrying a large basket. The other one was more birdlike; she wore glasses and her head darted as she peered; she lunged as she looked. They were chatting comfortably. Sebastien knew that they, like him, felt that the early morning was private time.

Halfway down the lane they stopped for the younger one to pick some wildflowers, and the older one moved the basket to her other hand. He wondered if they were mother and daughter, but he thought not: the tone and cadence of their voices was more polite.

Aunt and niece, Sebastien decided. He crouched as they resumed the pace, but not because he was afraid. They drew up to a back door, stepping high over the damp weeds, and here they paused once again, this time showing a slight hesitation, and the younger one took off her hat, carefully running the pins back through the empty crown. They glanced at each other and then disappeared, with only a slight squeak of the door hinges. The return of tranquil solitude was so sudden that he almost wondered if he had seen them at all.

He had been scouting for an hour, moving quickly, recording only the large features and the general plan of the place. The Retreat lay on a rising island of trees, a tip of higher land, with a small creek and the broad river on two sides, and the flat brown fields and pastures stretching off far in the distance on the other two sides. It reminded him of Mont-Saint-Michel, which he had visited a few years earlier, when they still spent holidays in France. Sebastien liked the feeling of natural boundaries, as if the Retreat had been designed to be defensible, even if just for a last hopeless stand, the house a keep, the fields an ageless source of sustenance that could become, overnight, a plain of war. This timbered island, with its own winding lanes and dwellings, was his spot, his place on earth. Sebastien knew that he had found what he was looking for, his center. He felt it like a burn.

He'd been around the house, a faded yellow stucco with red tile roofs. This was not at all what he had been picturing, not what any of them had pictured. Old gardens ran to the edge of the creek. There was a stone pier jutting out a few feet, and then a wooden dock, a line of pilings stretching almost halfway across the water. Completing his circuit, he passed a graveyard; the rusted steel arch of an arbor marked an entrance now blocked by unclipped hedge. Through the leaves he read the names on a few of the tombstones— Mason, Mason, Mason—but he didn't feel any blood pull from these dead Americans yet, only the accident of a shared name and place.

He waited a few more minutes after the colored women went into the house, wondering if these women might be mistaken for intruders. But when he had slipped out earlier, his family was all deep in exhausted sleep, breathing in the air of these large, uninhabited rooms. Simon had kicked off his covers and his nightdress had worked its way up on his chest, his penis and scrotum white and cold in the first rays of dawn. Sebastien had always understood that he needed to watch out for both of them. He threw the sheet back over him as he left, feeling a familiar ache for his defenseless little brother, cheerful in his ignorance. Only at night, when nightmares gripped him from behind like voices out of the dark, did he seem to suspect the real truth of his life.

Behind him he heard the shuffling of animals, and he wheeled around quickly, to see a line of cows marching along the fence line at the far end of the park. A man was herding them along, but Sebastien was staring straight into the rising sun and could not make out any features of this figure. Sebastien tensed, angry at himself for letting the procession come almost upon him unobserved, and he made a run into the thick, drooping canopy of a copper beech tree. He continued this duck-and-cover until he realized they were heading for the farm buildings, separated from him by a marshy tongue of water in a deep but narrow gully, a moat between farm and mansion. Sebastien stayed on his side and watched, and when a large barn blocked the sun, he saw this man clearly. He was black; he was staring right at Sebastien, and he smiled menacingly when their eyes finally met.

Sebastien ran. The first few choppy strides were instinct, the unconscious choice of flight over fight, but the motion felt good after this furtive game, and he settled into a lope through the park. He could feel the muscles and ligaments stretching through the inside of his groin, up his buttocks, and into his back, like small bolts of lightning following the contours of a tree. With each footfall he sprang up from the crusty dry loam; he felt the oxygen being filtered from each lungful of air; his head was proud. He was not dissatisfied with what had happened. He did not mind showing his back to this Negro; he headed back for the house with the sense that he was no longer on uncharted ground and was no longer alone.

When he turned onto the lane, he saw smoke coming from two of the chimneys, one in the main house and one in an outbuilding at the end of the kitchen. He slowed when he reached the line of shacks and sheds, which ascended in size as they approached the back door. The younger black woman appeared at the door of the last outbuilding, and she froze. She looked directly at him through her glasses and then immediately lowered her eyes.

Sebastien did not know what to say, so he said hello.

She mumbled a greeting.

"Good morning," he said.

"Morning."

"I'm sorry," he said, meaning that he hadn't wanted to startle her. The one thing his mother truly scolded him for was sneaking soundlessly upon her, sometimes scaring her, sometimes overhearing her thoughts.

The woman was behaving very differently from the servants—back when they still had them—in England. The timid maids at home acted as if they were afraid of losing their jobs, curtsying and bowing and apologizing, but this woman seemed afraid of much more than that.

"I'm Sebastien Mason. My family arrived last night from England. Perhaps you heard."

She nodded.

"My father and mother and brother are still asleep," he said, but then reflected that they might have risen, that his mother was almost certainly awake. "Have you seen them?"

She shook her head. "No, sir."

The voice of the older woman came through the screen door. "Valerie. Who you talking to?"

Valerie looked at Sebastien, as if the other woman would hear this silent answer. The lack of response brought the other woman to the door, and when she saw Sebastien, she came through. "You one of the master's sons?" she asked kindly.

"I'm Sebastien. I'm the oldest."

"That you which was spying upon us this early morning?"

"Yes, ma'am."

"Oh, don't 'ma'am' me, boy. I'm Loretta. This here's Valerie."

He said, "Yes, ma'am," again.

Loretta laughed. "You a real polite Englishman, Mister Sebastien, but you keep colored folks' time, I see."

Sebastien was very surprised that she had referred to herself this way; his mother had been telling him that when they met Negroes in America, he shouldn't make any sign that he noticed their skin. "I wanted to see what everything looked like. It was night when we arrived."

Loretta told him it certainly was beautiful out here, under the big trees with the water so close, and in the heat of the summer there was always a little air moving off the creek.

Sebastien was confused by this longish speech; he wondered why she was saying all this. He'd already decided that Valerie was a little off, which would account for her fear. But Loretta seemed to know everything about him and about this house, and he knew nothing.

"I expect you're hungry," she said finally. She held out a hand and patted him through the door into the kitchen.

Sebastien came into this large space, already warm from a fire in the Glenwood, already fragrant with the smell of bacon and bread. It was a large, rectangular room, with the chimney and stove placed like an altar at one end; the plaster above the stove was shiny with grease and puckered here and there by steam. He sat at the scarred worktable in the middle, and Loretta gave him a plate of eggs with something he learned was called grits, and a cup of hot milk. Valerie, limp with steam from the laundry, went in and out the back door with piles of bedding. Loretta sat down to smoke a cigarette and gave him a smile.

His mother came down about an hour later. He watched the women scrutinize her when she entered, still in her bathrobe and holding a roll of toilet tissue. She said, "Does the plumbing work?"

"Yes, ma'am," answered Loretta. "Robert turned it on this morning."

"Robert?"

"The hired man."

"Well, thank you," she said, and was quickly gone.

Loretta and Valerie smirked as they heard her heavy steps jogging up the stairs, and compared notes silently before Loretta said, "Why, your mama's a regular black-haired beauty. Yes, yes, *yes*. You got a little of her coloring, seems. All the other Masons is red-haired, like your daddy."

"You've seen him this morning?"

"No. We only heard."

Edith introduced herself when she came back, and then, as Sebastien had so often heard her do, she flooded these women with questions. Asking questions was what she did when she was nervous, and Sebastien had long ago realized that in these situations she never listened to the answers; it was the asking that helped her. But the women did not seem to mind, and they told her where they lived—in a settlement at the edge of the Retreat called Tuckertown; how they got here—they walked; where the food came from—from the farm, on their way through; who asked them to come this morning—nobody. "Nobody, Miss Edith. They's just work to be done, is all. Valerie and me gonna take care of you, just like I always did at the Retreat. Can I fix you breakfast? We got eggs and fine bread, and what all."

"I was wondering," said Edith, "where I might find a wet mop."

Loretta ignored her question. "You go get comfortable on the porch. I'll bring your breakfast round."

—

EDITH DID AS she was told, retraced steps taken in the darkness of the night through the long, musty hall and toward the vast porch on the water side of the house. The women had thrown open the French doors, and the sunlight on the straw mats was as yellow as butter, and the air coming through was flavored with box bush and marshland. Edith walked out under the low overhang of the porch, out to the stubby columns, and gazed over the overgrown terrace gardens, brown with tall weeds gone to seed. She thought of her mother, never happier than when streaked with dirt from her garden, perhaps even bleeding slightly in the forearm from a thorn or bramble. She had always tried to outdo her neighbors with her garden, even the wealthy of Lake Forest, all of whom had full-time gardeners. From her childhood Edith remembered only the heat and the boredom; it seemed sad to her then, this lonely conversation with the soil. Perhaps it was her mother's minute attention on these small things that had made Edith vow to live her life on a grander arc, but now that the trajectory had turned downward, taking pleasure in small things, things she could control, began to make a whole lot more sense. Perhaps Edith would try her hand in this garden.

Valerie walked up behind her with the breakfast tray. "Can I put it here for you, Miss Edith?" she asked nervously, placing the tray on an iron table that, like the wicker furniture, had not been there last night.

Edith turned. "Thank you," she said.

"Right smart of cream in your coffee, Miss Edith?"

It had been a number of years since Edith drank coffee, but she nodded, and watched Valerie drop a long strand of heavy cream into the cup. Edith gazed out at the water while she ate. There was everything reassuring about these placid water views, about McCready and these black women, about the self-contained universe they seemed to inhabit. When Mr. McCready had used the word "home," that's what he had meant, that she and her family could come here and nothing would change for anyone, and no one would ever have to leave. It would be okay, for a bit, to give herself to this most improbable refuge. There was much to do: carve out some portion of the house as their living area; figure out about the boys' schooling. But otherwise, maybe it was time to rest, to trust the hours a little, to wait.

Which she did, a few minutes, perhaps a half hour, with sounds of work coming from the kitchen behind her, the fields beside her, and the waters in front. She was there still when Edward burst out onto the porch, tripping on the step, almost as if shoved. "Ah," he said, regaining his balance. "Look at this. Perfectly splendid."

"What?"

"The view."

"Pleasant, maybe, would be a better word."

"Yes, yes. Superb."

"You slept well," she said. He had snored along as she fought with her childish fears in the dark; she almost woke him up several times and, in the end, lit a candle on her bedstand that burned until dawn.

"Very well. Perhaps it was all those Mason ghosts standing watch." He patted his stomach, the confidence of food to come. Apparently he had already met the women and had placed his order. "You look quite lovely here," he said. "A Southern lady. Southerners and their porches, after all."

"It isn't just the South. My grandparents in Indiana lived on their porch in summer."

Edward remained full of cheer. "Quite right. Quite right. Perhaps it is simply a matter of the length of the season. I suspect we'll still be sitting here comfortably in November."

"Do you really expect we shall pass the winter here? Now that you've seen it?"

He looked at her with alarm, trouble on his face disturbing the calm. "Well, certainly. It's what we planned, was it not?"

She said it was. It was what, before they left England, she had agreed to do: follow him here for a year and see how it worked out, and if it worked out badly, she would have to look for a better life for herself and the boys. It was a harsh thing to say to him back then, but it had helped her to imagine a schedule of sorts, and it hadn't really bothered Edward. She did not know that her father had given Edward a similar deadline along with money for the passage: If in a year he was not adequately providing for his wife and children, he should expect a call from Sidley & Austin, the law firm in Chicago. But her ultimatum already seemed silly to her. Already, only twelve hours after she arrived, she recognized that the Retreat was not a place upon which one imposed schedules and plans; one simply tried to trust what it held in store.

"Then we have a great deal to do," said Edith.

"Yes. I'm very eager to get together with McCready. Much to plan, I'm sure."

Through the day, Mr. McCready and Robert made runs back and forth from the Love Point ferry landing. Robert seemed in his late thirties, thin and quick, like a snake, not at all in the beefy image Edith had of farmworkers. Sebastien recognized Robert as the silent figure who had been observing him this morning, and he fell in at his side with the ease of a co-conspirator. He joined McCready and Robert on their trips, which Edward viewed as quite proper, the son taking a place on the truck seat between his father's workmen. When they came back the first time, Sebastien had acquired a straw hat of exactly the same style as Robert's, and he looked the part, looked like Huck Finn, and just two weeks ago he had been a rather downcast, sallow English boy.

Edward ventured forth that morning on a tour of the estate. Simon, his pockets still full of treasures, came along. Edward put a large palm on those small shoulders and drew him to his side. In the months before their arrival, Edward had pictured a tidy little farmyard, busy with life but compact, like a scene in a Morland or Herring print. This was not the case at the Retreat, which was spread out in an apparently random sprawl; only the long licks of water, jagged as flames, gave it any sense of plan. For the most part, the Masons seemed to have spent the last three hundred years building little outbuildings: kerosene shacks, harness lockers, chicken coops, corncribs, granaries, icehouses, and meathouses. He and Simon poked into each one in turn, and Simon immediately began to assign them uses in a proper English village. The kerosene shack was a pub, the potting shed a greengrocer's. "This one's the jail," he said about the corncrib.

"Is there such a need for a jail?"

"Of course. There are always bad people."

They shuffled along through the yellow dust of the barnyard, which seemed littered with stray farm implements and building materials. "I shall have this cleaned up," said Simon officiously, which was precisely what Edward was saying to himself. "Simontown will be the cleanest village in all Maryland."

"Oh, it's Simontown now, is it?"

The boy looked up at Edward, an open-eyed expression with a hint of anxiety. "Can it be?" he asked. "Please?"

They were in the middle of the yard, surrounded now on all sides by buildings, by the smells of farming, and by the sounds of animals and men. How comfortable this all seemed. Edward was filled suddenly with a very private elation—the antidote to all of his unspoken, unacknowledged despairs—and with warmth for his son, with love, actually. He took Simon in front of him with both hands and said, from deep in his heart, "All of this is yours, Simon. You can call it Simontown, and someday it will perhaps be Simontown. You only need to hold what you want in mind. Do you understand?"

"Yes, Father."

Edward gave him a last squeeze. "You shall have to help me, though. You'll be my assistant." Simon loved hearing this, and Edward was pleased, though he knew he ought to be saying this to his firstborn son, for whom it could really be the case. But he could hardly imagine saying such a thing, at least with such playful joy, to Sebastien, and was it his fault? The boy was sullen to him; where was the joy in such conversation?

Edward mulled this dark turn in his thoughts as he and Simon worked their way back toward the Mansion House. There was a large stable, with cupolas rising almost like spires, topped high with weathervanes.

"This is the church," said Simon. "And this," he said, pointing toward a dilapidated cottage, which must have been the coachman's residence, "is the rectory."

"Perfect," said Edward. And it was, even more so when they pierced into the darkness of the stable and found, just as he had hoped, the immense form of Miss Mary's Packard, delivered months after she died and put up on blocks the day it arrived. Edward pulled back the tarps and ran his hand over the polished surfaces, feeling that he could already detect the smooth purring of its sixteen cylinders. Over the years he had tried to think of an excuse for having the car shipped to him in England, and today he was glad he hadn't. In Simon's church, this immaculate automobile promised salvation.

The day after this tour, Mr. McCready came calling with the account books. He was drenched in acrid perspiration. They had both been anticipating this moment, whether as a beginning or an ending, neither one could be sure. Edward sat him down on a side chair in the library, took the books to his Chippendale slant-top desk, and made a show of putting on his glasses and sharpening two pencils. Edward's professional eye skimmed the orderly rows of figures: How much money, after all, were they talking about here? Could the family live on the income? McCready's account books, though smudged and smelling unmistakably of manure, were impressive. They equaled the reports Edward got monthly from the Machine Tool: a meticulous accounting of a business going nowhere. McCready's contained such entries as "3¢—nails" and "$1—bull, second return." There were few expenses and not much revenue, but most of it was profit. They could survive on it. He closed the books with a thump.

McCready stood and took a pace or two backward, waiting for orders. Edward had expected that in this first meeting he would lay out his strategy for a new era of abundance at the Retreat. But he found that his prepared remarks about making the most of the resources, creating a more productive work routine—the thing he had done at the works with good early success—seemed inappropriate. This farm was McCready and Robert and, during certain times of planting and harvest, a crew of ten or twenty fieldworkers. It wasn't the kind of operation one engineered; it was something one could nudge, at best. His eyes wandered from McCready's expectant face to the shelves rising behind him, the sets of Kipling and Trollope, Longfellow's poetical works, Sir Richard Burton, Zona Gale, Freya Stark, Zane Grey and Clarence Mulford, Zola and Tolstoy in translation. Edward suddenly felt that his father was in the room; even to the dime westerns, Miss Mary and his father had read the same things. No wonder, thought Edward, she gave the place to his line of Masons and not the rivals, who now lived in St. Louis. "Well done," he said to McCready. "You've done an excellent job."

Mr. McCready was pleased to hear this.

"I'm an engineer, not a farmer," said Edward. "But I'm eager to contribute what skills I have."

McCready might have viewed this with alarm, but he did not show it if he did. McCready was happy to have them there; perhaps Edward would buy him a tractor. There was pride at stake here, and perhaps the possibility of mutual respect, even though at this moment his wife was in town describing the Masons as stuck-up, and in particular, describing Edith as a "sultry English tart."

"You have any questions, Mister Edward, be sure to ask."

"Thank you."

"We just been trying to hang on through the tough times," he said. "No question that things can be done better."

"I'll look forward to discussing them with you after I've seen the full operation." Edward was now wishing McCready would leave, but he did not. He couldn't imagine what McCready was expecting of him. Finally he asked if there was anything more.

"About the Kohler," said McCready.

Edward sprang to attention; he was surprised it had slipped his mind. "Yes," he said. "I should like to know what happened to it." He waved his hand toward one of the useless electric lamps.

McCready began in 1924, the year Miss Mary died. The winter had been extremely cold. Certain people, his brother-in-law and his first cousin, had suggested that a diesel must be run regularly in order to be maintained. Edward's mind wandered at this point, and when he picked up the thread, the Kohler was now on the farm running a compressor. McCready then explained that the wiring in the Retreat was unsafe, that squirrels had probably eaten the insulation and the humidity had corroded the switches and fuses. Unless the house was completely rewired, who could tell what would happen if they lit off a generator? He explained that this had been done at Conquest Farm, a house across Eastern Bay, and that it burned just a few years ago, in 1930, or was it 1931?

Edward raised his hand to stop this explanation. "Thank you," he said. "Let's drop the past and just move on from here."

—

EDITH DEVOTED MOST of her first few days to a survey of the house's contents, with Valerie close at her side. In the pantries they found nests of Canton platters, the largest big enough for two turkeys and the smallest just about right for an ashtray. She found enough ginger jars, tea tins, apothecary bottles, and spice canisters to satisfy Marco Polo. The crystal was lined up deep as an army; there were snake skins woven between the stems, and a rodent path down a center avenue of broken globes and toppled goblets, the way marked by a shine of dirt and a fleck or two of antique rat blood on some of the glittering crystal shards.

Simon followed along in his mother's wake, peering in at the flotsam like a sea gull. Early in the first day he found a chest full of board games and jigsaw puzzles, mah-jongg sets and chess pieces, all smelling vaguely of kerosene. He found croquet and badminton equipment, which he dragged out onto the unmowed lawn and left, discouraged, in heaps. Some of this equipment was broken, pieces were missing. The truth was that most of what Edith was finding was worn out, stowed rather than thrown away. It was beginning to make her ill; everywhere she looked, in each overbrimming closet and pantry, were things that needed some sort of repair or resolution, decisions put off for a hundred years. In one closet she had found, stuffed into a fishing-rod case, what she took to be the original deed to the Retreat, signed by a Charles Calvert, whoever he was.

In the attic she came upon a pile of Oriental rugs—put away in the spring of 1924, as was the custom, in favor of straw mats— and she called on Edward to help sort through them. Edward was knowledgeable about rugs; he had once gone partially into business with a man who said he was an Armenian rug dealer but turned out to be a Turkish colonel trafficking in the confiscated heirlooms of deported families. In the attic they also found a lockup crammed with silver. It took Edith, Valerie, and Simon most of a day to bring it down to the kitchen, where Edith thought they could at least catalogue it.

Edward watched this parade with a good deal of interest. When the silver was all laid out on the worktable in the kitchen, they all gathered to observe the display, not just flatware and tea sets but items like cake baskets and sterling bric-a-brac. Edith was appalled at the quantity and uselessness of almost all of it, but Edward showed no shame. "Will you look at all this?" he boomed. "Must be worth ten thousand dollars. Easily."

"You can't be thinking of selling this. This is your family."

"Yes. Certainly."

"But what a bundle," said Sebastien, who had reappeared for one of his rare visits back from the farm. Edith realized she had not seen him out of his straw hat in a week.

"Will you take that hat off inside, at least?" she said.

"A bundle," repeated Loretta. "Yes, yes, *yes.*"

Edith was glad that Loretta spoke but wasn't sure that she under-stood what Loretta meant. What could these women make of this wealth?

"The tea set is superb," Edward continued. He was holding the creamer, peering at the bottom for hallmarks.

Edith did not want to hear him trumpet more wealth, more

indecent dollar amounts, in front of the women. To head him off, she said to Loretta, "I imagine Miss Mary put on quite a table."

"That it was. Towards the end, naturally, Miss Mary kept more to herself. She done little with company."

"A fine woman," said Edward.

Loretta and Valerie exchanged a glance before Loretta answered, "Oh, yes. Miss Mary was a fine lady. The Retreat was the pride of the county."

"And we shall make it so once more," Edward announced loudly, a statement he seemed to direct as much to the table full of silver as to the women and children in the room. He continued this line of thought at lunch, which he and Edith took in the dining room. Above them only a few ragged remains of the ceiling lath and plaster clung to the joists; Mr. McCready and Robert had hauled away the worst of it, but Edith still felt as if she were dining under a carcass.

"It's an extraordinary tradition, after all," he said.

"What is?"

"This house."

"It's difficult to imagine this place in its heyday. At its best, I'm not sure it sounds like the happiest place in the world."

"Maybe. But you have done a fabulous job." She had: The main living areas and the bedrooms in the new wing were now quite habitable, almost grand, really, almost as they might have been. A little paint and some new wallpaper was all it would take.

"Thank you. But it still feels as if we are living in a ruin."

"I'll have the plasterer around on Monday."

Edith put down her fork and looked over at him. "Please, Edward. Please promise me that you will not pour all sorts of money into this house. That simply can't be. You must see that."

He snapped back: "A few necessary repairs are not 'pouring money in.'"

"You know what I am saying."

"I have to make decisions about the maintenance of this estate, don't I?" Edward went back to his soup noisily, but he was in no mood to quarrel. Edward hated quarreling more than anything in the world, and especially with Edith. "I'm sorry," he said after Valerie had cleared.

She accepted this apology with a nod.

"I'm simply stating the obvious," said Edward. "Things could be quite grand here. We should have made this move years ago. We might have avoided some of our most difficult times."

—

WHEN EDWARD HAD looked forward to making a go as a gentleman farmer, he had expected to approach the problem professionally, beginning with a reading of texts. He was delighted to find at the Retreat over a hundred volumes with such titles as *Newbank's Hydraulics & Mechanics* and *Letters upon Cultivation*. He did his best to absorb them, even the slightly appalling *Useful Things to Know about Manure*. He concluded that Mr. McCready, for one, couldn't possibly know or care what happened to the phosphorus content of pig manure just before farrowing. He wondered if Miss Mary had known these useful things. One two-volume set called *Facts for Farmers* came embossed with a quote from George Washington: "Agriculture is the most healthful, most useful, and most noble employment of man." Edward had never quite thought of farming in those terms, but he took the point seriously. The key to the trade, in most of these texts, seemed to be good values and habits. There was a diptych in *Facts* comparing the trim and orderly scene of "Farmer Snug's residence during his lifetime" and the disrepair portrayed in "The same place under Farmer Slack's management." Even the trees had died under Farmer Slack.

Now and again he pawed through Miss Mary's account books

and records, the history of the farm as recorded by her own hand. In her herd books she had identified each cow and bull by name. Over the years she must have christened a thousand calves, many with reassuring British names: Raleigh Fair Jessica, Fairy Lad's Martha, King Lear's Golden Tulip. Could one imagine taking time to do such a thing? Edward might not have learned much about farming from this, but he got all he would ever need or want to know about Miss Mary. Cows that displeased her, that gave too little milk and not enough butterfat, that produced only bull calves, that had ugly switches and tongues, were consigned to the abattoir with a vicious pencil scrawl. Favored beasts received eulogies when they died of old age.

He visited afternoon milking frequently, following the line of cows into the dairy, their spiked haunches and open vulvae smeared with manure, tail switches crusty, pink udders bulbous and veined. Edward couldn't imagine, once he'd seen this sight, ever eating a dairy product again, but he held his breath and kept at it. Every time he walked into the operation, Mr. McCready yelled the same thing across the backs of the herd: "Mind yourself, Mister Edward. Watch your city clothes."

Edward didn't like the tone, but there wasn't much he could do about it. All he could do was persist. After a few days he found a place at the intersection of two lines of stanchions where he could survey the scene without getting his shoes and socks soaked in a steaming river of piss. Sebastien was always there; Robert had taught him how to milk a cow, and though he could not produce anything like the urgent pulse of white that came out of Robert's black fist, he did pretty well. Edward wondered what these long, penile teats felt like, enclosed in one's palm, but he had no desire to make a spectacle of himself by asking to try. Behind them all, in the milk room, Mrs. McCready cleaned the milk pails and cans. It sounded to Edward as if she were dismembering an automobile—the dense shattering clank of heavy, stainless pails hitting concrete, the brighter ping of the handles dropped to one side.

At dinner, in the flicker of candles and kerosene lanterns, Edward detailed his plans to Edith and the children. "I think we can bring this place back," he said assertively one night. "The key is the herd. We've got to restore the herd."

"Restore?" said Edith. Outside, a cool wind billowed through the porch columns. A week ago the air had changed, the breezes off the water now quicker and sharper; the pecan leaves were yellowing. Edith pulled a shawl over her shoulders. The children, despite Edith's many misgivings, had started in at the town school. To her amazement, Simon had instantly attracted all sorts of friends, from respectable families in town; Sebastien seemed to be keeping to himself, which was not surprising but made her sad for him.

"The breeding's gone haywire, as far as I can tell," continued Edward.

"I'm sorry?" said Edith.

"The herd, as I was saying. Miss Mary used to get as much as three hundred dollars for an animal."

"I can't imagine anyone paying so much these days."

"No, not these days, anyway." Certainly the Retreat could not pay such a price. McCready had been hinting about a tractor, which struck Edward as a reasonable capital investment until he found out how much they cost. "But when things improve, we need to be ready with good bloodlines."

Into the slight pause that followed, Sebastien spoke. "Robert says registered herds ain't never going to pay like they did."

For a moment, Edward had no idea what he meant. But one thing was clear: He was tired of hearing about this colored man. He was fed up with being criticized and patronized by country people, with the ironic look in McCready's eye when he offered an item or two from his reading, when he suggested that certain changes in routine could make the operation more efficient. He came back at Sebastien full force, his booming voice rattling the china and tea set in the sideboard. "What does he know? What do you mean by inserting that hired man's opinion into our discussion?"

Sebastien held his ground. "He works on the farm."

"Farming is a very technical business. A hired man does not make decisions. He works with his hands."

Edith rose slightly, caught between up and down. Sebastien was still not giving in. "He grew up here," he said.

"You may be excused," Edith said to the boys. "I'll be up in a few minutes."

Simon popped up immediately, but Sebastien made sure his father and mother saw that he hesitated. Then he shrugged, as if there was no need for him to fight this battle, as if his father would learn the truth for himself soon enough. He went to the sideboard, picked up his candlestick, and left the room slowly, the flame illuminating a studied smirk.

As soon as he had left, Edith turned to Edward. "For God's sake, Edward. What is the point of jumping all over him? How are you going to get anywhere with him if you behave like that?"

Edward grabbed the brandy decanter and poured himself an angry red reply to this defiance. "His impudence is intolerable," he said.

"You have encouraged him to share his opinions. That's all he was doing."

"His opinions. Not that hired man's. He was comparing me to him."

"You're the one that's comparing. You don't need to, you know."

"I don't think Sebastien's comment was innocent."

She continued to hold him in her sharp gaze, but she had to admit, Sebastien's allegiance to Robert had become total, so complete that

Robert must be fostering it, which was troubling. Robert always seemed to be scheming behind his gratuitous half-smile. "If you don't like him, then tell Mr. McCready to let him go."

Edward nodded, but both of them knew he wouldn't do that.

"Give Sebastien time," she said finally. "He's fourteen. He's at that age."

Edward nodded again.

"We're all figuring out how to live here, Edward. Not just you. None of us expected to end up on a farm."

"So you made clear to me in England."

He sat, wounded anew by the memory of those difficult days, while he drank. She heard a thumping from upstairs. This house was always speaking, in its fits and starts; at night, every floorboard creaked; the curtains moved to wind that no one could feel.

"I apologize," he said, finally.

"Not to me. To Sebastien."

"Yes. Fine. I'll speak to him," he said, which Edith doubted, but he was wearing a chastised look; it seemed deeper than usual, more sincere, and she took it as a sign of hope.

"I believe I'm right," he said. "About the herd. I really do."

She thought of him, at work in his study on those dry texts, dutifully making his appearances at milking, following McCready through his tasks like a child. There were admissions in all this that hurt his pride, but he was taking it. But there was no place for him here. The people and the farm itself seemed to have accepted Sebastien as a native son, just as this household seemed to have made room for her and Simon. But there was no place waiting for him, just an owner's prerogative, more respected the less it was used. Poor Edward, she thought; he never had a chance in all this. "What you're trying to do isn't easy," she said.

"I never thought it would be. Just that it is worth doing. As a start."

She stood up. "Let me go up and check on Sebastien. Maybe you'd like to meet me in the bedroom," she said. She moved over behind him and gave him a kiss on the top of the head, and then brought her hand to her lips to wipe off the smell of wintergreen.

She knocked on Sebastien's door and found him lying on the bed, still clothed. She sat beside him but said nothing.

After a good while he turned his head toward her. "He's going to lose this place just like everything else. It serves him right, but what's going to happen to us? What's going to happen to the Toad?"

"Now, now," she said, as if he were six, but he wasn't; as if his fears were childish, but they weren't. She heard the bitterness and knew it couldn't be coaxed away, but she didn't have any other reply to give.

"Oh, Mother . . . Why can't you just face the truth?"

"I face a lot of truths that you know nothing about." They squared off for a moment, Edith wishing that Sebastien didn't know so much. "I wish you could stop being so self-centered."

"Well, what do *you* want?" he asked. He'd pulled himself up on his elbows and was looking at her intently. "What do *you* think is going to happen?"

A year ago, when there was absolutely nothing she could imagine that would make her happy, she would have dispensed with his question quickly. "None of your business," she might have said, or "Time to go to sleep." What would have been the point of going any further, when nothing was going to change anyway? But these days she was feeling like those farmers on the Plains emerging from the cellar after a tornado; unexpected things of beauty had survived the blow. "I suppose what I want," she answered finally, "is some sense of permanence."

"You see?"

"And I want you to be happy."

"I am happy."

"Are you? Good. Then get ready for bed now."

Sebastien dropped back onto his stomach and turned his head back to the wall. "Robert's been to France, you know."

"What does that have to do with anything?"

"Well . . ."

She had made her point but could not resist her curiosity. "Just how did he get to France?"

"During the war. He was in the army."

"There. Many men were in the war. Fighting a war has nothing to do with farming."

"Oh, Mother. Robert didn't fight. They wouldn't let him; they wouldn't let any of them. He was a mule skinner. He retrieved corpses. He dug toilets. That's what he did for two years. He dug toilets for white people."

She stood up. She was tired of Sebastien tonight and was happy enough to leave. She could let him stew; he wouldn't burn up overnight. She closed the door tightly behind her, and found Edward waiting for her in the bedroom. He stood up and kissed her hard, and for the first time in some months, she kissed back equally hungrily, and they fumbled at each other's clothes as in the early days, and it was all she could do to get her underpants off and release her breasts from her bra before he was pushing at her. She was not quite wet enough but didn't want to wait; she wanted his penis and took it in, and very soon they were both pushing and bucking toward their own orgasms.

The next day was a Saturday, a still-hot October day. She was a little sore, but all morning she kept thinking of sex, surprised at the fierceness of the night before. She felt as if desire had been released in her, by the heat perhaps, the hot sweat of a humid Chesapeake life, and by lunchtime she found she wanted sex again, not love, but the release of orgasm. She and Edward were sitting on the porch, and she was about to turn to him when she was interrupted by a loud noise, a ship's whistle, and they both turned toward the water, to see, brilliant in the sun, a white sailboat approaching through the trees. The whistle blew again and the boys, who had been having their lunch in the kitchen, slammed out the back door and took off across the lawns to the dock.

"Why," said Edward, boyish with delight, "it seems to be making for our dock."

Edith had figured that out and was equally enthralled with this white apparition, a timeless guest, putting in for the Retreat. How gay, she thought, not really recognizing how isolated she had been through this first month here, and that she might have missed company. Ever since Hazelton—the old eavesdropper—had told them about the demise of the steamboats she had come to think of the water as a dead space for her, a place for fishermen, or watermen, as they seemed to call them here, but a void for her. She had not expected diversion, much less pleasure, from the Bay.

Edward had already begun to make his way through the line of terraces, and Edith followed, wondering who it could be—some old friend of Miss Mary's perhaps. But that seemed unlikely—Miss Mary, it had become quite clear, had no friends—and all at once Edith guessed that it must be the very person she had just thought of, Hazelton himself. Maybe not the first guest she would have invited, but there wasn't a lot of choice. When she emerged from the high cattails and water grasses that had overgrown the path to the dock, she saw that she was right.

She waved, and Hazelton, wearing a captain's hat and white trousers, waved back, as did a younger man at his side. Though the boat was tied to the pier, there was much activity on it, two crewmen gathering canvas, putting order to a mass of ropes, and through it Sebastien and Simon charged.

"Mr. Hazelton," she said, "what a surprise."

He bowed, full of his own pleasures. A man with a yacht always wants to make an entrance, and this greeting from the Retreat must have been exactly what Hazelton hoped for. The day was perfect for the occasion, blue from water to sky, and the slight turning of the leaves gave a fresh brittleness to the wind.

"A fine craft," said Edward, who had been walking the length of it and looking it over from the security of the dock. He leaned over to read the name on the fantail. "*Candide*, best of all possible worlds, eh?"

Edith didn't understand the reference, and what she knew of sailboats had come from family visits to a lake in Wisconsin, where the girls had been allowed to go out in the rowboats, but the canoes and sailboats were for boys and men only.

"Mrs. Mason," said Hazelton, turning to her.

"Oh, really," she said, "just Edith. Please."

Hazelton bowed again, and then moved slightly aside to introduce the young man next to him. "My son, Thomas," Hazelton said.

Thomas—Tom, as it turned out he preferred to be called— came forward handsomely, a man quite a bit taller than his father, with much sharper and more refined features. His whole manner was ironic; he squeezed Edith's hand too hard, on purpose, but he was striking enough to make Edith behave a little silly, commenting on his rumpled and dirty khakis. He laughed loudly in return. He must favor his mother in looks, Edith thought. He was tanned to a Mediterranean hue, and his palms were rough, like a fisherman's. She guessed him to be perhaps thirty, even a year or two older, allowing for the fact that men always seem younger when standing next to their fathers.

He said, "We had no idea if the channel into Mason Creek was still there. Father said Miss Mary had it dredged before the war, but the bottoms change around here quickly."

Edith nodded, as if these foreign bits of information made sense to her. "But you made it."

He held up one hand and described a space between his thumb and forefinger, as if it were real danger they had escaped, and not simply a soft brush with a sandbar. "Four inches under the keel, I would guess. We can't stay too long or we'll lose the tide."

"Then you'd be stuck," said Edith. Tom nodded, and then gave a sly glance toward his father. She turned again to Hazelton. "Of course you'll join us for tea."

Hazelton agreed that this would of course be their pleasure. In fact, it seemed to Edith that they would have to shoot him if they wanted to keep him out of the Retreat.

"The house is really quite mad," she said. "I'll be interested what you make of it."

Edward began to show the way. "Edith has done a superb job," he said. "She has routed the raccoons, beaten back the mildew, made it plain to the ghosts that they're to keep to their places. The workmen," he added, "arrive on Monday. You're just in time to see it in ruins."

"Ah," said Hazelton, rubbing his hands together with the impatience of a grave robber, "I can feel the history from here." From that moment onward their guest talked nonstop, showering them with details, bits of Mason lore, explanations. Edward might normally have tried to keep up his side, but even he could recognize that what Hazelton was giving him was an invaluable tutorial. The next morning, in fact, Edward would awake early and try to write down everything he had heard. Edith listened, for a while, anyway, especially when he described Miss Mary's gardens, her near mania for flowers in every room, cut fresh daily. But Miss Mary was not her favorite figure in his family history, and she was happy to turn this tour, now venturing over to the farm, into a more leisurely stroll with Thomas.

"I think Father was afraid he'd die before he had a chance to get in here."

"How do you people keep track of all this family history?"

"It's his life's work. People's families."

Edith noticed this oddly neutral phrase. "The Masons, you mean?" She tried to recall what Hazelton had said in Baltimore. "Was it your grandmother, a Mason?"

Tom stopped walking. They were standing under a pecan tree opposite the stable; Edward and Hazelton had crossed the gully to the farm and had disappeared into Miss Mary's famous, extravagant hospital barn. She looked at Tom to see why he had stopped, and realized that he was smiling broadly, full of mirth. "That's what he said?"

"I think so."

He began to laugh, snorting, coarse guffaws. "Oh, Father," he bellowed. "How perfect."

Edith was not enjoying this, and she narrowed her eyes.

"I'm sorry," he said. "My father is hopeless. He isn't a Mason, Edith, not even by the tiniest drop of blood. My father is a Jew. His parents were born in Poland." Tom explained further that his grandfather had made a fortune with a small but very wise investment in the B&O in the 1870s. Once he had given this account, he continued again with his private enjoyment. Edith thought that some anger or expression of outrage was due, but Tom's laughter, finally dying down, was so complete, and so oddly full of affection for this person revealed now as little more than a con man, that she surrendered.

"That's really quite awful."

"Yes. But mostly harmless."

"Frankly, he does look a little . . ."

"Jewish?"

"Well, yes."

Again Tom threatened to burst into his nasal laughter, but he brought himself back. "Don't tell him. You'll spoil his fun. He's in heaven."

They started to walk again, down the yellow sandy path, toward the dense pack of cows waiting for milking under the shade trees. The wind that had brought these visitors in was gentle. For the first time, given an opportunity to show it off, she felt the Retreat was almost a home, almost something to take pride in. The feeling rushed at her in a giddy wave; the momentary flash of joy—the voice within that told her everything was all right—was light and young.

Tom continued to nudge her into complicity. "He was beside himself after he met you. He said you were one of the most captivating women he had ever met."

"Oh, please, no. That isn't necessary. His secret is safe."

"Don't blush. That's what he said. He said you had caught him staring at you and let him have it."

"He was eavesdropping, not staring. But I forgave him."

"It was your eyes," said Tom.

"My sisters used to call me Coolie." She stuck out her teeth and pretended to be Chinese, but she liked these compliments and could enjoy them for a second or two, couldn't she? "But that's nice of him to say."

"My father isn't especially fond of women, young women, anyway."

"That must be why he's so interested in that terrible Miss Mary. I'm sure she didn't like young women either."

He let out another laugh; he seemed to find nothing but humor in life. "I'll have to tell him you said that."

"No. You wouldn't."

He said he would not pass this statement along, though Edith had the distinct feeling that he would. Tom seemed to be a man who enjoyed nothing more than passing along little and big indiscretions, just to see how everyone behaved. If it hadn't been done with such evident relish, and with such tolerance, she would have steered very clear of him. She knew the other type of troublemaker, back in England, the people who lived on the wings and whispers of hurt. But she was far away from those people here.

"And what do you do?" she said.

"Not really very much, these days. I've been sailing."

"I figured that much out."

"I've just come back from the Caribbean, actually."

"You mean really sailing."

"Yes, I'm afraid I do."

"Odd to come back in the winter, isn't it?"

For the first time, Tom's expression turned slightly reflective; his voice, still warm, turned a little deeper. "Actually, I'm trying to start a boat-building business in Annapolis. I have some ideas about boat design. Not that anyone much is buying boats these days."

Edith would have liked to ask him more, but up ahead, Edward and Hazelton appeared, finally satisfied. Hazelton came forward with an anxious gaze at his son, perhaps trying to decide whether Tom had unmasked him, but Edith could see him now almost as Tom did, harmless in his small chicaneries, and she had no desire to hurt him. She decided that she would not tell Edward, either now or later, because Edward would feel it his duty, as a gentleman and a Mason, to expose him. She smiled warmly at Hazelton and complimented him again on his knowledge about their family, and as the four of them all turned toward the house, she fell beside him and took his arm. She felt a small startled shiver, and then a tightening of his arm in pleasure, and she had the sensation all the way back that if she hadn't been holding him, he would have risen like a balloon.

Loretta had prepared an elaborate tea, but Edward and the Hazeltons soon discarded the tea for brandy, and by the time they came to their feet, the tide was apparently dead low. Indeed, it would rise so late at night that, in a few brushstrokes of conversation, it was decided they would moor in the creek for the night and return for dinner at eight.

"Well," said Loretta, "we having a party. Mister Edward is true to his word."

"Do we have food?"

"Certainly, Miss Edith. You go get dressed."

Edith thought long and hard about what she would wear. She wanted to dress right and looked with some desperation at her closet of clothes. She held up her gray wool favorite; it was long-sleeved, but it showed off her waist. When she wore it, Edward always ran his hand over her rump. It would do.

From his dressing room, Edward called out, "A fine man. These Masons are quite a diverse breed, wouldn't you say?"

"Yes, dear," she answered.

She slipped into the bath, looked over her breasts and flat stomach to her long legs with satisfaction, and emerged feeling the old excitement, the delights of attire and company, the warmth of a house. She dressed, sat in front of her mirror, hairbrush in hand, and asked herself if it could be true that someone had described her as "captivating."

Simon let himself into her room, and she was happy to have him crawl into her lap. They looked at each other in the mirror for a few moments, and she put down her hairbrush to hold him. The sensual boy folded softly and neatly below her breast. "Isn't this fun, dear?" she said. "A party?"

"Will I be allowed to sit with you?"

"At cocktails. If you're good."

"Neat!"

She reached for a handkerchief, softened a line of makeup with a corner, and then blew her nose to the left of his ear.

"Yeow," he squealed. "You're deafening me."

"Sorry," she said. "Will you ask Sebastien to join us?"

A dark shadow in his face came back to her from the mirror. "I don't think he will."

"Why not?"

"Sebastien says that families are all rot."

"Oh, perhaps he's right." She nudged him out of her lap. "But it can be fun, too." He headed off. She inspected herself one last time in the mirror, and when she glanced out the window, she could see the mast of the boat, and then a line of movement through the cattails, and then the guests emerged, perfectly dressed in evening clothes, magical visitors from the sea. It was suddenly many years ago in Edith's mind, perhaps many decades, perhaps an earlier era, and she was hiding in this protected vantage point like the daughter of the house, spying down for a look at the young man whose black tie was now being set straight by his father, and perhaps he was the girl's only love since childhood, and this was to be the most lovely night of her life, and the only thing standing in her way was her father, Edward, pacing downstairs, fretting about the wine and wondering if his breath was sour.

4

FALL AND FALLEN. Fall and cold. Warm and cold. The rhythm
of cold, the rhythm of firewood and coal. Firewood and coal for
rich people. Hot and cold. Cold and cold. Robert spat this beat to
himself as he shoveled, dug through the black dust and dark of this
basement, home of snakes, nest of rats, dungeon of ghosts, river of
mold, stones of sweat. That's what it was like, working in someone's
asshole. Shovelful by shovelful, coal and dung: "Now you head on
up to the Mansion House and bin that coal, and don't never talk
about all your snakes and ghosts, you hear?" He stopped, straightened up, mindful of the spiderwebs and beam splinters, leaned on
his shovel handle. "You hear," he said out loud. "You hear?" he
shouted.

There was a thump on the floor directly above him, from the
kitchen, and a high scolding cry. Robert smiled. "You hear?" he

shouted again even louder, and this time could faintly pick out a few words of Loretta's answer. He followed the sound of her limp across the floor, just inches above his head, and suddenly a sharp wedge of sunlight came to him from the trapdoor, followed by her voice. "What's all this?"

"Why, you're just hearing things. I ain't said a word." Robert must have been only a day or two old the first time Loretta poked him, prodded him, scolded him.

"Oh, now," she said.

"I'm telling you the truth. You must have heard them old slave drivers calling to you."

"You hush up with that," she said sharply, warily. Robert could hear the caution behind her voice. "I've got work to do." This last call was muffled; she was looking over her shoulder.

"I ain't stopping you."

"Boy . . ."

"You can mind your own business," he said. "All of us down here are fixing to party, ain't we?" He called out a few names, Masons, names from the graveyard, one of his other least-favorite places of work. "Ain't that the truth, Anna Maria, *be*loved companion of . . ."

A good laugh came down the stairs; the problem with Loretta, Robert had always thought, was that sooner or later she'd laugh at even the dumbest damn jokes.

"You send Val down here." He pretended to plead. "Ask her to tell the ghosts to stop distracting me from my work."

The laugh was over. "You keep out of her way," she warned. "You leave religion to itself."

"Okay. Then you come down and help me finish this coal."

"No one gave me time for your jokes," said Loretta. "You better get that coal finished yourself. Mister Edward ain't a man to be disappointed." She lowered the trapdoor with a thud, and the light stopped as if cut by an ax swing.

For a minute Robert's eyes flickered somewhere between blindness and light, broken spots of fire in the dark of this awful hold. "Mister Edward," she had said. "Mister Edward ain't a man to disappoint." Robert knew people like Mister Edward; he knew them like a surgeon, cut down to their soft quick and flowing marrow. Robert had seen them in France, had gone out to gather them in no-man's-land in the dark: white men, English men. He saw them fresh and whole; he saw them scared, with dried white stains on their pants; he saw them in pieces, a hand reaching to retrieve a face, a single foot still arched as if to keep on running away.

Robert was barely sixteen when he and Perry Gale—Loretta's nephew—joined up. When his unit first arrived in France, he was afraid that some young officer would give him a gun and send him out into the leaden air. He needn't have worried about that: the white men took the privilege of dying in battle all to themselves. They made Robert sick. Robert knew this man, Mister Edward, and he was not worried about disappointing him. Robert didn't think Loretta was, either; he'd heard her stories down in Tuckertown, in town at the Rainhollow Grille. Wouldn't all those white people be surprised at what came out of Loretta's mouth when she took her comforts, her cigarettes and her rum? She weren't afraid of Mister Edward. Not even McCready was afraid of Mister Edward, not like he was of Miss Mary.

The thought of Miss Mary made Robert pick up his shovel once more. He was ready to be done with this basement today, and it was the coal that was keeping him here. No matter what, he'd rather be here than picking crabs or cleaning out tomato cookers. He knew he was lucky to have a job when so many didn't. He might not like it, but he knew it was history that made a place for him on the Retreat, his one inheritance from his father; it was family that kept him there, even when, a couple times a week, a dry white man or two came off the dusty road into the farmyard and asked McCready for work, looking at Robert and saying, "How come this here nigger got a job and I don't?" Oh, Robert heard that, and he was supposed to hang his head and look down at his feet while McCready said, "Well, now, it ain't rightly my choice in the matter, but the boy puts in a fair day's labor."

At lunchtime Loretta banged on the floor. Robert came up the bulkhead and back around to the door of the summer kitchen. Valerie and Loretta were already sitting in their chairs when he got there, and his plate was waiting on the ground. "You a sight," said Loretta as he settled down. "Black as coal." She laughed: Robert's skin was dark to begin with.

Robert did not respond but stared out at the creek, which had been filling every night with ducks, geese, and swans, so many that when they left in the morning, the water was green with their droppings and smelled like fermenting corn. Robert hated the fall because it made him feel old, because it made him ask questions that he couldn't answer about what he had done with his life.

"What you hear from that brother of yours?" he asked Valerie. Her brother was Perry Gale, the buddy he enlisted with.

Valerie was cautious. "He don't write too much."

Loretta laughed again. "Come on now, Valerie. Has he ever?"

"He gets word to us, is what it means."

"Then what's the word, up there in Boston?" asked Robert.

"His boy started high school this September. Can you imagine?"

Robert could not imagine that it was true, that Perry—even with his light skin—was really up North with a job and a family, with kids getting an education. All through their childhood, Perry was bigger but slower than Robert. "It's what the man *says*, ain't it?"

"Then why you ask," said Valerie, hearing the bitter tone. "Why you ask about him if all you ever want to do is call him a liar?"

Loretta raised her hand to stop the bickering. She turned to Robert. "You had your chance to go with him. Far as I can tell, you made the right choice. It don't make sense to go so far from kith and kin."

She was right enough, Robert thought. He had had his moment, when they got back from France, and Perry took one look at Tuckertown, and took stock of his chances around there, and said he was going North. Perry hit on Robert to come with him, but both of them knew their situations were different. Perry was nephew to the Retreat, and to Windolit, where he had worked before the war, and to Mile's Acre and Blaketon, not son to any of them, the way Robert was. He had the canneries to look forward to, road labor at best, and he'd be out of work now either way.

"Things is looking up here, anyway," Loretta continued. After Miss Mary died she went to work picking crabs. Her hands were thick with yellow scars, from punctures and tears that took months to heal in the gritty brine. "Ain't they, Val?"

"Val don't have her mind on this life anyway, just the one beyond," said Robert.

Loretta sent the back of her hand his way with a sharp flick, the way Robert knew she would. Truth was, Valerie didn't need Loretta to defend her, which they all three knew well enough. Loretta kept up the talk. "You say what you want, Robert, but Mister Edward has got plans for this farm."

"He's got plans. First, poison the cows."

Loretta laughed deliciously; the whole county had heard the story, Mister Edward making McCready give the milkers some potion he had read about in one of his books. Three of them died. "Oh, now, weren't that an *action*."

"Can't even *read* correctly," said Robert. "That's what he supposed to be best at."

"Mercy," said Loretta.

"Thing is," said Robert, "he still blames McCready."

Loretta's tone changed. "How you know that?"

"From the boy," said Valerie. "From Sebastien."

Loretta's face, full and fleshy, turned troubled. "I'll tell you something," she said to Robert. "You giving me concern about this boy. You be careful."

"The boy ain't nothing." He went back to eating his sandwich.

Loretta wasn't done. "That boy is one sneaky child. You talk about plans? He's got plans, only no one knows what they are, not even him. I'm warning you about him. He's not a bad child, just the kind that can get you into trouble without knowing it."

"I'm just teaching him dairying. There's no harm in that."

"No," she said. "But you be mindful anyway. You keep away from your politics. And one more thing, you keep your mouth shut. Sebastien tells you things, you say 'Uh-huh' and then you forget it, you hear? You keep away from that white boy, as much as practical."

"Yes, ma'am," said Robert, standing.

"It's only for your safety."

"You the boss. You my mama and my daddy now."

"Yes, yes, *yes*," said Loretta. "Sometimes I got so much wisdom in me I think I'm going to explode. No wonder himself couldn't take it."

Robert laughed. She was talking about her long-dead husband, Harvey, a pearly dandy known as Snooter in the Rainhollow Grille. Robert thought about Harvey as he descended back into the darkness, groped around for his shovel, and leaned back into his task. Harvey hurt Loretta just about every way possible, but he was a man with soul and he gave the heart to Tuckertown. It was just a line of houses, nine of them, off the road to the Retreat, but they had everything back then, a school, a church. There was a mulberry tree in front of the Gales' that swept a little measure of shade across each house as the day passed, and at the end closest to the road, in front of Loretta's house, there was a watering trough carved out of an oak trunk big enough to swim in. As a boy, Robert sometimes tried with all his heart to imagine any place or any life that might make him happier, and he couldn't do it.

But first Harvey Gale died and took the joy out of it, and then Miss Mary ruined Robert's father and took the hope out of it. Tuckertown today was a place with no comfort to give. It wasn't just him. No one laughed anymore, except Loretta maybe. Robert spent his days with McCready, not such a bad man, but he wouldn't get a joke if it spat in his face. These days there was so little life on the porches of Tuckertown that maybe McCready was right, maybe it was just a bunch of shacks. Robert couldn't take offense, because years ago he had moved out of Tuckertown and into a place in the woods, `an old fruit house that *was* a shack, and he lived there alone, and had for a good while, and was satisfied with the arrangement even if people were starting to call him a hermit.

———

TWO FLOORS ABOVE, Edith sat in what she had started to call her sewing room, a small alcove that was once a second-floor butler's pantry. It had one large window that looked out on the water, and because it was over the kitchen, it offered a refuge from the damp chill.

Edith had admitted in a letter to her mother that she was thinking of doing some gardening the next summer, and for weeks the mail had been full of seed catalogues and pamphlets, annotated with scrawled comments and some—how it pleased Edith—smeared with dirt. The hasty notes her mother included with these packets tried to be cheery but always ended with a line or two about how uncomfortable it made her to think of Edith living in that awful wreck of a place. Her father had also written, a long, formal letter. It started with concern but turned quickly into anger and demanded that she write and apprise him fully what steps Edward had taken on the farm and whether she believed her husband would ever prove himself an adequate provider. He closed with the statement that he had already made a similar request to Edward, which Edward had not satisfied.

What could Edith say? As far as she could tell, the farm was providing for them more than adequately, the food was plentiful, she had all the help she needed. In many ways, the life was just as Edward had promised and predicted; they had not been to parties or to Washington, but Edith had never wanted that anyway. What she wanted was safety, and to a certain degree the Retreat was safe. Edward had always had difficulties with money—investments, loans, impulsive gestures with petty cash—but here, on the Retreat, there was no money. The land and houses seemed all but worthless. She hadn't touched a piece of currency in months; even in town one saw very few bills going back and forth. It was an economy based on pencil scratches, and who would spend a lot of time wishing they had more of those?

Edith could write back honestly that Edward was providing extremely well, and that he was being true to every word and commitment he'd made about devoting himself to the farm. She could say this, paste on a stamp, and know she'd told the truth, as far as it went. But things were not going well for Edward. He had no talent for this kind of work. Who would have said he did? When those cows were dying, he spent days in the hospital barn, and the veterinarian had come out and called him a fool right in his face. Sebastien told her this. Edward endured this moment with dignity, but after the third cow expired, he wept. She held his hand as he cried out his shame and frustration, and she told him that she was proud of him just the same. "You've always had very high standards for yourself," she said. "You've tried to do the most difficult things."

He looked up at her, eyes searching; these wounds went deep into Edward.

"These people all grew up with farm animals. It's not that they're smarter than you."

He pulled out his handkerchief. "Forgive me," he said, feeling better, needing more.

"I think anyone with your talents would have succeeded brilliantly at almost anything conventional, Edward. You've just never been willing to do that."

These words had helped, because she believed them, mostly. For years she had been the dark figure at his side as he charmed the room with his extravagant speech and manner; everyone loved him. Then it was as if the Depression had thrown a switch, and everyone wanted something quite different; he became stunningly unfashionable in a world run by those, like her father, who had plodded along a narrower path. By the end, people thought Edward a fool and looked at her—still at his side—with pity. Back then she'd felt she deserved pity, felt it for herself, but even as Edward hurt her, she knew that others were being unfair to him.

She was three thousand miles away from all that now. He'd done his best at farming. He seemed willing to keep at it, which made her sad, the kind of empathy one feels for a child trying to be liked at school. Edward was back at the farm right now, meeting with McCready about repairs to some of the structures, and she knew that he was good on such things; it was part of his training. There was room for him on that level, room with respect, but it would not be enough for him.

Edith could only realize these things and tremble. Edward did all his damage when underemployed, when empty of pride, when he believed that the only recourse was what over the years he had called "boldness." Edith sat in her sewing room that morning, feeling the warmth come through the floorboards, clutching a cup of her newfound passion, Loretta's teeth-grating coffee, and she felt the old, sick feeling, the companion of so many months, a crippling dread that got into her joints like arthritis. It was the fruit of the choices she had made, to know with such certainty what it was she must fear. Edward was getting ready to "take forthright steps," to make "bold decisions." What could Edith do? She had to find a place for him, here, somewhere. She had to find a way to live his life here for him, live it more fully than he could, or the voices inside him would begin to whisper, then to speak quietly with a slight taunting tone, and then to shout at him, daring him to prove that what they said wasn't so. Edith could see this progression in his eyes. She had not heard him use that word yet, but when she did, she would know they were in trouble, and everything she and the children had found in this most unlikely refuge would once again be gone.

—

"I WAS WONDERING whether we shouldn't have some people around," she said to Edward at lunch one rather wet and grim midday. "Now that Mr. Rhodes is putting things to order."

Mr. Rhodes had served as Miss Mary's carpenter, and when he walked in a few weeks ago, his face had registered the full disgust at how far the Mansion House had fallen. "You should have seen it when Miss Mary had it," he had said. By now, Edith had realized that any tradesperson who spoke admiringly of Miss Mary was not to be trusted; it would have taken more than fair wages to endure her abuse. But still, she had allowed Edward to hire him to repair the worst flaws, the ceiling of the dining room, the drafty windows in the kitchen.

"You're right. It's time we began to make our way," Edward

said. Her suggestion produced an immediate lift to his spirits. "We did pretty well with the Hazeltons," he added.

Yes, thought Edith, they had done well that night. It had been the kind of dinner she had thought might never again happen for her, bright with talk. Every time the subject of the Masons came up, she and Tom had shared a silent laugh, and before too long the Masons were left behind for other topics. Edith had listened mostly, drunk much too much, and enjoyed every drop. Though most of the Hazeltons' stories about Baltimore society had been rather catty and mean, they had made the life in that city sound full of fun. Halfway through the evening she had realized what was odd about their guests: This was a father and son who enjoyed each other's company. The more Tom mocked his father, the more the elder Hazelton liked it. By the end of the evening Tom was ridiculing him each time he opened his mouth, and the older man—confident that his secrets were safe—simply roared with laughter. They had gone off in the moonlight, down the box-bush avenue to their boat, arm in arm.

"Perhaps we should have the Hazeltons back."

"You certainly found young Tom charming," he said.

"Oh, Edward, stop it. They were both lots of fun."

"Well," he said curtly, "just Eastern Shore for our party, I would think." His enthusiasm built as he thought through a possible guest list. "The Pacas, I think. One of them signed the Declaration of Independence. Miss Mary's papers are full of correspondence with the neighboring estates. I should think we could attract a fine group. Leave it to me," he said.

"In December, early," she said.

"You could wear your black dress."

"If you'd like," she said, "though it might be too cold in here for that."

"This is the South, Edith. The winters are mild."

Edward left the table full of sudden cheer, and in the weeks ahead he threw himself into the task. Edith could relax for now. He would open his house to people of education and wit, entertain them marvelously and flawlessly: a new start. He had always taken the lead in their parties and he usually did it well. He went to the county library to research his guest list. The Eastern Shore appeared to have fewer surnames than China; one distinguished generations and cousins, class and influence by the barest and most random-looking typographical hints and by small details in their addresses. The people in the post office had helped Edward sort all this out. He considered that the Pacas would be his best catch, though they must be in their seventies. The others had good families: DeCourcy, the Cookes, the family from Blaketon; now that the trees were thinning he could see the yellow chimneys of this fine old house across the creek, and because the winds usually blew from that direction, he had often heard bits of voices. While in the county library boning up on other families, Edward took a moment to review the highlights of his own clan. Hmmmm, he thought, intimates of Lord Baltimore, delegate to the First Continental Congress, key figure at the Battle of Yorktown, a foolish but brave Confederate general: quite impressive. The Pacas had no right to be smug.

The menu he planned was quite simple: a crab bisque, fried oysters, and roast beef. From the tip of Cape Charles to the Delaware Canal there was not a wheel of Roquefort or a drinkable Burgundy or claret to be had, and for help locating these critical elements he had called upon a man he once thought of as his enemy, the manager at the Belvedere Hotel, who was performing admirably.

He kept Edith informed of these preparations and was pleased to see that she was looking forward to the party as much as he was. But she had gotten into a big snit over his plans to enlist Robert as a butler.

"You can't mean it," said Edith.

Edward was beaming. "Of course I do. There's a whole closet full of uniforms. The man said yes. Good opportunity for him, if you ask me."

"But he's a farmworker. You've said so yourself. You can't do this to him."

"I've done nothing *to* him. I made it very clear that it was optional."

"Oh, Edward. How is he supposed to say no to you?" She walked off disgusted, leaving him stung. Edith never had any imagination for fine things, he concluded; too much Illinois in her, he'd often thought over the years. But, no. He would not go into all that. Edith had been more than supportive to him over the past few months, and delightfully interested in sex. He kept his mind on his project, where he found, for the moment, relief from the cows and the crops.

On the morning of the party he drove over in the Packard to Love Point to meet the ferry and collect the Roquefort and wine. Simon came along with him, as he often did on such errands, though he was so small he could barely see out the windows of the immense car. He hummed to himself, which meant he was happy, especially because Edward had promised him a stop at the soda fountain in town on the way home. At the landing, Edward checked the vintages: a 1916 Romanée Conti, a 1921 Corton-Charlemagne, and, the most splendid and ruinously dear, the one even he knew he should not have ordered, an 1899 Lafite. After everything was loaded, and after he had sent a check of stunning size back with the Belvedere Hotel porter, he paused long enough to pry the lid off the cheese. He leaned down to breathe in the pungent youth of that ancient mold, the warm seep of those French caverns, the marbled fate of that caked sheep's milk.

"Ick," said Simon. "It's smelly cheese."

Edward hardly heard him. These heavenly essences were so sharp that his eyes watered, and the smell unleashed a barrage of memories of the joys and riches so missing in the dull gray of this Maryland life of pleasures far removed from farming and dairy beasts, even if that was precisely where the cheese came from.

"Are you going to eat that?" asked Simon.

"My boy," Edward answered, "if I could, I would devour every crumble of it, right here and now." He pretended to pull it into his mouth and growled like a monster. Simon giggled and danced around, darting to avoid the wide swings of the monster's paw.

The guests had been invited for eight, and at seven-thirty Edward made his last inspection. He thought back to that doleful arrival, not so long ago, and he was satisfied. The house was brilliant in candlelight, the table gleaming with just the right amount of silver— Sheffield and sterling with unassailable hallmarks. The carpets cast a warm glow upward; Mr. Rhodes's repaired ceilings were smooth and unblemished. He took his place under the hall chandelier just as Edith began to descend the stairs. She was in black, her Chinoise silk; he could see the muscles of her legs and buttocks flexing with each step. There she was, thought Edward: the old Edith, the sharp-eyed gamine beauty, the odd one out of those three sisters spending the summer in Paris at an utterly bogus "art" school, the summer of 1921. Edward and his friend Mickey Fox had planned to bicycle through the Low Countries, but once he met Edith, Edward never left Paris. Had he ever told her Mickey's nickname for her before they formally met, Madame X? She paused at the bottom of the staircase and gave him a coy flick of one bare shoulder, and it was as if he were glimpsing her for the first time. Wasn't this what parties were for, to recapture a moment or two in time? Edward and Edith, once again ascendant, a team?

At the sounding of eight, there came a knock on the door. Robert, dressed in a black tailcoat, manned the door as instructed, and took the guests' coats. They turned out to be the DeCourcys, whose forebears had bought a large parcel of the Retreat in lean times after the War of 1812.

"Welcome," said Edward. "Delighted you could come."

Mrs. DeCourcy came out of the foyer with the gaze of a private detective sent to retrieve stolen property. The DeCourcys were perhaps forty, a couple who appeared to have forsworn speech in favor of hooded glances and silent reproach, a manner Edward hadn't encountered since the first evening he met Mrs. McCready.

The next arrivals were the Cookes, a family related to the Masons in all sorts of tangential ways. Cooke pumped Edward's hand vigorously, introduced his young wife, and thanked Edward when he passed along flattering remarks he had heard about Cooke's sloop, the *Slipper*. Edward had always been good at suggesting that his flatteries were simply truths that others, out of jealousy, perhaps, wouldn't mention. He accompanied them into the hall, where Cooke exclaimed, "Ah, the Retreat."

Edward suggested that he might not find it all that changed from Miss Mary's day.

"I wouldn't know," said Cooke. "This is the first time we've been inside. Miss Mary didn't entertain."

"So I have gathered," said Edward.

"Especially not a Cooke," the guest added.

"And why so?"

Cooke turned to Edward with a sharpening of focus. "Why," he began, "because the Retreat is rightfully Cooke property."

"I beg your pardon?"

"We don't need to wade into that swamp," said Mrs. Cooke. She was heavy but exuded a nice, buxom energy. "If you ask me, we should line up all the Mason and Cooke men and shoot them."

Finally, someone with wit. He was pleased with his retort. "Is there no other way to solve this?"

"Intermarriage," she answered, leaning slightly toward him.

Behind them there was an assertive knocking on the door, which brought Robert to attention. Edward glanced at his pocket watch and discovered that it was only a few minutes past eight. One thing that seemed plain to him about entertaining on the Eastern Shore was that everyone was punctual, not a good sign. Farmers were punctual; people of ideas were late, distracted by something mad along the way. He pictured a lineup of automobiles at the head of their lane, with cars peeling off one by one at assigned intervals.

At least the new arrivals were the Pacas. Paca was white-haired and blotchy, but his eyes were still sharp and he moved with the agility of a sportsman. He helped his wife, a tiny person, take off her mink, handed it to Robert, and then stood for Robert to help him with his Chesterfield. "Thank you, boy," he said to Robert, the first person who had acknowledged Robert in any way other than to accept his service. Edward came forward to give them a deferential but warm greeting.

Paca looked at his wife quizzically. Edward wondered whether he had said something offensive.

Mrs. Paca said to her husband, directly into his ear, "Mr. Mason says we are welcome to the Retreat!"

The man's face brightened. "Fine." He bowed to Edward. "Delighted. Thank you."

Edward showed the new arrivals to the parlor and introduced them to the group, and each time Mrs. Paca translated in her high, clear voice, and each time Paca responded in his courtly but ultimately hopeless and blank fashion. Edward's heart was sinking fast, and Edith did not seem pleased as she struggled through the new introductions. He began to view his dinner guests, one after another, as a succession of gray faces; it was what used to happen to him when he went to church now and again, when all the faces became indistinguishably, obnoxiously, well-meaning to him. The evening was in trouble. The problem with Americans was that the families played out into boredom and not into madness, the way all his friends' families in England seemed to have done. The wives seemed, for the most part, more interesting and quicker than the husbands—the reverse was true in England—but they were awfully bossy. One of the new arrivals, in fact, had pointed out that a lamp chimney was being blackened and ordered Robert to take it to the kitchen for cleaning.

As Edward was accompanying some plump individual into the parlor, Edith was in the midst of the unexpected appearance of new guests, who had arrived on the water side and announced themselves by plastering their faces childishly on the French doors.

"Oh, it's Frank and Bitsy," exclaimed Nancy Cooke. "They always travel by water."

Edward realized she meant the Howes, from Blaketon across the creek, and he let them in. It might have been an exotic picture, this couple in evening clothes out on the water, like Venice or Amsterdam, rather like the Hazeltons. But the Howes came busting in noisily, just as he might have imagined from the sounds he had been hearing from across the water. They were perhaps a few years younger than he and Edith; along with the Cookes, they seemed to be considered the next generation, the newest flow of old blood. They entered with the confidence of a young prince and princess. Even Mr. DeCourcy rose to greet them and courted their attention.

"Sorry we're late," said Howe. Actually, it was only eight-fifteen, and Edward had not planned dinner until nine-thirty. "There's no dock light. If it weren't for the full moon, we'd be halfway to Annapolis by now."

Edward tried not to recoil. "So much to do to bring the place back, after all," he said.

Frank Howe looked around, and then made a rather bug-eyed

face. "Miss Mary would hardly approve," he said. Several people laughed.

Edward could either smack the man or play along. "The only reasonable course would be for me to give this house to the plasterer, and then lease it back when he's done."

When the laughter died, Edward remarked that he had deserted his post, and walked unhappily through the hall and out onto the landing. He surveyed the automobiles; there were drivers in two or three, the glow of a cigarette, the low scratch of talk. It was cold enough for the moonlight to sparkle on the grass and dead leaves. By his count there was still one couple yet to arrive, though he couldn't say who they were. Who cared, really? What was any of this for, he wondered, laboring with these people? Was there no end to labor? Was there no person in this bloody world who would allow him to be himself? Edith, perhaps, but there were many selves in marriage, too many to choose. Edward could think of only one person, one person who listened to his stories without impatience, who laughed at his jokes. Simon. What did it mean about life if your only real audience was six years old?

He glanced around, out into a bright night haunted by goose calls. Could it be that once again he was in the wrong place? All he had ever wanted was an arena—who cared how large or small— in which to distinguish himself. He had hoped that Maryland would be such an arena, a place for bold thinking, but that hope was fading quickly. Well, perhaps something would come along yet. He had an idea or two, in fact, some that could raise an eyebrow at this somber gathering if he were ready to reveal his thinking. In the meantime, he would go in, get to work, find the right moment to make just enough of a fool of himself to break through the ice; he would attend to Mr. Paca; the table would be splendid, the food fat with marrow and with memories of better times.

When he returned, he discovered that the men had taken up a

discussion of farming. DeCourcy turned to Chase and asked after the corn harvest at Windolit. The rest of the men leapt for the topic gratefully, though none of the estates seemed to be doing particularly well. As they went further, they all adopted bits of the Eastern Shore accent, the round o's and mumbled speech of their farm managers and fieldworkers, as if that were the only proper way to speak of such matters. Edward felt he might just as well have invited McCready, who was at least the genuine article and honestly wasn't aware of his patronizing attitude. Edward didn't think for a minute that any of these men knew more about farming than he did, even if they had all grown up here. During a lull he announced that he was devoting his efforts to restoring the herd.

"Miss Mary Mason poured thousands into those Jerseys," said Frank Howe. "As far as I can tell, she never made a dime."

There was a pause in the room, a polite shuffling. Edith heard these words with a chill; she had been doing her best, and the women seemed friendly, all of them chatting about gardens and children, a fine enough conversation for her these days. She liked Bitsy Howe, though she'd already realized that Frank was a problem. But she was also keeping an ear on Edward, and she knew that agricultural discussions were just what Edward did not need, especially because everyone in the room must have heard the story of the death of those three cows.

"What?" said Mr. Paca, hearing the muffled outlines of the talk. He had been seated in the very middle of the couch in the very middle of the room, with his wife to one side and the dowdy Ruth Chase to the other.

"The Jerseys," said Mrs. Paca, in her admirably compressed shorthand. "Mr. Mason is rebuilding the herd."

"A registered herd?" he asked Edward, straining forward to hear better.

"I shouldn't think so," said Edward. "Not sure it pays anymore."

Paca did not need to have this translated. "Quite right," he announced. "Jerseys are the wrong breed, anyway."

Edward had been standing at the door during this conversation, his arms folded in front of him. Edith knew only too well that bruised look in his eye as Paca deflated the last of his plans; her spirits drained with a sick tug on her stomach. Tomorrow her troubles would begin again. She hardly knew how to get through the rest of this evening. But mercifully—she had sent word out with Valerie that Loretta should do whatever it took to feed them as soon as possible—Robert came up behind Edward and mumbled into his ear. "It's dinner then," he said. "We shall toast the wrong breed."

"Hear, hear," announced a male voice behind Edith. Everyone stood, and they made their way across the hall to the dining room, where the Sheffield chandeliers cast their tangled and flickering shadows on the walls. Robert appeared with bowls of bisque, placing them carefully. She had held her breath for the first few, but in fact Robert was doing this well. She hoped her gratitude was in her voice when she thanked him for her plate, but he did not respond. She set to her own work, sawing through a few topics of conversation with her dinner partners as the dishes came and went. Edward was trying to keep things lively at his end, and she glanced up to reassure him that his efforts—Loretta's oysters were complimented roundly; the Romanée Conti was a huge hit—had been worth it, to her anyway, whatever the lack of sparkle at this table of dour aristocrats.

Robert cleared the main course and laid out the dishes for fruit and cheese. After a minute, and then a few minutes more, Edith realized that things were delayed. Mrs. Hollyday nervously adjusted the placement of her empty fruit plate, and Howe said loudly that he might have another glass of Burgundy as long as something seemed to be holding up the claret. It was a few more minutes before Robert finally came back in the room with the serving plate, and Edith could tell immediately that he was frantic. When he advanced fully into the room, into the elegant flicker of candlelight, Edith saw quickly enough what the trouble was, that the wheel of cheese he placed before Edward was a pile of bits, shattered into small chunks. She couldn't imagine how this would have happened. Edward looked down in horror, and the conversation at the table, which had been struggling onward, slowly dimmed. "What?" said Edward, turning to Robert. "This is the Roquefort?"

"Yes, sir," said Robert, backing off a little.

"What happened to it?"

"It was spoiled," said Robert. "How was I supposed to serve it? It weren't fittin' to eat." Edward was still barely hearing Robert's words, and Edith had her eyes only on Robert, but from around the table there came the beginning of a titter. "After I cleaned it, there wasn't nothing left."

There was again an interrupted sliver of silence, and then Edward slumped back down into his chair and began to bellow with laughter, hysterical laughter. Robert stood there. Others started to laugh. "Cleaned it," she heard someone repeat. Edith had her eyes on Robert, and she saw in him at that moment something of rage, a rage she had never been near before. She looked at Edward as he continued the ridicule almost triumphantly, for no reason in the world other than to save himself. She rose to her feet, but she didn't know whether it was to defend Robert or to protect Edward, until she heard Paca, who had missed what made everyone laugh, asking, "What? What did he say?"

Mrs. Paca leaned in front of the other guests and said, "Wanted to clean the cheese."

Paca heard this and suddenly his face darkened, and then he muttered, mostly to himself, "Oh, the poor boy."

This expression of sympathy was all the encouragement Edith needed. She caught up to Robert in the pantry. Loretta and Valerie, Simon and Sebastien, were sitting slightly bored in the kitchen. Edith turned to Robert. "Robert, I'm so sorry. They had no right to treat you like that."

He stood, his mouth curled, breathing hard through his wide nostrils, rubbing his hands. "I couldn't serve that rotten stuff," he said.

By now Loretta had realized that all this had to do with Robert, and she came forward, her large head peeking around the door. Edith turned to her. "Why did you put that cheese in the pantry? Why not just hand it to him?"

But Loretta didn't seem to hear her, had no interest in anything but Robert; she had read the disgrace and rage in an instant. "You go on back," she said, and Edith thought at first that she was talking to Robert, but she wasn't. "You go on back now," she repeated, and there was no "yes, yes, yes" in her voice now, just a dark warning, an order. "You go on back now, Miss Edith," she said one last time, "and we'll carry forth."

Edith returned to her seat to find a crumble of cheese and a pear served in front of her, and the smell of that cheese seemed as rancid and foul to her at that moment as it must have to Robert. The conversation had gone on, Howe was gulping the 1899 Lafite as if it were grape juice, but Edith could hardly move. Robert came back in and asked Edward, as he had been told to do, whether he wished coffee and brandy here or in the parlor, asked as if nothing had happened, or if it had happened, he was not angry at Edward for laughing, and the incident had passed. "I'm so sorry," she had said to Robert, but she couldn't imagine how he would forgive it.

"In the library, thank you, Robert," said Edward, beckoning to his guests that it was time to decamp. Edward stood up, and though he continued to act the part of the host, his manners, as always, intact, Edith knew that this evening, this dinner, had fed the creatures of hurt in his soul, and they were now whispering to him, and he was listening.

5

VALERIE HAD SEEN it coming, this winter of '37. Her dreams had showed her snowfall in December, a white world, the creeks and rivers frozen out to a thin, black trickle down the channels. She'd pictured the cold morning air, hard as a brick, and the crunch of ice crystals as she and Loretta walked to work in the dark. She had felt the cold, wet reach of the water coming to her from the river, heard the wide, empty call of starving waterfowl, a momentary echo across the silent corn stubble.

Now, as she stood chattering at the end of Tuckertown, waiting for a ride, any ride, to town, Valerie wished she had not been so right. Her thick glasses were fogged; the chill was working at her through her thin ankles. Behind her the wind rattled through a high stand of loblollies, but at least she was sheltered here. She was grateful for that, and for the warmth of her own house, hers, though she shared it with her sister, her sister's husband, and four kids. It was the oldest one in Tuckertown, a foreman's house, or maybe a coachman's cottage, the only building left from the Tucker estate, which had burned some years before the Civil War. Valerie knew the old Tuckers; they visited her now and again.

She stamped her feet on the hard yellow froth of frozen clay and sand; when she got to Tubman's Market, she would sit on the bench with her feet all but touching the stove, the heat piping up her skirt. She would be warm for the first time in a month. Miss Edith said that they were used to being cold in the wintertime, and that the Mansion House wasn't so bad, but if that deathly chill wasn't bad, then Valerie didn't want to discuss what was. At the end of the day at the Retreat she was so chilled even her bed couldn't stop the shivers. She looked up the road toward the fork, where Mason's Neck Road came in. She was early enough to catch McCready, if he had business in town; the Thompson boys, who worked Butler's Cove, could be coming along. The only colored from here on up who had a car was Shaky Little, at Windolit, but the last she heard, he didn't have any gas.

A vehicle pulled around the bend and started to come toward her. She couldn't make out who it was, but it was not a truck, which was a bad sign. The car drew closer, and now she saw that it was Howe, Mr. Howe, the man who owned Blaketon. She never would have expected a ride from him, but he stopped a few yards past, stopped with a short grind of frozen sand, and backed up to her. He leaned over to crack the door. "Get in," he said. "You're the girl that works for Mason. Right?" He sounded winded; his breath was stale with drinking.

Valerie didn't have any choice. She took the door handle and pulled the weight off the man's arm, and she climbed into the car. "Yes, sir."

"What's your name?"

"Valerie Gale," she said. "My mother was Mary Lee." Her mother had worked for Howe's parents before she died. Valerie was five when that happened, and she reckoned that this man might have been about ten. "Perhaps you remember her." She hoped maybe this was why he'd picked her up.

He was slowing for the turn onto the state road. The icy haze hit the windshield like grit. "Lots of girls worked for my mother," he said. "So how are things making out at the Retreat?"

"Fine, sir."

"Coldest damn house on the Eastern Shore, I hear."

"I wouldn't know about that. It's a right cold winter."

He turned his head quickly to glance at her, and she got a chill all over again. She didn't like being looked at by white people. He laughed to himself, but it was nothing that she was invited to share, a snort, the kind of thing you do when you talk to yourself.

"That Mason. How would you describe him?"

"I wouldn't, sir." Lord help me, thought Valerie.

"Well . . . He a good farmer, would you say?"

"Seems so to me," she answered. Since the cold started, Mister Edward had not set foot on the farmyard. Instead, he'd been in the house, driving the place to distraction; he seemed caged. Lord, the noise Mister Edward could make just asking for a cup of tea.

"Oh, hell. The man's a fool," said Howe."

Valerie heard this and she gripped the door latch. "Mr. Howe," she said, "you gotta let me out right here." They were still six or seven miles from Cookestown, but it was only a few minute's walk back into the woods to Spain, where her cousins lived, and she could wait there until she got a ride back home.

"Oh, now, I don't neither," he answered. "Don't you worry about a thing. I ain't going to say anything more about your master." He drove for a few minutes, long enough for Valerie to hope he'd done talking.

"So," he said, "how's Old Man Walker?"

Walker was her great-uncle, and he had lived a free life. "He's just fine, Mr. Howe. Getting along just fine."

For a moment, Howe seemed to be considering Walker, a man as much loved as forgiven, remembered by most as a great baseball player on the Tidewater League teams before segregation.

"Walker has got more stories than a cat," said Howe. He thought Walker liked him, that was plain enough. Valerie knew white men such as Howe only spoke fondly of colored people when they thought the colored liked them. "Still out with the ladies?" he asked.

"Yes, sir. I expect he still steps out," said Valerie.

"Sap still rises in that tree," said Howe, as if he knew things in confidence.

"Yes, sir. Maybe so." They were passing the Kent Island Road, cutting across the Markson place, fields so carefully harvested and harrowed that they looked swept. Mr. Markson bought the place just before the Depression hit; it was said his brother bought him out of their family dairy in Pennsylvania. The barns came into view on the right, and the whole place shone. There were three tractors in those sheds, Valerie knew. It was the only farm around that was making money, and the Markson boys called everybody, white and black, ma'am and sir, and lots of folks hoped they'd get so rich they could buy every damn place in the county.

"You tell me now," said Howe. "That Edith Mason. How's she getting on?"

"I couldn't—"

"I said, 'You tell me.'"

Three minutes to town, Valerie said to herself. Oh, Lord, how much trouble could she get into in three minutes? It was just as Loretta always said: Familiarity with whites brings nothing but trouble on colored, nothing but trouble and danger. She said, "Miss Edith, she's a hardworking woman." This was saying a lot, too much, to this man. Miss Edith was doing right fine. "The whole family is hardworking. Fine people," said Valerie. "They's a quality family."

They were coming up through the colored district, past the Rainhollow. He hadn't asked her where she was going, and she figured he'd dump her out any time now. She was almost safe, and if so, it could have been a lot worse. No way the heater in the Thompsons' truck could have warmed her like this Hudson; damned if she wasn't sweating a little now.

"Sure, sure," said Howe. "Goddamn beavers. But how long do you figure they'll last? A year or two? If I was you, I wouldn't plan my life around the Retreat."

"No, sir," she said. If she were him, she wouldn't count on much either. Valerie had often wondered if these white landowners had always been this lame, in centuries past. If so, how had they become so rich?

They were driving down Commerce Street now, with the court-house coming up on the left, and Tubman's Market just a block away to the east. "I'll just thank you for this ride, Mr. Howe."

"Going to Tubman's?" he said, with an edge now, as if Tubman's were the only place in this town that would have her.

"Yes, sir, that is correct."

He slowed and stopped fast, and she got out, hoping not to show him that she was lifting off this imprisoning seat with the flutter of a bird; she would have skipped, now that the door was closed and he was pulling away, if she had thought he might not see her.

—

ON SUCH MORNINGS, Edith began her day by shaking Simon awake. His big room was filled with the sharpened light of winter; its news was brutal, but it filled her soul. This cold, which she hadn't felt since she left Illinois, was reawakening an almost rustic energy in her, an energy that was a drug and a source of pride. She'd come to think of herself as one of those vigorous creatures that didn't hibernate, and to think of Edward as one who did. When he wasn't in his office, he stayed in bed, sometimes for days, odd books and texts and scribbled notes overflowing his bedstand. When he rose, he wandered to the dining room and bathroom with his topcoat over his dressing gown. The cold had settled in a few days after the party, as if to put him on ice, dissatisfactions and all, and suspend all the crises for a later date. He seemed content to wait the winter out, his schemes little more than diversions for evenings in front of the fireplace, and Edith knew that they were all safe for now, but she worried about the thaw.

Simon slept with so many blankets and quilts that she was sometimes not sure he was still in there, and when he was, it was cruel to demand that he come out into the frigid air. He clung to his comforts, like his father. Usually she had to reach under the covers, hands bony with chill, and pull on him, and as soon as his shoulders crested the covers, he darted out the door, down to the kitchen, where Loretta would have laid out his clothes for the day. She often heard him yell, "Coooold," as he ran barefoot down the stairs.

Robert came at five to fill the furnace and stoke the Round Oak parlor stove in the hall. No matter how soundly Edith might be sleeping, that first tiny and distant scraping of Robert's shovel, the barest tin squeak from the basement, woke her up with a start, ungently, in the blue night. By the time she got down to the kitchen in the morning, Loretta would be there, drinking her coffee and smoking her first cigarette. Edith would sit down beside her, and they'd talk about the weather, and about vegetable gardens, and sometimes Loretta shared gossip about the colored, about working people, and about the men.

Often during that winter she thought of the work going on at the farm, the milking twice a day in all seasons. She saw the cows being reluctantly shooed out into the pasture, and she felt sorry for them. Their white udders and teats seemed so piteously exposed that she crossed her arms in front of her breasts. She would have worried far more about the men, out in this weather, if her occasional chats on the road with Mr. McCready weren't always so cheerful, and if he didn't react with such embarrassed sputterings when she expressed even mild concern. Sebastien was out there with him as much as possible after school, and neither he nor McCready nor Robert ever complained; they all seemed to like the winter because Edward left them alone.

Sebastien came down on his own schedule, and they ate breakfast together until Mrs. McCready's sour car honk signaled time for school. She drove them to and from school and spent most of the time—so Simon had reported—saying mean things about Edward. When the boys got back in the afternoon, the life resumed in the kitchen. Edith had dragged a second worktable in from the potting shed and upholstered side chairs from the parlor, and had placed them at the opposite end from the stove, as much out of the way as she could, and it was here, in the Retreat's only real warmth, that the family lived. She studied her gardening texts and helped Simon with his arithmetic, which was a problem for him. Early on, she and the boys had whispered at their end, of the kitchen, and Loretta and Valerie had mumbled their conversations at the other, but they had all long since gotten over this hesitation. The room was now full of voices, from the pure ring of Simon's soprano to the husky and milky roll of Loretta's exultations, the food and the lessons mingling, the day passing, the sounds of study and the smells of cooking all speaking of some kind of promise. When the sun began to fall, Loretta lowered and lit a kerosene lantern hanging from the ceiling on a pulley and chain, and this lantern was so big that it gave off a central glow of heat and roared like a blast furnace. In years to come, every once in a while a particular clatter of cooking pots, or the smell of kerosene, or a phrase of the children's lessons, would bring these days in the kitchen back to Edith, and she would have to stop what she was doing, sit down, let the flood of memory occur, feel the yearning in her heart for those times.

Edward's one surviving pretense that winter was to take dinner in the dining room, and if the wind was not from the southwest, which it usually was, the dining room was not unbearably cold. They often discussed his latest readings, especially those from the Retreat's large military library. He became captivated with the battle of Gettysburg, and Edith listened, not unhappily, to minute discussions of strategy. It was better for him, and for her, if he was engaged with a battle that had happened more than seventy years ago. Once he mentioned, out of the blue, that the Retreat would make quite a good artists' colony of some kind. She did not need to respond to schemes that were patently ridiculous. Lately Edith had noticed that the ceiling, so freshly repaired and as yet unpaid for, was sagging, as if this house would not permit this room to remain in one piece; as Edith ate and talked she glanced from time to time above their unprotected heads, with a vague sense of doom.

—

THE DEEPEST FREEZE came at the beginning of February, and it was so tight that tidal ice rose high above the creek banks. Edith had never seen anything like it, these geologic shapes of striated ice, veined with strands of seaweed. One day she was looking out the window of her sewing room into the crystal winter sunlight, and she saw, far out on the frozen river, the figure of a lone skater doing turns and leaps, twisting jumps and long swooping glides. At first she thought it was a seabird, an albatross, perhaps, diving against the hard surface. She came downstairs, poked her head into the kitchen, and yelled to the boys that they must come outside. "I have a surprise."

Simon could tell that it was not a present or a sweet, and he said he was happy making cookies with Loretta. But Sebastien, tense with unused energy, grabbed his coat and hat in a single swipe. Together they walked down the avenue of hoary box bush to the dock and ventured tentatively out onto the ice. The surface was smooth and seemed pure black until they observed all manner of plants and fishes, and even a perfectly preserved Canada goose, encased as in glass. The skater was far out into the river, but the shearing of the blades on the ice sounded right at their feet, and they could tell by now that the skater was a woman.

They drew closer, close enough now to pierce the solitude of the skater, and she looked up so abruptly in midturn that she almost fell. It was Bitsy Howe, looking as young and healthy as a teenager. They had not met since the party, though Edith had visited Nancy Cooke a couple of times and she and Edward had put in an appearance at the Tillbourne Christmas tea. Edith did not need to be reminded of any images from the end of their party, when Edward had tried to make the best of things with the last guests while she confronted Frank Howe. Howe might have thought he was funny, with his hand on her breast, but there were tears on his cheeks when they finally got him into the DeCourcys' car.

A half mile from shore on the frozen Chester River, Edith could hardly pretend that she and Sebastien were on the way to Queenstown to buy fish. She recalled the sensation of Frank Howe's hand as she stood there now, in front of his wife, but whatever Bitsy knew or imagined, she showed no awkwardness. "You startled me," she said, breathless. "I thought you were Chessie."

"Chessie?" Edith wondered if this was someone from the party whose name she had forgotten.

"Chessie is the monster that people say lives in the Bay," explained Sebastien.

Bitsy smiled. "You're Sebastien," she said.

"Yes."

"I've seen you," she said. "Along the bank."

Sebastien looked away; Edith could tell he was embarrassed, but for herself, she could not resist anyone who treated one of her children with warmth.

"You look wonderful out here," said Edith. "We couldn't stay away." As she said this, Edith noticed that Bitsy was even more striking up close, with her long, thin legs, her fair skin and red cheeks; Bitsy was a real American beauty. "You skate so gracefully."

"We have a few of our talents left. It's what's left of our youth." She did a little pirouette as she said this, and then returned to Edith with a bow. Despite the slightly odd use of the "we," it was quite charming.

"I never imagined people doing winter sports here," said Edith. "I really didn't imagine winter here at all, actually."

There was regret in Bitsy's voice when she answered. "This is the first time in my sixteen years on the Eastern Shore that it has frozen like this. I didn't grow up here. I learned how to skate in New England, at Miss Walker's and at Smith."

Sebastien had wandered off, heading farther out onto the river. "I thought . . ." Edith said.

"That anyone who lives here has to be born to it?"

"No. Of course not. It's just hard for me to picture that others are outsiders. Everyone knows what I do not, even Sebastien." She nodded toward him, quite distant now.

"He shouldn't go too much farther out. That's one thing he doesn't know. There won't be much ice in the channel." She skated off after him. The sun was dazzling; Bitsy's sharp strides left luminous arcs on the ice. Edith watched as she caught up to Sebastien, skating circles around him as if they knew each other and were picking up where they last left off. Sebastien thought she was pretty, that was easy enough to tell.

Bitsy turned him back toward safer territory, and returned to Edith. "I've persuaded Sebastien to try skating. He can borrow Frank's skates this afternoon, and my daughter, Alice, can teach him."

Edith hadn't imagined quite this, especially with these neighbors that she had been thinking of, for months, as enemies. "How nice," she said.

Bitsy's face fell a little at these words, though the smile remained. She sighed. "If that's okay with you," she said. For a moment the smile left altogether, and Edith understood it all: these mad, wild spirals on the ice, this lone skater. But Bitsy was not going to apologize for her husband's performance, and Edith knew all about that. Edith knew that apologies didn't start things, they ended things; she knew that when she had to go around to make soothing words, it was too late.

"Our husbands didn't hit it off," said Edith. "But that doesn't have to mean anything."

Bitsy's cheer returned at this, and she leaned down—she was a taller woman anyway, and the skates added a few more inches—to give Edith a hug. It was unexpected, close to inappropriate, but Edith gave in to it immediately. Bitsy's body felt wonderful, the smooth and cool skin of her cheeks, the fragrant warmth of her cap and hair. Edith hugged back as if she'd been friends with this woman since childhood, and suddenly there was a deep affection between them, not only an instant history but a long future; in a second or two Edith imagined doing all sorts of things with Bitsy, walking, taking trips, going to the city—whatever city—as friends. A sense of things to come filled Edith with eagerness as if it were suddenly safe to look past the spring, as if she were waiting for more than just Edward's next step, as if there might be something coming that she could embrace without fear, as she had embraced this new friend.

They parted and looked at each other like lovers who have gone too far, too quickly, but have no regrets. "That's settled," said Bitsy. "We're friends."

"Good," said Edith, and there was in this single word perhaps more of the truth than Edith intended: a gratefulness, a rest from despair.

Bitsy seemed to understand all this. "We're not the only lonely women on the Eastern Shore," she said. "The place breeds them like chiggers."

Edith had not really thought of herself as lonely, at least not especially so here in Maryland. In the last several years in England she had stopped trying to keep up with people, except for her friend Cecily, and no one had exactly rallied around. But she did not want to go into this now, so she said, "I have missed my friends since we left England."

"I've often thought of your Miss Mary, you know. Alone with her cows. She was an absolute bitch, I'm sure you've heard that."

"Not really. All I hear is how lovely the Retreat was when she had it, and what a wreck it is now."

Bitsy waved her hand along the frozen shoreline, the crumbling banks breached by fallen pine trees and caved-in storm hollows. Every once in a while, shining in the piercing blue light, Edith could see the heavy presence of a rivershore estate. "All of these places are sliding into the Bay," said Bitsy. "I could list the crises one by one. All these old families are coming to the end, finishing off with a lot of bitter old spinsters and widows, like your Miss Mary."

"It hasn't really seemed that way to me. The men seem to devote their lives to these places."

"Exactly. It's what ruins them, living by the graves of all their damn fathers. You can see it their eyes." Bitsy mimicked the expression of terror, glancing from side to side. Edith laughed. "None of them want to be the generation that lost it all."

Edith thought of the Retreat, nearly finished off before they arrived; she thought of what it could be and should be: a place that could give room to her sons. "You don't make it sound very pretty."

"It's not." Bitsy blew into her mittens. "But the thing about your Edward is that he's not trying to hold on. He seems not to have cared all that much in the first place."

Edith was taken aback; she wasn't sure how Bitsy had figured this out, though Bitsy and Edward had talked for some time during the dinner. What had he said to her? She wanted to leap on this statement and ask her to repeat the conversation. Often in the past this was how she had learned of Edward's plans, stray little bits he had dropped just to keep things going with a dinner partner. But Sebastien had returned now. They spoke of getting together soon and said good-bye, and she and Sebastien watched Bitsy skate off, receding toward the high clay banks of the shoreline and the yellow chimneys of Blaketon.

In the afternoon Sebastien went back out for his lesson with Alice, and much as Edith would have given to be there and to overhear Sebastien with a girl, she could only strain to see around the spruce branches that blocked the view from her sewing room. Sebastien looked quite uncoordinated, and once Edith saw his feet and legs lift so completely out from under him that for a moment, a long moment, he seemed suspended, floating, until he hit very hard. She held her breath while Alice leaned over him and then dropped on one knee to talk to him, and soon it seemed this had become a conversation on the ice, and Edith was filled with joy, with parental delight, as if all in the world were now loveliness and possibility. She had a friend now! A girl was talking to her son! She could not resist calling to Edward, who happened to be in the next room on one of his prowls.

"Is that the Howe woman?" he said sourly.

"It's their daughter, Edward. A girl."

"The man's a rotter, of course."

"We're not talking about Frank Howe. That's your son out there."

"Oh, yes," he said.

"Well, I think it is marvelous," she said. "It's what is supposed to happen." She let him head for the door. These days, anytime his eyes fixed on her she could feel the desperate need, the pleading that could draw her in like a fishing line. In the past she had always given in to these supplications. In the past, she would have listened and then opened a back door of escape for him, and off they'd be, refugees from yet another private war. She wasn't going to do that this time.

"Edward," she said. He stopped abruptly on hearing her tone and turned.

"My dear?"

"I'm very happy here, you know."

"Yes, certainly. I'm glad. It's what I hoped."

She shook her head. "Thank you, but I mean it. I haven't felt like this in a long time. I wish you did too."

"Oh, don't worry about me," he said plaintively.

On Friday night Sebastien told Edith that Bitsy—he called her that, which shocked Edith for a moment—had invited them all to come out for a skating party. Sebastien relayed the message that Frank was busy and would not be joining them. He told her, eyes wide, that the Howes' servants would bring some chairs out and would build a fire on the ice. Edith felt certain he had misunderstood this last detail; surely the fire would be set on the shore. But the next afternoon, perhaps the coldest one yet, she and the boys dropped off the dock, walked to the mouth of Mason Creek, and saw a small sitting room set up on the river.

"Miss Edith, I wouldn't do this if I were you," said the Howes' man, Archie Gould, as they drew up. He was nervous enough to show a little anger; his wife, Rebecca, was standing well away from the flames.

Edith was surprised he knew her name. She knew who they were, of course. Loretta had told her all about him and Rebecca: the sadness of three children who did not survive, Rebecca's fragile mind. They came to her with the intimacy of characters in a novel. "Do you think we'll fall in?"

"Miss Elizabeth says it's okay, but I say even a fool dumb enough to build a house on sand still wouldn't build no fire on the ice. No disrespect."

But Bitsy came back, and she reassured Edith that she grew up doing this; that the lakes in northern Connecticut, where her family had a country estate, were always ablaze with these warming fires in winter. Edith recalled the fishing shacks that used to dot the lakes in Wisconsin; this seemed not so different. They sat in their Queen Anne chairs and watched Alice and Sebastien skate. Simon ran behind them, and at one point Sebastien tied a scarf to him and made him pull them. Alice didn't skate all that much better than Sebastien, which made sense, since she couldn't have had much more occasion to learn. She was big and broad-hipped, full of health, and her face was lovely. She smiled quickly, with a friendly, even conspiratorial, laugh. Edith remarked that Alice seemed very used to spending time with boys.

"Alice has grown up with boys," Bitsy said. "All the children in the crop were boys. I once spent some time figuring out that there wasn't another girl Alice's age within fifty miles of here. On this side of the Bay, of course."

"Do you have friends on the western shore?"

"Oh, yes. There's a packet of ladies that meets in Baltimore. We have lunch and shop. It's lots of fun."

"I've almost forgotten what a city feels like."

"Then you must come with me. We'll go to the Owl Room for

drinks. It makes all the men nervous. I'll show you the sights: the Bromo-Seltzer Building. We'll buy you something nice. Purple would go well with your coloring."

Edith wasn't sure she wanted to buy anything for herself, and especially not something purple, but no matter. "That would be lovely. In the spring."

"Of course. Old Smokey can't get through this ice anyway," she said referring to the ferry. "But it's decided: the first chance we get, we're going to town."

Edith took a bowl from Rebecca, and the warmth of the soup and heat of the fire filled her. She was happily surveying the frozen vista in the falling sun when she saw Edward's dark form come down to the dock, hesitate, pound the surface with his heavy boot, and then set out for them. "Absolutely marvelous," he called when he was close enough. "Damndest thing I ever saw." He came into the firelight. "Mrs. Howe," he said, "you have given me the sight of a lifetime."

"Bitsy. Please," she said. "Would you like some soup?"

He declined the soup. His large face was red and his mustache whitened with frost. He was wearing a cap, found deep in a closet, that smelled of raccoons. He'd brought the last bottle of his Lafite with him, and he set it down on the table with a thump that carried down the legs and into the ice. From his pockets he pulled three crystal goblets, and he filled them with wine, ruby in the reflected light of the flames; he sat, full of cheer, and offered a tip of his glass to the two women. They drank the cool wine. He and Bitsy quickly fell into conversation, and Edith heard him tell her that he had been working quite hard lately on Retreat business, that he had been much influenced recently by the work of Henry George, especially his *Progress and Poverty*. "I'm considering," he said, "whether we should investigate creating a demonstration of the single-tax theory."

Edith drew in her breath. Was this—whatever it was—the dark flowering of his long night?

Bitsy appeared to know all about the man and the book. "His ideas aren't exactly the kind of thing that is popular down here."

"Of course not. His ideas are extremely bold," Edward said. "Something like that would work here, in theory."

Edith kept her attentive smile while she fought back the impulse to scream. She grabbed the carved arms of her chair to keep from leaping up. "Edward," she said, measuring her breath, "the Retreat is a farm. It's not a theory."

He looked crossly at her. "Of course," he said. There was a long pause while Bitsy tended the fire, and then the children came back. Bitsy and Edward cautiously resumed a conversation about reading, about Bitsy's love for Dickens and, as she said, the "forgotten genius Trollope." Edith had long ago stopped trying to pretend that she was much of a reader, and she turned to Alice. "Have you ever seen ice like this before?"

"Not here," she answered. "But we go everywhere by water. It's just the same, isn't it?" Her voice was warm.

"Do you like boats?"

"I love to sail," she answered. "Daddy has just bought a Comet."

"A boat?" asked Sebastien.

"It's a brand-new one-design. Do you like to sail?"

Sebastien shrugged. "I've never tried."

"What fun. I'll teach you this summer," she said, and though Sebastien tried to shrug a second time, as if maybe he would fit it in, Edith could see the pleasure on his face. Yes, she thought, we will have the summer here; Edward can cook up schemes about a single-tax demonstration, she said to herself with sudden confidence, but we will not sink with him this time.

It was now quite dark and very cold. Edith leaned in to tell Edward and Bitsy that they ought to pack up. Archie had returned to the bank with a wagon and had reappeared on the ice, still shaking his head. He kicked at the fire tentatively, and was surprised to see that far from melting a hole into the depths, it had hollowed out only a slight indentation.

The boys and Alice went on ahead, pushing chairs and tables across the ice toward the dimly visible beacon of the horses' exhalations, and the adults followed. They thanked Bitsy in this most improbable place, standing in the middle of the creek that separated their land, and then they headed home. Edith turned to take a last look at the fire, burning now unattended; she thought, as she often did in Maryland, that others would now take her place in front of the light—watery hoboes drawn to a campfire—and she wondered if she would ever do this again.

The next day the weather finally turned. The air from the south, which had been blocked for months, came in like cream; the animal and plant fragrances in this fecund invasion were almost overwhelming to Edith, after the mineral purity of the freeze. By the first of March the ice had begun to shatter and jam, carried in murderous shapes on the tides. Sebastien spent a few afternoons on the dock watching the breakup and looking over at Blaketon. Edith spied on him now and again, as usual. She would have given anything to know what he thought as the ice parted, but she didn't have a clue; back behind the cool eyes of her son there was a darkness, there had always been a darkness. She raised her own eyes to the river, liquid again, but still she searched for the imaginary red glow of their camp, a flame in her memory.

———

EDWARD OBSERVED THE breaking of the cold in a self-centered frame of mind. His studious and reflective winter was drawing to a close. He stood at the land-side window in his study, looking across the fields and pastures as they turned to ooze, a fecal and foul soup. He reflected that the surface of the earth was nothing but a layer of rot and decay. Oh, God, he thought, in a week or two McCready will be wanting to plant some damn thing in this muck. He'd come calling, straw hat in hand, and they'd discuss seed corn. He'd tell Edward the teams were all lame. He'd ask to buy a tractor. He'd ask for electric power in the sheds, a water main to the hospital barn. In the meantime, if Edward gathered correctly, there would be calves popping out all over the place, fur matted with mucus, followed by tremendous, pulsating sacks of afterbirth, and by green splatters of manure and a steam bath of piss, all of it ground into a paste by the foot traffic around the scene. This whole dairy operation, with its udders and vulvae, its odors and fluids, was unbearably female. It occurred to Edward that Miss Mary, the meticulously dedicated herdswoman, was not such an anomaly after all. If Edward followed her example during this calving season, he would spend his nights in the hospital barn, and if asked, he'd grab hold of a breeched pair of legs and yank a slimy creature up from the depths of the cow's womb. He'd be there waiting with Miss Mary's herd book, his pencil sharpened to record the first impressions. It was no damn life for an industrialist, a man of vision. Edward Mason did not think he was put on this planet in order to comment on, much less to attend to, the newborns of any species.

He sat back down at his desk, a slant-top at which a Mason forebear reportedly wrote the first draft of the Maryland constitution. This historic fact had been told to him by one of his guests at the party. Which one? He could not remember. The party was a smudged memory, crystallized only in the horrified and enraged look his wife had given him about that goddamn cheese. What exactly was his crime, except trying to save the evening and, in the process, to show that poor black bastard that there was no harm done? God, thought Edward, no one in America laughed at himself; these country people didn't have the wit to see that most of what happened in life was a goddamn joke and might as well be enjoyed. "You humiliated him," Edith had nearly screamed. Life is humiliation, he had wanted to tell her; in that respect, we're all created equal, he reasoned.

Edward shuffled through his papers. He had been working on a number of alternative ideas for the place in the course of the winter. A businessman was always looking for the highest and best use of his assets and resources, and Edward could hardly imagine that dairy farming was it. Edith could have her house, but there was potential in this land, if nothing more, as collateral to pledge for capital. There was a little merit in every one of his speculations: artists' colony, college of applied engineering, airport, single-tax community. Perhaps a little farfetched, but each had merit. By fall, if indeed fate kept him imprisoned here until then, he'd make a move, and damn-all Edith if she couldn't see the logic.

But the Retreat was not what he was working on today. In fact, as he shuffled a little farther through the onionskin airmail letters and reports from the works, he was beginning to confirm a rather curious fact. In the past six months, business at Machine Tool had been slowly but steadily increasing. Connolly, his manager over there, did not elaborate in his reports but did inform Edward that orders from aircraft companies had been picking up.

There it was: Business was up. Connolly even mentioned the necessity for a slight expansion of the plant, and unlike McCready with his bloody tractor, Connolly could demonstrate a reasonable rate of return. Even more to the point, Connolly had written that the accumulation of profits in the past nine months (Connolly did not draw attention to the fact that Edward's absence had allowed them to accumulate for the first time) gave the company, as Connolly wrote, "the means to control its own destiny." Edward was entranced by that phrase, describing a state that was, for him, novel and unexpected. For weeks Edward had been wearing a new hopefulness like a fine pair of shoes, giving a spring to each step. Perhaps, just possibly, the long descent might have ended; maybe he was going to get another chance after all. But it was too soon to tell, too soon to know what it could mean for him, and he hadn't suggested a word of this news from the works to anyone—he had decided to keep it a secret for the time being, until the possibilities were clear.

There was a knocking on the door. It was Edith; when Valerie brought tea to his study she tapped timorously and had a very odd habit of refusing to set foot over the threshold. Edith had never seemed very comfortable in this room either; she often complained that it was cold, even when it wasn't. "Yes, dear," he yelled.

She came in, and he was pleased to see that she had brought a cup for herself. "Valerie is off," she said.

"I'm delighted. Let me pour."

She balanced the tray on the candlestand beside his desk, looked around anxiously, rubbed her arms, and then backed into his old, brocaded wing chair. She looked small as she sat stiffly in this monstrous piece of furniture. He found all this nervous motion immensely trying and quite unlike her; tense people, especially women, had always grated on him, because sooner or later they would turn their anxieties and skepticisms on him. He handed over her tea. "Are you cold?" he asked.

"No. It's quite comfortable. I'm sorry," she said, and then paused on a thought for a second or two. "How is it going?" she asked.

"My work?" He beckoned toward his piles of books. "Fine."

They drank their tea quietly. He said, "It has been a long winter, hasn't it?"

"We survived. It wasn't easy for anyone."

"But you . . ." Edward realized his heart was pounding, yet he could not completely understand his nervousness. "But you have been doing much more than surviving."

"Oh," she said, "I learned how to keep warm. How to be content in the cold. That's not something you or I was ever very good at, in the old days."

He didn't like this criticism: it was fine for her to say such a thing about herself, but he wasn't sure that this was true of him. He used to have a fine time, thank you. And he wondered what she meant by "the old days." "Is that the way you think about home?" he asked.

"Home?"

"England, dear. Where else?"

She looked him in the eye. She was asking, Edward knew, what the plans were for next year. He realized suddenly that that was what she had come to discuss, as if to force his hand. He didn't have any plans, just the beginning of hope.

She waited for a second or two more and then said, almost like a challenge, "Next winter I'm sure will be milder. That's what Valerie says."

"Valerie predicts the weather?"

"Well, yes. She does. Some of the colored farmers plant according to her predictions." She relaxed with this odd piece of information; thinking about the colored people seemed to have given her pleasure. She leaned forward to collect her cup from the stand. "Nancy Cooke says I would have an unfair advantage in the garden club. I think I'll try."

"Is there a rose show?"

"Something like that, wouldn't you think?"

"Yes. Naturally."

"There must be some lovely things in Miss Mary's old garden. Perhaps I'll try my hand at bringing it back."

"You always loathed gardening," he said.

"Mummy only let me weed. I suppose it's time to forgive her for that."

"Yes," he said. All this talk of next winter, and of gardening—

he couldn't let that go on too much longer; at this rate, he'd never get out of Maryland alive. He took out his handkerchief and blew his nose, as if to announce a radical change in subject matter. "There are a few decisions we must make at the Machine Tool. Quite a lot to decide, really."

"The news sounds good, from your tone of voice." She did not sound surprised.

"Well, I wouldn't say good. But it could be. Of course, it's extremely difficult for me to tell, being so far away. Something is going on. Maybe this damn Depression is really over."

"Perhaps it is," she commented. "What decisions?"

He really was not prepared for this conversation; he had been pondering how to walk her carefully down this path, but instead she was careening ahead of him, threatening to disappear around the next bend. "Decisions about expansion. Things may be turning around."

She leaned forward. "Then there's really quite good news in those letters?"

He couldn't help smiling, but he tried not to beam. "Damned if I know why, but yes."

"Then you must be there to look after the affairs."

He could hardly believe his ears. She had jumped right to the main issue so fast, he had to ask her to say it again. "What?"

"You must go over. You can't run things from here."

His whole body felt jolted by these magic words. Back to England! Home from exile! Could this really be it, so easily, and with so little negotiation and pain? Just one fiercely cold winter? He said, "I didn't want to push you into such a thing. But you're right, I really should be there."

"Yes. But don't worry, we shall be fine."

He was confused by this; then an inkling of the truth came to him: She had veered off onto a new path and was now leading their lives in a direction of her own choosing. He said, "The boys won't be . . . disappointed?"

"Oh, they'll miss you, of course."

"Miss me?" said Edward. "I'm not sure I understand."

"While you're gone, but certainly it won't be for too long. A few months, would you say?"

"My dear, I have absolutely no intention of leaving you here. I wouldn't abandon you in"—he waved a hand contemptuously—"this wreck. Your father would have me arrested."

"You're not suggesting we all come back with you?"

"Yes. Of course. You're my family."

"No."

"What? No? That's all?"

"I will not go. I am happy here. The boys are happy. Can you guarantee to me and the boys that there will be a sufficient living for us in England?"

"Yes. Well, not exactly." Again he waved his secret correspondence at her. "Business doesn't work like that. We would be taking risks, naturally."

"Then it would seem premature for all of us to return."

Edward slumped back into his seat. Of course it was premature; that's why he hadn't mentioned any of this to her earlier. He'd known well enough that she would demand some sort of security. Thoughts of England began to recede in his mind.

"But," she said, "that doesn't mean you shouldn't go. If there is an opportunity to reap some reward from all your hard work, then you must go. You must be there to seize the chance. Connolly certainly can't handle it alone."

Never, in all their years together, had Edith asserted herself in this way. How quickly and perceptively she had cut to the chase. Should he be there, at the works? Of course he should; that seemed the one inescapable truth, now that Edith had spoken of it. Did he want to go to England? With all his heart. With every deepest prayer, he had hoped for this. But why did he feel as if she were throwing him out the door? He hadn't felt this way since he was expelled from the third form at the Choate School in 1912; much as he had loathed that place, it still hurt that they had bundled him off halfway through the spring term, like a dormitory thief.

"Then what will you do here, alone?"

"I won't be alone. The boys and the women will be with me, and Bitsy has become a dear friend."

Ah, thought Edward, the Howe woman. In some way, this rebellion was her doing. He snapped back, "Then things will be quite perfect for you. I see that."

"Oh, Edward, you can't be feeling sorry for yourself. Isn't this what you dreamed about?"

"I'd say I've done a good bit more than simply *dream* about it, Edith. If the company still exists at all, it's because I gave my life to it."

She leaned forward to take his hand, which he didn't want to give. But even in the darkest hours, Edith had never made him feel like a failure. He could not accuse her of anything but loyalty and patience to a fault.

"I'm sorry," he said. "This is all rather sudden."

"We will miss you. We will all keep busy, you at the works, us here. I am really quite excited about the garden. And I've decided this summer to read Dickens." She beckoned toward the complete set on the shelf to her left; the whole time they lived in England, Edward had been telling her that she should do this.

"Ah," he said. "Poor little Paul Dombey."

"See? We shall be fine."

She gathered the tea things and departed; her business had been tidily accomplished. She left him feeling thoroughly manipulated. He was stunned by this turn in his life, and remained so for a week.

He had dragged her here kicking and screaming, and look what had happened: She'd fallen in love with the bloody place. She'd spent a winter plotting, and now, at the first chance, she was throwing him out.

But there were, of course, pleasures to be thought of as well. He could hear the whistle of the *Normandie*, a chesty and masculine call. He glanced at the French Line schedule that had been in a pigeonhole since they arrived, frequently opened, scanned with regret; for a month, ever since this first news began to trickle in from Connolly, he had denied himself the pleasure of referring to it, but now he snatched it out. May 18. The *Normandie* would sail from Pier 88 in New York on May 18, bound for Southampton. The whistle called for him. He unleashed a flood of images and sensations: the air perfumed with Chanel No. 5 and sharpened by the slight tang of fuel oil; the satin gaiety of the violins; the gentle rocking of the bed; even the reassuring vibration of the propeller shaft, turning the screw through the black water on the passage home.

The weeks began to pass; the date of departure approached. Back to England! He imagined the landing in Southampton, knowing that awaiting him on the dock could be a modest but sufficient purse for his expenses, which would take him to London by evening, dinner at the Ritz, a few days' visit with Lord Belsen, and then— and this was the source of the most joy, this was what was new, this was what he had saved as his most distant ambition—to Manchester, to begin work, to remake himself at age forty-two, to take up the challenge tendered to him by fate, and by his wife. He looked around at his study and it was suddenly lovely, like a memory. He thought that if he were a religious man he would fall on his knees and give thanks, and then he did just that, dropped forward with his knees creaking, his folded hands on his desktop as on an altar rail, and thought, "Thank you, thank you, thank you." He tried to conclude the prayer with a snatch of verse from Isaiah, and from the depths of his early schooling came the words "I heard the voice of the Lord saying, Whom shall I send, and who will go for us? Then said I, Here am I; send me."

When things were finally set, he called the household into his study and announced that pressing business was calling him back to England, and that he might be away for the summer. Simon heard this news and he began to whimper slightly. "But, Father . . ."

Edward was touched deeply by this display, and he went over to his son to give him a comforting pat on the shoulder. "Just a month or two, a blink of an eye for a six-year-old," he said, jocularly.

"I'm seven," said Simon.

"So you are." He turned to Sebastien, in time to see that he had been staring aggressively at his mother, who was avoiding his look. For a moment, Edward paused and tried to imagine what this meant, this silent demand in Sebastien's eyes. Edward shook off a flickering of suspicion and continued with his prepared remarks. "And you," he said to Sebastien, "will have to assume many of my responsibilities, especially regarding the farm."

This expansive gesture had the effect he anticipated. "Yes, sir," said Sebastien.

"Oversee the summer plantings, of course, and your mother will need help with the affairs of the estate."

Sebastien tried not to show how happy this made him, but Edith's eyes filled with tears of gratitude. Yes, thought Edward, this is all as it should be. The way is now clear. The emotions in the room were larger than anything Edward had ever before imagined in family life, and he did not scold the boys when they could not restrain themselves from leaving the room at a run and whooping in the hall—even Simon was now captured by an obscure elation. Later, Edith did what pleased him so much, which was to take his penis into her mouth, and he leaned back with his arms folded above his head as she gave him this pleasure, and before his body began pumping out its juices, he shed an honest tear of joy.

The following day he took the Packard to town and spent the morning at the telegraph office, with cables to Connolly, to the French Line, to Lord Belsen, and to Marston, his once and future gillie. A week later, with little explanation to Edith, he went over to Baltimore for a night, packing a rather oversized bag for the trip. Edith did not remark that this bag clanked as Robert took it to the car, but Valerie shot him a menacing look. Edward certainly did not like this implication that he must apologize to the colored girl for decisions about the Retreat's furnishings. The manager at the Belvedere, who had arranged meetings with two silver dealers, and the gentlemen themselves treated this matter of the sale of a few pieces with a great deal more respect. Indeed, quite a bit of silver and other decorative arts had been leaving the Eastern Shore in the past decade, and it served no one to suggest that families were doing this because they were hard up for cash. Before returning home he wired most of the proceeds to the French Line.

In the midst of these preparations, McCready appeared for a consultation on crops. Because it no longer really mattered very much to Edward, he was happy enough to sit through a long description of the plans. He thought, too late, of inviting Sebastien to join them. "I was thinking," said McCready haltingly at the end of the conversation, "of buying a tractor. I've seen a John Deere that's priced right."

On the wings of the mood that had borne him these past weeks, he responded patiently. He had seen, he said, no figures to support the notion that a tractor would pay for itself, and besides, he had decided that they would continue to funnel whatever profits came off the place into the buildings, the buildings and, of course, certain household expenses.

"No, sir, Mister Edward," said McCready. "I weren't supposing you'd pay for it."

"You weren't?"

"No, sir. The missus and me is going to buy it."

Edward was more than a little shocked; he had time to imagine how he would have felt about this news if his own affairs had not turned around slightly. "You have the money?"

"Yes, we been putting aside. Most of the horses ain't much good anymore anyway."

"Well, then," said Edward. He waited for McCready to speak again.

"Then I was wondering if I would have permission to bring it on the Retreat."

"Yes," said Edward, still incredulous. "Whatever you wish."

McCready was very uncomfortable, miserable, really, but something else was pushing him forward. "Then I was wondering w-w-w-whether we needed to make some business arrangement. With it being my tractor, and all."

The truth was that McCready could well have a case, but where was all this savvy coming from? Edward said he would not want to be pressured but would be willing to consider a proposal on the matter.

McCready thanked him vigorously, promised that he would think through how this business might be conducted, and left gratefully. Edward walked out to the porch after seeing him off and glanced across the silent lawns and fields. There had been a change of fortune for all, even for McCready, and the misfortune that had seemed to be following Edward for the past few years, after his early triumphs, might perhaps have finally been frozen clear of him by the coldest winter in many decades. Go! said the scene in front of him, as if he were a young man of ambition contemplating an escape from farm life. You can trust us, said the land and water, the clay and the stone. Leave your family with us, and go forward.

The last day, the family gathered in the vestibule, where Mrs.

McCready had sat that first mournful night. Robert had brought down the trunks, into which one or two additional pieces of silver had found their way, and packed them in the car. Edward had taken a long time with his bath. It was hot again, and he had chosen the light heather tweed and gray topcoat for his traveling wear. He shaved with caution and then powdered his cheeks and mustache lightly. He snapped his shaving kit together and gave Robert the last bundle. He came down the stairs slowly; the family faces were turned toward him. Sebastien was first in the line, and they shook hands; Edward even began to believe that his relationship with his older son could now become, in his absence, the mature affection of mutual respect that Edward had hoped to enjoy with his own father. Simon was next, and perhaps because Edward was so taken with this image of Sebastien as a young man, he saw Simon as a very small child, and he did what one did with a child, picked him up, and in the process he bashed him into the chandelier. In fact, he opened a small cut on the boy's head, from which blood flowed. There was much commotion, with Loretta running for a damp towel, and Edward apologizing to the boy but avoiding, at all costs, getting bloodstains on his suit.

As a result of this injury, his parting with Edith was not what he had planned. He had meant to tell her he loved her, with the courageous love of the long-married; he wanted to tell her that the example of her courage and strength had sustained him for many years, and would continue to do so when they were apart. He had planned to vow to her that if he had a single talent, a single skill learned, an ounce of energy to expend, all of it would go toward the Machine Tool, that from now on he would be measured by what he accomplished every day. He wanted to say, finally, that she should wait for news from him.

"You better run," said Edith over Simon's howls. Robert was waiting with the car.

"I . . . I . . ."

"Don't worry. It's just a small cut. Good-bye."

"My dear . . ."

"We shall miss you," she said. "Go."

The train was standing at the siding when they arrived. The trainman and conductor loaded his things, and he took a dusty seat at the middle of the car. This was a farm-country train, a whistle-stopper that ran back and forth on the peninsula like a horse harnessed to a mill wheel. But the first lurch of motion was enough, finally, to push Edward's thoughts ahead, to the *Normandie*, to London, beyond. He settled back, a free man, laughed slightly at himself over that terrible blow to poor little Simon, thought of Edith not as she was when shooing him off—which was what she had been doing since early March—but as she had been in bed that night with him, her lips running up and down his penis, and how he wept as he came.

6

ACROSS THE BREACH of many years, Harry Mason can imagine his grandmother, Edith, on the landing of the Retreat as Edward's car draws slowly down the lane. In this one juncture of the story, his grandmother comes to him with the clarity of a photograph. He pictures her in her youth, almost as a teenager: her dark hair is soft and lovely and invites caress; her skin is untouched and unscarred. But Edith is not a child; she is not coy about her charms and careless about her future. Edith has been through disappointments—some of them perhaps of her own making—and she has struggled, and she has been loyal to this difficult man she has just sent off to England. She knows some of the costs of life.

The hand that has just finished her final send-off to her husband has landed absently on her cheek, and she lets her fingers palpitate slightly, as if to remind herself that she can give pleasure with her touch. She notices that there is a small stain of Simon's blood on her thumb, and she licks it off, the salty essence of life. She feels the pumping of her own heart, slowly recovering from the last anxious moments; her sinews feel as if they have been wound in tight spirals but are now uncoiling, and with each breath she expels one more lungful of trouble, and a calm reaches deeper within, until she feels that she is only breath, only this most private air. Her own name comes to her mind as a surprise and a gift. She is not quite ready—Edward's car is barely on the state road by now—to feel safe and free; that will come soon enough, but for this moment, as Harry imagines it so fiercely, she is free to stand there and wait.

Simon, Harry's father, has been withdrawn to have his wound washed and bandaged, and his whimpering has been hushed. Silence comes over the scene like mist, gently filling the spaces Edward has just abandoned. It still seems almost impossible to Edith that these events have played out as they have, that she and the boys are not being trundled off at this very second to England like Gypsies, that instead, they have been left in this calm and this stillness. All winter and into the spring, little white pulses of hopefulness had flashed before her, and she had snuffed them out quickly because she could not bear to watch them die slowly. But then, a gift: Sebastien came to her and said, "Mother, talk to Father about the Machine Tool," and she asked why, and he answered, "Connolly wants him back."

She glances over at Sebastien, sitting on the steps, a long stalk of grass hanging out of his mouth. He's grown; he's old enough to slouch. She doesn't want to acknowledge her debt to him, because he will tender it soon enough. He'll make demands; he's always been a listmaker, a recorder of favors received and owed. But she wants him to feel the freedom they have earned, and she wants him to make the very best of it.

"Well," he says harshly. "It's done."

"We shall be fine," she answers without really thinking; for years she has used this phrase at each moment of change.

"Oh, Mother," he snaps. "We shall be much better than fine."

She thinks she ought to defend Edward, but nothing of that sort comes to her mind. She recalls instead the day her sister Rosalie went off to boarding school, and her own sense of rapture—she was ten at the time—as she recognized the small freedoms that began to accumulate in her life.

"Well, don't you think?" Sebastien insists.

"Oh, I suppose."

A half-century later, Harry can hear the equivocations, the half-truths in her answers. She's survived her adult life thus far because she has given up trying to believe and has settled for supposing; she has given up hope and consoled herself with waiting. Who would have handled things differently, or better, than she? But even as she uses these words to keep Sebastien slightly at bay, she's racing ahead in her mind. Oh, yes, they will be better than fine. They will prosper this summer, grow new like Miss Mary's garden. She looks over again at Sebastien, and he is still waiting for her to give him what he wants, but for a second, she is not even there. That's how Harry has decided she must feel. The eagle pair that lives in the white pine by the water is hunting above them, squawking at each other as they swoop, and she imagines flying with them, high enough to see that the Packard, with Robert at the wheel and Edward in the back, has made it to the passenger siding, that the train is there, and he is getting on the train. She can now, as she settles back onto the porch once again, take up the gift of time to herself.

During her silence Sebastien has wandered off into the high grass under the pecan trees. The door opens, and Valerie leads Simon back out, a swatch of his red hair turned orange with iodine. He gives Valerie a hateful look, his small mouth fixed with thoughts of revenge. "It hurts," he says, about the iodine, after Valerie leaves. "I hate them."

"Shhh."

"Well, I do."

They sit together and she gathers him in, silencing him. The wind off the water is scented with fish and gasoline. This place, the land, sea, and air, all of it, is abundant with life and honest work, and that's how she feels, sitting there with her arms around her younger son.

"Are you all right?" she asks him.

"Is Father coming back soon?"

"Yes. Just a few months. But we'll have fun, won't we? You can have your own garden, if you want."

"All mine?" he asks quickly.

"Just yours. You can plant chrysanthemums and dahlias. Some pansies, maybe."

A shout comes from Sebastien, halfway across the park. "Come," he yells. "Toad. A snake!"

Simon jumps up, and Edith follows, and they gather around an enormous blacksnake, thick as a log, lashing at Sebastien's stick. "See," says Sebastien, "it can't move. It's eating." The back feet of some small rodent are protruding from its mouth.

Simon yips with excitement. "Get the ax, Sebastien," he says. "I'll guard him."

Edith looks at the snake, eyes buggy around its prey, and wonders whether this long tube of gristle can sense fear and danger. She and Simon watch for a moment as it tries to force the lump down its throat, if a throat is something it has. At length Sebastien returns, and Edith thinks there is no reason to cut this thing in two, and perhaps good reason not to, but she backs off. It is time to let the boys go.

She walks back into the house and goes upstairs. She wanders into her bedroom, and then into Edward's dressing room. It is by far the nicest room in the Retreat, much airier than hers in summer, and sunnier in winter, but she has no desire to take it over now that he is gone. Valerie has already retrieved the last of his laundry, put away the stray bits of clothes and accessories, and covered the furniture with cloths. The loud voice left in this intimate space is muffled by the folds, and when Edith walks back out, she closes the door behind her.

The next day Edith assembles Valerie and Loretta after breakfast and tells them that she has in mind a thorough spring cleaning. Actually, what she has in mind, has been planning for a while, is to strip the place bare. "All this clutter," she says. "I want it removed." Loretta resists change, but Valerie approves. Back up to the third floor lockup go the silver, the china, the crystal. "I don't plan to be entertaining," Edith explains. "One set of china will do nicely." They empty the closets out onto the floor—the moth-eaten coats, the broken games, the rusty implements. Valerie and Loretta take home what they can repair and give to their families; Robert hauls the rest out onto the point and heaves the pile over the bank into the creek. As they strip and empty the recesses of the house, the one thing Edith gathers and saves is the papers—sheets of foolscap and record books, notes and photographs; she deposits them in her sewing room and will spend the following winter cataloguing them.

But otherwise, Edith is ruthless with the contents of the house. Loretta says, "These is Mason things," as if to say Edith doesn't have complete leave to move them, and Edith responds that Mason things or not, they give her nightmares. Robert and Valerie pack the knickknacks, the busts, the priceless flotsam, into wooden crates and pile the crates in the old icehouse. Simon is allowed to keep out the arrowhead collection; Sebastien selects an alabaster monkey, principally because his mother finds it hideous and ugly. Edith keeps, as a warning, a miniature of a young man—Miss Mary's brother, who killed himself in his teens—because it seems her life must now be given over fully to her boys and to the future.

Bitsy comes over as this is all happening, and Edith greets her covered with cobwebs, her shirt nearly damp through with sweat. Bitsy has a sour look on her face; she's depressed and wants to complain about life, but Edith is too full of energy to sit, and too full of cheer to be much comfort. The labor has felt wonderful; she feels radiant. "Doesn't it look marvelous?" she exclaims.

"If you say so, dear. The place always did look like a pawnshop."

"Are you all right?" Edith asks, because she has to.

Bitsy waves her hand as if to avoid answering but then stops this motion and says, "The Eastern Shore blues. Always comes about this time of year."

"But it's so lovely."

"Of course it is. This is the only season down here. It's the best there is, the best my life gets. You see the problem."

Edith has spent a number of springs hoping for renewal and knowing it wouldn't come, but this one will be different. She succeeds in getting Bitsy back in her car, promising that as soon as the cleanup is done they will make their trip to Baltimore. "Next week, perhaps," says Edith, and Bitsy drives off hurt and miffed.

Once the house is organized Edith sets to work in the garden. She's been watching for blooms shining out of the thicket, and marking the spots where there seem to have been tulips; she's found rhododendrons marking corners of most of the beds and has discovered, beneath the ground cover, a series of herringbone brick walks. McCready releases Robert for a week, and Edith works with him side by side as they hack and dig their way through the weeds. She is curious about spending this time with him—she hasn't been alone with him since the disaster at the party. The first morning she instructs him on what to dig out and what to save, until she realizes that he knows far more about flowers and gardens than she does; she realizes that he must have worked in these gardens as a boy, probably planted much of what was there. By the end of the week she is asking his opinion and taking his advice, and on Friday they stand back together—with Simon, who has been at her side far more than she would have expected—and congratulate each other.

"Looks right fine, Miss Edith."

"It does. Doesn't it?"

"It does, ma'am. We done good."

That night she soaks the grime out of her pores and the soil from her fingernails, and when she is dressed for bed, she looks down at this orderly scene through the moonlight. Harry imagines her there, in the window, taking stock of all that she has accomplished. The house is clean and spare; the light summer breezes pass through it without obstruction. The garden is tilled, the young plants are taking root. She has never had so much, been given so much. She is free to do with it what she will.

—

"I WAS BEGINNING to think I'd never get you out of there," said Bitsy. They were sitting in the dining room of the James River House in Baltimore. "I thought I was going to have to hitch a team to you to get you off the Retreat. It's not healthy." The room was full of ladies dressed formally enough for the opera, and they were all having cocktails. Bitsy had introduced Edith as they worked their way across the floor, and at last they had reached their table. An elderly waiter, his white coat spattered with soup, made a show of holding Bitsy's chair for her but seemed to ignore Edith.

"I've never felt more healthy in my life." In fact, a day or two ago Edith had been astonished and delighted to notice that the muscles of her forearms had become denser and sharper from her labor. Holding her highball glass, she could feel her physical strength.

"You know what I mean. The only people you have talked to in weeks are those colored girls."

Edith tried a small joke. "I talk to the ghosts. All those dead Mason women," she said. "They're quite diverting and I find them quite suitable companions."

Bitsy leaned forward over the table. "That's *just* what I mean. It's as if you are disappearing, Edith. You be careful with all this history over there. It's time to burn it all, if you ask me. It's not as if that has been the happiest place all these years."

"Well, no," Edith admitted. "But that doesn't mean I have to be unhappy, does it? I'm done with that."

Bitsy eyed her, as if she had just stepped over the line into disloyalty; she was warning Edith not to talk about happiness, not to find contentment in these places. "Here's what *I* think," she said. "I think these big family places run out of luck, sooner or later. I think bad things begin to happen in them."

"Oh," said Edith, wishing, sort of, that she could think of some comment to make about this.

"History is prophecy," said Bitsy.

"Really, Bitsy. This is getting tiresome. I thought we were going to be gay."

"Okay," said Bitsy. "You're right. Let's dig in." The waiter had brought their lunch—there seemed to be no menus and no choice here—and the fish was poached almost to mush. Bitsy spent the rest of the lunch talking about the things she was planning to buy for Alice—Edith had begged off this part of the trip with the question, What do I know about dressing a girl?—and as they parted, they agreed to reconvene at the Belvedere's Owl Room at four. "It's *filled* with men," said Bitsy.

—

OUT ON THE street, Edith decided to explore. Bitsy had listed the cultural must-sees and high points—the Peabody Library, the Walters Art Gallery—but Edith was happy simply to stroll, to sample city life with the pleasure reserved for one who didn't live there.

She wandered and climbed, and eventually she found herself in a rather stately square, somewhat like those in London. This park in the center was marked with circles of lawn, and in the middle she saw three Negro nursemaids, dressed in uniforms with high Victorian collars, leaning against the base of a statue. The women were talking casually, but their charges, three girls in white dresses and hats, stood stiffly and unhappily to one side. Edith wanted to go to them and tell them, For God's sake, for your own sakes, try to be happier. She'd had a happy childhood, even if her sisters had picked on her, and the three of them were almost ready to leave girlhood squabbles behind that summer they spent in Paris at art school. This had apparently been a finishing touch advocated by her father, and her mother had gone along, the gardener from Winnetka, and spent the months looking utterly bewildered. Edith's art teacher, whose name she had forgotten long ago, had told her that her art needed passion, that French was the language of love, and he took her to a café one afternoon to announce that he would be willing to initiate her in the joys of sensual pleasure. As she reddened and searched for a way to escape, a large, noisy, bumbling charmer—an American she had noticed that summer because he affected a student cap and riding breeches—began wading clumsily toward her between the tables, attracting the outraged stares of the waiters and bringing the painter to his feet as if ready to draw a weapon. When Edward Mason reached her, he said, "Do you think you're lucky or unlucky?"

Edith kept walking down the square, noticing that for all the architectural grandness of the houses, most of them were in poor repair, with dirty windows and façades missing pieces of ornament, with white marble stoops that seemed scuffed and uncared for. But the side streets still seemed fashionable, the houses slightly smaller and more practical, the tone quieter and more protected. At the far end of the square, she stopped to consider where she might head next, and suddenly she realized that a man had walked by, tipped his hat perfunctorily, stopped, peered at her, peered again, and then let out a cough. To her surprise she recognized that it was Tom Hazelton. She couldn't speak, even though she tried.

He waited for her and then, with a hopeful look on his face, he introduced himself.

"Yes, of course," said Edith. "I'm sorry. How extraordinary to see you here."

"Extraordinary? My father lives here. This is Mount Vernon Place."

"I mean me. I'm just over here for the day with friends. My husband is in England," she added, immediately wishing she had not.

He smiled broadly. Yes, said Tom, this was Mount Vernon Place. She had just walked past Miss Mary Mason's house, in fact. This was the part of the city where people of good family routinely saw each other out walking. When he said "good family," he winked. "Actually, my father's house is just a few blocks north."

"How *is* your father?"

"He's well. I'm just on my way to have tea with him. Join us. He'll be in ecstasy."

For a moment, Edith almost accepted, despite the fact that she had only a few more minutes before she had to meet Bitsy. "I couldn't now. But another time it would be lovely. You and your father are the only people I know in Baltimore," she said, as if that explained why she thought it would be nice to visit them.

Each paused for the other to speak. He looked splendid, tanned and fit, and she almost said so before he broke in.

"You look absolutely marvelous. You've been outside, I see."

She explained about her gardening, and once begun, she told him about her spring cleaning, and then about Edward's business in England.

"My father won't approve," he said.

"About Edward?"

"No. About the Retreat. About you tampering with his family's ancestral home." They both laughed.

"And how are you?" she asked.

"I'm living mostly in Annapolis these days."

"Building boats?"

"Yes. In July I'm going to be sailing my new one to Havana. We'll run circles around every boat in the Caribbean. Want to come along?"

"I'm sorry," she said, looking into her purse. "I seem not to have packed my bathing suit."

He smiled, but there was a pouty expression on his face when he said that it really could be arranged, with the boys, too. "You seem like someone who enjoys a change of scenery."

"Perhaps when my husband gets back."

"Of course." He said this with a small thread of irritation in his voice. It was clear to her that for all his humor, Tom didn't like to be told no. Perhaps she had backed off perceptibly; perhaps what she was figuring out had made an arc of expression on her face that was easy for him to follow. He was quick, then, to cover with a smile, at first a forced one, and to add that Edward would of course be welcome.

They stood awkwardly, long enough for Edith—had she wanted to—to bid him a pleasant, even jocular, farewell and be done with him. But she didn't want to do that, so she smiled back and stood her ground. "Edward only goes to sea on the *Normandie*," she said.

"Your husband has great style," he said, but she could not tell if he was being ironic.

"Perhaps we're mismatched." Edith, again, was not sure why she had said this and wished she hadn't, but Tom had been so willing to flatter her last fall, and was giving her such attention now, that she could be forgiven for fishing for compliments. But this time he did not say anything, but simply reached out and, for an instant, took one of her hands. His palm was rough, as she had noted the first time they met, but now hers was too, and when he gave her a squeeze, she felt the pressure all over her body.

"I really must get back. My friend Bitsy is already mad at me."

"Where is she?"

"At the Owl Room. We had lunch at the James River House."

"Dreadful."

"The food is always dreadful in places where women have lunch. Don't you think?"

"I wouldn't know."

"Of course. You wouldn't. Would you? You've never been married?"

"No."

"If you had, your wife would have dragged you there at least once, to show you off."

"I'll give you a ride," he announced. He pointed the way up a side street, and as they walked, she kept a noticeable gap between them. She needed this distance, and needed very much to go home now and think about the strands of pleasure and danger that were in this meeting. That seemed what he wanted as well, but as they drew up to a line of parked cars, he headed to a space where a large, black motorcycle was standing.

"You're joking."

"I said a ride, didn't I? My car is in Annapolis."

She made a motion toward her skirt, but it was, in fact, fuller than many she had; besides, she'd always wanted to ride on a motorcycle. He stepped over the motorcycle, brought it vertical, and pointed behind him to a passenger seat perched over the rear fender. She put one foot on the pin he pointed to, swung her other leg over, and landed firmly, her kneecaps just brushing his hips. He stamped once or twice until the engine caught with a fat gurgle of fuel and smoke, pulled her hands to his waist, and then jolted out into the traffic.

He took what she recognized as a long route, up and down several of Baltimore's famous hills, and once she stopped fighting the lean of the motorcycle on the corners, the pure excitement of speed and motion caught on. She could sense the sinews of his legs working as he shifted and braked, his flirtation with this piece of machinery, a coupling with steel, like a rifle on the shoulder.

Later, she had the uncomfortable vision of passing down the streets with her dress blown up to her waist, but she did not much care. As they pulled up to the restaurant a couple of ladies stared, and she could see one whispering to the other, as if she knew who Edith was or Tom was. Edith wanted to stay there, her clothing ragged, her hair a mess, like a display for all the ladies of the afternoon, even for Bitsy, but she slowly swung her leg over onto the sidewalk, holding on to Tom's neck like a handle.

He turned off the engine but remained on his machine.

"Does one thank someone for that?" she asked, her breath still coming out in pants. "Scaring one to death?"

"If one liked it."

"Oh. Well, then, thank you for the ride." She looked around again; her audience had scattered.

"*Candide's* in the water," he said. "Perhaps the boys would like to come out for a sail."

The boys, thought Edith, yes, the boys. "They'd be thrilled."

"Lots of nice day trips over there on the Chester." He was almost trying to sound spontaneous, but Edith suspected he'd already charted a course, even before this meeting.

"Yes. Lovely," she said. "I have to go." He gave her one last scrutinizing glance, then an inwardly directed smile; he seemed to like what he saw.

"Good," he said, stamping the engine to life once more, and he disappeared into the traffic without any other good-bye. She stood there, feeling the lingering strain up her groin, the chafe and heat of the motorcycle on her calves, the burn of wind on her face. She felt as if she had been carried by an eagle and then deposited on this spot with only a slight talon-pinch to prove that she had been there, aloft.

———

A LETTER CAME from Edward, postmarked Manchester, a detail that Edith noticed immediately, because it meant he had not stayed in London, the locus of so many of his vices, but had done what he'd said he would do: head straight for the works. He spoke tenderly of her and the boys, with inquiries after Simon's head wound, and then devoted a page or two to the new England, an energized place, the papers full of talk about Hitler and the Continent, debates in Parliament. Edward reported these things as if he had known them all along, as if he had discussed politics frequently and had a body of opinion from which to draw. Edith was now separated from him not only by an ocean but by a phantom former life; he had become a person with a different history altogether. He closed by saying that there was even more business to attend to than he had imagined, and that certainly it would take the full summer, if not into the fall.

At dinner she told the boys all about these things, and they both listened quietly. "You should be proud," she said. "Your father has important work to do."

"Will he be coming home soon?" asked Simon.

"She already said. Not until the fall." Sebastien was so happy with the news that he was squirming in his seat.

"Oh," said Simon. But later, when she put him to bed, he asked again. It was Simon's way, when troubled, to keep asking the same question over and over again, which was one of the things that his older brother found frustrating. "Is Father coming home soon?"

"No, sweetie. Probably not until winter. He's doing very important work."

"Yes," said Simon, settling for his father's importance in the place of his love. She put him down and lay beside him. She tiptoed out when she thought he was asleep, but when she came back from the bathroom to say good night to Sebastien, she heard the two of them talking in Sebastien's room.

"Is Father coming back, Sebastien?" She felt Simon's hurt right through her body. "Is he going to forget about us?"

"No, Toad. Don't worry."

"But he's in England."

"Yes, he is."

"That's so far away."

She knew that in private, just the two of them, Sebastien would never be mean and sarcastic to Simon, especially not when he needed so much, but she heard the tone of his voice change. "Look. You've got Mother and me, right? You've got your friends at school? Friends are better than fathers. You can trust them."

"I trust Father. That's mean to say you don't."

Edith heard Sebastien's arm settle on Simon's shoulders. "I know it's hard for you," he said, "but think of it this way. We're happy here, right? If Father doesn't come back until the fall, we'll have the full summer to do things together."

Simon's voice sounded perkier now. "Will you take me out to the point field with Robert?"

"Sure, I will."

"And let me drive the team?"

"Sure."

There was a satisfied sound as Simon settled on the bed; he clearly felt a little better.

"Look, Toad," said Sebastien again. "You'll see. If Father never comes back, as far as I'm concerned, that's the best news of the year."

Edith wished he hadn't said that and thought of bursting in and scolding him, for Simon's sake. But she could not. She had never imagined that so much could change deep within her, right into her soul, that her husband of more than fifteen years could be gone as quickly and completely as a dinner guest. But he really was— six weeks gone and quite forgotten. She took what Sebastien said to heart and tiptoed into her room. Simon *was* doing well, with his pet bunnies and his friends; no one could say he was being injured by his father's absence. Could they? School was now over, and Sebastien had returned to his beloved fields, a young man now, with muscles across his back. The small family was thriving here among the cultivations and harvests, the tides and winds, the flat-open invitations of the land and water. Edith was being called to live this life fully, all of them were, and she knew what made sense was to answer.

Two weeks later—Sebastien had seen letters over and back on the subject—the Hazeltons' boat, *Candide*, came into the creek out of a morning haze. Sebastien sat on the porch and watched it pick its way through the channel under auxiliary power, the crewman forward nosing the bow one side or the other with a pole. Sebastien was alert to every nudge, to the slow advance of this boat into his life. So much to understand. His mother had been enticing him and Simon with visions of the boat for days—its kitchen, its bunks, its tall mast. Why was she so interested in this trip? Why did it seem to matter to her so much? A few days ago he had said offhandedly to Simon that anyone who liked sailing—which Sebastien did; he'd been out several times with Alice in her Comet and it was like becoming part of the air—that anyone who liked to sail was a fruit. His mother yelled, "They are not," practically from the other end of the house. He had never seen his mother so happy.

Sebastien kept his eyes on Mr. Hazelton, a straight and tall figure in the cockpit, with a voice as sharp as an air horn. This man: Sebastien knew he was his father's rival. Yes, thought Sebastien, Mr. Hazelton could deal a hand to his father and they'd all get to watch him squirm. But his mother was acting almost giggly, and Sebastien was not sure he liked seeing her this way, distracted behind a slight smile that she would not explain. He understood what she was hiding; the truth had never been difficult for him. It wasn't information he cared about. He could tolerate almost anything from his mother but secrets. They could go out on this boat, but Sebastien wanted her to remember that at the end of the day, after they had gotten home and eaten, and after Simon had been sent off to bed, after everything, she owed him her thoughts, she owed him her deep feelings, like a confession.

He gave a yell into the house and then proceeded to the dock. The boat had been made fast; he heard the muffled sounds of men below. Soon a large sail bag appeared through a hatch, followed by a pair of hands and, finally, the head of the crewman. He was a boy, maybe a year or two older than Sebastien; they looked at each other wordlessly, the boy with a rather superior expression, and

Sebastien doing everything he could not to show that he was jealous of this boy's job.

Hazelton emerged into the cockpit aft, and gave Sebastien a greeting and invited him aboard. Mr. Hazelton was wearing a captain's hat and bright blue linen pants and a white shirt, a costume that Sebastien found silly; rich grown-ups were often such goofs. Sebastien heard Mr. Hazelton call his mother Edith as she approached. He turned to find himself face-to-face with the crewman. "Hey," he said.

"Hey," said the boy. He was busy coiling the mooring lines.

"Where are we going?"

"Don't know. Mr. Hazelton said it was up to you."

"Up to my mother, he meant."

"She your mother?"

"Yes."

"Nice," said the boy with a swagger.

Well, yes, thought Sebastien, I suppose so. She was wearing shorts, which she rarely did. Hazelton had shown her to a seat in the cockpit; she sat stiffly and nervously, her smooth white legs crossed in front of her. The next second Hazelton's voice barked the boy's name, Larry, from behind, and Larry jumped. Mr. Hazelton seemed to be Captain Bligh rather than Admiral Hornblower. Edith and Simon settled in the cockpit with Hazelton; she was trying with every cell in her body to appear enthralled as Hazelton repeated the procedure for finding the channel. Sebastien felt the slight heave of the keel brushing the sandbars and thought it might be funny if this whole elaborately planned excursion ended a hundred yards from the dock. He would have been curious to see how Mr. Hazelton behaved. But he didn't want this to happen, and once they had made their way well clear of the mouth of the creek, Hazelton turned into the wind while Larry raised the sails; he cut the motor, and for a moment there was a confused and violent flapping, and an uncoiling and snapping of lines, as if the whole boat would begin to disintegrate. Hazelton's commands were sure but curt. Edith clenched her hands very firmly on Simon, wincing from the spray that came over the bow and a wind that seemed less to blow on them than to pull them as it flew past. The noise of the sails and the shouting and the wind rose until, with a delicate hand on the wheel, Hazelton caught the wind and suddenly there was not a sound but the warm creak of stretching Manila and a gravelly scraping of bubbles on the hull below.

Sebastien watched his mother as she turned to Mr. Hazelton. "How exciting!" she said, with a slightly dubious smile on her face. If they started to sink, she'd probably keep that same smile on her face, telling Hazelton that she enjoyed a little dip in the ocean now and again.

"Getting under way always seems a little like a Chinese fire drill."

"Don't apologize. That was quite a show. Wasn't it, Simon dear?"

They were moving now, slicing hard along the rivershore of the Retreat, heading up the Chester River. The cornfields, where Sebastien had been working just yesterday afternoon, were ribbed with furrows, now beginning to take on the hue of the first shoots. The land seemed to be going one direction, the water another, and this boat was now the powerful center, as if the earth were revolving around it.

They came around Piney Point and past Reeds Creek, and from there made the open dash across the mouth of the Corsica. The water was thick and heavy here, and grayer; though the sun still shone, the light off the sea seemed to reflect weather to come. Sebastien looked up the riverbanks and saw the docks and steamer landings, jutting out at quite regular intervals, and behind them, often separated by a side patch of lawn, he could see the houses, some hidden behind neatly clipped hedges of box bush and solemn rows of arborvitae. A few, even from this distance, looked all but abandoned. That's the way the Retreat must have seemed all those years, overgrown and shuttered, a closed eye on the shoreline, a dark memory at night.

"So where's your daddy?" asked Larry. They were sitting side by side, their feet through the lifelines.

"What do you mean?" Sebastien answered, though he was already light-years, lifetimes, ahead of this boy. He was always ahead of other boys, soon bored by them; he didn't enjoy not being liked at school, but he couldn't pretend, wouldn't, that their opinions were anything but stupid.

Larry tipped his head back toward the stern. Hazelton had opened a bottle of champagne—which Sebastien knew his mother loved—and they were both holding glasses. Simon had taken the wheel; Hazelton had an arm over his shoulder and was making slight adjustments now and again and whispering pointers into his ear. Oh, look at this, thought Sebastien; just imagine how things could have been. His mother laughed, bringing her hand to her mouth, as if someone had said something wicked. Oh, imagine this. Sebastien looked back at Larry, a boy with clean skin and straight teeth, almost certainly the son of one of Hazelton's friends. What did it matter what anyone knew? "He's dead," said Sebastien.

"Uh-huh," said Larry. "You mean your father," he added, after Sebastien didn't continue.

Sebastien nodded. What was this feeling like, he asked himself, to say this? Wasn't his father's absence enough?

"So how? In the war or something?"

"What war?"

"In France, I guess. You're English, right?"

"I'm fourteen," he said. "How could my father have died in the Great War?"

"Well, hell, some damn war or something."

—

Edith let the champagne bubbles burn her tongue. The air and the sun were glorious. She looked ahead, happy to see Sebastien getting along with the crewman. He was some sort of distant cousin of the Hazeltons', a possible pal for Sebastien. Perhaps she should send Sebastien to school in Baltimore, a place where all the boys went, St. Paul's, she believed Hazelton had said. Simon was still sitting at the helm, feeling important; he avoided his mother's eyes, as if to tell her that his life had changed and he no longer had time for games with her. Tom Hazelton had won Simon's love forever from the moment he asked him if he wanted to steer. It was so easy with boys, she thought; just toss them the tiniest bits of duty and power, and they practically weep with gratefulness. Why was this so hard for Edward to do?

Edith did not want to think about Edward; she didn't really want to think about the boys, but she'd dragged them along and had to make sure they did their best. Everything was fine. She reached for the champagne bottle and poured more than she wanted toward her glass, but the wind turned it to droplets on the way down and they splattered her face, her shirt, and the cushion she sat on. "Damnit," she said, leaping up. "How stupid."

Tom laughed at her. "Haven't you ever heard about pissing into the wind?"

Simon giggled.

She glared as she patted the champagne off her face. Pissing into the wind, thought Edith—is that what it meant? How silly, how male. "The cushion will stain," she said.

"You know how we clean cockpit cushions?" he asked. She was about to say that she did not, when he pulled it out from under her and threw it over the side.

"No!" she said. "You can't."

"Man overboard!" he shouted, and took the wheel violently from Simon. "Jibe ho," he barked, and when Larry jumped up, apparently in the wrong direction, he shouted, "I said jibe, goddamnit. Jibe." The boat heaved, dipped its low rail under as they turned, and then dipped on the other side as the sails filled again. Edith was getting thrown from side to side; the boom had passed overhead with a whistle, but as the boat settled on a reverse course, she noticed that Tom was wearing a large and extremely self-satisfied smile. She realized, as she sprawled about, and as the boat careened recklessly, he had been looking at her legs. Midway between anger and modesty, she felt a sudden flood of desire. She rode that stretching of nerves for a second or two, aware that Tom had forced it upon her, just as he was forcing this big boat to double back upon its course almost in defiance of the winds and currents.

"Good job, crew," said Tom. They had come alongside the cushion and seemed to have stopped dead, all of it done in a minute or two. If the cushion had been a person, even a nonswimmer, like the boys, he would hardly have gotten his hair wet. Edith could not help looking impressed.

"My father used to do that. 'Man overboard,'" yelled Tom, in what seemed a good impersonation of his father's nasal voice. "It made me furious. He didn't know a thing about sailing."

"Fathers and sons on the same sailboat seems to cause trouble." On the lake, in Wisconsin, she used to hear fathers screaming at sons; it was one of the many times in her childhood when she was glad she was a girl.

"What do you mean?" he said quickly, even defensively.

"I don't think men are very good teachers."

"That's ridiculous."

"They don't let children make mistakes."

"Then let's see, shall we?" he said. He stood and called out for Sebastien.

"Take the helm," Tom yelled, across the wind.

Edith looked on with surprise and gratitude and alarm, as Tom gave the wheel to Sebastien, surrendered it as if Sebastien had spent his entire life doing this. "Aim for those silos," he said, beckoning toward two distant landmarks, and then passed by her roughly on his way below. She began to protest but then kept her mouth shut; if this was to be a test of someone—perhaps of her as much as any of them—then she would see it through. When Tom was below, she said softly to Sebastien, "Are you okay? This is a bigger boat than Alice's."

"Mother," he answered sharply, but he could say no more; he had his hands full, and she watched as his eyes darted from the compass to the objective ahead to the sails. The *Candide*, with its unfamiliar skipper, sliced less sharply through the swells, and then a large wave pushed it slightly off course. Things began to rattle, lines suddenly loosened, and the sails began to flap. The crewman glanced back, the beginning of a victorious smirk on his face. Sebastien fought indecision, and the rattling continued while he nudged the wheel first one way and then the other. Edith was ready for the contest to end when Tom poked up his head casually, and said, "Try shutting your eyes. Sail by ear."

Edith quickly gestured to Sebastien, silently, that under no circumstances should he close his eyes. He didn't intend to, but he took the advice about listening and followed the sounds from the rigging to bring the boat back on course.

"Wonderful, dear. Hooray for you," she said.

They were coming to a bend in the river, which had been narrowing for a time, the banks drawing closer, the houses passing like gaudy steamers, and as they rounded the point, she saw a town with a bridge barring the way.

"Chestertown," said Tom. He had slipped back into the cockpit and took the wheel in a wordless change of command.

She waited for him to compliment Sebastien, but that didn't seem part of the exercise; no words meant he had done fine, she supposed. "This is as far as we can go?" she asked.

He waved toward the bridge. "There's a draw span, but the Chester turns pretty shallow from here on. Smells like a cesspool up there. We'll tie up at the steamer clock. Time for lunch anyway."

"Yes."

"We'll leave the boys to their sandwiches and grab a bite at the hotel in town, shall we? It's quite good."

"I'm not properly dressed."

"A yachtsman's luncheon," he said. "It's the custom. You look marvelous."

They ate at the old Washington Inn, in a dining room whose former splendor was now decayed, with waterstains on the ceiling and a pervasive scent of cooking oil. There must have been forty tables in the room, but the far end seemed unused, with cleaning tools and extra chairs piled along the wall.

"So much of this life seems to be just hanging on," she said as they sat.

"It's true. I think the Eastern Shore is reverting."

"To what?"

"Oh, Edith," he broke in. "I don't care about the Eastern Shore. Let it sink. I care about you."

It came as a slap, something that she might have deserved. The room was quiet, and she glanced quickly at the other party; the two men and two women were dressed no more formally than she was, with open necks and bare shoulders; perhaps none of them were married either, to each other, anyway. There were so few barriers in her road, nothing but a spiky moment or two aboard the boat, which had been resolved gently, with both boys triumphant;

nothing to keep her away from a new life, but there was still everything, nothing and everything. "Please," she said finally.

"You deserve better, Edith."

"Don't."

"I won't push," he said, though Edith had felt nothing but push from him since the minute they met. "But you want better. I know that."

Edith, her stomach in knots, picked at her crab salad for a minute or two, but she was very hungry and soon was enjoying the food, this place, this company. Tom ordered a bottle of wine, which, she gathered from the hooded gestures and folded bills, was not something the hotel normally provided, perhaps even was against the law. She wanted to ask him about the women in his life—was there someone she would be supplanting, and who was she, what was her name?—but had to be satisfied asking questions about his boats, and listening to his plans for the Caribbean. Whatever his theories about boat design, she was sure he would do well; he had not an once of doubt. She kept her own stories neutral, speaking of England, mostly, living there as Americans, fresh, unmarred faces in a land whose people were still exhausted by the Great War. She did not talk about, but remembered at that moment with the sharpness of her teeth biting her lip, the feeling she had that every woman there wanted any man who had survived the war, would steal him if she could. She remembered the feeling she had when a few of them did steal Edward away to the glitter, while she and the boys passed evenings in a cold goddamn flat. How close, she had always wondered, did he come to leaving them for good?

Tom was paying the bill when she realized that her conversation had faltered, and that she was drunk. "I'm suddenly quite tired," she said haltingly. She passed one hand across her brow.

"It's the sun," he said. "I should have warned you."

Warned her? she thought. Did he mean about the champagne?

"Perhaps we should get back." She stood, and found that this was at least possible, with her calves propped against the chair and her thighs against the table.

"Let me help you," he said, coming around to offer his arm.

"Oh, dear," she said, weaving.

"What? Can I help."

"Oh, hell," she said.

He gave her an arm, and once they were back out on the street in the fresh air, things became a little clearer, and she could thank him, apologize, apologize again, and then keep his arm for the walk down to the river. The sail back to the Retreat was agony; when they rounded the point into the wind and chop, she went down to the head and threw up, and was for several minutes stymied by the flushing instructions and panicked that she would not be able to clean up. Even when she mastered the damn thing, she knew that she was fooling no one, certainly not Tom Hazelton, and that this day was now a disaster, one she richly deserved, though, for leading this man on. What was she thinking of, wishing he were the father of her children, imagining herself in bed with him.

—

SEBASTIEN WATCHED HER slowly return to the cockpit. She was a wreck. He watched Mr. Hazelton rearrange cushions so that she could stretch out in comfort, which she did, her feet practically touching his side. Sebastien let himself imagine Hazelton touching his mother's foot, but it made him angry to think of it, because he suspected his mother would like it. As sick as she looked, when she and Hazelton came back on the pier after lunch, they were walking like a couple, and Sebastien had to fight the urge to go up and shove Hazelton away from her.

But on the way back, a slow and hot dead run, Mr. Hazelton let him take the helm for an hour or two, and the way was silent and purposeful, drowsy with rest. Sebastien didn't want this day to end, and he knew that if his father were still in America, the day wouldn't have happened at all. Sebastien could feel all the rival emotions of this moment, though he could understand few of them: He wanted someone to hurt his father, but not Hazelton; he wanted his mother to be happy, but not with another man. Sebastien understood already that somewhere along the line, possibly quite soon, he would have to make a choice. He wanted to be able to choose, but not to suffer if he chose badly.

Mr. Hazelton had planned things carefully, and by the time they stood off Mason Creek in the yellow late-day light, the tide was right once again for them to inch their way through the channel and up to the dock of the Retreat. His mother had roused herself, and though there were certain chores to be done under Mr. Hazelton's direction, she seemed to want the boys to give their thanks, say their good-byes, and be off.

"I'll be along," she said. "Quickly go and tell Loretta we're back."

Sebastien said they would, and they left the pier, but once they got into the cattails he sent Simon along, and he waited. Through the sharp leaves and tassels he could see Larry at work on the boat, and he saw that his mother and Mr. Hazelton had stopped halfway down the pier. The wind that had blown them home now brought the conversation between them straight to Sebastien, and he did not even need to strain to hear.

"Thank you," his mother said. "It was lovely. I'm ashamed of my performance."

"You have no need to be. Nothing feels worse."

"Yes. I'm sure I haven't felt worse for a good while."

They paused; the wind eddied around Sebastien as he crouched. He knew everything about grown-up voices, how they pinched when they lied, how they trailed when they were bored, and how they bumped and lunged when . . . when, if that's really what it was, what was happening, when they liked each other, when they might be looking at each other and waiting for a change of heart.

"I'll be back in September."

"I don't know whether . . ." his mother said.

"Edith."

Her answer was so low even the wind couldn't carry it, or maybe it was just a small sound in her throat.

"Edith, I won't force trouble into your life, you can trust that."

Again, a sound from his mother, perhaps a thank you that she didn't mean.

"I'll only come back if you want me to," he said. He dropped his hands to his side; they had been up, as if to accept an embrace.

She took two steps away from him and then turned back. "Will you come back?" Sebastien could hardly breathe. "Please?"

This time it was Mr. Hazelton who mumbled something, and they parted stiffly, no handshake or gesture, and he walked up the dock to his boat. Edith came Sebastien's way, and it was far too late for him to escape, so he hit the ground and held his breath. As she passed not two feet from him, he heard her say to herself, "Oh, God, what am I doing? What have I done?"

Edith awoke the following morning still feeling sick, sick at heart. She would write Tom a letter, which she would sign "cordially," or perhaps, perhaps she could allow "affectionately." Would it matter? Dear Tom, she would write, My duty is to my husband. Something like that. Something stupid and pointless, enough to make all her stirrings of joy a complete waste, to sacrifice herself to a husband who, for all she knew, could be living as man and wife with someone else right now, waking up beside another woman and running his hands up her nightgown to her breasts, and maybe she would do what Edward always wanted on such mornings, which was to purr dreamily and then roll over to him, and not, as Edith usually did, move his cold hand away in surprise. Maybe that's what this was all about, his trip to England, to leave her chaste and neglected, with no rivals that he had been able to discern in his surveys of the surrounding farms and families—except, of course, he hadn't thought of the sea, had he?

She almost felt that morning that the sea would forgive her. If she fell in love with a sailor and had a mad affair with him, perhaps it would not be adultery, perhaps not even love, but something different whose name was a word in ancient Greek that had no modern translation, a Homeric escape from Anglican vows and American virtues. She could say to Bitsy, in all honesty, "It's not as if he's ever *driven* here." The sea was perhaps like the dark, one could steal away in it, and if she offered herself in silence, it could be nothing but a dream.

As teenagers, Edith and her sisters used to ask each other whether it was more important that their husbands be interesting or nice. Rosalie had chosen interesting, and had never married; Meg had chosen nice, and married a man her father could order around. Edith had never been willing to choose, so Rosalie told her that she would just run off with some handsome ne'er-do-well, someone deceitful and full of himself. Rosalie described this man to Edith as a punishment, but Edith could see the yearning for romance in her unhappy sister's eyes, the jealousy in advance for what Edith assumed would never happen.

Maybe Tom Hazelton was nice *and* interesting. Maybe you could have someone who was both. He was self-assured, even manipulative, but he was fond of his own father and had been sweet to her sons. Maybe that was the key. Edith had never imagined that she should look for a man comfortable among other men when she chose a husband. Of course, thought Edith, should Edward trust Tom Hazelton? And if Edward shouldn't trust Tom Hazelton, why should she?

Her thoughts kept tumbling like this for the rest of that weekend, and for the following week, and the week after that. She and Simon, often with an hour or two of help from Robert, turned Miss Mary's old garden into the envy of the county, and ladies came by twos and threes to admire and to find fault. But even though weeks had now passed, every time she picked up her trowel and settled to work, she became so entwined in her feelings that she thought she would go mad. She spent hours composing and rewriting her letter to Tom, reciting out loud (she feared) an imagined letter from him, one that by its cleverness and attention to detail offered a way out that had not occurred to her, a work of magic that could help her to leap over the complete mess she had made of her life into pleasant routine. But she did not expect Tom to write, and he didn't.

—

SEBASTIEN COULD NOT fabricate these deliberations in all their richness, but he could get pretty close. Just by looking at her during pauses in her attention, lapses that even Simon noticed, or by watching her fiddle with silverware and writing implements—she hated people who fiddled with things—he could tell she was trying to decide whether to fall in love with Mr. Hazelton. Sebastien didn't know what he wanted, but he did know that it was up to her, that he and Simon, Mr. Hazelton, his father, all of these men and boys, were waiting for an answer from her, and when it came, they would have to know what to do—how to fly, to remake a fabric, to stretch it taut as sails. The merest sign, a white handkerchief on the Retreat's flagpole, a puff of blue smoke up the chimney, and the next minute the *Candide* would be poking its way into the creek, its pennants flying. Sebastien figured that was the way he'd learn of her answer, and each day he spent out on the rivershore fields with Robert, he glanced now and again out onto the Chester, out toward the Bay, looking for the sails.

7

THAT SUMMER, THE summer of 1937, Sebastien grew muscled and tough working on the farm at Robert's side. He learned how to work, how to lean into the pitchfork and pivot the weight up over his thighs; how to cut off a herd like a sheepdog, playing the angles, not oversteering; how to swing a load wide through the gates; how to back a wagon up to the corncribs and haymaws saying "Ba, team, ba" in a firm singsong. He had an aptitude for these skills already, seemed to have been born with it, though McCready and Robert could still give him plenty of pointers; all he had to do was watch. Robert called him Spook. Robert laughed each time he called him this. "Spook," he said, entertaining himself, "you stop giving me the Eye."

It was morning, September. Sebastien was out with Robert in the forests of corn on the rivershore fields. School was waiting for the harvest, which would be early this year, so dry and hot in August; in a week the men from Tuckertown, and a few white men from elsewhere in the county, would show up in numbers. The school in town, filled with the children of shopkeepers and lawyers, would crowd the harvesting schedule; the farm schools might not start for another month.

They had been at the Retreat for a single year, though it seemed far longer than that. England no longer existed for him; the last flat, with its smell of sewer gas and its buckled parquet floors, was gone; they had never spent weekends with Lord Belsen, who got drunk and grabbed for Sebastien's crotch while rubbing his own. Forgetting had been Sebastien's purpose for the summer, remaking his accent, coarsening his unlined face, turning his hands yellow with callus. His father wouldn't recognize the boy he had left. The months had passed, and only Simon brought his father up, mentioned his name. There had been a few letters that their mother had read to them, things about Europe mostly. Sebastien hardly listened, anyway, and his mother's heart seemed not to be in the recitation. Sebastien's most sheltered hope had grown into a suspicion that his father might never come back.

"You giving me the Eye," said Robert. They were shucking a single load of corn for the cows; they had wrist hooks over their gloves, but it was hard work and Sebastien could match only one ear for Robert's five.

"I just wanted to see how you did that," Sebastien protested. He didn't love being teased; he wasn't out there, out there under the sun, ripping his forearms raw on the sharp edges of corn stalks, not out there to be teased.

"You want to know how to do something, you just ask me."

Sebastien knew Robert was one to talk. The reason Robert called him Spook, Sebastien had come to believe, was that someone had once called Robert that. It would make sense. He knew Robert was always watching him; they shared this, shared it like blood. Sebastien could feel it at milking, across the fetid sweat of the cows, those eyes on him, as if plotting.

"What are you doing out here, anyway?" asked Robert, pausing to tighten his hook. "Owner's son. Rich white boy."

Robert had asked this question a hundred times. This was the way Robert talked, themes and repetitions, refrains on his thoughts. "How 'bout you?" said Sebastien.

"Working. Working for the man." Robert snorted, one of his coarse and obscure laughs.

"Which man is that? McCready or my father?"

"Don't much matter which."

"Why is that?" said Sebastien. This was the kind of conversation he loved; he realized Robert was about the only person in the world he had ever felt loose around.

"You making fun of me?"

"No, sir," answered Sebastien.

"Okay," said Robert, "it's like I told you before. The colored are going to take it all, sooner or later."

"Is that true?"

"Yes, sir, I should say it is. The whole Eastern Shore, a colored state. I can see it now."

They went back to work, yanking their way down a row, the team following along. From across the honeysuckle-tangled fence line, in the section of field they called the tobaccolands—though tobacco had not been grown at the Retreat for almost two hundred years—they heard the popping of McCready's John Deere. Ever since it arrived, Mr. McCready had seemed to Sebastien a changed man: a man with a mission and a plan, and the means for getting there.

"Yes, sir, the man got hisself a program," said Robert. "Got to admit, the man is going places on that tractor."

Sebastien could see it easily enough. More silage, more cows; more cows, more milk. He knew McCready was doing the arithmetic; it turned out he'd been working on these equations for years. His John Deere, with rubber tires and a three-bottom plow, cost a thousand and fifty dollars. "Where did he get that kind of money?" Sebastien had heard his father bellowing, peering into the account books as if cheating were the only possible answer. Sebastien knew a pig would sing before Mr. McCready cheated someone. He'd just been doing those equations, year after year, a dime or two into the pot each chance he got, a whole life focused on buying a tractor, a fixed stare ahead at something better—unlike his own father's wagging glances around at everything he wanted. This tractor was just the beginning. Now McCready wanted a combine, and a New Departure cultivator. Next summer they could start building up the herd, and it was Holsteins McCready wanted; he'd done that equation too: big brute Holsteins, a thousand, fifteen hundred gallons of milk a year. Just after Edward left in May, McCready had asked Sebastien whether his father really meant to restore the Jerseys—was this really what his father thought the farm should do? Sebastien had told him not to feel insulted, but that his father had forgotten the herd ever existed. I thought so, answered McCready. That was what I thought.

"McCready's got everything on his side now," said Robert, still with his eyes following the steady green travel of the man and machine a half mile away. "He surprised hell out a lot of people."

"You too?"

"You bet."

"Father too. I wish I'd been there to see it."

Robert went back to his work.

"You know what I mean? The surprise on his face?"

The repetition straightened Robert up once more, an ear of corn in both hands. "When you going to lay off that daddy of yours?" said Robert.

Sebastien thought it was a joke, Robert deep in one of his bitter ironies, but he saw the narrow focus of Robert's eyes, the look he wore when telling the truth. "What?" Sebastien asked. "What do you mean?"

"A man don't have to be perfect, do he? A daddy's one thing, maybe the onliest thing, that don't have to be perfect. It's not right for a son to ask for that. He should know better."

"Perfect?" Sebastien almost shouted. "Perfect? You say that after the way he's treated you?"

"What I think of him don't mean anything to you. I just work on his place. But I wouldn't pay it no mind. You fourteen, boy. It's time you took things on your own and stopped blaming your daddy. That's the truth."

Sebastien held his ground. "I'm on my own. I don't expect anything from him," he said, wishing it were the truth. With every year it became more true, and for as long as he could remember, his life had been tinted by one vague but always present hope: that he could grow up enough before his father lost everything. He had felt doomed to come close, but not close enough, like missing a ship by a single yard of open water. "I don't expect anything," he repeated.

"Good," said Robert. "That's good. Keep your feet on the ground, you'll be okay." The team had wandered off a bit, making the throw too long, and he went to bring them back. There was a rustling to the left, and then a wave of skunk odor, and then the white and black of the animal's tail marking its flight in the opposite direction. The horses snorted.

Robert and Sebastien shucked slowly out to the water, then around the long perimeter of the point, then back into trees. When they were along the river Sebastien kept his eye out for boats, but all summer, except for an occasional passing schooner, the only sails he saw were those of Alice's Comet. They had spent many afternoons out there together, and they had spoken about school, about what they wanted to do with their lives, about their fathers. But mostly they just sailed, and when there was heavy wind, he pushed closer and closer to the limit, to the line between flying on the edge and going flat and squat into the Bay, a tangle of wet sails and lines. When they were about to capsize, Alice would swear at him and scream, "I told you to fall off," before they both went headfirst into the Bay, into the jellyfish and tepid brine. The water held him like oil; he fought back to the surface feeling baptized.

"Looking . . . for your girlfriend?" said Robert. He spoke in the rhythm of his work, the quick yank of the hook, the light toss of the ear, the clunk as it bounced off the hitting board and into the wagon.

"Bloody hell."

"Ain't nothing . . . at all wrong . . . with a girlfriend."

"How do I know?" said Sebastien. He'd heard the way the men in town spoke of themselves as fools with no chance of winning with women, and of love as something they never got.

"I seen you out there," commented Robert, pausing before throwing the ear in his hand.

The one thing about his sailing lessons that Sebastien regretted was this. He'd hoped Robert wouldn't see him, but he should have known better—those eyes took in everything, even through the shimmer and glare.

"Nothing wrong with a girlfriend," Robert said. "It's the boat is a problem. Nothing but bad out there on the water."

Sebastien wanted to end this conversation. "She isn't going to be out there today."

"Why's that?"

"Mrs. Howe is taking us all to Tolchester Beach." It was an amusement park, so Alice had told him, with a roller coaster and a dance hall. Sebastien had been pretending he didn't want to go, but he did; he'd barely been off the Retreat all summer, and he longed for colored lights and doughnuts; inadmissibly, he longed for a touch of the city.

"Is that a fact?"

"Have you been?"

"What? What you say?"

"Have you been to Tolchester. Alice says everyone goes."

Robert twisted to look back at him, his eyes angry. "Of course I ain't been there. What you think?"

Sebastien wanted to shrink; of course Robert hadn't. Sebastien had noticed that even if Negroes from the city could go to places like amusement parks, farm Negroes never went anywhere except to places of their own.

"I'm sorry," he said, but the apology fell into the air; he'd gone over the edge, the line that kept Robert from his dreams. There were so many secrets—not just Robert's, but secrets the black women kept, silencing each other in glances. It was as if he and the Retreat were floating on an ocean of Negro truths, and if he fell in, he might drown.

They had finished shucking along the fence line, and when they reached the spot closest to the farm, Robert stopped. "You get on now," he said to Sebastien without turning. "No work for two here."

Sebastien had expected this, but it hurt nonetheless.

"You get on now. You go on to Tolchester with your girlfriend and let a man earn an honest wage."

"Robert . . ." But it did no good. He stood on the baked earth, feeling as if he'd been put off a train. Robert was back at work, the muscles on his neck and arms tensing in an even flow, but his body was rigid, as if preparing to spring.

Sebastien headed down the furrows until he reached the fence line along the lane. He glanced right, past the vast yellow stable and the trim coachman's cottage. Simon called this cottage the rectory because he had decided the stable was a church. Sebastien had his own plans for that small house; he dreamed of living there alone, like Robert in his house, and of waking up each morning and pulling on his boots.

He looked back out the lane toward the fields one last time, catching the distant sight of Robert in the cornfield. He trotted up to the house and went in the kitchen door. Valerie looked at him, narrowing her gaze through her thick lenses. "I thought you was going out with Miss Elizabeth."

"I am." Sebastien poured himself a glass of water; he felt the women watch him drink.

"And Miss Alice," Loretta added.

"So?"

"Well, mercy, Mister Sebastien," Loretta said; she loved to talk about him and Alice. "What's the girl to think if you show up for a date in overhauls?"

"What date? And who says I want her to think anything?" He said this angrily, too angrily even for him.

"Oh, now, you just leave off being so unpleasant. Ain't nothing but a nice question. You got no call to snap at me."

Valerie said to him, "Now you done it."

Sebastien knew he ought to apologize, but he was sick to death of being teased about Alice. Besides, what he said was the truth. He didn't really know what he wanted her to think, and he wished he didn't care so much. He didn't know why the others, including his mother, were paying so much attention to this; their interest made him feel used. He could feel the hunger himself, a sudden need that seized each organ in his body, the raw spreading of desire. But those feelings were private, if anything was.

He left the kitchen and came out into the hall. Through the porch overhang he saw his mother in the garden. It was still a remarkable sight—his mother bent over the dirt and soil, tending plants; she used to make fun of people who gardened. Under her wide-brimmed straw hat, in her long and quite dirty brown skirt, she looked, from there, like a Negro, a farmworker. She was secretive about her plants, like a cook who wanted every dish to be a delicious surprise. Maybe she wasn't sure anything would come of them. Valerie had brought some slips, and his mother took her to one side before asking what they were and how to plant them. When Simon asked her what she had planted, she said, "We shall see!" with a little singsong in her voice, as if this were Christmas. Simon could still be hooked in this way, but not Sebastien. It infuriated him not to know things. His mother had been keeping secrets from him all summer, and without his father around, she could keep them well.

He went up and changed, washed his face, hands, and arms, and—because earlier in the summer his mother had mentioned that he might do this now and again, if he wasn't going to bathe properly—his armpits. He put on his linen pants and blue cotton shirt and felt rather handsome as he came down the stairs. The Howes had arrived, and Bitsy was a vision in blinding bright yellow. Alice was in a sundress, arms and shoulders bare. But his mother was still in her gardening clothes.

"You can't mean it," Bitsy was saying.

"I'm sorry."

Sebastien reached the hall. "Mother, you're not coming?"

She turned to him. "I have lots to do in the garden. You go have fun."

Simon had been waiting on the porch all this time, and as soon as he figured out what they were talking about, his small face began to struggle.

"See," said Bitsy. She was angry. "See?" You've disappointed Simon badly."

Edith went over to him and explained that she just didn't feel like a day out right now, but that Sebastien would take him on any ride he wanted, and at this, Alice looked over at Sebastien with a crushed expression.

"Edith, I don't like what you're doing."

"I'm not doing anything. You'll just have to go without me."

The five of them stood in the hall for a moment, the whole day in question, but nothing seemed to move his mother, not Bitsy's anger, not Simon's complaints. Sebastien had never seen her like this, and he knew there was a reason for it. Bitsy took her to the other end of the hall, and while they talked, the three young people moved outside.

"It's okay, Toad. We'll have fun."

"But why isn't she coming?"

"Just let her be, okay?"

"Mummy will be furious," said Alice, like a threat. Her tone was haughty and superior. "This is very impolite."

"Now look here, Alice. If Mother doesn't want to come, what's the big problem?"

"Well, she and Mummy had a plan."

Sebastien did not want to continue this, and didn't have to. The door slammed open, and Bitsy brushed by, telling them all to get into the car. No one went back to take leave of Edith, and Bitsy's anger continued as she backed and filled jerkily, everyone's head bouncing. Sebastien cast one look backward, but the dry autumn roads sent out a dense cloud of clay dust, and soon they were out on the main road and headed for what was supposed to have been the celebration at the end of summer, the treat before fall, a bonding of friends.

———

FROM HIS DISTANT spot in the corn plants, Robert watched as the Buick clattered over the washboard and accelerated out of view. There was no mistaking a car being driven angrily, and Robert thought it was interesting, a fight among the white people. Perhaps he did feel a little bad for having cut out Sebastien; the boy was trying to understand, and someday Robert would explain to him that he shouldn't try. Oh, hell, let him have his fun. He was too burdened as it was.

By the time Robert was twelve he was earning his own keep, him and Perry Gale, and the world felt new and bright. Robert was the skinnier of the two, bony as a mule, but they set out each morning before sunrise, the men walking on ahead while the boys made bets on every damn thing that was to come that day: cows milked, fence posts set, haycocks bound and hefted, corn shucked, bushels of parsnips and potatoes dug and stored, amount of cane put through the mill, juice boiled, firewood sawed and split, coal shoveled, ice cakes cut. They made their boasts in the dawn mists all the way through Tuckertown and through the woods, and when they came out on the lane, with the Retreat to the left and Windolit on the right, they shook on it one last time. Then in the evening they met up again, each boy hot and drained, quieter now in the reddened afternoon glare, and it never really occurred to either one of them that the other would be padding the results as much as he, and so, win or lose the bet, both went home smarting with defeat and woke up the next morning determined not to lose again.

Robert could still taste that life, now way in the past. Everyone had work, everyone had food. The air in Tuckertown was always filled with the scents of baking and roasting; the buttermilk up from the springhouse was so cold it hurt your eyes to drink it. There was time to visit in the summer, plenty of wood to burn in the winter. Robert's memories came to him like the red taste of whiskey, alive and smooth. Tuckertown was Jerusalem, and all of them, the Gales, the Morrises, the Goulds, were the chosen.

And then he'd gone to France, and come back to find his father's beautiful face scarred into a torture of flesh on one side, the eye blinded and white. That was Miss Mary's work, tossing a pot of scalding coffee, thick with sugar, at him as he stood in her office, waiting for orders. What had he done? Who knew or cared? He had somehow found his way back to Tuckertown, the burn sinking still deeper like acid the whole way down the road, and he had howled in pain and terror, "In my face. She threw it in my face." A minute later Dr. Rawn had arrived, because Loretta had called on that telephone that used to work, and told him there had been an accident out at the Retreat, and to head right up to Tuckertown. Dr. Rawn was a drunk and a fool, the only doctor in town who would call on colored, and what he did for Robert senior was not too much; for weeks the infection turned the bandages yellow, and the smell was like death. Robert senior lived a few more years, but he was used up by then, so used up he couldn't even hate the woman who had ruined him.

Robert was out at the far end of his turn, along the rivershore, and he stopped to give the team a taste of grain. He gazed outward on this water, thinking again of Sebastien, and he noticed that a boat seemed to be heading this way, a big sailboat. He hadn't told Sebastien why he really hated the water: that the only time he'd gone to sea was in a troopship headed for France, and they'd put all the colored soldiers way down in a hold, and the second day out he'd realized they were trapped down there like slaves.

The mare shook her empty feedbag and stamped, asking for more, but he took the bag off her face firmly and gave her a light slap on the nose. "No more for you till lunch, honey," he said, and they set off again. They jolted down the longest leg toward the barns, worked along the road, and turned out toward the water, and by the time he got back to this spot, two furrows closer to the center, the big sailboat was standing off the mouth of the creek. The tide was low; he could see the riffle of water over the sandbars. The boat was anchored, and a man was rowing into the creek in a small boat. So, he thought, Miss Edith's got a visitor, and that was that, he thought, and contemplated other things as he shucked, until suddenly the rowboat reappeared with a passenger in it, Miss Edith. Well, ain't that something, he said to himself, and he spent the whole next pass around the field trying to keep track of events through gaps between the corn plants. By the time he had come out of the corn and had a clear view again, the boat was gone.

Robert stared out at the water, looking for the sails.

"What you up to, Robert? Something broke?" It was McCready, who had walked up from behind.

"Just catching my breath."

McCready wasn't in a scolding mood. "How much you think I already done this morning?" he asked when they were facing each other.

Robert was getting tired of this with McCready, that white face grinning; he looked as if he'd die of glee. He'd been looking like that for a month, as if Mason leaving and the tractor coming were gifts from the Lord. "Can't," said Robert.

"The whole damn tobaccoland!" He waved in the direction of the far fields. "That ain't been turned over since before the war, and I did it in a morning. Damn," he said, pounding his side. "Hot doggie."

Robert turned to loosen the harnesses.

"Thought I would tell you I'm thinking of hiring up."

Robert was wondering why McCready had come over, and this

was it. He didn't like the sound of it at all. Depended who or what he hired was the thing. "You got someone in mind?"

"A boy goes by the name of Lance Farley, from Kent County."

"Lance," said Robert. "Don't know no Lance." He didn't say the next thing, that farmwork at the Retreat was work always done by coloreds, but that Lance weren't a colored name, now was it?

"Young fella. Lots of ideas."

Robert nodded. He thought of Sam Morris, Tunk Smith, the Gomers, good men—not that Robert would have called them friends—and you didn't have to go to Kent County to find them; they were right down in Tuckertown, or would be overnight if there was work offered. "Young fella," Robert repeated. "Lots of ideas. You got work for a man extra?"

"It's like I keep saying. This modern machinery don't take away jobs; it makes jobs."

Robert couldn't recall McCready saying this to him, and it sounded just a mite too clever for McCready to have figured out himself. "Hell now, Robert, don't you be nervous, now. Plenty of work to go around."

That wasn't really what Robert was asking, but he was relieved to hear it. He hated his relief, especially with McCready talking to him like a child.

"What's England say about that?" Robert asked. He'd been calling Edward that since long before the Masons had returned.

The question produced a flicker of doubt in McCready's eyes. McCready had played this a certain way, that was clear to Robert. He had a plan of some kind and neglected to include the owner in each piece of the plan. It wasn't Jersey cattle McCready was buying and breeding, for one thing. "I'm the manager of this place," he answered finally.

"Yes, sir, you is."

The pleasure began to come back into McCready's simple eyes.

"Got to make decisions whether Mister Edward is here or not. Things don't wait, do they."

"No, sir, they don't wait is sure."

McCready tried to throw off the last of his doubts and fears. "Nineteen hundred and thirty-seven," said McCready. "Mark it down, boy. A year to remember."

"Uh-huh."

"We worked hard for this, you and me, all them years."

Robert hadn't worked hard; he just worked. He hadn't worked for "this," because whatever this was, he wouldn't get the benefit of it. Thing was, would McCready?

"You got lunch?" McCready asked.

"Uh-huh." He pulled it out of the toolbox, his sandwiches and a jar of cider wrapped tight, and showed McCready.

"You didn't tie up that lunch, now did you? You got a girlfriend down there in your shack? Is that it?"

This one he had to answer. "No, it's Loretta makes it up for me."

McCready's expression turned—the Masons again. "Loretta? What you hear up at the Mansion House anyway?"

"Don't hear nothing." I don't hear anything, he thought, but I just seen something.

"The boy tell you anything about Mister Edward's plans?"

Robert could tell McCready the truth, that the boy didn't talk about his father but had his own big plans. McCready might feel clean rid of Mister Edward just in time to run face-to-face with his son. There was always a new generation on these farms, after all, and if these families didn't have a son coming along, they'd marry one of their daughters to someone who'd be willing to change his name to inherit the place. That was what Miss Mary's parents had hoped to do, so Robert had understood: keep a Mason line going at the Retreat. But Robert had no quarrel with McCready and no reason to remind the poor bastard of all of this. "He don't tell me nothing," Robert answered. He looked out onto the water, wondering if he'd see the boat coming back, but there was no sign of it, just watermen out there, and seine haulers working the bars over by Queenstown.

"Okay," said McCready, getting ready to leave. "But you tell me if you hear something I should know."

Robert watched the man head down the lane for his lunch, double-timing because he was late and his wife had been known to give him a good smack when he failed her. Robert had seen her do it, a hard, fleshy palm on the side of his head, though he had to pretend he was looking the other way. McCready was all right, maybe even more than all right, and he better be, because Robert had spent most of the hours of his life with him, harnessed together like a pair of mules, side by side with perhaps an occasional hoof in the flanks. That was the life they lived, those two. Sickness and health, richer, poorer; that's right, thought Robert—it's as if I'm married to the man.

Robert had been married, which was something McCready didn't know. In fact, he supposed he still was, unless she'd divorced him, not that it mattered to him. He still made out down at the Rainhollow, whenever the need was too great to ignore. God bless her, is what he thought; just keep her over on the western shore, where she belongs. Baltimore County, where she said she was "in business" instead of "working in." That was where she came from, first laid eyes on Robert in his army uniform at Union Station, married him in his father's suit, and left him in his overalls a few months later. She'd been back a few times, just to check on whether his fortunes had changed, the last time not so long ago, but there he was, still living in his old fruit shack. She said she wasn't going to live nowhere that didn't have electric, that was what she said. "Ain't you country colored ever heard of the REA?" Maybe all that meant was that

Robert had been unlucky with women, with Miss Mary and with a wife whose name he would not repeat. But still, it had made him cautious, had kept him watching when Miss Edith came back here. Maybe she'd throw a pot of coffee in his face. So what was she doing out there in that boat with that man, that's what he wanted to know.

—

EDITH AND TOM spoke little as they sailed around the point and into a small cove, dropped anchor, and then turned to face each other. Edith asked herself whether this moment was worth all that it might cost. What had Edward been feeling, those times that he had been unfaithful to her? She felt as if one side of her was torn open and bleeding, as if a child had been ripped from her womb; and the other side was taut and tuned, a drumhead for touch. She knew that in any other time, with any other man, she would have been given a slow and manageable progression of small decisions before she reached this point—an evening as a dinner partner; a night at the theater; yes, a sociable day on the water. At any one them she might have decided that he talked too much about himself, or not enough about anything at all, that perhaps she had been wrong, that it really was just a slight infatuation, that he really didn't appeal to her all that much and she could go home with Edward that night no longer feeling quite so trapped in her marriage and tricked by fate. But this time she wasn't given this luxury.

Tom, nearly blackened by the Caribbean sun but flushed with success, had sailed back to Annapolis in three days, abusing his crew—which no longer included the boy Larry—ignoring a hurricane warning. He had arrived with a cracked mast, transferred to the *Candide*, and sailed across the Bay alone, to be here with Edith. Tom was not troubled by the niceties of courtship and the exquisite suspense of small decisions. He wanted to hold Edith, wanted to undress her and see that shape nude; after so many months, he wanted to know the feeling of her body. As long as Edith had asked, that was what *he* wanted.

"Well," she said, breathless. They were facing each other across the cockpit, and the boat was bobbing a little from the wake of an unseen passing ship, but the air was hot and still in this cove, the shore grasses tall enough to give them the time they needed. "You're not being coy, anyway."

"No. I don't believe in coy. We have two choices. We can set sail or we can go below."

Yes, thought Edith, I can have all or nothing; I can still choose.

He stood up, gave her his hand, and gave a slight tug toward the ladder. In her mind, this tug was the invitation, after all the flirtation, that she could accept or decline. In any event, it was all he did. He tugged, and she fell, smooth and slick, down the ladder into the awkward spaces of the master cabin, and they undressed and began to caress, and Edward became nothing for her but a point of history. In Tom's arms she was a different Edith. For a few moments, she almost felt she could watch this new Edith as she lay back naked on the bunk, but that moment soon passed, and she, as one, was there and only there. He was touching *her* breasts, it was *her* back and buttocks that he rubbed, *her* clitoris that he went for and found. Her joy and delight, the most powerful sexual desire she had ever felt.

Their whole affair had been rushed and episodic, so they did not wait any longer, and for a few moments she almost had an orgasm, but instead she was content to fall back from that peak and move with him, and the boat, until he finished, in the confidence that the next time she would.

The *Candide* was deep in the cattails and water elms of the cove—a surprisingly deep cove, Edith realized on subsequent visits throughout the fall, when the boys were at school and she'd given up trying to deceive Bitsy or, God help her, the women of the Mansion House. She felt secure as a pirate behind the lip of a sandy point, an anchorage hidden in a thicket of sea grasses. Falling asleep at night in the Retreat, she could recite every blip and bleat of this apparently featureless landmark, seen out the small porthole as the boat slowly shifted on its mooring, as she and Tom lay dripping and slick. They pushed that cover just about as far as it could go, using every last bit of it, every patch of sand, just as she pushed her body as far as it could, which was much further than she had ever imagined. She wondered where he had learned some of the things he did to give her pleasure, and to take his pleasure from her—with nice girls from Baltimore or a whore in Havana? What she did she merely improvised. Lying in her bed at the Retreat in her flannel nightgown, she recalled these things with a slight disbelieving cringe, but they took on the momentum of experiment. Her discoveries were driving her back not to her early marriage but to her adolescence in Winnetka, back to when there was a "me" in her life, a demanding and insistent me lodged in the center of her chest, allowed to thump, unconscripted into the sisterhood of loss.

That first afternoon, Edith lay dreamily on the deck while Tom fussed with the rigging. The air was lightly tinged with swamp gas. She had no idea that a mere ten feet up one could see for miles across the lowlands of Eastern Neck, could see easily back to the Retreat rivershore or across the Bay to the dark skies of Baltimore. From twenty feet up, not even to the top of the *Candide*'s mast, if one knew where to look, one could see the gay pennants and flags at the top of one of the Eastern Shore's smash attractions, the Ferris wheel at Tolchester Beach. And perhaps it was at that moment that Sebastien, with Alice clinging alluringly to his arm, came to the crest of the wheel, and though he did not see the single guilty spar jutting above the expanse of landscape, he did see everything else: the river, Hail Point, the Retreat, Baltimore, and in a moment of triumph over his father, and a moment of betrayal by his mother, he realized that the sails were out there, the sign he had been waiting for.

—

ROBERT GAVE ONE last sweep of the eye into the western sun, but he couldn't really make out anything or tell the difference between oystermen and seine haulers heading home and a yacht making a dash, with the tide high enough to make it quicker, to keep a lid somewhat over a pot of secrets. Robert didn't feel good now. He often got the blues at the end of the day. This nation, Robert thought: what a sad place, in the end, such loneliness all around, starting with himself. Miss Edith could do what she wanted, make her best deal. That's what he had done, as pathetic as it might seem to him now. He didn't choose his solitary life—he thought the fruit shack was just for his honeymoon—but when it chose him, he didn't put up much of a fight. Robert was thirty-eight years old, and it didn't seem now that he was going to make much of a difference in anything.

He went into milking in this mood, silent in the face of McCready's crowing, and when cleanup was done, and the fever of the locusts had slowed its pulse, and the sun was magenta, he headed home down the lane. Through the trees of the Mansion House park he saw Valerie backing out the door with her basket, and he stopped at the gate to wait for her.

"You waiting on me?" she asked when she got close. She treated it as a joke.

"Well, hell," he said.

"You was going to carry my basket? I declare, *Mister* Robert."

"I'll take your basket. Give it here." He reached out for it, and she looked at him warily before handing it over. It had a turkey carcass in it, three thick pieces of corn bread; in a couple of hours it would be soup, a fine meal.

"You okay?" she asked.

"Sure."

"Something plaguing your mind?"

"Oh," he said.

She fixed him in her stare again, but then cut it off. Years ago she might have persisted, but not now. They walked along together.

"Where's Loretta?"

"Miss Edith sent her home right after breakfast. She gets tired in this heat."

"So what's happening in the Mansion House?"

"Nothing. Why you ask like that?"

"I seen Miss Edith on a boat."

"Them Hazeltons, from Baltimore. An old man and his son. Can't be nothing to that."

"Old man?"

"Old man. That's right."

"Honey, you see the future plain as day, but what happens in front of your nose is all mystery to you."

"You just got a dirty mind," she said, but Robert could tell she was thinking it over. They walked along side by side for a few moments, down the line of linden trees, with the rivershore fields on their left. To the right, down the state road, was Tuckertown, a mile and a half away; straight ahead, in the woods, was Robert's home.

"So what you think, Val?" he asked. "What you think is gonna happen?"

"Happen to what?"

"To us all. To Loretta. To Miss Edith and the boys. To you and me."

"Robert, you ain't *ever* talked like this. Are you really asking for something this evening?"

He stooped to pick up a perfect oyster shell out of the pink-and-white dust of the crushed surface of the lane; he supposed this shell had lasted because it was so much stronger than the rest, an oyster with a gift, a champion oyster. He rolled it in his palm, thumbing along the sharp edge, and then flung it into the field. It flew like a wafer.

"Forget it," he said.

She walked along with him until they were about ten paces from the turn. "Come back with me," she said suddenly. "Come on back and have some of that supper you're carrying."

"Nooo," he said.

"Come on. You go down and set with Old Man Walker while I'm fixing soup. You want to know what's going to happen? I'll tell you. Walker ain't gonna be with us too much longer. You know he miss you."

"I'll see him at the Rainhollow some evening presently."

"You will not. He can't hardly walk and you know it. You owe him a visit out of memory to your daddy. You know that's true."

"I got something I have to do," he said, and he knew that he'd keep arguing until Valerie gave up, which she did after a few more tries, and he knew what she was painting for him was sweet, an evening in Tuckertown, maybe like the old days, around people that loved his father and had been loyal to his son no matter what. Robert knew that whatever Valerie's reasons and whatever feelings she had for him, she was giving him permission to come home, but no. "Nooo," he said again.

She took the basket from him. "That damn shack is gonna fall in someday with you in it and all your mess, and you'll both just rot away, ungrieved upon."

"What are my choices?"

She was walking away now, but she turned. "Your choices is

turkey soup and corn bread, or some dry old lump of pig and turnips. What more choices you need?"

"I thank you."

She started to sing a hymn. "Come here, sinner, your savior waits," she sang. She turned around one last time and sang the second line, though it was more of a shout in his face, a challenge and a taunt: "Behold, before you, those heavenly gates."

He slid into the woods, into the beech and loblolly, the tangles of holly and poison ivy; his path, over this soil so dense with clay, was packed harder than bricks; it was a yellow road through the green forest. He walked up to his shack and stood in the yard, scratched bare by the chickens and further polished by his sweeping. The walls were still more or less plumb; it didn't look to him as if it was about to fall in on him. One end of the yard was a square shape cut into the woods, where he had once planned to garage the Model T he hoped to buy. He inspected the shack before going in—two very small windows on either side of the door, a small pile of stones under each corner, and a KEEP OUT sign left over from the days when the Retreat grew and stored a good many peaches, pears, and grapes, pecans and pine nuts; they made wine out here, mostly pear wine, and the walls still smelled of that sharp taste of alcohol. Robert remembered well as a boy, a little boy, coming out here with his father to shell pecans that had been drying in the loft.

He lit a lamp when he got in; it was always dark in these pinewoods. He looked around: his chair, his bed, his dry sink, his plates and utensils. The stove was a Home Comfort, a good one, a wedding gift from Tuckertown. Robert's house was clean and neat—it always was; Robert hated mess—but Valerie was right about his dinner, a pot of beans and what was left of a pork shoulder. He scraped enough meat for the meal and warmed up the beans, and when it was all done, he took his plate out into his yard, sat on his chair, and looked out the woods toward the sunset, broken in a thousand pieces like a stained-glass window. Robert sighed, a long breath that picked up a little pained voice at the end. Oh, this lonely place, he thought, this terrible lonely place.

8

When the fall came and the *Candide* was finally put into its cradle—Tom's father had been insisting it was time for weeks—Tom and Edith met in Annapolis, and in Easton, and in Baltimore. The Bay no longer rocked them. In the hotels Edith felt like an adulteress; the rooms felt cold and deceitful, but the crazy desire and joy were the same. In January he went back down to the Caribbean, and she counted the days he was away—boats, bringing them together, boats pulling them apart.

Bitsy visited Edith often during that fall and winter, driving the long marshy route around the deep fingers of the creek. She made these trips out of a sense of duty, not because she really wanted to have tea in those cold rooms. With the leaves off the trees, she could see glimpses of the Retreat almost the entire way, and it didn't look like a happy place; it never had, all those years with its shutters closed and the ghost of that mean old shrew rattling around, still screaming at the help.

Bitsy had many feelings about what Edith was doing, starting with the aborted trip to Tolchester and continuing with those visits by the *Candide*. This person she had considered her friend, off with a lover—it seemed unfair to Bitsy. Everyone in the world was getting love and she was not. She had once been lovely, she had once been daring, but she had never been held by a lover, just by Frank, who was now drunk every night and often impotent, not that they had tried recently. Edith had never had to deal with *that*, as far as Bitsy knew, with Edward. Edith knew nothing about the despair and loneliness one could feel on this hollow landscape, the flat, unrelieved, and empty world. Bitsy had not befriended Edith in order to feel abandoned all over again; she had thought she was safe from hurt with Edith, a sister. Bitsy had to fight these feelings each time the *Candide* made its silent way to the creek; it was difficult to ignore such a public gesture.

"Christ," she said to Edith one afternoon, "why not take out an ad in the *Record*? Why not just diddle him in Courthouse Square?"

"Please don't be so crude."

"I'm just telling you that you aren't being discreet. All boats may look the same to you, Edith," she said, "but do you think *anyone* on the Chester doesn't know *Candide* on sight?"

"You don't have to worry about that. *Candide* is out of the water. Tom's going to the Caribbean next week for the winter."

"Is it over?" Bitsy asked, as if she thought it would be done that simply.

"No. Why should it be?"

"Because it's wrong. A bad idea from the start."

"It isn't. It wasn't. I need this. I deserve it. Edward left me no choice."

"Oh, Christ, Edith. *My* marriage is the mess. *My* life is pointless. You, whatever Edward is up to, you have a chance. I've told you. Get out of here. Leave the Eastern Shore. I hate it here. I hate the Eastern Shore."

Edith waited for Bitsy to cry, but she did not; Edith had never seen Bitsy cry. She put her hand out to comfort her friend, but Bitsy swatted it away.

"I'm sorry," said Bitsy, now offering her hand as a truce. "I know you're not asking for advice, but here it is: Forgive Edward, whatever he did to you. Let him forgive you. And then get on with it. You've still got to use your *head*. What are you *thinking?*"

"I don't know. Perhaps that's why I'm so happy." She could not say this word—"happy"—without feeling it, a quickening of her heart; she saw Tom in front of her.

"Don't you have to think about the money?"

"What money?" Edith was shaken out of her dreams.

"Edward's. He *is* making money over there, isn't he?"

Edith had begun to realize that Edward was making a lot of money over there, but the farm income had been sufficient, over these many months, to support them. She was prouder of this fact than of almost anything else. "I don't want his money. I don't need it."

"I'm not talking about you. I'm talking about the boys. It's their money I'm trying to protect. You let Edward spin off out there and he's going to meet someone new, and they'll have kiddies, and your boys will never see a dime. Be practical, please."

Edith understood well enough that she was not being practical, but Edward's money had come and gone before, and probably would again, and it was hardly an issue she had to face now.

"And what *about* Edward?"

"Oh, Edward has found himself. He's found his life, after all this time. You're wrong to think that I am punishing him for those years in England. He earned the chance, he paid dearly for it, and now he's grabbing it. I'm proud of him."

"Does that mean he's never coming back?"

"Not to live, I shouldn't think."

"Will you divorce?"

Edith had not used that word to herself, and she had not supposed it would be necessary. She did not pursue the logic of her thoughts out into imagined events, but it seemed to her that Edward—ah, Edward, father of her children—would simply be "off." That was all. "Where's your husband?" they would ask when she was ninety, and she would answer, "Edward is off," and at that point she would probably mean that he was dead, but it wouldn't really be that different. Frank Howe would be long gone from Blaketon, and there they would be, Bitsy Howe and Edith Mason, Miss Elizabeth and Miss Edith, as they would be remembered, remembered single, decorated with their husband's names and titles but relieved of their attentions, two old wives as chaste as nuns, virgins restored like monarchs.

"Bitsy, nothing is going to happen. Nothing has to happen."

"Edward is going to find out, you know," said Bitsy. "Then what will he do?"

"How's he going to find out?"

"How? Someone is going to tell him, that's how. What you do here on the Retreat isn't just your business. The more people there are who find out, the more people are going to get nervous. This is a community, damnit. When the mayor's taken a turn for his secretary, the city gets nervous. The colored all know about it."

Edith had realized from the beginning that no secret in the house could be kept from Loretta and Valerie, so she hadn't really tried. Loretta had not concealed her disapproval, either. Still, Edith had assumed that the women, out of loyalty to her, would not tell anyone else what was going on.

"Loretta isn't your friend, you know. She's the biggest gossip in the county. Why do you think there are always so many people visiting her on Sundays?"

For a moment Edith was hurt by this truth, but the colored women, or Edward, these weren't the people she was worried about.

"Okay, Edith. You do what you want. But don't forget. You've got two boys to take care of."

Edith snapped forward in her chair. "The boys don't know. You'd tell me if you knew the boys know, wouldn't you?"

"Of course I would." Bitsy seemed, at last, satisfied that she had gotten Edith's attention. "But they'll find out, won't they? Don't you really think Sebastien has already figured it out?"

"No," she said quickly. "He hasn't. He won't. Besides, Sebastien wants me to be happy. That's always what he has wanted. He hates Edward."

"He loves you."

"Yes."

"Well?"

Bitsy kept her eye on Edith as she reached for a cigarette and lit it. Edith, finally, wanted Bitsy to leave. She wanted to throw her out, but she could not, any more than she could forget about Sebastien and Simon. She never had, not once during the fall when her avenue of lies was opening up her affair with Tom, in the necessary secrecy and privacy of love. The lies were for the boys, and she had to believe they were working, even on Sebastien.

"What about Simon?" Bitsy said finally.

"I have to think that I will make it right for him. I have to think that somehow this will be better for him, don't I?"

"You do. If you didn't, you wouldn't have started it in the first place. But Simon needs his father. You know that. Boys do."

"It's not as if Edward has not been gone before. Simon will have to get over it."

"Get over losing his father? Edith, don't be so cruel."

Edith leapt to her feet. "How dare you?" she snapped. They faced each other. "Simon will adjust because he *has* to, just like Sebastien."

"Sebastien did not. He needs his father too. That's his problem." Bitsy was now gathering her things to leave, her work done. "I'm sorry, Edith. I love you and I'm sorry you're in this mess. Nothing good can come from it."

———

THE WINTER WAS nowhere near as cold as the year before; the creek and river did not freeze in, though there was plenty of ice afloat, green with clumps of seaweed. When the west wind blew, the floes ground onto the shore and against the Retreat dock. What would Tom do, Edith wondered, if the winter took out the landing? He was writing from the Caribbean, and telling her that when he came back he wanted her to make a decision, to choose. Sebastien brought her these letters from the mailbox, and each time she saw one of them in his hand her heart stopped, as if he could read them with his touch. Oh, she would say brightly, a note from Mr. Hazelton. How thoughtful of him, she would add, as if she could make Sebastien believe. She would put the letter down and ask him about school, and he wouldn't answer, might just stare at her for a second before leaving for the farm.

Inside the Retreat, there was little of the fellowship in the kitchen that winter; there was no real reason for all of them to huddle together in the warmth of that communal space. But Simon had noticed that Loretta was being crabby, and Edith had answered that it was nothing, just something in Loretta's mind, all very complicated. This hadn't really done it.

"When is Father getting back?" Simon asked.

"Oh, I should think—"

"No," he insisted. When he was angry and upset he spoke through his nose. "I mean *when*."

"He's not sure," she answered.

"I want to see Father. I don't like it here," he said, deliberately trying to hurt her. "I want to go home to England."

"But, sweetie, you have so much here, don't you?" Just last week, Simon had been invited to spend the night with his friend Billy Warren, whose father was the president of the savings bank; Edith had never imagined that children did such a thing, but she was pleased he was asked. "Wouldn't you miss Billy if you went to England?"

He didn't answer, so she reached out for him, and he responded by bolting for the door. "No," he said. "I hate you. I want Father."

This conversation bored deep into her for days. How could Simon say that he hated her? How could he turn this all against *her*? Simon hardly knew his father. Edward was the one who had brought them there to Maryland and then left them to survive as best they could, which was what she was doing. And about Edward's return she was speaking honestly. His letters were full of his work, and of politics, of that fool Neville Chamberlain, who wouldn't see what Hitler was doing until he marched into Whitehall and dictated the terms of peace. Edward spoke of airplanes as the only chance now, and of expansion of the works to build parts for them when the time finally came, and of meetings with ministers, and again of airplanes. At the end of his letters there were lines about missing her and the boys, saying that he grieved to be apart from them and held them all tenderly in his heart. Once or twice he seemed even to be trying to entice her to come over, describing a house he had taken for them all in Manchester. Very good, Edward, thought Edith—good manners, as always. And then he usually closed with a few words about when he expected to return, but "perhaps in November" had become "certainly at Christmastime" and was now "when we see what Hitler has in mind in Austria." Edward's timetable was ruled by armies in Europe, not by the needs of a woman and two boys. Edith tried, genuinely, to make Sebastien and Simon proud of what their father was doing, of his importance in the world, but he had made his choices, and she had made hers. Simon, it seemed, responded to the whole thing simply by hating his mother.

Who could she talk to about this? There was no one. She and Bitsy still got together now and again that winter, but after their long conversation in the fall, there was nothing really to talk about. Bitsy's slightly sarcastic tone had hurt her as much as Simon's childish pique; Edith didn't want to be told she was stupid anymore. Sebastien was her only friend now, but she couldn't fool herself; he'd figured out some of the truth. Sometimes they talked as they had always done, for an hour or two into the night, chatting like spouses, but then he would turn cold. The winter days passed, and Tom's return drew closer. She gave Sebastien room; she let his anger float without scolding him. I'll give him time, she thought. He doesn't love Edward. He wants me to be happy. He'll see.

When, in the spring, Tom came back, the *Candide* was the same, though brilliant in its new paint and varnish, and the cove was the same, if more open at the mouth after a fierce winter blow. Edith and Tom came together with a winter's store of passion, but the outside world was not the same, and events that spring and summer of 1938 were beginning to tug now, tightening the lines a little, giving a little pull on the ropes, which were fast uncoiling to the bitter end.

—

AT SCHOOL, THE boys called Sebastien Prince Boy and made fun of his accent. He was big and strong, like his father, and they had learned from earlier shoving matches and an occasional punch not to mess with him, but they called him that name in his earshot, and he could hear them in the corridor mimicking his answers in class. He spoke only when the teachers called on him. He reacted as any boy would, by trying to shove the boys' ignorance back into their faces, but they laughed even harder.

This year he had moved on to the high school, and now the buses brought the older children, the farm children, into town. He had told himself that the town kids were all jerks anyway, but the farm boys didn't like him any better, and they were bigger and stronger than he, and everyone knew it. The few times he had tried to talk to them about farm work, they spat and gave him looks so filled with ridicule that he had to walk away in silence, his eyes stinging.

After Christmas the principal, Mr. Swenson, had called him into his office, offered him a chair, and asked how he thought things were going.

"All right," Sebastien had answered.

Mr. Swenson had spoken sympathetically. "I was wondering whether you'd like to talk to me. You seem to have so much on your mind."

"I'm fine. I don't want to talk about anything."

"Is there anything we could do to help you fit in? Mrs. Dobson and I wondered whether you'd like to join the Math Club."

No, Sebastien said.

"We're just trying to help. We know this is difficult for you."

Sebastien said nothing. He wondered what Swenson meant by "this": going to an American school after a childhood in England, or being his father's son?

"Boys can be mean, at your age. But it seems to us that there are several who could make companions for you. Dilly Egger, Bob Tanner. I'm sure—"

"I don't want companions. Things are the way I like them. Is this all?" He saw Mr. Swenson bristle at this response; he heard the controlled anger in his voice.

"We had only thought to offer help, Sebastien. You are not the only boy who has social difficulties in adolescence. I do not think disdain for others will get you anywhere in life."

"Can I go?"

Mr. Swenson stood up, reminded Sebastien that his door was always open, and said that he would check in with him in a month or two, but Sebastien figured he wouldn't. Swenson had done his duty, and to hell with the boy, irritating and arrogant Mason. Swenson had maybe thought they'd seen the last of his race here when Miss Mary died. Sebastien spent the day worried that word of this session would get out, and when he saw Dilly Egger in science class, he probed those pathetic, scared eyes for some sign that Swenson had taken him aside, but there was nothing.

Some of the girls spoke to him now and again, and one or two may have thought he was cute. Sebastien thought Mandy Stevens was pretty, and she sometimes sat with him at lunch and told him she thought the other boys were stupid. Yeah, Sebastien said. She told him he could act nicer, though, and he agreed, but nothing came of it, and nothing came of Mandy Stevens. Her friends didn't like Sebastien, and he didn't like them, and when they rode home on the bus they all sat in the front and talked about who was dreamy and who was swell, and it wasn't him.

Sebastien was the last student to get off the bus, at the last stop, where the state road ended on Mason's Neck. The driver was a woman whose husband ran the feed store, and she usually had a word or two for him; she was willing to listen to his news of the farm—what they were going to plant and how the milking was doing. He liked her and was grateful for her kindness, but she always spoke of the farm as McCready's, and once or twice he tried to correct her, to tell her that it was the Masons', that it was his father's and soon to be his. "Oh, now, son," she said, with a sympathy and an impatience he did not want to acknowledge, "you don't need to fight with me."

Sometimes Simon was waiting for him at the bus stop, and Sebastien could hardly admit to himself how much he needed the sweetness his brother brought into his life. There were times during the day, standing alone at recess, that the thought of seeing Simon's little red head brought comfort. Sebastien could be himself on the Retreat with Simon, and be loved in return. No matter what anyone else had said to him all day, Simon spoke to him with reverence and admiration.

"Hey, Toad," Sebastien would say, and he would feel his voice relax, and as they took up walking side by side, he would loosen and move. They had a game called Crusher, in which they found large rocks that McCready or Robert had picked out of the road gravel, and they smashed one on the other to determine the champion, the one with the largest bit remaining. When Sebastien brought his rock down on Simon's, he pictured his tormentors' heads.

By the time they reached the house on those days, or even by the time Sebastien reached it on days Simon did not meet him, he always felt better, safe again. School was gone, in the past. He was home. The Retreat was his magic; his insides relaxed, his fists uncurled, his world was right again. The women were always there, Loretta and Valerie, and his mother. When he had started school they used to ask him about the day, and what he had learned, and what he did, and his mother asked especially who he had eaten with, and who he had played with during recess. Sometimes he made an answer up, and sometimes he informed her that he never "played" during recess, and sometimes he said that he had spent the time by himself. "Oh, by yourself. How nice," his mother would answer, with a cheerful and encouraging smile, which he hated. Along the way, she had stopped asking him those questions, and instead she listened while Simon described his day, his own games with his "gang." Sebastien thought this was just fine, as long as they left him alone.

That winter, Sebastien often wondered if and when his mother was going to tell him the truth. He could forgive her anything if she would only tell him the truth. If only he could have found a way to make her understand that it was her secrets that hurt him, and not whatever it was she was doing. He could have helped her; he had plans and thoughts that might solve her problems. If only she had not shut him out, after all they had lived through together.

There was plenty of opportunity, in those long evenings after the women had gone home and Simon had been sent to bed; it was their time together, and she told him about her day. She told him his father's news, and he listened intently to her voice, searching each pause and inflection for the information he wanted. She said "your father," not "Father," or "Edward." She didn't say he would be "home" soon" but said he would be "back" when the business could spare him. Earlier, when he had asked about the summer or next year, she used to say "We'll have to see"; now she said she hadn't decided. Sebastien heard and understood these subtleties like words and paragraphs. It amazed him that she still believed she could fool him, or even that she still bothered to try.

Once or twice he brought up Mr. Hazelton, just to watch her face. It never lied; when his mother's face tried to lie, it spoke all the more plainly. Her eyebrows rose a bit and her cheeks filled slightly, and he waited for her to give a sigh and say, as she had done in the past about all sorts of things, "I might as well tell you; I can't keep *anything* from you."

But she didn't say that, not once over the winter, when it would have been easy, closed in by the cold, to share secrets in the candlelight. If she had, they could have prepared together for what was coming, just as they always had; together they could have decided what would be best for Simon. Now it was spring again. Whatever Sebastien believed about his father, he could not imagine that he would stay away yet another season. His father would be coming back on the wings of success, with money in his pockets, ideas in his brain. It was at times like this that he did the most damage. The past year had been breath, it had been harvest. Sebastien would flex his right arm, and rub over the ridges and mounds of his muscles, and wonder if he was strong enough, if all those days in the fields, working his body under the hot sun and cold winds, had gotten him where he needed to be; he wondered if he was man enough for his father's return.

—

IT WAS MAY; planting was finished and the farm boys at school, who had missed weeks during April, were now back to finish out the year. All the lessons had rushed forward without them, and then doubled back when they returned, and Sebastien was bored out of his mind. There were boats now out in the Bay and the river, yachts once again, and he knew that at least once Mr. Hazelton had come over.

Simon was waiting for him at the bus stop one afternoon, and as Sebastien stepped off, he yelled excitedly and happily, "Father has sent a telegram!"

"What did it say?"

"Um."

"Come on, goddamnit, Toad. What did it say?"

"Gee, Sebastien. I don't know. It means he's coming home. Doesn't it?"

"How the hell do I know," he answered, and took off on a jog.

"Sebastien, wait for me."

But Sebastien could not, and he ignored the beginnings of Simon's tears and kept up his jog until he got home. He burst through the doors into the kitchen. "Where's Mother," he demanded.

Loretta glared at him, about the doors, about Simon following him in tears. She made him work for it but then told him that Miss Edith was in town, that the telegram had said that Mister Edward would be calling her at the bank at three sharp. Sebastien wanted to howl with impatience, but there was nothing to be done but wait, all four of them, even as the room began to darken. When at last his mother drove back up and walked in the door, Sebastien could see that she was stricken, nearly drained of all emotion, and that she could bring herself to speak directly only to Simon, with the kind of fake delight that might be expected when talking to an eight-year-old. Yes, Father was coming back, she said, just as soon as he could get away. There were a few things that had to happen, questions about the government, because Father was now quite important and could not be spared for a few weeks yet. But, she said to Simon, isn't that lovely? Father will bring you a present, she said.

Sebastien waited for more, for a sign from her that what she had concocted for Simon would be followed later by details, by—he still believed he would get it—the truth. But she would not answer his questions and kept her eyes on Simon, and finally Sebastien glared at her one last time and then marched from the kitchen, letting the butler's door swing and crash. He stood in the hall for a few moments, next to the permanently closed door of his father's study, and fought a wave of panic. That man behind there, blowing his flatulent nose, dreaming his dreams like liquor, and then opening the door with a wave of stale ethers at his back: Sebastien couldn't bear the thought of that life resuming.

His father would be coming back on the *Normandie* this summer, soon, soon. He wanted to go to his mother and demand to know the specifics, but she had left the kitchen now and had withdrawn to her room, and he knew she would not come out. He was afraid to anger her; he was afraid of losing her, even as he realized that she couldn't, perhaps wouldn't, help him now.

He walked outside into a fine mist. He stood on the stoop overlooking the creek and breathed deeply. A fat muskrat, straying too far from the safety of its marsh, waddled into the box bush; he saw a catbird, and he wanted to fly with it. He stood until he was damp, and until Valerie came up behind him and spoke from the porch.

"Mister Sebastien. You all right?"

He turned. He wanted to go to her and ask what to do, but what could Valerie say? "Yes," he answered.

"We all knew he would be coming back. It's the man's home, ain't it?"

He looked her in the eye. "You don't believe that. It's ours, all of us. But not his."

"It don't have to change things all that much," she said.

"But you don't understand. He's not coming back to stay. He's coming to take us back to England. He doesn't want this place. He doesn't care about it, about the farm, and you and McCready and Robert and Loretta. Valerie, I promise you: he's forgotten your name. He won't know who you are when he walks in."

"It don't matter. He can forget my name anytime he wants."

"What's going to happen to Mother? Valerie, you tell me, what's going to happen to Mother?"

For a moment, Valerie looked as if she were trying to guess what he knew or didn't know. "I don't know that. Your mama is going to have to make her way now. Won't be easy, but it will happen."

At dinner their mother was full of chatty bits and details about nothing. Sebastien knew she was barely in control; she was talking to them as if she were coaxing dogs into a kennel. Maybe she had been drinking wine up there in her room. She was as tight as wire. This woman, thought Sebastien, my mother, is acting crazy.

"Won't it be smashing!" she said, about Edward's return.

She didn't say she was glad; she described their father's return with a word she'd never used before, Sebastien felt certain, in her life.

"The end of the summer at the very latest. And guess what?" With the childish turn in her voice, Sebastien knew that once again she was talking only to Simon. "He's bought a new automobile. He's picking it up in New York and driving it down. Isn't that exciting?"

"What kind?"

"What kind of what, dear?"

"Of car, Mother."

"I don't know. Just an automobile And that isn't all. He has directed Mr. Rhodes—you remember Mr. Rhodes . . ."

Simon did not, so Sebastien said, "Right. He's that carpenter who kept coming by for months after Father left, looking for his wages."

She straightened the silverware around her plate and moved her water glass precisely into the corner of her place mat; she ignored him. "He has directed Mr. Rhodes to proceed with electrification of some of the house, with *two* telephone lines into his office. The study will be quite different."

All this news, and especially her frantic delivery, was too much for Simon. He looked to Sebastien for support. "No more candles!" he said. "But I like candles."

"So do I," said Sebastien.

Their mother looked at them both and sighed, as if they had ruined her fun, as if they were sticks-in-the-mud. She sighed once more, and now she spoke coldly. "There will be changes," she announced. "Of course there will. We can't expect everything to remain . . . remain . . ." She stopped. The clock ticked; the women had gone home.

"Mother?" said Sebastien. She didn't answer, so he watched her through the candlelight, and in the flicker he began to see the shine of tears on her cheeks. She was sitting there, her place mat perfectly arranged, her hands folded in her lap, and she was crying, and the tears weren't the dry crystals he expected his mother to cry, the accidental sand. The tears were flowing, oily, hot. "Mother?"

Simon was stone in his chair, and she raised her arms and invited him into her lap; he crawled in like a toddler, and Sebastien sat while she took the comfort of his brother's soft hair on her face.

She resumed: "There will be changes. I can't tell you what they will be, but we've had fun here, haven't we, in this big old house." She was saying this for Simon. "Remember how cold it was the first year?" Simon's head bobbed a little as she bounced her knee. "Brrrr," she said, "old Mother West Wind. Remember the night we arrived, with Mrs. McCready in the vestibule? I'll tell you the truth. I thought she was an old witch."

Simon brought his face out of the crook of her neck, gulping a few deep breaths. His movement seemed to bring Edith back, and to reassure him enough to go off and start getting changed for bed. They watched him go before she turned to Sebastien.

"It will be hard for you, dear. I know it. But we will all do our best, and perhaps in the end things will work out right."

"Are we going back to England?"

"I don't know. If there's a war . . ."

"That's stupid. I won't go."

She stopped at this thought and said nothing for a few moments, but he did not interrupt her thoughts. "Your father will be proud of you, of what you have done here."

"I don't care what he thinks. It's what he has done to you that matters."

"Sebastien. You can't fight my wars. Your father . . . is a forgiving man, and you must be too. You are the child of two people, your father and me, not of a marriage. Promise me you will try to understand that."

Sebastien could not stand it anymore. "I know everything. I know what you have been doing and he deserves everything he's gotten. He's the one that must ask for pardon, not you."

"Don't fight my battles, and don't interfere."

"It's my battle too," he shouted. "It isn't just yours."

"No. It is just mine. You can't help. I'm sorry."

"Why are you turning me away? Why have you done this. We can do this together, can't we?" His voice was breaking.

"No."

"You lied to me. You said you never would, and you did."

"I just wanted you to be happy. I'll do anything to make you happy again."

"Then stop keeping secrets from me. Please, Mother."

—

THE NEXT MORNING Edith arose early to the sounds of birds, to the brush of honey locust branches on the sides of the house. She waited for the boys' departure, dressed, and then stole out the side door. She walked down to the dock. Bitsy had been wrong, saying to her last winter that all boats looked the same to her; *Candide* was a smudge across the river, but it was clear to her eye. She didn't know why, exactly—the slightly cream-colored jib, perhaps, or the way it pitched when it reached the tops of the swells. She glanced at the water on the pilings and saw that the tide was high enough for him to enter the creek. She waited while he drew nearer, occasionally dropping her gaze and looking toward the chimneys of Blaketon. Bitsy would have seen him by now, everyone would have seen him, including whoever it was who had written to Edward to say that his wife had taken a lover, we thought you should know; the letter was signed, said Edward, by no one.

"I won't ask you why," he had said. "I don't need to." That voice, familiar even as it crackled under the sea, down the long threads that bound her to him, came from a man she no longer knew. "Perhaps it's too late, but it's time I came home." Maybe this man was the Edward she had hoped she was marrying in the first place, but that was too long ago now for her to know whether she still wanted him. Maybe this man was the better self he could become only apart from her. He said yesterday he had neglected her for many reasons over the years, and now it was war that stood between them, not their war, but war just the same. There was little time, he said. He asked, "Can you forgive me *now*?" and she had not answered, simply stood there in Mr. Warren's hastily vacated office, while nervous and ripe-smelling farmers waited for conferences on this year's financial crisis, while Neville Chamberlain prepared to go to Munich to search for a way to avoid the death of Europe.

Candide was in the creek now, and she could see Tom's face, mouth tightened, an even line of doubt. He'd been angry on the phone yesterday; angry for them both. She needed to know whether he'd let her bounce softly and cushion the fall, whether he would show her love. Instead, she got anger.

He cast her a line as he nosed into the wind, and idled the diesel while she pulled the rope fast. The water closed between them, and she stepped over the lifeline into his grasp. He began to cast off.

"Wait," she said.

"Why?"

"I need to talk."

"Well, let's talk."

"No. I mean here. At the dock. Please tie up."

She could see him argue with himself even as he did what she asked. He sat down in the cockpit. "There," he said.

She beckoned to the cushion beside her and held out her hand. "I won't talk to you unless you hold my hand."

He took it, and she watched as the anger drained out of his face. "I'm sorry if I seemed selfish," he said finally. "You have too many selfish men in your life these days."

"No. I don't. I'm the only one who has been selfish."

He whistled through the small gap in his front teeth. She used to think this was funny, when they were out on the water and she told him things that surprised him or shocked him and he made a sound like the wind, as if to say, Who could ever understand what fools people are. "I am thinking of you," he said. "Of what's best for you."

"Tom, I was never just me, even when I thought I was. What's best for me is past."

"Why. Because that bastard has decided after all this time to come back?"

"Don't," she said. "He doesn't deserve your indictments. He's not asking for that." She had always realized that Tom understood nothing of her marriage to Edward; it had never before mattered, but now that Edward knew about them, nothing mattered more.

"What is he asking for?"

"Me, I guess. The boys. That's all he's ever really asked for, you know."

"What are his conditions?"

"For letting me back?"

"Yes."

"I don't think he has any. That isn't the way Edward thinks." As she was saying this, it struck her how true it was. "Edward has made enough mistakes in his own life not to judge others so harshly."

"He's caused you nothing but sadness. He's the most selfish person that ever lived. He's a fool to have treated you the way he did, and it serves him right that he lost you."

"Don't say that."

"What? That he lost you? Are you telling me that he hasn't?"

"Don't make this so hard."

He had dropped her hand, and his anger had returned. "What is he offering to you? What are his plans?"

"He's got business here in America, he says, but I'm sure he'll want to return to England as soon as he can. He has no life here."

"But you do." The mean cut in his voice returned. "With me. This is stupid."

"My problems are stupid, Tom? Is that it? My life is just made of stupid things?" It was beginning to astonish her how quickly and completely the long-expected event was leveling this love affair; the truths were falling on the felt like playing cards.

"Of course not."

"Are my children stupid, Tom? What about them?"

"Of course they're not. We'll talk about them. You know I care for them."

Edith remembered the kindness he had shown to the boys, the few times they had been together, but kindness was not enough. They had to be part of him, part of his soul, and they weren't. They could never be.

"They'd be happier here," he said. "They don't want to go to England."

"Why are you so sure? What do you know about my children?" About three that morning, at the time when she always felt the ghosts were on the prowl, she had gone into Simon's room and sat with him. A little boy who loved his father, beyond all reason or recompense. She had peeked in on Sebastien; could she give up and allow him to spend his life hating his father? Would Sebastien ever be whole if he did? Wasn't that a little of what she had learned watching him, that there was no damage to the heart more persistent than going through life hating a parent? "Simon loves his father."

He stood up, and paced in the cockpit, where she had spent so many hours. This boat, Tom's boats, they seemed frivolous just now. "And what about Sebastien? If Edward has his war, he'll be drafted in England."

In sudden fury, Edith leapt up, steadying herself with a hand on the boom. "Do you think I haven't thought about that? Is there anything you wouldn't do to get your own way?"

"Edith, I love you. That's what matters."

She jumped up onto the dock. "It isn't the only thing that matters. It doesn't even help very much. My life is with my children. They're the only thing that matters now."

"But Edith," he said, and then paused, his face screwed tight with his effort to show his love and not his anger. "Life with the boys doesn't have to be with Edward, does it?"

"I don't know. But for now, I have to believe it. I have to let you go in order to find out what is right for the boys. I'm sorry I asked you to come over today. Please," she said, kneeling down to untie the mooring lines, "please go now."

"What if I won't? I won't leave you."

She turned to him. "You will. Please. You will or I'll ask the men of this farm to come here and make you go."

9

SIMON HEARD THE telephone ring. It was the bright, hard sound of magic. During the summer, while his father's arrival hung out there in the shadowy world of adult delays and excuses, he had watched Mr. Rhodes and his men fish wires through the walls, and cut holes for electric boxes. He had believed in Mr. Rhodes. The men had put electricity into his father's office, and into the kitchen. They had put electricity into one of the bedrooms upstairs, which Mother said would now be Father's room. But best of all, Mr. Rhodes had put in the telephones, two of them, as Mother had promised.

Simon had sneaked into his father's office a few times during the fall, as they waited for his arrival. Miss Mary's stuffed calf was in the trash, along with the ostrich plumes and sharks' teeth. The books and the bookcases were gone, and in their place, stretched across the blank walls, were two immense maps of Europe and Asia. Simon had stood in front of those maps, mouthing the names, running his small fingers across the magenta borders, reading the political divisions as nothing but the raised ink of engraved printing. He looked at England and found Manchester. Manchester, he whispered. His father was there, or he had been. Now he was at sea, maybe here, he thought, touching a watery spot at the extreme edge of the map, maybe here, he guessed, moving to a small speck of dust on the wall, where he believed New York must be. Maybe he was already driving here in his new car.

There were now two desks. The small one, on the far side of the mantelpiece, had a large black typewriter on it. Simon had rested his hands on the keyboard, afraid to touch, unable to resist. He had hunted out the letters S-I-M-O-N, spoken the sound of each letter as he located it, pushed on the keys hard enough to begin the travel of his name toward an imaginary piece of paper. The ribbon, shiny with the promise of words, rose up in between. Inside the typewriter, he heard the whisper of gears and rods. He let the letters down gently. To the right of the typewriter was a wonderful lamp with a long, segmented neck, ending with a head for the bulb. He was blinded when he turned it on.

He stepped over to the larger desk. He ran his hand over the expanse of smooth leather, traced as much of the gold filigreed border as he could reach. He sat in his father's chair, felt the cool embrace of the leather seat, and the spring back uncoiled slightly when he pushed; he held his breath at the sound, and listened for footsteps. He would have liked to open the drawers, but simply could not. He mustn't. That was the sort of thing Sebastien would do.

He raised his view slowly across the desktop. A black cord came into his line of sight, and then another, and he followed them back to the telephones. The two telephones sat side by side, lovely and black. The heavy ends of the receivers draped over the cradles, held there in a grip, at the ready, like a cowboy's revolver. The world was in those telephones, the whole world in a parcel. His father was in there. He had not told anyone how much he missed his father, but he would like to pick up one of these telephones and tell whoever it is that answers. My father is coming home, he would say. He's been building airplanes in England for the king, and now he's coming home. I'm nine, he would add. Well, nearly. My mother is sad. I think my brother is mad at me, but I'm not sure why. Hello? Hello? Did I mention that my father is coming home?

And now, in late November, the telephone rang. He was in the kitchen when it happened, kept home from school for the occasion, and the whole house jumped at the sound. Loretta let a spoon drop; Valerie spilled her tea. It rang again, and Loretta said, "Well, I declare." Simon heard his mother's quick steps on the staircase above, and the telephone kept on ringing as she crossed the hall. Simon went to the door of the butler's pantry and swung it open enough to watch her enter the study. She was in her slip; she'd been dressing for this day. She picked up one receiver and said Hello. Simon could feel the weight of it, the smooth shine of it on his ear. She said Hello again, but the ringing didn't stop, and she reached for the other receiver Hello? she said, holding both of them to her head. Yes. Perfectly, she said. Hello, Edward, she said. In New York? She listened, glancing around as she did. Then about two, it will be? she said. Fine. Yes, yes. I'll tell the children. Yes. Of course. Good-bye.

She hung up, stood there, brought her hand up to her face, and absently rubbed her ear. She looked around, let out a sigh that, even from this distance, Simon saw washing from the rise of her chest to the slumping of her shoulders. He let the door swing back to its center and retraced his steps into the kitchen.

"Your daddy?" asked Loretta.

"Yes. I think so."

"This is a big day, ain't it. You got to look your *best* for your daddy."

"What time?" Valerie asked Loretta.

"Well, I don't know," she answered querulously. "I weren't eavesdropping, now was I?"

"I think about two," said Simon. "He's in New York."

"New York," said Loretta. "No, thank you."

Six hours later they were all there, sitting in the hall. Simon was wearing a tie for the first time in months, and his flannel pants itched, but they were long pants. His mother, seated behind him, was dressed in green. Sebastien, in a suit, was pacing a little to one side. Valerie had brought a chair out of the kitchen for Loretta, and stood beside her, just a few paces into the hall. The clock ticked. Simon tried very hard to picture what his father looked like, his red mustache, his large nose, his broad chest. He had no trouble hearing the voice and could feel the great rushes of air and sound that his father made as he moved. Simon couldn't imagine him fitting into this house anymore, big as it was; he couldn't help thinking his father was too big to get in the door.

Sebastien was out in the vestibule now, peering through the narrow door lights. Suddenly he came to attention. He looked again and said, "Okay. That's him."

There was a confused bustle as they all jumped for the door and fanned out under the portico. A car, black and shiny, was slowly making its way down the lane, pausing to go gently over the ruts, and when it reached the gate into the Mansion House, it stopped. Simon could see him now, in the driver's seat, looking intently at the stone piers before inching at a crawl between these obstacles.

"It's a Buick," said Sebastien. He seemed pleased, which made Simon happy. The great chrome prow of this car was churning toward them, the large form behind the wheel seeming to be the engine powering the whole thing, willing it onward, and finally it crunched to a halt right below where the household now stood. The car settled into its space with a sort of hiss, the last gasp of arrival.

His father sat for a moment, and then, in the most deliberate unfolding of limbs, he stepped out. Simon heard his mother let out an odd little closemouthed cry, right at the top of her throat. His father's face came back to him in an instant, the instant of one who had been lost, and was now found. His father was thinner, it seemed, but maybe Simon had been wrong to remember him fat. He was dressed differently; Simon always thought of his clothes as having lots of flaps and buttons and pleats, but now his dark suit was smooth and plain; it reminded Simon of Mr. Koren, the principal of the elementary school. His father was still his father, and he still loved him, but he wasn't exactly the person he expected.

"Edith," Edward said. He spread his arms, pulling up a sudden show of white shirt between his waistcoat and trousers, and referring to everything in his sight—the grounds, the house, the family. "You all look marvelous. Thank you."

Simon could not wait any longer. He skipped down the steps, hesitated between a handshake and a hug, and accepted instead a large rounded hand on his head and a palm on one check.

"Simon," Edward said. "Perfectly extraordinary."

Sebastien was next, not because he followed Simon down the steps, but because his father walked up and sought him out. "Sir," he said to Sebastien, gave out a hand, and bowed.

"Hello, Father," said Sebastien, and returned the handshake.

He backed up a pace. "I salute you, boy," he said.

Sebastien said nothing, but Simon started to laugh, though he didn't know why, and Valerie brushed past the group, giving a very quick curtsy to Edward, and came down to shush him up.

Edward now took note of her and of Loretta, and though there was no bow, he met both their eyes and said, "Ladies, how kind of you to greet me. I thank you for my family."

Through Valerie's arms Simon saw that Loretta was quite stunned by this, and she backed off with one cycle of her limp and step.

At last he turned toward Edith. "It feels good, Edith," he said. Simon held his breath to hear everything.

"Edward, you look very well. You really do."

"As do you, Edith." He pulled one of her hands up, across a slightly awkward gap between them, and caressed his cheek with it. "Is there room in the house for me?"

This last phrase struck Simon as very odd indeed. Of course there was room; Mr. Rhodes had even specially put electricity in a bedroom that Mother had said would now be just Father's. Had Father forgotten because he had stayed away so long? He wondered even more, because his mother blushed, her lips trembled, and she seemed to take it as a serious question, though an unexpected one, and seemed to be considering it almost as if she might deny it. It was a moment of mystery to him, and at last a source of impatience, because there would be presents, he thought, somewhere in that car, and he wanted to get on with them.

"Welcome home, Edward," she said finally. "You must be very tired."

With this common phrase, there was motion again, the more expected spin of arrival, and the women went back to the kitchen. Robert was sent for, but it was Lance who appeared. Edward eyed him with some surprise, but he accepted Valerie's introduction of him as the new hand, and directed the unloading of the car, which, as it turned out, was stuffed with things: file cases, one huge steamer trunk—a new one, Simon observed—other parcels and boxes. One of them was so heavy that Lance, a look of surprise on his red face, had to set it down for a rest on the steps. Most of this luggage went straight into the new office. Simon followed along, and could not resist pointing out to his father each of the wonders—the telephones, the typewriter, the maps. His father paused at the map of Europe. He raised a long finger to it, much as Simon had done, but the slightly yellow nail landed not on Manchester but on Germany. "Do you know what this is?" he asked Simon.

Simon looked. "Yes, sir. It's Germany."

"Good boy. Do you know who lives there?"

Simon thought, but could not really imagine. "No, sir."

"It's Hitler," his father told him. "By God, evil incarnate." His voice quivered. "But I'll tell you, that man is in for one bloody hell of a tussle." He remained a second longer, boring a fiery gaze at the spot, until, apparently refreshed by the effort, he turned. "Now let's see what is in my luggage for you."

The family was called into the living room, and they gathered, Sebastien last. From the packages now arrayed in front of him, Edward selected one, pretended to hand it to Simon, but drew it back quickly. "I've brought something for the help," he said, peeling enough of the wrapping aside to reveal a bolt of wool.

"How thoughtful of you. But don't tease Simon. He's practically undone anyway."

This time the package was given to him, the most joyous moment. He ripped open the paper, removed the red cardboard top, and saw in front of him, each one stitched by a single thread to a stiff backing, an array of lead knights. The Battle of Agincourt, he read with difficulty, scripted along the top, gay colored banners forming the capital letters. There were mounted knights, fierce and hooded in their armor, horses clothed with flowing robes; there were foot soldiers, shields held up in front of their swiveling arm thrusts; archers; and pages; and, more wonderful than he could ever have hoped, a wagon with six horses and four spoked wheels spinning on their axles.

"Can you say thank you to your father?" his mother asked.

He wanted to close the box back up and take it to his room. He was unable to speak.

"Leave the boy alone," said Edward. He handed the next parcel to Sebastien, who removed the wrapping to reveal a leather case, and opened the case to see a shaving kit, with silver-handled brushes. Sebastien, more proper, thanked his father formally, but Simon could see he liked his present very much.

"My father used to say," said Edward, "that no matter what happens, a man is still a lord if he has his razor."

Edward turned now to Edith, and there was a fur, a luxurious fur. Simon thought she thanked him so quietly because these wonders had all been beyond dream, because joy of this kind was like eternity, deep and boundless. Released at last, Simon took his knights up to his room and stared at them for a while, the tiny grunting expressions on their faces, the red flare of the horses' nostrils, until he could stand it no more and unlaced them from their mountings. He and Sebastien ate dinner in the kitchen—the women had stayed late to cook a welcoming feast for their parents. After dinner Simon sat with his parents while they had their drinks. He listened to his father's stories about the works and the government, and about Hitler, and when he was sent to bed, he found his knights arrayed, as he had left them, in a long march across the counterpane.

There was a light under the door to Sebastien's and he went in. Sebastien was there, sitting in his chair, looking at the shaving kit.

"See? See?" said Simon. "I told you."

"Toad," Sebastien said, shaking his head slightly.

"See? These lovely things? See?"

Sebastien looked at the kit. "It wasn't his father who said that about a shaving kit. It was Lord Belsen, that fat old fairy."

"Stop it!"

"Quiet."

Simon yelled, "Stop it. You can't say that." He was crying, hysterical. "Stop being so mean!" he yelled again, and suddenly his mother was at his side, and he was moved out of Sebastien's room, and his nightgown was dropped over his head, and the knights were moved carefully, and he was kissed and patted, and he fell asleep.

She kept patting him lightly as his breathing settled into rest. She would have liked to stay there all night. She had anticipated many things about this day, as it drew toward her jerkily through the summer, Edward's return playing cat and mouse with the possible outbreak of war. It would have been better, she could argue, if Edward had never come back—but he had always been there, a candle burning in his younger son's heart, a black void in his older son's soul. Who could account for this division of allegiance? Children simply seemed to choose which parent to favor; Edward had behaved the same way toward both. Edward had been there for her, too, as the judge and arbiter of everything she had done, in the firm grip of memory of their early years together. Edward had been revolving around them for these months like the moon, waxing and waning, whether any of them liked it or not. So when the news came that Chamberlain had succeeded, that he had given away much but secured "peace in our time," she was relieved, for herself, because it was time to move forward. If Edward never came back, they would never stop waiting for him, so it was good, now, that the waiting was done.

Edith breathed deeply, calming herself. Edward is home, she said to herself. He had come back with talk of his work and the war and news of friends; she knew the sound of half-truths and embellishment, and she had heard none of it so far. He'd done better with this arrival than she would have believed possible, with gifts that did what gifts should do: they had created the illusion that she and the children had been in his heart from the moment he left, that there had been a picture of them, as family, in his eye during the months when he was gone, his wife and his two sons seated in front of him at the hearth. That picture had never been taken, but now perhaps it could be. Perhaps, in the frankness of hurt, and with time, she and Edward could make it happen.

She adjusted Simon's covers a last time, and thought for a moment of going in to check on Sebastien, but what could she say to him, or for him? She could barely speak for herself and for Simon now. What could she do for Sebastien?

She went downstairs and found Edward standing in front of the portrait of Oswald Mason, a hero of the Revolution. He straightened his tie, as if the portrait were a mirror. "Not so bad, do you think?" he said.

She wasn't sure what he meant. "I've grown fond of him," she said, about the portrait. "Maybe there is a smile behind his scowl."

"He was probably quite ugly, of course. They can't have all looked like Leslie Howard."

"Shall we sit?" She went to the door and called out to Valerie.

"Sebastien is such a handsome boy. He's filled out so well," he said as they waited.

She took this as a compliment to her. "It's the fieldwork. He's thick and strong like you, in the middle. Robert and Mr. McCready treat him like a man."

They paused while Valerie brought in the fried oysters. He took a bite before she left and threw his head back in extravagant pleasure. "Ah, the blessed mollusk," he exclaimed. "Done to perfection."

Valerie bowed awkwardly. "Yes, Mister Edward. I'll tell Loretta you're pleased."

After she left, he reached for a lemon half and squeezed all of it onto the oysters, took a scoop of horseradish, and then vigorously covered his dish with salt. He munched away in uncomfortable silence. Edith did not want to be the one to break it.

"Is Sebastien still so enthralled with Robert?" he said at last.

"Robert has been good to him. He's taught him a great deal."

"Yes, yes. You always defended him. But hardly a proper teacher for a young man."

Edith was tired, too tired to defend Robert, but, oh, what she might have said: that Robert had been a father to Sebastien during the past two years, that he had provided a love no more impenetrable than a doting father's.

"Got to get together with McCready, of course," he said, leaning back for Valerie to deposit the beef in front of him. "I'd be the first to admit that I was wrong about him. He and I, eh?"

"He and you what?"

"Oh, I can't say that . . ." He wiped his mouth with his napkin. "McCready and I. Well, he seems to have made a success of things. Given the chance."

"He's a kind and hardworking man, and he deserves everything that has come his way."

"Yes, he deserves a very good arrangement," he said, but his eyes wanted more from her at this moment. She knew what he was thinking: Perhaps I am not kind, hardworking, and deserving, but have I not labored against my faults?

"You know I'm proud of you. I'm happy for you."

"Oh," he said quickly, the plea gone in a second. "I've been very fortunate. I owe it to you, for the time you've given me so generously."

"Edward," she said.

He held his silverware above his plate, his ear cocked.

"You are being very kind to me."

"But?" he said, after she had paused.

"Well, kindness isn't really enough for us now, do you think? We have to talk."

He put down his fork, almost regretfully. "What about, just now."

"Well . . . your plans." He took this in but for a moment seemed to think it odd, her asking this, as if they had just gone over his plans an hour earlier and she had forgotten. Edith had to think back to make sure she hadn't. "What are your plans?"

"I have business," he said. "I can't tell you much about it. The Roosevelt administration is trying to help us, but the situation is awkward. I turn out to be a convenient messenger, for the moment. I expect us to have quite a few visitors out here at the Retreat, away from the Congress and all."

"And when it's done?"

"Hitler means to have war, and if he gives us just one more year, we shall be ready. We need that year, I can say that to you."

"Edward, can we leave the Nazis out of this? I am asking you about us and our family. Must I beg?"

He gave a last glance at the remains of his dinner, now cold, and at hers, untouched. He poured himself a glass of wine and reached for a cigar, but neither of these symbols of gracious dining appeared to give him pleasure. "I had hoped," he said, "to simply return as if all was normal. I'd hoped to begin with a clean slate, again," he said. "I'd hoped the children would welcome me back. Forgive and forget."

"I'm not asking for forgiveness," she said. She really wasn't sure she wanted it yet, not forgiveness, with all its hard bargains.

He said sharply, "I haven't said you must ask for it, have I? I was talking about myself."

"Oh. Yes. I'm sorry."

"I know I am not handsome and dashing, and I know I am not blameless and pure. But still, I have come to win you back. Sad, isn't it."

"No. It's not sad. We can try to win our marriage back." She paused, listening to the creaks in the house, the passage of ghosts, perhaps. Suddenly she was very hungry—she couldn't remember eating all day—and began to eat her cold dinner. She said, "I need to know what you expect. That's what I was really talking about."

"And I need to know what you intend," he said.

"Me?"

"When the business assignment is done, I have to return to England. I have bought a house in Manchester. Nothing grand, but it is comfortable. I want you and the children to come back with me."

Edith could not answer; she could only sense the burden of the choice. His decisions were simple: they were just for him. Hers had to count for three people, and those three did not agree. She could trust no one but herself.

"Would it be safe," she asked finally, "if there was war?"

"I believe so. We have our air defenses, a whole new science, if you want to know. But I can't lie to you. I have no faith in the French."

"The boys. Sebastien. He won't want to go. He's at home here. Do you understand that, Edward?"

Edward could only agree, but he could not bring himself to say it out loud.

"Be careful not to be hurt by Sebastien. You musn't expect too much of him all at once."

"I don't."

"Give him time to decide what he wants. There's no reason to throw this all at him right away, is there?"

From behind her, in the hall, she heard a sudden scratching of wind, a breath and a creak. Edward heard it too, and for him it was nothing, just this old house. But Edith knew that it was Sebastien, Sebastien himself out there, prowling for information, guarding himself against betrayal.

—

SEBASTIEN CREPT BACK to his room, stinging with rage. What he had heard made him sick. His mother was coaching his father on how best to lie to him.

This was his reward. This was what his loyalty would win in her heart, more lies and secrets. Sebastien felt he had been listening to her lie since the day he was born: Things are wonderful, don't worry a bit. When he was very young he had figured out that if he wanted the truth, he'd have to go looking for it himself. And what was the one piece of truth he had discovered time after time? That his mother was lying to him.

But okay. If she wanted to be clever, so would he. No reason to lay it all out. He'd be smart. He would stay nimble and would pay out the line an inch or two at a time and see what he caught. That was decided. He could go to bed now, and rest, ignore that scratch at the back of his throat that meant what he really wanted to do was cry; rest, because the man was talking about war, and he would get it; they all would get it.

He awoke the next morning to the sound of his father bellowing into the telephone. The house would be awakened that way often over the coming months, through the winter: Edward shouting down the imperfect tube of the transatlantic telephone cable, talking of schedules, of tolerances met or exceeded, of raw materials and finished assemblies. Sebastien was almost impressed by his father in this new role, giving urgency to the tasks, delegating to others.

Later that morning, as Sebastien was hanging around, keeping his ears open, his father invited him into the study. So this was it, thought Sebastien; this was the first step in something his mother had planned for him. His father closed the door behind them and, with a great deal of effort, tugged out a smudged and rough box from under his desk. Sebastien tried to ignore it, but his father handed him a hammer. "Open it."

Sebastien hefted the hammer in his hand, shrugged, and pried off the top. He stared at the bed of excelsior.

"Take a look. It's something I wanted to show you."

Again Sebastien made sure his father saw his lack of interest, and then parted the wood shavings to bring up a small assembly, spotless, from the rough pebble of its castings to the crystal surface of the machinings.

"Quite something, eh?" said his father.

"What is it?"

"It's part of a landing gear. Something our company makes. Look at the rest."

Sebastien did as he was told, pawed through and pulled up an assortment of machines, bushings, housings, bearings. He paused slightly over one or two, sampled the articulations; he admired them for their weight and shine—there was no reason to deny that. He could hear his father's thoughts: These were the best, impeccable British engineering and manufacturing, good enough for the king.

His father was being clever here, not rushing anything, as his mother had suggested. But when the unpacking was done, and the two of them were sitting looking at bits of excelsior all over the carpet and a pile of cold steel, he could not resist asking Sebastien what he thought of it.

"The Toad says you are making airplanes."

"Well, we're making what goes inside. It's the more important part of it, wouldn't you say? Besides"—he offered a laugh—"I could hardly pack up a Hurricane, now could I?"

Sebastien stood up to go. The place was a mess.

"I thought you would be interested in what we do," said his father. He seemed disappointed, but Sebastien said nothing more.

After lunch a prissy young woman named Sally Baker, "Miss Baker" to everyone, arrived to begin work as the typist. She reminded Sebastien of the English girls who worked as assistants in the store where his mother used to buy her hats; they, like Miss Baker, had perspiration stains and smelled sour. Sebastien gathered that the authorities, in Washington he supposed, had located her for his father; she was a graduate of some business school in Salisbury. She was clumsy and spilled her tea in the kitchen, but when she sat down to work at the typewriter, the whole room shook, the whole house rattled as if sprayed with machine-gun fire. She let everyone know that she had been "cleared," by which she meant that she was allowed to know military secrets, and in days to come she all but refused to speak to the family. Loretta asked her if she was having a busy day, and she answered, "I'm not allowed to say."

"She can just take her tea in the hall," Loretta announced after she left.

In the week after Edward returned, McCready was summoned and arrived at the Mansion House with his bundle of papers and account books under his arm. Ever since McCready had heard Edward was coming home he had been in a condition of feverish activity and dark anxiety. Today, as Sebastien opened the door on him, he was so nervous that he affected a limp. Sebastien could see Mrs. McCready sitting in the truck, looking up at them. Edith came up behind Sebastien and also saw the distress on McCready's face. "Mr. McCready," she said, "what's wrong?"

"Oh, no. Nothing wrong." He held up the bundle. "Business with Mister Edward, if he's in."

He looked so miserable and anxious that she put a hand on his sleeve and said, "But you have done so well with the farm. Edward knows that. He told me himself."

"Yes, ma'am, that's right kind of you to say."

"I shouldn't think you'd have anything to worry about."

"No, ma'am, I ain't worried," he said again, and swallowed hard. She knocked on Edward's office door and opened it briefly to tell him that Mr. McCready was there, and then left. Sebastien and Mr. McCready stood facing each other.

"You don't need to rest here, son," said Mr. McCready. He shifted back and forth on his feet.

Sebastien wandered off into the dining room, but he made no show of pretending to be gone, just lurked a foot or two out of sight. He heard McCready cough once, as if to tell Sebastien he knew he was still there, but Sebastien did not move or make any further sound.

After ten minutes his father's door opened and he called McCready in with a big noise of welcome. Sebastien slunk back into the hall just in time to see McCready disappear, and to see Miss Baker step out, looking quite annoyed. Sebastien moved forward. They knew a little about each other, things about secrets and about their feelings for territory. Miss Baker understood immediately that he wanted to get near the door to hear what he could of this meeting, and she set her mouth, folded her arms, and barred the way. Sebastien wanted to punch her in the face, but he knew she had him in her beady sights. He shrugged and for a second tried to disarm her by whistling. It got him nowhere, and he broke into a scowl. He and Miss Baker faced off like this for a few minutes, and when it became apparent that the meeting in the office was going to take a while, he moved his listening post into the parlor, and she pulled a small chair to where she could keep the guard in better comfort.

When at last the door opened again, Sebastien heard McCready's voice shake with pleasure; when excited, McCready tended to spit a little, and he must have been splattering the walls now, as he thanked Edward and bid a good morning to Miss Baker. It had to be a combine, thought Sebastien, maybe even a baler. His father was rich now and could afford it.

Several times during the fall and winter his father went off in his Buick to Washington, where he stayed for a day or two. Most weeks when he did not make these trips they were visited by tight-lipped American men, who usually stayed for an hour or two, while their drivers sat in the cars with their motors running. Sebastien knew these men had come over on the ferry at first light, hoping no one would take notice of them. He asked one of them straight out if they were from the government—he knew they were; he just wanted to hear how the man would answer—and the man went "ho ho" and tried to patronize him. Sebastien had never seen a worse liar; it struck him that if the Americans were going to get into this war, they'd have to be a whole lot smarter about it than that. His father, with all his rhetorical indirections, his mannerisms and blusters, could weave these guileless bureaucrats like a rug.

So this, Sebastien thought, was war, his father's war—meetings in Maryland, outside the grasp and pry of newspapers and spies. In these very rooms, if Sebastien believed what he had been told by his mother, similar men in different dress had plotted during the American Revolution. Sebastien understood now that his father had come back as much because his masters in England had sent him as for the family, and this insight filled him with some hope. In the absent hours of this ominous twilight, this time once again of waiting, he wondered when his father's masters would reel him in. When that happened, Sebastien knew, his own war would begin.

—

"SO NOW WHAT?" said Bitsy. It was a rainy day in February; 1939 was starting gray and damp. The two women sat down in Bitsy's sunroom with their coffee and Bitsy's cigarettes. The bright yellow linen cushions of this supposedly gay place seemed to be waiting for a happier party in a warmer season.

"Edward thinks there will be fighting by June, July at the latest."

"And?"

"I'll have to go back with him. Before it starts," said Edith.

"You will?"

"You always knew I would."

"I didn't. I always said I thought you should, though now I wish with all my heart that you wouldn't. I was being selfless, to say that."

Bitsy took another cigarette, though one was burning in the ashtray. "He's never asked about you and Tom? You've never had a conversation, you know, make you beg for forgiveness or something? Outpourings of the truth? Promises you can't keep?"

"I think what's happened to him in England is enough for him. I think success has simply filled in enough of the holes in his life."

"And Tom?"

"Tom will do just fine. I don't want to talk about him."

"Men," said Bitsy.

"The problem is," said Edith, "I have two sons. They love each other; one hates their father; the other worships him."

"You're doing the best you can for them now. Sebastien and Simon will have to work out their differences after we're all gone."

"Maybe." It was a comfort to think of the two brothers in years to come. But Bitsy was wrong; Edith didn't have the luxury of the future, just the burdens of the present. "I need to ask a very large favor," she said.

"Of course. What?"

"Sebastien."

"The only favors you've ever asked for concern Sebastien."

This might have been true in the past, but it wasn't now. She was asking as much for Simon as for Sebastien, for herself and

Edward, too. It could all be all right. "I'm not taking Sebastien back to England. I won't force him. He'll be called up, you know. I'm not letting the army get him."

"Then what?"

"The only thing that makes sense is to leave him here. The farm is the only thing he cares about. It's all he wants."

"But he's only sixteen. As far as he's concerned, he'd be happy to move in with Robert, but you can't just leave him at the Retreat."

"No. I want to know if I can leave him with you."

"With me?"

"Of course."

"And . . ."

"And he would finish school, and then he'd be ready for college, and perhaps this war will be over, and perhaps everything will look different. It's just the next year or two that are the problem."

"Lord knows we have room." She waved around the big, empty backdrop of Blaketon, a house built for twenty or thirty souls. "But I'm not sure it's a good idea. What about Frank? I'd think you'd have reservations."

"What do you think? He's your husband."

"Oh, Frank. Frank is Frank. He's unhappy, but he isn't a bad man. If you want to know the truth, I think Sebastien would be a good influence on him."

"I've thought of that."

"But still, Edith. You'd do this? You'd give him up?"

No voice within her argued that it wouldn't break her heart to leave him at the dock, and she knew that it would force Simon to choose between his brother and his father, but she knew what choice Simon would make. This is what it had come to. The four of them could not work; they could not be made to work. The only peace was in three. She had cast lots, and the lot fell on Sebastien, as it had on Jonah. He would dive over the side willingly; he was always leaving, after all. She had always loved him best when she could look at him from afar, which she would now begin to do: a young man ready to be on his own. When he was gone, she would draw Simon close to her side and never let him go.

"I'll do what I have to do," she said to Bitsy finally. "Wouldn't you?"

—

THE AMERICANS WERE all but hopeless—not an ounce of history in their veins, thought Edward. He was sitting at his desk. Miss Baker had left for the day, and he'd taken this moment to enjoy the solitude. She was a dreadful, graceless creature, he thought, not, not like . . . But no. That was over, those English office girls who would type and file throughout the day and then go home and with those same clerks' hands guide their boyfriends' salty penises into their mouths, would turn on all fours for the thrust, all flesh and voice, Here, love, let me help you, yes. English office girls practically yelping like dogs: God, how *dirty* they could be.

No, said Edward to himself. The English girls could still ruin him. That had to be over. He glanced around the room, clearing his mind with the manifestations of work, the papers and machines, the maps that seemed already in flames, cities burning, lowlands mucked with the tracks of tanks. He couldn't blame these Americans, these men so much smarter than he, men who could rest in the smooth course of their uninterrupted careers. These were the men he once envied in England. He could see them in front of him, a line of manikins, faces immovable. They wouldn't remember him—he was just a passing moment of awkwardness for them, as if a "Who was that?" could serve as his epitaph—which would make it all even sweeter, the look of uncomprehending surprise on each face as he went down the line, one at a time, giving each a vigorous knee to the groin.

His moment had arrived with his sure and certain knowledge of what was coming, his epiphany. Saint Paul on the road to Damascus, fresh from his stone-throwing episode, off to martyr a few more dangerous fools, got whacked with the truth. Yes, thought Edward, that was the way it was in religion and in war. A vision: a bird's-eye view of battles not yet fought, the conviction of things not seen. War and religion, same damn thing, really. Edward did not take joy in the future he saw—he sometimes had to remind himself of that, to pause in the full breath of work for at least some kind of reflection—but as long as it was coming, he thanked God that it had come to him.

Edith was off, over there at the Howes'. From the moment the letter had come to him, he had blamed Edith's affair on Bitsy Howe, this husky-voiced and rather loose woman—no one could say that *she* wasn't finding a little extra outside the home. But he had always liked Bitsy, maybe even found her sexy, and he had thought she rather returned the interest. Blaming Bitsy had all the ambiguities of cheating your best friend at cards.

But there was little ambiguity in a note that said your wife was being unfaithful, sent by "a person who values decency." Edward had cried when he read it. Earlier in their marriage he might almost have expected it, with all the admirers Edith attracted. The images of men had burned in him, as he imagined them with Edith, especially in the tender aftermath. When the letter arrived, he was stunned; he let the paper drop from his hands.

After that he had made many plans of revenge and spite, all of them, thankfully, unacted upon, because after several days had gone by, the truth became very simple to him: He didn't want to lose her. He wasn't entirely sure that he wanted her, but a part of him needed her desperately. It was like hunger and thirst—who questioned the need for food and water? So he had waited a month and then called and said, "Edith, I want permission to try to win you back." He had practiced saying it so many times that it came out as if he meant it; and when he said it, he did mean it. There had been silence from the other end, until she said, finally, "I'll tell the boys you're coming."

Edward brought his handkerchief to his forehead. His mission was coming to an end on schedule. Patience was his ally, had been his ally for months and months in the grit of Manchester, where he headed off to work each morning at an hour when he could become friendly with dustmen and lamplighters and spent months in a flat that a monk would consider adequate but drab. His peculiar circumstances had placed him in a position of unique usefulness, and he had done his best. But fomenting a civil war between the executive and legislative branches of the United States Government had never been his plan, certainly not a skill, and in any event, things were just about to overtake him. The conspiracy, as the American papers were beginning to call it, had moved up a notch, and estimable lifelong servants and schemers in both governments were ready to take over. Edward's place was at the works. His sacrifices would be rewarded at the works. The works would save him, his marriage, his family, his sons.

He had asked her to come home with him, and unless he was misreading her, she would come. It was time now to claim his sons, and he knew he was halfway there: Simon, a sweet child, a pretty child, had offered the affections of a child. Sebastien never had; he was always older than that. Edward understood Sebastien, not that either the boy or Edith ever gave him credit for it. He gave him everything his own father had not given him: room and privacy. Things would build between them because, through luck and as a result of war, he was ready and had something to give Sebastien.

Edward remembered taking Sebastien to the works years ago, and, God bless him, he had seen it not as the pathetic little concern it was then but as a place of magic and power. Sebastien gathered sharp spirals of brilliant steel from under the lathes and beamed when he was given a box of defective machinings, of which there were all too many in those days. Sebastien was so proud of being there, the owner's son, that he walked with an odd little stiffness, hardly bending anything, like some sort of beetle. It was the only time that Edward had ever felt anything like love from his older son, and since then, damnit, since then Edward had prayed, against hope and against his own many failings, that he and his son could meet again on that production floor.

And yes. At last, yes. Those prayers had been answered with such abundance that it took Edward's breath away now, sitting at his desk in Maryland; even at such spectacular distance the perfume of his success at the works intoxicated him. Sebastien had behaved about as he expected the day he showed him the machinings he had brought over. It was enough that some of the objects were interesting to Sebastien; he would make a fine engineer. That damn box had caused complaints and curses from porters and cabbies and stewards and customs officials all the way from Manchester, but it was worth it. He had to fist his nails into his palms to keep from saying to Sebastien, You always thought I was a fool, and maybe I was, but look at these things.

Patience. Patience over the days and weeks and months. Edward was dancing for time through this winter, consumed with work, proud of what he was trying to do, proud of his efforts at home, dancing as spring began with its feathery buds on the tulip trees, its warming of the Bay winds, its sputtering and bubbling of the wet soil.

That time was now running out. Neville Chamberlain had brought "peace in our time," and although Edward had known that the man was an imbecile to think it would last, he was also grateful to him, because he had given Edward a chance for his patience to work. But perhaps peace in our time wasn't going to last quite long enough. War was coming, and even the Tories had begun to figure that out, even Chamberlain himself was realizing that it was time to say "Oops." So the question was, to Edward: When would it be time to fold this American operation and get into the bunker?

He had not avoided this subject with Edith, keeping her posted almost daily; there was no reason to spring anything on her. Lately, in fact, she had seemed far less resistant; perhaps patience had done the trick. But April and May were now gone, and the summer was here, and the time had come.

Edith was in the kitchen, talking to Valerie about the rosebushes. Edward waited until they paused and turned to him. "My dear," he said, "could we talk for a moment?"

"Of course. I'll be right in." She went back to her conversation with Valerie and a few minutes later joined him in his office. He asked her to sit down.

"The situation in Europe is falling apart. The time has come. We have to go home."

She considered this; she fiddled with a stray thread on the arm of her chair.

"Should I explain further? Can I give you some information?"

"No," she said. "There's nothing really to explain, is there? We've always known this. They need you and you must go."

"I mean all of us must go." He ran through some of the arguments he had prepared. "We don't have any idea how long it will take. It may be quite a while. And"—he faltered but went on—"I need you. I can't do what I have to do without you."

"I understand, Edward. But what about Sebastien?"

Edward was taken aback by this question. "What about him?" he asked. A sick feeling began to grow from his gut; his ears searched for the sound of a half-understood warning.

"He doesn't want to go."

"Have you talked to him about it?"

"No. But nothing has changed."

"Something has changed, at home, at the works. He's got nothing but opportunity ahead of him, as far as I can see."

"I can't think ahead. I'm just thinking of what would be best for him now."

Edward was beginning to lose patience. "Edith, I really don't think you have a right to say it like that. I am his father, and I'm Simon's father. My decisions have always been made with them in mind."

"Then please consider this." Her tone offered this as something to discuss, but her eyes had the force of an ultimatum. "We'll be ready to go with you, Simon and I will, whenever you say. I'll mourn this place I love, but I think it will be for the best, for all of us."

"Then what about Sebastien?" he bellowed. The boys were at school, but the whole house could hear this phrase explode through the thick doors of the study.

"I want Sebastien to stay here."

He was struck as if shot. "Stay here? Alone?" He was suddenly short of air; the "Alone?" came out as a falsetto cry.

"No. He could live with the Howes at Blaketon. Bitsy and I have discussed it. He could finish his last year of high school, and then we would see what was next."

Edward was struggling to speak. "With Frank Howe? Sebastien?"

"Frank Howe is everything you say, but Bitsy is very strong. It isn't ideal, but it works."

"This is bloody outrageous. I will not have my son living with my enemies. Besides"—Good God, he thought, am I to lose him just now when I can win him back?—"I need him at the works. I've built that whole establishment for him. That is his place in the world, not here. His place is as my son at the works. It's only right."

"His place is here."

"Why?"

"Because he's happy here. Because he takes the family and the birthright you gave him seriously. Doesn't that tell you something?"

"Have you discussed this with him?" The thought that she might have discussed such a thing with Sebastien behind his back was insupportable.

"No," she said, doing everything she could to keep the conversation calm. "I haven't, but I know what he wants. He believes his place is here on the Retreat, running the farm."

"But," he sputtered, "that's not possible."

"It is. Mr. McCready has shown what can be accomplished."

"No. I'm telling you, damnit, it isn't possible."

Edith began to speak again. She had clearly expected these flat refusals; she'd expected loggerheads. She had intended to speak past them, through them to the heart of the thing: what was best for all of them. Edward knew this was how she had planned it. "Of course it's possible. Why wouldn't it be possible?" But then she stopped, and in an instant, Edward could tell she had grasped his meaning. "Edward?" she shouted. "You . . . ?"

"Well, yes. I mean, of course I did. What use is a farm in Maryland to us? McCready wanted it, and he offered a plan that made sense. As God is my witness, Edith, I thought you would be pleased. I treated him very generously, just as you asked me to."

Edward didn't know what she would do next. She was still sitting in the wing chair, but her face was red, her hands were trembling; she suddenly seemed old and frail, but if she had had a pistol in her hand, he thought, she would have shot him.

"Well, it must be undone," she said, after a long pause.

He was baffled; he had forgotten that the issue of Sebastien's staying was what had brought this subject up. "Why are we talking about this? It's done, sealed, recorded in the damn book of deeds.

You have never in the past showed any interest or concern with such matters. It never occurred to me to even ask you about the farm."

"Then we are now living in the *McCreadys'* house?" She put her full astonishment into this question.

"I didn't sell him this *house*. Not the house and our grounds. I kept a hundred bloody acres. Isn't that enough? I always expected that we would visit, after the war. Maybe build a new house in the point field. If the war goes badly, we might need it again."

"You didn't sell my house, but you sold Sebastien's farm? Oh, Edward, you made the wrong choice. Oh, Edward, you've made a terrible choice. How could you do this?"

"How could I know it was so wrong? The boy doesn't speak to me. You told me nothing."

"Did you do this to get back at me?"

"No. Sebastien's place is with me, at the works."

"Is this my punishment?"

"No, no. No," he insisted, but there had to be some rub of truth in what she said; when he had signed McCready's papers, he'd given it an extra flourish, believing that this whole sorry chapter—the cows, Edith's unfaithfulness—was now irretrievably cut out of his life.

Edith got up from the chair. "This is not done, Edward, but no matter what happens, promise me that you will not tell Sebastien that you have sold the farm. You will not tell him."

"Yes. No. Of course. I don't want to hurt him. I love him," he said, as she flowed on past him, liquid almost, flowing to the door. He opened it to follow her, to explain further—though God knew what he could say—but he saw that she had already crossed the hall, and that Valerie was standing there, a dust mop in her hand, and that Edith was falling into her arms.

Oh, how Edward wished that this place had never existed, that it had never been rebuilt after its fire in the eighteen hundreds, that it had fallen in from neglect, or been sold generations ago. If it hadn't been here, they would never have left England in the first place, and as it turned out, in six months' time the long slide would have been over. If only they could have held on for six more months, the good life would have come back, better than before. How these dead Mason faces seemed to mock him. Go to hell, he thought. All of you. This place, not a gift from Miss Mary Mason, but a trap, a spiderweb, a curse, her last spiteful legacy to those that made her what she was.

10

A WEEK HAD gone by. It was almost July. Edward and Edith had barely spoken. In fact, Edward had been in Washington for two days. She could hardly bear to look at Sebastien. She would have no idea what to say to Mr. McCready: Congratulations? Good luck? To Mrs. McCready: Thank you for stealing my son's birthright? Loretta stood by, waiting for orders: Was you wanting to pack up? Mister Simon, he's already done and packed. *Yes*, yes, yes.

Early in the morning, Edith took a few things with her, and put them in the Packard. This ridiculous boat of a car was as conspicuous on land as the *Candide* was on the water, but she didn't care now. Simon was in town, spending the night with his friend Billy. Sebastien was in the fields, his beloved fields, and he would see her drive out, but it would not matter.

She drove through cornfields, past farmyards and pastures, the men all out at work, the women inside cleaning up after breakfast, preparing for lunch, stopping only once or twice to look longingly out the window. She drove through Cookestown, down the hot, dry center of it, past the Texaco, Mitchell's Market, the courthouse, and Lawyer's Row, and then out the other side, back into the farmlands, here and there framed by the bright flash of water in the morning sun. Along the road, buildings were going up: a new dairy barn, a milk plant, an implement dealership, hardly begun but already proudly displaying the red-and-white Farmall insignia. All around her, a land blessed with plenty and privilege was stirring after years of Depression and hundreds of years of somnolence, and young people with ambition were setting out on their own paths to a piece of the promise. It was a nation she saw, a nation, as Roosevelt had been saying, on the move, and it was leaving her and her son Sebastien behind.

She reached Easton at ten and checked into the inn. Here for the theater, Mrs. Mason? the clerk asked, reading her name off the register. Yes, the theater, she said. She took her small bag up to her room, and after the porter had brought coffee, she pulled the curtains and lay down on the bed to wait for Tom. Two days ago, when she had called him, she had told him that Edward had sold the farm. She had been hoping to erase it, had persuaded herself that he might know a smart Baltimore lawyer, someone who could undo the hen scratches of a little old lady, a registrar of deeds, with some clause about families and estates, the consent of the generations. Something like that.

She heard his footsteps in the hall as he hunted for his room number. She heard him thank the porter, as clearly as if he were in the room with her, and then she heard his door close. There was silence for a decorous moment or two. Her heart beat, and she was standing at her door, cracking it, the moment he raised his hand to knock.

"Tom," she whispered. She tugged him through the door. He came through with a startled look. She smelled the exhaust from his car ride, the coffee from his breakfast, the shaving soap from his bath. She pulled away to look up at him, tall and handsome.

"I've missed you," he said.

"So have I," she said. The part of her that loved him hadn't disappeared the day she threw him off the Retreat.

He pulled her over to the bed, and took off his jacket and shoes before they lay down. The springs creaked, and outside, from the porch below, she could hear two elderly women complaining about the rector of their church. She did not resist him. His hands were under her shirt, and they had found the catch on her skirt. She asked herself: Do I really believe that Edward sold the farm to get back at me for this? He took off a piece of his own clothing for each of hers, and the hot flesh folded back into the close, darkened air of this hotel room. His body ran with sweat, hers with points of desire. She remembered what a liquor these feelings were, that whole first sail they took to Chestertown, their first time in the cove, and for this last moment, she was drunk again.

They lay beside each other when they were done. "Was that good?" He always used to ask that; it had become her last pulse of orgasm, to hear him ask, to speak shamelessly about these private ripples.

"Yes," she said. "It has been a long time."

"But with him?"

"Oh, Tom. Yes. With him."

Tom sat up, his bare chest slick in a sliver of light. She stayed on her back, her body oily, under the sheet.

"Well, there it is," he said.

"Tom, please. No bitterness. I can't take it." He turned on his elbow to argue, but she cut him off. "This is good-bye, a better good-bye than the last."

"A month ago I wouldn't have even talked to you on the phone. You didn't have to behave that way to me."

"I know. I'm sorry."

He lay back on the bed. She tried to count the number of times they had been together.

"You know," he said, "that you and Sebastien can stay here. All you have to do is give the word."

"What about Simon? Did you forget about Simon?"

"Of course not. Simon too. I just meant that it's you and Sebastien who have the strongest needs right now."

She fought a sudden rush of rage, hearing him opine about the boys. He could not begin to understand the force a nine-year-old can exert on his mother's life; Tom could not understand the calculus of decision and and consequence, hurt and fear, that was now the only way Edith was making sense of her love for her children. She breathed in and out, to let the anger go. "Simon is the one person in this family who knows exactly what he wants. He wants his father."

He let out a long sigh. "Then it really is over. You're going back to England. The littlest one wins." He pulled his legs from under the sheet and sat at the side of the bed.

What an odd thing sex is, Edith thought, to have induced her to spend so much of her energy and passion on it this past year; to think of what she risked for this physical coupling with someone so young in everything that mattered to her. If she had concentrated more on what mattered, perhaps things would not have gotten where they were. Perhaps she would have poured her energy into letters, making Edward understand that she was not bitter against him anymore, that the Retreat had given her a chance to mend, a chance she had never expected and for which she was grateful; that for the boys, every parental choice could mean a lot, and they better think carefully, together. If she had told Edward the truth and had

not been forced to hide behind the deceptions of a love affair . . .
If they had behaved like parents were supposed to . . .

"Your husband really did it this time. Didn't he?"

"When I look back at what has happened, I can see perfect logic
to it all. If I had been paying attention, I would have seen it coming
in time to prevent it."

"But just to piss it away? Give it to a damn farmer?"

"Edward doesn't attach to places. He doesn't have a clue what
it means, or could mean, to anyone. It's just a farm, a business he
would have failed at. So who else do you sell a farm to but a farmer?
What happens now seems out of our hands, mine and his. It's
slipped away. He believes that as much as I do, no matter how
much remorse he might feel." She put her feet over the bed and
searched around on the floor for her underwear, wishing that this
country inn offered private baths, or a bidet; she did not want to
wash herself from the basin, in front of him. "It's not as if Edward
got so much money for the farm."

"I'm sure not. And not any cash."

"But the Retreat would be quite valuable, to the right person.
The house is sound."

"Perhaps."

"Edward has made it clear that he considers the house mine. If
I sold it, I could buy Sebastien a new farm. Maybe it's silly, but I
have to ask."

He had put on his shirt and tie and was hiking his trousers up
when she said this. He stopped in this ridiculous pose and stared
at her. "Ask what?"

"If your father wants to buy the Retreat. Then he could be a
Mason for real." She gave this a little smile, a hopeless reference
back.

Still holding his trousers around his waist, he began to laugh.

"Why are you laughing at me?"

Her question nearly doubled him over, and he fell heavily back onto the bed to catch his breath. "Haven't you learned anything since you've been here?"

"Stop it, Tom. Don't insult me."

"My father doesn't have any money. He's been selling things off for years. I bought *Candide* from him and he's just about used that up. He's busted, Edith."

Edith's hand, holding her hairbrush, stopped in midair. "That's not possible."

"I told you at the time. He makes a hobby of this."

"But you didn't tell me that he was lying about everything."

"Of all the things he has lied about, money is the least of it."

"It's still wrong. It's all wrong," said Edith; she had once been charmed by Hazelton's game, but that was before she fell victim to it.

They were now clothed and brushed, remade for the outside world. He took her hands, and at long last he was almost tender about it. "It is a silly idea, Edith. Forget it. Sebastien will have to grow up, just the way I did. Do you think my childhood was without surprises and disappointments? He's a smart boy. He'll figure something out."

"I have to go," said Edith. "I have made a terrible mistake coming here."

"Edith—"

"I can see, it's almost funny."

His expression turned; the laugh was gone as soon as she said the word "funny." "Is this why you came here to be with me? To get me to buy the Retreat?"

"No. I wanted to say good-bye."

He shook his head. His disbelief spread through his face; his mouth was open. "I don't believe this," he said. "You came here to screw me so I would buy the place?"

"Don't say that."

"And you tell me my father is a liar? He's never tried to sell his body, Edith." He stood for a few moments, looked at her once more in stunned rage, and was gone.

She pulled into the Retreat about three, went upstairs, took a bath, and went to her sewing room. The air outside sizzled with the locusts, and gulls were crying on the long, flat pan of the water; she breathed into the silence of these sounds, stilling her body.

A confession. Yes, she thought, I must confess. I have sinned. Isn't that what the Catholics say? I have been given a life to do what I can with, and I have failed. I have treated my life with disrespect; I have thrown much of it away. I have wasted so many, many hours. I have failed my children; I have failed my husband, and I have allowed him to fail me. She could hear her sister Rosalie behind these self-accusations: "Mother, Edith lost her hat. She is *so* irresponsible." "Mother, I saw Edith talking to boys today." Edith heard these familiar sounds and she welcomed them. Yes, Rosalie, you always were right, and now we will pay.

The air was cooler now. She still sat in her stiff sidechair, looking out the window. Behind her she felt the presence of all the women who had lived in the Retreat, the Elizabeths and Marys, the stern and bitter hags and the bright, cheerful nymphs. She felt them come up to her as one presence, and she opened herself to it. Let me hear your condemnations, she thought. Have you come to hear my confession? The presence was silent, but it impinged on her forcefully. She felt it did not care about what she might have done— the chapter and verse of her mistakes was not the subject. It did not want to hear her; it wanted to give testimony. We have witnessed so much, it wanted to say to Edith. We have been forced to see the same mistakes over and over again, mistakes of love and hatred. It whispered a message to Edith: Life can all be so simple. Why do the living make things so hard?

—

VALERIE HEARD A different sound from the graves. She heard trouble; she heard voices everywhere. They were in the Retreat, in the scrape of a chair leg and in Loretta's dense pounding on the pastry board. They were in her house on still nights, and in the woods, breathing out of trees. They spoke harshly in the far-off *kraah* of the terns, in the tree-high crackling of the eagles, the death cry to all below; the musical plovers and yellowlegs were silent. She felt eyes from the usual frightened perches, in the hall, at the top of the stairs, at the door of the study, wide-awake and feverish at their watch. She saw them walking, a stray fold of cloth moving across the lawn, or a startled presence warming itself on a cold hearth.

In the fear of the early morning she packed her basket and walked down the Tuckertown lane to Loretta's. There was no light on when she got there. She was worried as she moved through the door, stepping over the sleeping twins on the kitchen floor, past the gruff and startled shout from young Walker's room, down to the end of the hallway. Loretta's huge form was inert under the covers, and Valerie might have already begun a prayer if Loretta had not bolted up on the bed. "Who's that? Who's there?"

"Loretta, what you doing? I declare."

Loretta was still mostly asleep, her eyes darting sightlessly.

"It's me. Loretta, you give me the fright of my life." Valerie was shaking Loretta's heavy round hip and pulling on one of her forearms.

Loretta was finally aware of what was going on. "Here now, girl. You stop on that fussing. You leave off with that." She yanked her arm free and tried to give Valerie a good sharp smack.

"What you doing in bed? I thought you was dead. What you all doing asleep in this house? It's five-thirty already."

"You foolish girl," said Loretta. "It's Sunday. I'm feeling poorly enough to be denied my rest on Sunday." She leaned back heavily. "Oh, Lord, Val. You behaving crazy these days. What's wrong with you?" she asked.

"It's a mess of trouble."

"Concerning who?"

"Mister Edward, Miss Edith. The family."

Loretta gave her a disgusted snort. "Stop that. Mister Edward, he comes and he goes. Ain't much a man to concern ourselves with, now is he? What difference does it make to us? I declare, we put up with Miss Mary Mason for all those years. Now that was trouble. You go back home, Valerie, and don't worry me or yourself about that family no more."

Valerie knew Loretta had a right to these opinions—daughter of slaves, child of the South, raised as handmaid to Miss Mary Mason, as close as the devil had ever come to these parts. Valerie remembered the rejoicing Loretta did on the day Miss Mary died, when she, a girl of ten, had brought the news to Tuckertown.

"The dead is all out and about. I never seen nothing like this before. I seen Robert senior with his ruined face. Next it'll be Miss Mary herself, waiting for one more lick."

Loretta motioned to the door with her head, and though Valerie didn't care a bit about what Walker and Esther said about her, she got up to close it.

"Pray to the Lord to forgive you, honey. This is all in your head."

"No, it ain't."

"Well, you see it your way, if you choose to. But that's for the Masons to contend with. That's the Retreat's concern. You are safe here in Tuckertown; you safe with me." She took Valerie's hand.

"I fear for Miss Edith," said Valerie. "I fear for those boys. Miss Edith and them boys are going to pay for what that family done here, all those centuries."

"It ain't as if they haven't added a sin or two theirselves. Hell, Miss Edith is just a common adulteress, you ask me. If that's what's to be, then that's justice. That's fairly justice. You talk about Robert senior? There's payment due on what Miss Mary done to him. If that happens, it was meant to be."

Valerie shivered. It was cold in this house; she was hardly ever in it, and couldn't remember the last time that she'd been in Loretta's bedroom. Valerie felt too close; there was a dark spot in Loretta's eyes, and she had it fixed on her. "You don't mean that," Valerie answered, hoping to make Loretta look away.

"I surely do. I mean that Miss Edith and those two boys haven't been bad to me, but you never saw what I saw. I'm sixty-two years old and I seen a lifetime of blame. Oh, I'll remember Miss Edith for her good intentions, but I won't forgive her *nothing*." Loretta was shouting. "I won't speak on her Judgment Day. This is Jesus' promise to us colored, that *we* will inherit the earth. I'm sixty-two years old," she repeated, gaining power deep in her breast, "and I am sick to my bones, but I just hope I live to see the day. Ain't no one's sadness going to diminish my joy on that day, you hear me?"

"Mama?" came a voice behind the door. It was young Walker. "You okay?"

"I'm just fine. You go to sleep."

"Can't sleep with you hollering."

Loretta looked over at Valerie and smiled. She whispered, "You tell that grandson of mine that I can't sleep for all their rutting, night after night. Most indecent marriage I ever heard of. Lord. And she's just a few weeks away from delivering."

Valerie turned away. She wouldn't know much about the subject, as Loretta knew; it was an unkind thing for her to say. "Well, then, I'll leave," she said, hurt.

"Honey, you forget about those Masons. I'm awake now, so give

me my privacy for a moment, and then we'll eat and see what the
Reverend Accelyne has in store for us sinners today."

Valerie did what she was told, and the biscuits were good, and
the church was full. She confessed to her faults, gave thanks for
her blessings, and sang as well as she could, which was never very
good. But during the sermon, about the woman at the well, she
realized she was being called to help Miss Edith, and whatever
Loretta said, she was going to try to help her and the boys get back
to England in safety.

In July, just after the Fourth, Sebastien was helping her put back
in the lockup the last pieces of silver and china they had brought
down nearly three years ago. It was hot and breathless in this attic
space—even the mud daubers were just resting inside their burrows,
and the snakes, if they were there, had crawled over to find an
updraft under the eaves. She said to him, "Mister Sebastien, you'll
be ready to leave, early August? That suits you?"

"In all my life I've never wanted to do anything less. You know
that."

"Well?"

"What more is there to say? I'm going to England with my
family. Mother needs me. The Toad needs me. My father wants
to make me chief of the works or something. It's all planned. Who
the hell cares what I want? No one does. No one cares." He stomped
off and left her there, and for a few days what he had said convinced
her that all would go smoothly, that come the beginning of August,
they'd be standing out on the land-side porch, waving good-bye,
and then turning to close up the house for the next long wait.

But she didn't really believe it. Sebastien was going to try something; she could feel it. The signs were there, in his eyes, a kind of
peace that belied the torment he laid claim to; when she looked at
him, she did not see a boy about to do the thing he wanted to do
the least in his whole young life. Mindful of her future judgment,

and to ease possible burdens of her soul, Valerie made one last try in all this, with Robert. She waited for him one evening at the head of his path, and when he approached, she yelled, "I got something to say."

"What you got to say to me?" he asked, his expression cautious.

"It's about Mister Sebastien, is what it is."

The expression didn't change. "Ain't seen him. Been busy with my own affairs."

"Oh, now, Mister Foreman." She called him this to be funny, but she was proud of his new role on the Retreat; everyone was proud of Robert, foreman to the new owner, McCready.

"Valerie, you say your business."

"I always do. Don't have to be invited."

"Then say it. I ain't inviting you, anyway."

"That boy's planning something, and I want to know what it is, and I want you to tell me, over the memory of your dead mama and papa, that you got nothing to do with it."

He thought for a moment, but not long enough for her to suspect he was making up a lie. "I don't know nothing about no plan of his. I don't know what you're talking about."

She changed direction on him. "It ain't the boy I'm concerned about. It's you, you black fool. You get messed up with this and you never going to be clean again."

Robert came back with the question that Valerie, in these weeks, had never asked herself. "Then why you messed with it? Same goes with you. Something goes wrong, and you'll be in as much shit as me."

"Well, I'm trying to stop it," she said.

"Stop it? Hell, a dog knows not to try to stop a truck in the road, don't it? Hell, a damn dog knows that stopping things is where it gets real delicate."

"Okay," she said. She was getting ready to give up. "You keep out of it and I'll keep out of it. That's between us."

He said okay, and she thought that would have to do.

"When they leaving, anyway?"

"Two weeks. Two weeks last Monday."

———

SEBASTIEN KNEW HE had to careful. Especially careful with Valerie, who had been spreading alarms all over the Retreat. He was careful with his mother, in long talks in the afternoon up in her room, telling her that he always knew they would be going back, that he wasn't happy, but that he accepted it. He had seen every dart and bend of her mind played out, and he had met each one. She would realize that others can lie too. She'd thank him for it, because in the end, still, after all she had done to him, he was trying to save her as much as himself. Just as he had many months ago, he had found a small trapdoor in his father's schemes, an escape hatch big enough for a woman and two sons. He had found more than a year of freedom in the letters from Connolly. This time, he believed, they could drop back into a small bit of history, a tiny backwash from all those propellers churning now on the ships and warplanes of England. It was what she would do herself, if she could, he knew that. She would do it herself, if it weren't for Simon.

Sebastien was breathless with the possibilities raised by his father's war. His father had drawn him aside and said he must not say anything to his mother or to Simon, but the sailing on August 3 would almost certainly be the last, and it could be dangerous, but he shouldn't worry, because the *Normandie* was the safest vessel on the sea, faster even than the *Bismarck*, and with any luck the summer passage would be rough, as it often could be, and the U-boats wouldn't stand a chance, even if war had finally come. He had told Sebastien that no matter what happened, they would be on that ship when it sailed on August 3. And now that was only a few days away. Even the moon was cooperating; the French Line had made sure that the *Normandie* would be at sea when the moon was new.

For the past month Robert had been avoiding him. He had hidden himself so completely that Sebastien marveled at the skill of it. They were in one of those slack moments of the farmer's year—the first cutting of hay was in, and the corn was not quite ready. Mr. McCready was spending his time in the shed with his tractor, and with his new purchase, his silage chopper. But where Robert was during these days, Sebastien did not know. He must have been slipping in and out of milking clothed in his own darkness, and however he got to and from his shack, it wasn't by his old route down the lane and into the woods. But he couldn't hide. Sebastien knew where he lived. He'd never been in there, but he'd seen the shack through the trees in winter, a gray form. In the evening, two days to go, two nights left, Sebastien was there when the man got home.

Robert came from behind the shack, and he stopped when he saw Sebastien, stopped dead.

"What you doing here?"

"I've come to say good-bye."

This brought Robert out of the last branches and into the clearing, but Sebastien knew Robert didn't believe him.

"That's it?" asked Robert.

"Why does it have to be anything more?" said Sebastien.

"They's always something more."

Sebastien started to speak but could not go on. Why was Robert treating him this way, avoiding him, secreting himself away? What was Robert hiding? Sebastien was only sixteen, and nonetheless everyone was against him. What had he done? His eyes were stinging and his throat aching. "Why are you being so cruel?" he said finally. "I thought you liked me. All that time we spent together?"

Robert stood where he was, but Sebastien could tell he was feeling his pain.

"Everyone has given up on me," said Sebastien, "but I never thought you would."

"I ain't given up. It's just things in the world."

"What things? That's what I want to know. I want to know what things."

"You. You're a white boy. A man now."

"So what?" he said, trying to understand. "What difference does that make?"

"It makes a lot of difference. You tell me you can't see it." He motioned around the bare mud floor of his yard, the shack.

"That isn't what I mean," Sebastien insisted. "That's money and things like that. There's money on this farm for everyone now, now the Depression is over."

Sebastien could not see the look of pity on Robert's face when he mentioned this.

"I'm not stupid. I see how they treat you. But doesn't it matter that I don't care that you are colored? Just between us?"

"Look, Mister Sebastien. Ain't no problem to me being colored. Ain't nothing for anyone to apologize about. Ain't no damn problem me being who I am. You understand?"

Sebastien stopped. He was beginning to understand, beginning to understand how things might look from Robert's point of view. "I . . ." he said.

Robert's anger left as quickly as it came. "Don't trouble yourself. It's the way of the world. Ain't your fault, that much I know."

"It's the way things used to be. We're going to change it, aren't we? Isn't that what we used to talk about?"

"It was, boy, but maybe we was just passing the long hours in talk. Maybe things is never going to change between white and colored. Besides, you are leaving in a couple of days anyway."

"I'm not."

"What?"

"I'm not. I'm not leaving." There, thought Sebastien. Finally, I've told someone. "I'm not getting on that ship."

"How are you going to do that?"

"Isn't it better that you don't know?"

Robert nodded his head, looked at him with something like gratitude. But he asked, "You going to take care of yourself okay?"

"Ain't anything to it. Don't worry."

"What's that mean?"

"It means that it's simple. If they can't find me the day after tomorrow, my father will have to leave anyway. There's no more time. He has to go back. The government wants him back."

"Your daddy ain't going to leave you here lost. No man would do that."

Sebastien wanted to scream. His father had taken everything away from him all his life, everything that mattered, and now he'd persuaded everyone to trust him. Simon, Mother, Robert. He said, "You are fools if you trust him. He isn't a man; he's a monster."

Robert shrugged. "Okay. Then what?"

"Well, he'll be gone. He said so himself, this is the last ship."

"What about your mama and your brother?"

"If I'm not there, she won't go. She'll have a reason, an excuse." Sebastien saw that there was a grimace crossing Robert's face, very slight, but something there. "What's wrong? My father has to go. He's the only one who has to go."

The cloud on Robert's face darkened; he was struggling.

"What's the problem?" repeated Sebastien.

"Don't do it. You got this all figured out, but things aren't like you think. Hear me, boy. Go back to England with your family. Your daddy's not a bad man, I been telling you this. Forget all this now. Don't do this."

—

IT WAS A simple plan, he recognized that from the start. It was as subtle as Hitler's Panzer Corps; as sure as an ocean liner; as plain as the new moon. Hide for two days: gone the first night, when the family expected to be in a hotel in New York, gone the second, when the *Normandie* sailed with the tide. It would cause no great pain, except for his mother's worry, which might have to be extended a few more days, just to be safe. He didn't expect to be thanked when it was over; he could imagine all manner of punishments, but how bad could they be? He was sixteen. He could be sent to war in a year or two in England. Would his mother prefer that?

At bedtime the next night, Simon wanted to talk about the hotel in New York and the ship and the lovely pastries at tea, which they would take on the Promenade, but Sebastien sent him away angrily, to make sure he went and stayed gone. His room was cluttered with boxes and suitcases, but he got into bed with a hopeful heart. He rehearsed what he needed to do. It would work. He felt the forces drawing his father out of this land, away from this place. The next morning the government—whose, he didn't care—was sending a truck to take the luggage on ahead, to get it on board the *Normandie*. He could hear his father saying, "But if I don't go, our luggage will be lost." "Then you must go," he heard his mother saying. "Go. We shall be fine. Sebastien can't be far. We shall be fine. Go. Go." Sebastien could see the hunger on his father's face. "Oh, well," he heard him say, "if you think it would be better, my dear, perhaps I will just make that sailing after all. Business, of course. Got to build those airplanes for His Majesty. And by the way, I think I shall take that tea set. Fetch a handsome price— American silver is very much prized in England these days."

He heard ten gongs being sounded on the grandfather clock. There was a slight puff and ruffle in the curtains. He dressed, and heard Simon rolling in his bed. The Toad. He had a job in life, to guard Simon, and this was the best way to do it, but he didn't think Simon would thank him. No, this was not a simple plan. There was hurt in it, the hurt of two brothers. "A certain man had two sons," his father had said. Should he give up the whole thing? Was Robert right? It was a glorious August night. In the air there was the promise of wind. He gathered his mackintosh and an extra sweater and slipped down the back stairs, into the kitchen, stopping at the bread cupboard and fruit bins, and then out the door.

He walked out to the end of the dock; behind him, through the dense domed canopy of the Mansion House's trees, he could see a light, a lamp in his father's office. He was all but safe now, and he rowed the dinghy out to Alice's Comet almost careless of the noise. Alice would forgive him for stealing her boat for a day or two. The oars moving through the water sent back swirls of phosphorescence, produced by tiny, ancient creatures that make their own light even when darkness is on the face of the deep. He was more mindful when he came alongside the Comet, because the thud of two boats colliding was a sound that would travel.

He rigged the boat in the dark with no trouble; he had practiced this many times during the summer, doing it with his eyes closed. Just as Tom Hazelton had said, he had sailed with his eyes closed. The canvas came alive once released, and the flapping worried him. He grabbed the sheet and then the tiller, sat, took a very deep breath, and cast off.

He let the boat fall off. He was moving slowly and silently and could measure his progress only by the slight rearrangement of the large shapes on the land. The light from the house flickered in and out of the leaves. He did not need to say good-bye to this beloved landscape; he'd sail back in with the full celebration of daylight, probably accompanied by a launch or two, because there was no question they would have been out looking for him, and when they got close to the Retreat, the launches would blow their sharp whistles, like the tugs in New York Harbor, and his mother and Simon and perhaps Valerie would be on the dock in an instant, and his mother would be wearing the most angry, the most tearfully furious and grateful look he had ever seen in his life.

As he rounded the point, the river's evening winds hit him, and they were good and fresh, everything he could have hoped for, but they chilled him to the bone. He already had his sweater on, but he was shivering. The cold was inexplicable to him. As the wind drove at him, his hands were so cold that they couldn't grip the tiller, and the sheet payed out painfully through his palm, and in the cutting wind he heard voices and a single cry in them, his mother's voice, a cry from the dock, a scream. The boat now seemed to him foreign and displaced on the water, graceless as it took the swells broadside, a wreck.

Sebastien made a lunge for the tiller and brought the boat back on course. The terror was past. The voice couldn't have been his mother's—he was well upwind of the dock; it was the air in the rigging, the old siren's call that used to plague frightened sailors. He looked around, took his bearings again from the dark shapes visible in the moonless night: the pecan trees at the Retreat, the open cornfields of Blaketon, the deep void of the rivermouth. He was surprised that he had fallen off so far, that his momentary lapse seemed to have lasted so long, but no harm was done; in fact, as he felt the warmth of the August night breathe on him again, he thought it was good that it had happened now rather than later.

What he had to do was all very clear, and this fresh wind would make it possible. Tonight he had to get all the way across the rivermouth, up the bight to Love Point, and around the point into the Bay itself. He had never before made it that far, but he had never had enough time to do it. Time was his now. His father's tight clock ticked, each second measured, but Sebastien's time was now boundless. He had to get around Love Point and then fall off due south into a dead run. He had a chart—stowed forward with his food, his clothes, his water jugs, and Alice's life preserver—but he doubted he'd have to unroll it. The shapes and thrusts of this careless shoreline were his friends, and when he needed to find shelter in them, he'd be guided by the faint hollowing of the dawn.

Sebastien was surprised by the night. He realized he had imagined that, new moon or not, once he was out far from the shadows of the trees, out onto the unobstructed reception of open water, there would always be light of some sort, the illumination of the sea, a luminous secret. But he had to strain so hard to find his landmarks that his vision was thrown off by bright flashes, as if he had been pressing his palms hard against his eyes. His cover was complete, had come in behind him like a veil, but it was also in front of him. He had no sense of distance out here, and once, as he neared the shores of Hail Point, he jibed in a panic, thinking he was only a few feet from land. Once around, he looked forward and saw that the opposite shore seemed not much farther away, although he knew it must be about three miles. Sounds didn't help either; the lapping of waves on the shore, an occasional rustle of rockfish and rays, or small beasts in the grass, these sounds came from everywhere and nowhere.

He was completely alone, more alone than ever in his life. He told himself that this was what he wanted, but the reassurances sounded a little false. Perhaps when he got back he would make more effort to be popular at school, more like Simon. The girls could like him, as Alice did. Alice was the only girl Sebastien had ever spoken his mind to, in this very boat, and he had missed her this summer—she was spending it in Connecticut—and would miss her in the fall when she went off to college in Massachusetts. He'd have to meet some other girls, talk to them. Maybe he'd bring Simon along as his entrée, because the high school girls thought

Simon was cute; they patted his red hair and asked him to say things so they could copy his English accent. No one had ever treated Sebastien like that, no one.

Sebastien guessed it was about midnight. His head bobbed up and down a little until he forced himself to stretch, to splash hot brackish Bay water into his face. There was nothing to hit way out here in the middle of the channel, but falling asleep would be dangerous in these strong breezes, and he kept himself alert with visions of capsizing into the black water, into the jellyfish, which were unusually numerous that year. He took the precaution of going forward and grabbing Alice's life preserver, with its confusing tangle of canvas straps and brass buckles, and resting it at his side.

He was lost in memory for a long time, voices speaking to him, pleasant in their music, sufficient to keep him mostly awake, and to fuel his way down the bight. As he passed Hail Point he was surprised to see it flatten; he'd always thought it was round, like a ball on the end of a string. Now he looked back and couldn't make it out at all. He was not worried, because there were faint lights coming from the drawbridge over Kent Narrows, and ahead, slowly making itself known to him, the Love Point beacon was waiting.

There was no question that the swell was building; the Bay was his ocean, not his creek, and it was broad and deep. His breath quickened; he cast around in the boat, as best he could, to make sure everything was ready. The beacon was getting nearer; maybe the new sound he was hearing was the pounding of waves on the rock piles. Sebastien had not expected this, the feeling that once he left the river he would leave what was known and secure and enter into danger. He headed into the wind and went forward for the flashlight and the chart, and when he returned to the helm, he unrolled it, trembling. The chart told him nothing, gave him no burst of insight; it was the same old chart, with its benign colors and picturesque place-names. He cast it aside, and when he turned off the flashlight he realized he was completely blind, helpless as a blind man in the middle of a street, sailing completely blind. He fell off from the sounds ahead of him, and clamped his eyes shut to clear them, but instead he was met by those familiar, now mortally dangerous flashes. He opened his eyes and waited, and though his night vision came back, it was as if he had sailed across a boundary and had now lost his way. The dark shore of Kent Island was to his left, but it was a hard and hostile line, not the feathery and forgiving fingers of marsh and grass he had expected.

He was sailing into the Bay. The wind and the swell were weather that he had never before experienced in this boat. He knew he must come about, but the thought panicked him. He'd lose the mast in such wind, he thought. He'd known this feeling before; it was something all sailors had experienced, momentarily afraid to take on the full belly of the wind. The sheet was beginning to burn his palm. He was heading right into the Bay now, and soon the swells began to come over the bow, to wash him, to clean him. His mind was telling him to stay with the boat, whatever happened, stay with the boat, and he was sitting absolutely fixed, rigid as one of Simon's knights of Agincourt, ready, like them, to be felled in battle, helpless to raise a hand to cushion the fall. The boat was swamped now, and he could feel the slap of jellyfish on his face and arms, though not their sting; as the boat slowed, Sebastien was thinking maybe this was what was going to happen, maybe this was his sheltered port, a waterlogged hulk, but the waves were rolling over him and one knocked the tiller out of his hand. He was going over the side. He grabbed for the life preserver and found a strap before he was in the water and the boat was gone.

—

In the Mansion House, everyone was asleep. Simon's head was stretched back, his mouth open to the air. Edith was curled around a pillow, her nightgown twisted by her movements. Edward was flat on his back, snoring, the sharp points of his mustache moving as he breathed. At the farm, the McCreadys were asleep, both of them content in their good fortune, the riches in their future. In Tuckertown, Loretta and Valerie were asleep. Only Robert was still awake, fretful and frightened, tossing on his cot, wet in the humid night.

—

SEBASTIEN GASPED FOR air, spitting out the Bay water only to have his mouth filled again. He struggled with the life preserver straps, knifing his feet to stay afloat and to free them from the tangle. He'd lost the boat, but if he could only get this life preserver in his arms, and stop screaming, he could think. He kept that idea in mind, and soon he had the life preserver at his chest, and he had stopped panting through his mouth and was taking in air through his nose; the jellyfish stings were all over him now, but the wind was calmer at the water's surface, and his legs stopped thrashing and began to pump with more rhythm.

He was a speck of sand in the sea. Okay, he said to himself. Okay. Okay. That wasn't very smart. That was stupid. That was unspeakably stupid. He rose and fell with the waves. How could these swells have scared him so? How were they sufficient to swamp the boat? It was almost embarrassing to think of it. Where was he now? He pictured his chart and believed that he identified the spot, about a mile into the Bay. He was calm and quite in control. The lucidity of his reasoning, now that it couldn't do him much good, was a cruel pass, but he'd take it, he'd swim on it.

He floated. It was perhaps two in the morning. He expected first light around five. The crabbers and clam diggers would be out well before that, but not this far out in deep water. The launches and the marine police would come looking for him by ten, he'd assumed.

By then his mother would have gone into his bedroom to remind him that this was the day, the day they were going back to England. She would see his bed empty and think it not particularly odd, quite normal really, that he'd gone out on a last solitary prowl. But then, absently stripping his bed and gathering his clothes, she would glance out the window, and something about what she saw would turn her to ice, and by the time she realized that what she had seen was an empty mooring, she would be running for help.

Sebastien was still figuring the plan. Say he wasn't found until nine, would his father have left by then? He was starting to think not. His father would not leave him here to drown, would he? Just for a war, leave him here? Would he? Father, would you? There was something wrong here, very, very wrong. The plan—could it have missed something? His father would not leave him to drown, but how was he supposed to know the difference between his son safely and stealthily hidden in the cordgrass, and his son alone on the sea?

A wavetop hit him; another. He was as low to the surface of the earth as anyone had ever been, the last peek lifeward before he was lowered. Oh, my God, he thought, it's true, I'm sinking. The life preserver was getting heavier; it was becoming a stone. He knew he couldn't panic. Time had passed, maybe a lot of time, maybe enough. It happened that way, he'd read—the long wait for salvation could really go by in a flash; it wasn't time as it could be measured by his father's watch. Maybe he'd been in the water quite a long time, four or five hours. It could be. Maybe it had taken that long for the life preserver to begin losing buoyancy, and at that rate, he'd still get some help from it for several more hours. Where was the dawn? He crabbed himself in an arc but saw no lightening of the sky. He was too low, he thought; up there, maybe it was springtime.

He started to cry. He wanted his mother and his father. He

wanted them to love him and be true to him. He wanted his Toad. Oh, his sweet, sweet, sweet brother. He was crying out in the middle of the sea, pushing the wet life preserver farther down, trying to balance on it like a saddle, but there was no horse to ride.

He cried for a long time, so long that now there was faint color in the east. Yes, he saw it, and it filled him with hope. Joy, actually. The sea around him was calm now, the night blow had gone out to sea. It was calm, quite flat, almost glassy. Oh, you Chesapeake, he thought, this is more like you, flat and oily, with the laziness of a drowned river valley. Those slack doldrums, those sailing trips that end with such exhausted calm, the endless trip home through the shimmer. Yes, thought Sebastien, this is what I was waiting for.

Then he saw a boat, an old sailboat about the size of the Comet. It was making its unhurried way toward him, and there was a man, or a boy, in it. In fact, it was a boy who looked quite like him— thin face, sharp jaw, sandy hair. He could be my twin, thought Sebastien, now riding quite comfortably. The life preserver felt like a cushion of air. The boat came over, and the sailor called out, "Do you like to sail? I love sailing. My sister makes fun of me, but I love to sail."

Sebastien, or what was left of him, of the boy, tried to think of the right answer.

"I often sail. Aren't you getting tired of swimming? You're quite far out, you know."

Sebastien knew that he was all the way out.

"Here." The boy in the boat leaned forward, arm outstretched. "Take a rest, anyway. Drop that preserver and take my hand."

—

IN HER HOUSE, Valerie came bolt up off her pillow and started to scream. Edith reached sleepily for her clock. In Germany, the armies were silent. As Mr. McCready shaved, he reminded himself with pride that when Mister Edward left, he would have in his pocket the first quarterly payment on the mortgage, two weeks early. In the shack, Robert was now finally asleep, sleeping past the dawn, as if drugged.

———

ROBERT WAS AWAKENED by a small shout from outside, almost like the cry of a bird. What time is it? he wondered. There was another shout from outside—definitely a person, a child. Robert got up to look out the window and saw that it was Simon out there, shouting at the shack. He quickly pulled on his pants and walked out to the porch.

"See?" yelled Simon. "See what you did?"

"What?" asked Robert. "What you talking about, Mister Simon. What you doing here at this hour?"

"See. I told you. Sebastien's gone. He's taken the boat. It's your fault. It's all your fault."

Robert knew the trouble had come now, to him. "Where?"

"I don't know where. None of us do. But it's your fault. You told mean stories about my father. You made him do this. I know you did."

"I didn't do nothing. You wait. I'll take you home."

"No! I'm not going anywhere with you. They're out looking for him now. You did this. I know you did." The boy yelled this one last time and then ran off through the woods. Robert stood on his porch, still sleepy, but there was not one single shred of doubt in his mind what had to happen next. He had to get out of there. Whatever good or ill came to Sebastien, sooner or later they'd come for him, and, oh, Lord, they would string him up. They would string him up for any misfortune of their own making—they always had, they always would. They would string him up for running, if he was caught, and they would string him up for staying, if he was dumb enough to try it. Matt Williams, George Armwood, Euel Lee, they'd all been dumb enough to stick around long enough to get caught, and look what it got them—what was left of George Armwood, when they cut him down, didn't even look human.

Robert got dressed, laced up his boots, grabbed his rifle, and headed out the back window. He ran a hundred yards, his legs instantly bloodied by the bramble, crouched down, and waited for his panting to stop. There was rustling in the woods but no tramping of human feet. He moved off another hundred yards, farther away from the farm, and paused again. Still no pursuit. They would string him up, for telling, or for not telling. Always had been this way and always would, just for talking with the boy, just for spending time with him. Did he really think Sebastien would go through with it, whatever the plan was?

No. He'd go hide and then get scared and come back. That's really what Robert had thought, or hoped, would happen. He moved again, just a few more feet, and thought he was safe there, unless someone brought dogs. Which they would, but not yet, not for a good while yet. What was he going to do? Where was he going to go?

He heard movement in the woods, off toward his shack. He crouched down, and sure enough, it was footsteps he heard, a man's. He listened. The man called his name, the call broken like static through the branches. It was McCready. "Robert?" he called. "You in there, boy?" Robert was breathing hard and he was trying to make out what the tone was. "You better come out, if you are there," McCready yelled. Was it an order or a warning? Was it really "better" for him to come out? Better for who? Robert couldn't tell. "Robert," McCready yelled one last time, and Robert was almost ready to answer, because McCready had always been fair to him, and McCready knew the truth. But Robert didn't answer just the same, because he wasn't sure, and if he had learned one thing in his thirty-nine years, it was this: If you ain't sure what a white person intends, then keep your head down.

So he kept his head down through the day, mostly right where he was sitting, close enough to keep informed but a good enough head start if he had to run. About midday he cut through the woods to where the pines thinned out into the scrub oaks and water elms. He looked across the water, and there were a couple of boats out, a workboat and a launch, and they were splitting the river crossways. It was a sight that chilled him. Sweet Lord, he thought, I let this happen. Maybe all he would have had to do was tell Sebastien that he didn't have a farm to come home to anymore, just a big old empty Mansion House, cut off from the land, no reason in the world left for it to be there, and no reason for anyone to live in it. They all knew they weren't supposed to tell Sebastien the farm had been sold. McCready had made that clear to Robert, and Robert had felt for the man then, because his face was screwed up tight with guilt, like he'd stolen it from Sebastien or something, like it wasn't hard work that had made the place his, but a trick. Robert could tell that wasn't the first time McCready had faced this thought. Robert knew if it was just up to him, McCready would have been happy enough to go on as before, but it wasn't just up to him: it was Mrs. McCready wanted ownership, wanted the Masons out of her hair, would do anything to raise enough trouble to make it happen.

He listened for traffic on the road, the sound of that Buick. He wondered if Mister Edward had left, gone back to fight his war. He couldn't imagine it, but Sebastien could have been right. Robert had always believed what he'd learned in France, that these people love their wars more than life, more than their sons, whom they gave up readily enough. Those English boys in France, they died yelling for their daddies, their duty, and their privilege, not for their mamas, not for sweetness and love; they died telling their daddies how good they done, going over the top, getting maybe ten feet on their way before a Betsy blew out their guts.

At nightfall Robert made his move. Both me and Sebastien, he thought, hiding out by day, getting ready to move with the sunset. He walked for a mile, and then judged it was time to head south, and just about when he expected to, he saw the road. He made a run across it and caught the faint lights of Tuckertown—first Loretta's, then the Shaw place, lived in now by someone he didn't know, then the Goulds' and then the Gales'. The house was quiet. He didn't know what room Valerie slept in, so he trusted necessity and tapped on the first window; a baby let out a muffled sigh. He went to the next. He tapped. Someone stirred and came to the window, raised the shade. He saw the white nightgown, and then the face; she didn't have her glasses on, but in the darkness she always saw best anyway.

"Valerie," he whispered.

"Robert? Is that you?"

"It's me."

"Where you been? Sweet Lord, where have you been?"

"Are they hunting for me?"

"Come round to the door. Quiet."

He crept up onto the back stoop and she let him in, took hold of his arm, and pulled him to her room. It smelled of violets. She closed the door with just the tick of the latch and motioned him to sit on the bed. He took a place as near the foot as he could, and she leaned against the headboard. "I been hiding. Did they find him?" he asked.

"No." Her voice was worried. She told him that Miss Edith was frantic for a few minutes, then so cold and composed it frightened her, then frantic again. Mister Edward had been on his telephones all day, now to England, now to New York, to the police, to other families that had motor launches, to Annapolis.

"Are they looking for me?"

She didn't answer right away. "You done a fool thing to hide, Robert."

"What could I do? What chance did I have?"

Again she didn't answer, and this time, she didn't need to. "Did you know about this?"

He had planned to deny it, but he couldn't with her. "Could I stop him?" he asked. "Was telling someone going to help him? Lord, Valerie, how could I stop him? He wasn't listening to reason. He would have gone whatever I said."

"Stop now," she said. "Don't trouble yourself anymore. It ain't your concern."

"What am I going to do?"

"You'll stay here, and tomorrow we'll talk to Mr. McCready."

"Oh, Lord . . ."

She reached the length of her bed to touch him, and he stopped. He could feel the sweat still pouring out of his body, as it had been in the hot thrash of his early morning; even before Simon woke him, he'd been pouring out his body in fear.

She pulled him, pulled him to her side, ran her hands through his hair, rubbed his neck and his back. Her fingers were like silk, but firm. She began to undo the buttons of his shirt, and he took hold of her hand, but she shook free of his grip and finished with his shirt. It fell damply to the floor. She left the room for a few minutes, and came back with a basin full of warm water and a washcloth, and she told him to strip the rest of the way. She gave him a clump of mint to chew, and positioned him in the center of her room; she bathed him in the darkness, as if to wipe off the fear of the white men, the scent for their dogs. She turned him so he faced the mirror, though there was barely enough light to make out their shadowy figures, and came up behind him, toweling his back almost raw. She dropped the towel and began to rub, pressing her fingers into the rock-tense muscles of his neck and shoulders.

"Relax," she said. He dropped his arms, let the weight of his hands pull them to rest. "That's better," she said.

He looked around her room, at her chair, with tomorrow's dress neatly laid out, underwear on top, at her dresser top, with its linen runner, a small china jar, a few snapshots poked into the mirror frame above. Her Bible was on her bedstand. He smelled the new purity of his own body, and the fragrance of hers, her fresh breath, the flowers in the room, and the clean pitch of spruce.

He turned, and she backed onto the bed, pulling her nightgown over her head. In the dim light he could see the shine of her skin, her body outlined against the white sheet, the flat of her stomach, the dense curl of her pubic hair. He wondered for a moment if she'd ever seen a man erect before; people didn't think so, but Valerie had her secrets, Valerie had always had her secrets. She lay back for him and he joined her, kissed her, her ears, her nipples, her stomach. Too soon, she was guiding him into her, and he didn't want this to end, but still, he wasn't going to fight her. He wondered if there would be resistance from her hymen, but nothing stood in the way, just a long smooth ride. He was on his arms, looking down at her, beautiful Valerie, the offerings of her soul. She rocked her hips to get him going, and it didn't take much, for him, because this lovemaking had always been in the dawn for him, far out of reach until he had the strength and wisdom to want it.

He lay beside her. Up and down Tuckertown, the families were sleeping, through the dark of this moonless night. He had come home to Tuckertown. In the morning, the songbirds were singing.

11

SIMON WAS VERY quiet. He sat in the kitchen with his hands under his thighs and said "Yes, thank you" and "No, thank you" when Loretta asked him if he wanted things. He thought he might go for a walk, go down to the stable and feed his rabbits, but then decided he would not.

In the house there was a lot going on. Men had been coming in and out since yesterday morning, and he recognized some of them: Mr. Howe; his friend Billy's father; Mr. Cooke. There had been lots of boats at the dock, big ones, with cabins; one of them had run aground on the sandbar, and several other boats were trying to pull it off. Mrs. Howe was with Mother. Sebastien was in a lot of trouble. He wondered what Loretta meant when she said something about "tanning his hide." Maybe it was something the police would do. They had been in and out, and his mother brought two of them into the kitchen, and he recognized one of them because he stood outside the school at the end of the day. Simon said "Hey" to the policeman, as all his friends did. The police asked him where Sebastien was, and he told them the truth: He didn't know, but Robert did. They asked him where Robert was, and he said he didn't know; he was at his house yesterday morning. Robert was very wicked. Today Valerie had not come in. She must be out looking for Robert.

He heard a car leaving, and it was Mrs. Howe going out. He was sitting in a good place to see everything. Earlier, the truck had come back with their luggage. The driver looked mad. Simon sat. His mother came in. She looked very frightened but she tried to smile when she asked how he was doing.

"Fine," he said.

"Don't worry," she said.

His mother had been telling him not to worry all his life, and it had been easy to tell her that he wouldn't, until now. He felt strange all through his body, which was why it seemed better just to sit where he was, very quietly, not moving a muscle.

His rear end was beginning to get sore, and he was about to move when he heard a truck coming in. He looked, and it was Mr. McCready: the black flare of his pickup fender, the yelp of his dogs, the rattle of the chains that were always tied around the tow hitch. There were two other people with him. It was Valerie and Robert that got out. He didn't know why Robert had behaved so wickedly, but now his father was going to punish him, which might help to make everything all right. After his father punished Robert, Sebastien would come home.

Loretta saw Robert get out of the car and she started to cry. "Oh, land, oh, Lord, oh, sweet mercy," she said. "Please. Please."

Simon went into the butler's pantry and cracked the door. One of the policemen was still there, and his father came out of his office, and the five grown-ups met in the hall. Robert looked very frightened, and Valerie had her hand on him to make sure he didn't run away. His mother saw him and said—well, she shouted it quite loudly—"How could you? How could you let this happen to him? How could you be so cruel to me?" Soon the policeman would put handcuffs on Robert, Simon guessed. All of them went into his father's office, and Miss Baker came out. She sat on a chair and lit a cigarette, and then, because she thought no one was watching, she picked her nose. Simon watched and watched, and his legs started to get tired. He squatted down on the floor, keeping the swinging door open with his cheek, his breath misting the varnish.

At last the office door opened wide and they all came out. The policeman had not put cuffs on Robert, but he did have a hand on Robert's shoulder. They went out the front door, and Simon ran back to his window in time to see Robert and Mr. McCready get into the police car. He wondered why they were arresting Mr. McCready also.

Valerie came into the kitchen and went straight for Loretta, who was clutching a dish towel, wringing it like wash, her black hands weaving a pattern in the white linen. Valerie whispered into Loretta's ear for a long time, and Simon watched her face, which still showed terror, but she was nodding back to what Valerie said to her, and her hands stopped working on the towel. Valerie backed off now, still touching Loretta, and Simon heard her say, "It's all right now."

Simon said, "Is Sebastien found?"

For the first time, Valerie took notice of him. "No, honey," she said. "It ain't that, it's . . ."

"But he will be soon?"

She left Loretta and came to him. "We pray that he will, is all we can do." She said this, but Simon heard the doubt in her voice. He went back to his seat and watched the comings and goings, listened to Mr. McCready's dogs, the interrupted buzz of the locusts, the closing and opening of doors, the bellow and bustle of the cows out in the pasture. The women gave him lunch, and he wasn't hungry but he ate a little. He must not be rude. The time passed. From somewhere across the water he heard the sharp smack of a rifle shot, and the answering blast of an air horn.

He wandered out into the hall. The luggage was still sitting in the vestibule—the trunks and footlockers, Sebastien's cases, his clothes. Simon looked down the other end of the hall, toward the porch and the water, and saw his mother standing there at the edge of the tile, beside the white columns, staring outward. A vine kept falling into her face, but she did not move; she simply brushed it away, and it worked back, and she brushed it away again. She was holding her arms in front of her, as if cradling a baby.

Simon went up to his room, which had been stripped for the departure that now must be put off because of the bad thing Sebastien had done. Simon did not remember very clearly the night that they arrived, he recalled only this bare feeling, only the musty smell of the place, the damp feel of the blankets, the flicker of the candles. At the time, he had thought they were just going to be spending a night in this place, that this was just a place they had borrowed on the way to Maryland. No one had told him that this was the Retreat. Maryland, he had decided beforehand, would have cactus and horses and water you couldn't drink. It was a day or two before he figured out the truth, that this ordinary place, with its ordinary peeling wallpaper and ordinary overgrown garden, was Maryland.

Suddenly, downstairs, there was motion. His father shouted and shouted; doors slammed and people ran. His mother began a stammering cry, something like an animal's. Simon heard the scrape of feet on the cement stoop right below him, the stairs off the porch toward the water. His father was running now across the lawn, down toward the water, the dock, running. Simon had never seen his father run before, clutching his waistcoat as his watch chain flew wide. Simon glanced ahead of his father, and there he was, Sebastien, in Mr. Howe's arms, and he was sleeping. He'd been gone for two nights, so he must be very sleepy. Simon thought his mother should be quiet. Shhh, he thought. Mr. Howe handed Sebastien to his father, and his father took him gently, so as not to wake him, and he came back up the lawn with him. Sebastien's head was back, and his clothes were wet. His mother screamed once and then was silent. Simon heard his father come in, and soon he was climbing the stairs, step, step, step, going right past his door, into Sebastien's room. Simon heard the bedsprings creak, and a small rustling of bedclothes, and he stood rigid in the middle of his room, and when his mother came through Sebastien's door to get him, he knew his brother was dead and he started to wail.

—

SIMON STAYED VERY close to his father's side during the last days on the Retreat. He stood beside him at the funeral and at the graveside, and though it was his mother's caresses that sent him to sleep at night, in the morning, when he awoke, it was his father he looked for first. He was with his father when he made the final announcement to Loretta and Valerie that the family would be leaving on August 29 and did not know when they would be returning. Simon sat with his father in the office while he made his telephone calls. He listened to his father discuss things with the works, and with the British consulate in New York, which was arranging their passage. They seemed to be upset that his father insisted on making the passage on the *Normandie*. "There is a British ship, the Cunarder *Aquitania*, due to leave at about the same time," his father explained after he hung up. "They're worried about what the French will do."

"Aren't they are our allies?" asked Simon.

"Indeed."

But Simon knew his father didn't like the French, so he decided that the reason they were going on the *Normandie* was that his father preferred the food. Simon remembered the sweet rolls and petits fours. Why hadn't Sebastien liked them as much as he did? Why hadn't Sebastien been happier? Simon had thought the *Normandie* was beautiful, except for the governess in the nursery.

He was at his father's side when they took their last walk to the farm. Simon watched carefully when his father shook hands with Robert; he had been hiding in the equipment shed, but McCready made him come out. Simon watched, and he could see the fear in Robert's eyes but could see nothing in his father's, or in his father's voice. As they walked back to the Mansion House he asked his father why he had shaken hands with Robert. "Because we cannot hold him to blame for anything," said Edward, but Simon wasn't sure. Maybe Robert should have stayed with his own people and not let Sebastien play with him. That's what everyone had been saying for years: Loretta, Mrs. McCready. So why didn't Robert listen?

In town, people on the street stopped, and some of his friends from school talked to him, but they were scared and didn't really want him to come play. People asked his father what would happen to the Retreat, to the Mansion House, and he said that it would be maintained in good repair, that it would not be allowed to fall as low as it had after Miss Mary died. "Hard to keep up when it isn't lived in" was what the grocer said. "Down here the weather and the critters undo man's work right easily." The stone of the graves and the sand of the beaches, the lumps of soil, that was about all there was that lasted.

On the last morning, Simon woke up early, listened to the locusts, already winding themselves up for the day. When he got downstairs, the luggage truck was waiting and packed, and his parents were gathering the last items. His father took his tea in his office. The walls were bare; even the maps, with their notations and marks, had been burned. The telephones were disconnected.

Simon finished his eggs, and he let himself be hugged and kissed by the women. Loretta was crying. His mother came in and got him, and then she and the women kissed and cried, and then his father came in to get everyone, and he did not cry, but offered his one arm to Edith and one arm to Simon. They walked out like this, banging awkwardly on the butler's pantry door, and Simon let go of his father's arm in order to follow. He liked seeing his father and mother arm in arm; he hoped he would see them do this more.

His father drove the Buick with his mother beside him, and Simon sat in the back, quietly saying good-bye to the buildings of Simontown, to the last view of Mason Creek, and then to the last distant treetop of the Retreat as they drove off the Neck and out onto the highway. His mother did not turn around, but he could see his father's eyes searching in the rearview mirror. They stopped at St. Paul's to visit Sebastien's grave, a mound already settled somewhat and clothed with the first shoots of new grass. They got back into the car and drove north, away from the rivers and creeks of the Chesapeake, across the flat, plowed country of inland Maryland and Delaware. They crossed the Chesapeake and Delaware Canal, and then the Delaware River, and they were in New Jersey, where the land suddenly began to roll somewhat, because it was more permanent, not a peninsula made of sand and eaten by the tides. They worked slowly north, and by early evening they were entering New York, and in the constant daylight of the city they arrived at their hotel. A man from the consulate, Mr. Boynton, was waiting for them.

"What news?" said Edward.

"None."

"Poland?"

"Not yet. Tomorrow, perhaps. The situation is very tense."

"The ship?"

"The *Aquitania* is scheduled to cast off at two. I understand the *Bremen* is also planning to leave early. It's an extraordinary situation. We would all feel so much better if you were on the *Aquitania*. There are rumors that the Collector of the Port will search all three ships. It could be quite a madhouse. Your dinner is waiting in your room," he said to the family. "Get some sleep, if you don't mind my suggesting it. It could be a very long day for Mrs. Mason and Simon."

"Don't worry about us," said his mother. "We will be ready."

The hotel was very full, and they were all put into one room, with Simon on a couch and his parents together in a double bed. Simon had never seen them lying in the same bed before. He heard his mother sigh and his father cough, and the three of them lay back in the hushed shout of the traffic below, their first night back in the world.

Mr. Boynton was waiting for them with a cab in the morning. Simon didn't know what had happened to the Buick and decided it was being driven back to the Retreat, to be put up on blocks beside Miss Mary's Packard. It was a hot day, and the air tasted of exhaust, and as they approached the piers, Simon could hear the tension in the voices, the angry shouts of men and women. Rising out of the crowds were the bows of three ships, each of them still and steadied by long, draping ropes. Simon heard people speaking German as they passed the entrances to the North German Lloyd piers. At the head of the Cunard White Star piers, he heard the English conversations, with their restrained trip and flutter, and he knew that he no longer talked like that. At last the cab stopped. Outside, French people were shouting at each other; a woman was shoving a man forward, who tripped and fell.

"Don't be frightened," his father said.

"I'm not," Simon said defensively, wishing he had his toad, wishing he had Sebastien, but still, putting his trust in his father.

"My dear, wait in the cab. Boynton and I will see what we can learn." Simon jumped out before his mother could stop him and grabbed his father's hand.

The pier was packed with people and luggage. They pushed past the crush at the third-class ticket office and reached the pleasant marquee designed to welcome and advise the passengers in cabin class, but there was no one there to answer questions. Simon listened; he would now have to listen very carefully, because Sebastien was no longer there to do it for him. The talk was the same: The departure would be held up for a thorough review by the authorities. Of the world outside, there were only rumors, some of them passed on by people whose eyes were filled with terror, about the U-boats, or about the safety of those at home. Has it begun yet? Is it declared?

Mr. Boynton came back with the new rumor that the French Line was considering canceling the trip. "The *Aquitania* will go in any event," he said. "I beg you to reconsider."

"We have made our plans. The *Normandie* is faster and safer and will reach Southampton first, which is the most important thing."

They left Boynton to his fretting, and went back to the street. Two policemen were arguing with the cabdriver, who gave Edward, coming out of the crowd, an angry frown. Edward ignored the cabdriver and the policemen and said to Edith, "It's chaos."

"Will it sail?"

"The French will make up their own minds. You know how they are. But they will not risk the *Normandie*. If it is safe, it will leave."

"Then the French Line will make our decision for us. We'll have to let this cab go." She beckoned toward the three exercised faces looking in at them through the windshield.

The crowd on the pier was now more angry; Simon watched a Frenchman rip his ticket up and throw the pieces into the face of a French Line official. Still, no announcements, nothing but questions. They sat on their luggage, next to the cabin-class gangplank, and after a while a steward pushed a tea cart down the slope and served little ham sandwiches. Simon ate five and asked for a cake.

Finally, around two, a groan of despair and panic began to build from the other end of the pier, and Boynton came running out of the crowd just ahead of the news: The *Normandie* would not sail. The crossing was canceled.

"If we hurry, we can get you aboard the *Aquitania*. We must rush."

Simon immediately jumped up and began to gather the bags that had been assigned to him. He looked at his mother and father, and they seemed to be frozen; they hadn't moved at all.

"Do we have any information from Europe?" his mother asked. Despite Boynton's urgency at her side, and despite the shouts and shoves from all around them, she was speaking with utmost care.

"As far as I know," said Boynton, "the war has not begun. We don't expect any warning, though."

"Edward?" asked Edith. Simon did not like her tone; he knew it had something to do with him. He pushed his way between them and looked up as his father spoke.

"The French must believe it has started. It's too dangerous now."

"And what of the *Bremen* and the *Aquitania*?" his mother asked Mr. Boynton.

"They will both sail. The *Bremen*, certainly, will not stay, and Cunard has been ordered to leave, no matter what."

"Then . . ." she said.

"Edith," his father said, resignation now on his face. Simon made his body big and started to push his mother away, in the direction Boynton wanted them to go.

"Then what?" Simon shouted. His mother tried to shush him. "What's going on?" He appealed to Mr. Boynton, who said nothing. "Father," Simon wailed.

His father knelt down in front of him and took him in his arms as he spoke to Mr. Boynton. "Mrs. Mason and Simon will stay," he said.

"Father. No!"

"We must hurry," said Mr. Boynton. "We'll have to go on foot."

"Father, you can't leave me. I want to go with you. Don't go with him," he yelled, now realizing that Mr. Boynton was an enemy, had always been one.

"Simon," his father said, with his arms tight on his shoulders, "we have lost Sebastien in the sea. We will not risk losing you."

"No," he cried again. "I want to be with you."

"You'll come later, when it is safe. Be a good boy. I love you with all my heart."

Boynton began to interrupt. "Well, then. All decided . . ."

His father paid no attention to him. He turned to his mother. "Boynton will arrange everything."

"Yes, yes, Edward," she said. "Go quickly now. You must. I love you."

"Yes, certainly," said Boynton, nearly squeaking. "Now, sir—"

"We shall be fine. You must go, Edward. You must be on that ship."

His father dropped his arms from his mother and knelt a last time in front of Simon; his father was crying, but Simon could not hear his good-byes. "You can't do this to me," he yelled. "You mustn't. I hate this place. I hate America. I want to go home with you."

—

THIS IS WHAT Harry Mason imagines: his father's pain, the pain of the child on the quickly emptying pier, the pain and terror of losing so much. His mother has him in her grip and does not let go until long after Edward is gone. Simon's eyes and nose are running; he has pounded her chest; he has told her he hates her, that he always did, that it was her fault Sebastien was dead.

They sit on the luggage. There are three or four other groups, sitting on their luggage. They all sit, and soon, from the gangplank, Simon hears the squeaky wheels of a tea cart coming down toward them, and on it is a three-tiered display of petits fours and mousse pots. The steward pushes it over to Simon. He looks at his mother, who says yes, he may have some; he may have as much as he wants. Another little boy, who speaks a language Simon does not recognize, comes over, and each of them takes a cake. Harry can picture the sheen of the hard white frosting of the petit four in his father's small hand, can savor the taste of the cake, too sweet, sharp with the flavors of brandy and tears.

Edith sits on her suitcase. She fingers her pearls, taps lightly at the hair below her hatband. The lights have come on in the pier and on the ship, and the colors are gay and welcoming. She sees a liner passing by on the way out to sea, but whether it is the *Aquitania*, with Edward aboard, or the *Bremen*, bound for Hamburg and already darkened for war, she cannot be sure.

Harry pulls himself out of these thoughts and glances across his desk at the clock. It is only a little past ten, California time, but he is very tired; earlier that day he and his family had flown out of Washington, D.C. The children are asleep, and Karen went to bed an hour ago. "I'll be along soon," he said to her. "I just have to call Pop and tell him about the trip." But what does he want to say? That they drove over the Chesapeake Bay, and from the top of the bridge might have seen, in the slate gray of the water on this windy June day, the spot where Sebastien drowned? Does he tell him that they met a man who must have been McCready's son, a man with enormous ears, driving a huge tractor that probably cost a hundred and fifty thousand dollars? Does he tell him that McCready mistook them for buyers come to see the Mansion House, for sale yet again, and that McCready had told him if *he* had two point five million he'd put it in the Magellan Fund? His father is waiting for this call, but not, Harry guesses, for tidbits like that.

Harry sits at his desk and thinks of Edith perched on her luggage. What could she have been thinking on the pier in New York? That everything was lost? That her life was a ruin? She had told Simon that they would be going to Winnetka, and that it would be fine, just temporary, just a little family adventure. Was she grateful, after all this, that she could return to her father's house in safety? Did she think that her father and mother and sisters could help her find hope again? Harry doesn't know. He imagines the sound of Edward's good-byes slowly stilling in her mind, the way a word or two can resonate for minutes after it is spoken, an unwelcome echo.

A few minutes later Boynton had come back, almost silly with relief. He had fulfilled his duty, gotten the bloody bastard on the boat, and to hell with it then; let the Germans sink the damn thing, for all he cared. He just had to mop up the details: get this woman and the boy back to the hotel, put them on a train to Chicago tomorrow, and then get back to work. Harry knows—this is one of the odd details of the story Simon has told him—that Boynton went back to England himself in a few months, joined the army, and was killed in the war. Simon makes much of this, as if the bullet that got Boynton would have been aimed at Sebastien.

Harry imagines his grandfather on the mute deck of the *Aquitania* as the vessel slips through the harbor, the pounding, brilliant roar of New York City receding into its peacetime night. The whole country spreads out behind the city, tendons reaching back into the heartland like telephone lines. Edward has done what he can in America, and has paid for this passage with the last flicker of his youth, the end of his dreams, the life of his son. "Ah, sinful nation," he says, a snippet from Isaiah. It makes him feel better, this lament and warning from history, a rearrangement of blame and the promise of prophecy. He has much to do. As the last blink of land falls into the sea, he leaves the deck and goes below to his cabin, where his mates, a captain of the Royal Guard and a Swiss diplomat, are unpacking their things.

The *Aquitania* and the *Bremen*, noncombatant sisters in the "phony war," dart in company across the Atlantic, the one fearful of U-boats, the other plotting its escape into the North Sea. The *Aquitania* arrives in Southampton as the German troops drive through Poland, and a car waits to take Edward to Manchester. To hear Simon tell it, in the fateful years to come, Edward became something close to a secret weapon, on a par with radar and Patton, as if, had Hitler known Edward Mason was thumping a map on a wall in Maryland in 1938 and daring him to pick a fight, he might well have reconsidered the whole thing. Edward became a British subject, and when the war was over he hoped to be knighted, but was not.

Edith and Simon spent three years in Winnetka, living with Aunt Rosalie, who is now in her mid-nineties and still writes Harry once a week, the handwriting a little spastic but strong. In 1942, with the blitz over and the fortunes of war turning, they went back to England, on an airplane, an American Liberator fitted out with bunks in its bay, and though Simon, now twelve, was reunited with his father, it did not last very long. After the war, smarting from the lack of public accolades and royal recognition, appalled at the coming of the welfare state, Edward sold the works and moved the family and his store of pounds sterling to Bermuda. Simon went back to America for college and was at the University of Chicago when Edward died, suddenly, in 1951. Edward had always said that Mason men did not live long, that the law of averages was against his surviving to sixty, as if by lowering the average, Sebastien had shortened his life.

Harry does not know exactly when the Mansion House was sold, but it was after Edward died. Edith had left Bermuda and gone back to Chicago to live with Rosalie. Harry remembers Edith from their occasional visits, her looks still exotic, black hair side by side with gray. Aunt Rosalie ran the house, and seemed to run Edith's life as well, which satisfied both of them. Even as a child, Harry had noticed that his father's manner was correct toward Edith, but that his real affection was for Aunt Rosalie, that he shared his news—always slightly prettied up—and his thoughts with her, that they spoke often of old events, the war years, his spotty college career, spoke of them as things shared between mother and child. Edith seemed to have no past other than the one Aunt Rosalie provided: tales of deep nostalgia for their perfect childhood. Often Harry found himself and Edith thrown together as the odd ones out, and she dutifully took him to the zoo, and to Riverview Amusement Park, bought him ice cream, and clothes at Marshall Field's, but as soon as they returned home she retired to her room, as if recounting the details of the afternoon would be too much like memory for her to endure. If she pretended that nothing had ever happened in her life, perhaps nobody would ask her questions.

For all the times that his father has told Harry tales of the Retreat, Harry has never heard it from beginning to end, just in details and snips of life, those that seem to make good conversation to Simon according to his many moods: in his bonhomie at the club, in his stern, fatherly lectures about good habits and the need to keep well dressed and groomed. Thousands of riffs, always on the same text: all of Simon's metaphors and analogies, references and comparisons, end up in the Retreat. Simon has put many spins on his family history, like a screenwriter—which he once hoped to be—pitching a story line: deep, dark tragedy in the crucible of the nation; a romantic tale about a waning era; gritty collision of race and class. They all seem plausible to Harry; his father seems to be within his rights to say it however the hell he wants to.

This unlucky man, haunted by his brother's death, has so often seemed thwarted but has never given up. He'd had a career in advertising that slid through a couple of firms in Los Angeles, and then was a copy editor on the Pasadena *Star-News*. Harry is an only child. His father said he stopped at one child because he wanted to make sure he didn't have two sons, but it wasn't really that: Harry's mother divorced him. His next marriage, to a ditzy woman everyone called Trinket, didn't last long either. Simon is now officially retired, from love and from work, but every once in a while he gets a voice job for local radio spots, and he calls up Harry in Marin and says, "Guess what? Your pop is a retired schoolteacher worried about drugs," or "You're talking to the voice of the United Way of Pasadena." He's really very good at this, as good with accents as one might expect of a person raised in such a fractured way. In college he was a star of the Dramat, but Edward wrote him—it was the last letter—that all actors were homosexuals, and Simon quit.

When Harry told his father that he and Karen and the girls were planning to visit the Retreat on their trip back East, Simon pretended he could not care less. "Why would you want to go *there?*" he asked, as if he'd hardly ever mentioned the place, as if it had nothing to do with the family story, a place only amateur genealogists and other busybodies would care about. He had been back only once himself, in 1967, to bury his mother alongside Sebastien in the graveyard at St. Paul's in Cookestown. But Harry didn't believe his father's protestations; he knew his father, at home in Pasadena, had been imagining this pilgrimage mile by mile, minute by minute.

"Why are we doing this?" his daughter Rosalie had asked from the backseat. "What is this place, anyway?" Good questions. Harry had answered that they were going because it was important to Pop. He explained that Pop had lived here before the war—World War II, he added. Your great-uncle drowned here, Harry told his children. It's been hard for Pop. I want him to know that what happened to him in his life is important to me.

Harry would have to call soon, not because his father would be in bed, but because the story was over. He could fill his father in on a few details he had gleaned from McCready: that both Valerie and Robert were still alive and living in Tuckertown; that Tuckertown itself seemed quite trim and prosperous, with fresh paint and green lawns; that there was now a historic marker at the gate of the Retreat announcing that this was "the ancestral home of the once-influential Mason family," a curious slur, Harry had thought.

And maybe that was all there was to it, in the end. We listen to the repetitions of family tragedies because we would like to think that something new will come out for the teller, but there is nothing new to learn. Perhaps Harry had hoped, out of love for his old pop, to bring back some balm, a final release from these painful things that happened so long ago. Harry had almost believed, for a few moments as they finally drove under the great trees of the Retreat, that he might find the missing part of his father, the part of him as a boy that seemed to have been left behind or lost in the sorrow and confusion of 1939, the part Simon seemed to be searching for as he told and retold those events. But this had not happened, and Simon had not asked for it to happen.

We recapture these lives of our parents and forebears to give us some testimony of the truth as it was once received, and we give honor to pain and forgiveness for mistakes, but the blood begins fresh with each child, and flows only within that child, and dries to dust in that body when all is done. There is sadness in that for Harry, because he would like to undo what was done to his father. But there is also mercy in it, Harry recognizes. One life, one's own, is plenty. He'd come home, carried the sleeping girls to their beds, and kissed his wife good night, and now that he had sat down to make this call, his deepest thoughts were only for himself. How grateful he was for his blessings. How hard he would try to preserve them and earn them anew.

ABOUT THE AUTHOR

CHRISTOPHER TILGHMAN lives with his wife and three children in central Massachusetts. He is the author of the story collection *In a Father's Place*, which appeared to wide acclaim in 1990. His stories have been anthologized often in *The Best American Short Stories* and in other anthologies in the United States and abroad. The recipient of numerous grants and awards, among them the Guggenheim Fellowship, the Whiting Writer's Award, and the Ingram Merrill Foundation award, he has taught at the University of Virginia and other graduate writing programs.